Berta De Luca

Book one of the Angels on Earth Series

To Marty
Enjoy Berta
Yours
Terry Suchanek

A Novel by Terry Suchanek

First published by Dog Ear Publishing
4010 W. 86th Street, Ste H
Indianapolis, IN 46268
www.dogearpublishing.net

ISBN: 978-1-4575-1263-6

This book is printed on acid-free paper.

Printed in the United States of America

This book is lovingly dedicated to my beautiful niece.

Meaghan Horan

Acknowledgements:

I'd like to thank my mother, Helen Horan, for her unwavering enthusiasm and encouragement while I wrote this book.

I'd also like to thank my friends and fellow nurses, Carol Perkins-McGraw and Shawnna Gannon, avid readers of fiction, for their sincere interest in the work of a first time novelist. Their suggestions and feedback were a huge help.

Also, I'd like to thank Angela Gonyer, editor extraordinaire and Esther LaPierre for taking the time to comb through this novel and catch the misspellings, omissions and grammatical errors that spell check/grammar check didn't. It was a terrific help!

I'd like to thank my daughter, Janell Suchanek, for her technical expertise, without which I would have surely lost my mind.

Last, but not least, I'd like to thank my husband, Dick Suchanek, for his patience and support while I pursued my dream of writing a novel.

PROLOGUE

Rosa DeLuca and her daughter Berta came to America from a small village outside of Genoa, Italy in the summer of 1917. Gaston DeLuca, Rosa's husband, worked as a stone cutter in Italy, but had left for America in 1915 after Italy joined the Allies in WWI, and declared war on Germany and Austria.

It was at the docks in Genoa that Gaston met a man, a padrone, who promised him steady work at high wages in the coal mines of Pennsylvania in America. The padrone's job was to recruit men to work in the mines for The Consolidated Coal Company. Gaston's passage, like so many other immigrant workers, was financed by the Stabline Bank of Boston.

Gaston knew that if he didn't leave Italy then, he and his wife and daughter would have no hope of escaping the horrors that the war would eventually bring. After almost two years of working in the mines, Gaston had finally managed to save up enough money to send for his wife, Rosa and their six year old daughter, Berta. They were to arrive in New York City, and then take a train to Pennsylvania to meet him.

Gaston awoke in his one room shack; it stood among dozens of other meager dwellings in the mining camp he had come to call home. He looked at the calendar and smiled. Finally, his wife and daughter would arrive at the end of the week. He couldn't wait to see their faces and hold them in his arms.

The horn blew in the distance, signaling the beginning of another grueling day in the mine.

Gaston reported for work at the pit at six fifteen in the morning, six days a week. He and the other men, eight in all, stepped onto the platform of the cage. It descended rapidly, jerking now and again, down the shaft more than a thousand feet. The men stepped off the platform; the sickening reek of mine tallow lamps filled Gaston's nostrils and nauseated him. The roof was low, forcing the men to hunch as they drudged through the sucking mud toward the wall of coal they would hack at for the rest of the day. A fierce rumbling stopped them in their tracks. They stood in silence, waiting for it to cease. Then, there was a sudden, deafening explosion.

CHAPTER ONE

$\mathcal{T}$he journey across the Atlantic was nightmarish. The ship was over-crowded and smelled of vomit and human excrement. Clean water and food were scarce. After what seemed like a life time, Rosa DeLuca and her daughter Berta arrived in New York City on a sunny July morning.

It was a relief to get off the boat and away from the putrid stench. Once in America, Rosa, Berta and the rest of the steerage passengers were put on a barge and brought to Ellis Island. They were herded through a huge barn-like structure: doctors and nurses examined the heads of every arriving immigrant for lice. Medical personnel marked a large "X" on the outer garments of immigrants that they deemed to be ill. Anyone with a fever or cough was suspected of having typhus or tuberculosis and they were immediately quarantined and sent back to their country of origin without exception.

Finally, Rosa and her daughter came to a big desk where a government inspector sat wearing a placid expression. He seemed exhausted by the monotony of his job, but when he looked at their paperwork his countenance changed. He looked up at Rosa with an expression of concern and sadness. He began to speak quietly. Then he let out a sigh and shook his head, realizing that neither Rosa nor Berta could understand anything he said. The gentleman summoned another worker, who returned with a man who was able to speak Italian.

The Italian speaking man was old with sparse white wispy hair and a kind face. He introduced himself as Mr. Tomasi. He took Rosa's hand in his and softly, in Italian, said, "Mrs. DeLuca, I'm so sorry. There was an accident in the coal mine. Many men were lost. I'm afraid your husband, well, he, he…"

Mr. Tomasi's voice trailed off.

Rosa dropped to her knees, covered her face with her hands, and began to sob. Berta didn't fully understand at that moment what had happened but she knew that it must have been something terrible. Mr. Tomasi brought them to a small room and started to ask Rosa a series of questions.

"Mrs. DeLuca, do you have family or friends in New York? Is there someone we can send word to?"

Rosa shook her head and said, "No, no, we have nobody. My husband is the only family we have."

Mr. Tomasi shook his head in dismay, "Returning to Italy would not be wise. You and your daughter escaped just in time. The war has ignited in full fury. Thousands have been killed; it would not be safe."

"What am I going to do? I have only a little money and these train tickets to Pennsylvania."

"Is there nobody in Pennsylvania that can help?" Mr. Tomasi asked.

"No, Gaston spoke of no one. I don't know what to do."

"Well, perhaps I can sell the train tickets for you. That will give you enough money to get a room and time to decide what you should do. I can give you the address of the Church of the Scalabrinian Fathers. There is a Sister Maria there, she is from Naples. She may be able to help. You may need some help with your daughter until you can get on your feet."

Rosa knew what Mr. Tomasi meant but both were careful not to let on to Berta. Rosa and Berta waited in the room for hours. It was near dusk when Mr. Tomasi came back. He took them to a boarding house not far from the dock. It was clean and modestly furnished. There was a fat middle-aged woman sitting in the front parlor. Mr. Tomasi went to her and spoke for a few minutes. The woman looked over at Rosa and Berta with a wary eye. She turned back to Mr. Tomasi, shook her finger at him, and said something Rosa couldn't understand.

Mr. Tomasi looked at Rosa and said, "You must understand that you will only be able to stay for one week and no more because the money will run out." He gestured to the woman. "This is Mrs. Gartner. She will provide you with breakfast and dinner. Breakfast is at seven and dinner is at six. I wish you much luck. I am sorry that there is not more I can do for you. God Bless you and your daughter."

Mr. Tomasi left. They never saw him again.

That week, Rosa and Berta walked the streets of New York City. It was wondrous and frightening at the same time. They were in search of the church Mr. Tomasi had told them about. Rosa told Berta that the church would help them, and that they needed to say prayers for daddy and light a candle. Berta had not seen her mother cry since the day at Ellis Island but Rosa's eyes were red rimmed and swollen. After walking for hours, Rosa finally found the church on Carmine St.

Rosa knew she had no choice. She would soon be out of money. It was one thing to have to fend for herself. She would get by somehow, but the idea of watching her child go hungry and not being able to keep a roof over her head was more than Rosa could bear. She wanted better than that for Berta. Rosa's heart was breaking. She knew she couldn't tell Berta what her intentions were before they got to the church. Berta would have been hysterical and Rosa would have had to carry her bodily through the streets of New York in order to get her to the church.

Rosa held Berta's hand as they walked up the steps to the door of the rectory. Rosa knocked on the door. A young woman in a habit opened it. The rectory smelled of incense and garlic.

"I'm here to see Sister Maria." Rosa told the woman in Italian.

She responded in Italian as well. "Is she expecting you?" she asked politely.

"Mr. Tomasi told me to see Sister Maria. It's very important. He told me that she could help us." Rosa looked down at Berta and put her hand on her daughter's head and smoothed her hair. Berta's attention was fixed on the young woman. It was almost impossible for Rosa to keep her composure but she had to for Berta's sake. The young woman motioned for them to come in.

"Follow me," the woman told them kindly. They followed her to an office at the end of the hall where an elderly nun sat behind a large mahogany desk.

"There's someone here to see you Sister." the woman said to the elderly nun.

The nun looked up at Rosa and smiled warmly. "Can I help you?" she asked.

Rosa looked down at Berta and spoke softly. "Berta, I'm going to talk to Sister Maria for a while. I want you to be a very good girl and wait outside the office."

Berta looked anxious; her eyes wide and questioning. "Alright Mama. I'll be right here," Berta said, as she climbed up on the bench in the hallway outside of Sister Maria's office. Rosa shut the door to the office and introduced herself.

"Please have a seat," Sister Maria gestured to the wooden armchair across from her desk.

Rosa tearfully told Sister what had happened and that Mr. Tomasi had told her about the orphanage. She asked Sister Maria if they could take Berta until she could find a job and a place to stay.

"I am so sorry to hear of your loss Mrs. DeLuca," Sister Maria replied, "But unfortunately there are too many children that need to be cared for. There are thousands of children living on the streets of New York City, abandoned or orphaned. There are even children who are exploited by unscrupulous adults. Berta is very fortunate that she has you. Many of the children here have no parent to look after them.

"Please sister, I beg of you," Rosa pleaded. "It will only be for a short time until I can get settled." Sister Maria finally relented and agreed to admit Berta into Sacred Heart Orphan Asylum.

CHAPTER TWO

One of Berta's earliest memories was of sitting on a long wooden bench outside of Sister Maria's office. Berta dangled her small legs back and forth and thought about how she couldn't wait to get big enough for her feet to touch the floor when she sat in a chair. She felt nervous sitting outside of Sister Maria's office by herself. At six years old she had never been to school and couldn't remember spending even one day away from her mother. The thought terrified her. After what seemed like a very long time the door of the office opened. What happened next was nearly unfathomable to Berta.

Tears streamed down her mother's face. She leaned over and held Berta close. "I am going to find a job so that I can take good care of you," Rosa whispered into her daughter's ear, "I will come back for you soon. I love you Berta. Everything will be okay. Be a good girl and listen to Sister Maria."

Berta's mother stood up, turned around, and began walking slowly down the long corridor. She turned around after opening the door that lead to the busy street outside, the afternoon sun flooded in behind her so that Berta could no longer see her mother's face but only the outline of her body. Berta screamed and tried to run after her mother but the nun held her tight. Berta never could remember what happened in the days immediately following that dreadful afternoon but she spent almost three and a half years at Sacred Heart Orphan Asylum.

Berta made many friends at Sacred Heart Orphan Asylum, many of them even spoke Italian, but her best friend at the orphanage was Chevonne O'Farrell. Chevonne didn't seem to notice that Berta didn't speak a lick of English when she arrived at the orphanage. For weeks, Chevonne cheerfully babbled on and on, seeming not to notice that Berta didn't understand a thing she was saying. Chevonne was five, but she carried herself with an air of confidence that made her seem older.

Chevonne had thick blonde hair, the color of corn silk. It fell in unruly ringlets around her chubby face when it escaped from her hair ties. She had large deep dimples that formed at the sides of her mouth; they made Chevonne look as if she would burst with delight when she smiled. Her clear, baby blue eyes always seemed to have a mischievous twinkle. Berta thought they were the happiest eyes she'd ever seen. Chevonne had a brother, Patrick. He was eight and had the same happy eyes as his sister but instead of blond ringlets he had a shock of red hair that he usually kept hidden under his newsboy cap.

For a long time Berta cried herself to sleep. At night when all the girls knelt at the side of their beds and recited the Pater Noster, Berta would add her own silent prayer, "Please God, please let mommy come tomorrow to get me, I miss her so. I promise that I will be good every day of my life and never make a fuss over anything ever if you will just let mommy come to get me tomorrow."

But Berta's mother didn't come to take her out of the orphanage the next day, or the next, nor the next, and the weeks turned into months. Eventually, she stopped praying for her mother to come get her.

The children in the orphanage ranged in age from five to roughly eleven. Berta missed her mother but she was grateful to have a warm bed to get into every night and the benefit of attending school each day. Sister Serafina taught the younger children. She was fun loving and creative and Berta worked hard to do well, partly because she wanted to impress the Sister. A compliment from Sister Serafina could make Berta beam with pride for days.

Berta could only vaguely remember her father but she felt tremendously fortunate that her mother was able to visit her, albeit briefly and infrequently. Chevonne and Patrick were not as lucky. They were from Boston. Both their maternal and paternal grandparents came to America from Ireland after the potato famine. They settled in Roxbury, an Irish shanty town. One morning before Berta was fully awake Chevonne came to her bedside and showed her a picture of a girl that looked to be about seventeen years old and said simply, "That's my mother."

Chevonne took the tattered picture out from under her pillow every morning and looked at it quietly for a few minutes. Chevonne's mother died giving birth to twin boys when Chevonne was barely two years old. The twins survived less than a week. Their father came down with consumption a few years after their mother died and Chevonne and

Patrick went to live with distant cousins in Lower Manhattan. It wasn't long before they were dropped off on the steps of the convent with a note explaining their plight.

Since Sacred Heart was a girl's orphanage, Patrick was directed to the Children's Aid Society. They recommended Patrick board "a mercy train." Some people called them "baby trains," but Patrick referred to them as "orphan trains." Patrick told Berta and Chevonne all about them.

"They take children who live on the streets of New York City to live with families who have farms. Some kids get lucky and they get to live with nice folks who feed them and send them to school, but I know a few fellas who left on an orphan train," Patrick told them. "They didn't have good luck and ended up running away and coming back to the city. They told me all about it. My friend Billy said he got whipped if they didn't work hard enough and they hardly fed him, so he ran away and came back. I don't know if I like the idea of being sent away to live with strangers. Doesn't sound like anything I'd want to do." Patrick declared. "Besides, Chevonne, you're happy here at the orphanage with your friends and I can come and visit whenever I want."

Patrick visited frequently and enjoyed telling Chevonne and Berta about his adventures and all the people and places that amazed and inspired him. He told colorful stories of his exploits and boasted that he knew New York City "like the back of his hand." He knew the best places to get a free meal and the best places to sleep and wash up. He knew the best places to go to stay warm in the winter and cool in the summer. One of Patrick's favorite places to visit was the library. The New York City Public Library was architecturally breathtaking. Patrick loved the Main Reading room at the top of the building. Light streamed in through the gigantic windows and it was nearly two city blocks in length. Patrick liked to pretend that he was a powerful king and the massive structure was his castle.

He told the girls how magnificent it was and told them about a very kind lady named Mrs. Wallace. At first Patrick went to the library to find a quiet place to lay his head down. He had been at work for hours as a bootblack on the busy corner of Wall Street and Broad. He was exhausted. When the librarian came over to him he thought sure she'd shoo him away. She was a smartly dressed, slender woman who wore her thick auburn hair up in a French twist. But she didn't shoo him away. Instead, she walked over to her desk, took a ham sandwich out of her bag, and offered Patrick half. She sat down next to him and they ate together.

"Do you know how to read?" she asked.

"Yes, I like to read. My father taught me when I was little. I've been reading since I was four years old." Patrick said proudly.

The woman smiled. "That's good. What's your name?"

"My name is Patrick O'Farrell."

"Well, that's a lovely name. I'm Mrs. Wallace."

CHAPTER THREE

After weeks of washing up in the train station bathroom, sleeping in the park and standing in soup lines, Rosa found work as a servant for a family who lived on the Upper East Side. She slept on a cot in a small room in the attic and shared a bathroom with the other help. Her pay was little more than an exchange for room and board, which made saving for an apartment almost impossible. There were so many poor immigrants clamoring for jobs that Rosa was afraid to ask for time off to go visit Berta at the orphanage for fear she would be let go and wind up on the street again. Three weeks after being hired, Rosa mustered the courage to ask for a day off.

Rosa was relieved to see that Berta was healthy and as happy as anyone could expect under the circumstances. The girls at the orphanage wore dark blue pinafores with plain collared white blouses underneath. Berta's uniform was clean but appeared to have been worn for many years by at least a dozen other little girls who had long since grown out of it. The sleeves of the blouse were thread bare. Berta's long chestnut hair was neatly pulled back in a ponytail. She assured Rosa that the nuns saw to it that all the girls combed their hair, brushed their teeth and washed their hands and face every morning and night.

Rosa and Berta visited with one another in the church next to the orphanage. The Sisters discouraged parents from coming into the orphanage to visit because it was difficult for all the children without parents to watch. Rosa and Berta said prayers together and lit a candle. They sat in one of the pews and talked.

"Are you getting enough to eat?" Rosa asked.

Berta nodded. "Yes Mama, every morning we have oatmeal and a glass of milk. Some mornings we get an apple too. At lunch and dinner we usually have soup or stew and some bread and cheese. It's not like the food at home but it tastes fine when I'm hungry."

Rosa didn't want to give her daughter false hope, so she explained to Berta during one of their visits that her job paid very little and that saving up enough to get Berta out of the orphanage would take longer than she had planned. Berta was visibly upset. "But mama I miss you so much." The tears welled up in Berta's eyes and her bottom lip quivered.

"I think about you all the time Berta. I miss you too. I'm going to come and see you every chance I get. It'll all be okay Berta, you'll see." Rosa held Berta tightly against her and rocked her and kissed the top of her head. Rosa could feel the warmth of her own tears rolling down her cheeks. Her heart was breaking, and though she'd never admit it to Berta, she couldn't imagine how she would ever be able to earn enough money to support her daughter.

Rosa visited Berta as often as she could, but the weeks passed quickly and those weeks soon added up to months. Eventually, Berta stopped crying and pleading with Rosa to take her from the orphanage. Berta eventually settled in and soon learned to speak perfect English with no trace of an accent. Rosa managed to visit Berta once a month or so. She loved to listen to her daughter talk about her new friends and their lives while they sat in the calm of the empty church. Rosa could see that Berta had actually come to like Sacred Heart Orphan Asylum and worried that the day would come that the nuns would insist that she take Berta out of the orphanage to make room for another less fortunate child. But one day, when Rosa came to visit, Sister Serafina came to the door with a cloth over her face. Rosa had to strain to hear the nun's muffled words.

"I'm sorry Mrs. DeLuca, Sister Maria has informed me that you can't see Berta today. Visitation will be restricted for the time being. I'm very sorry, I don't know more than that."

Before Rosa could ask any questions the nun closed the door. Rosa stood in front of it stunned as the sound of the bolt lock sliding into its latch on the other side of the door echoed in her ears.

CHAPTER FOUR

*O*ver a year had passed since Rosa and Berta had arrived at Ellis Island. Rosa was becoming accustomed to life in her new country, but it was harsh. She worked hard at assimilating into American culture. She was observant and bright, and although she had a heavy Italian accent, she eventually spoke English well enough to make herself understood. She had found work as a seamstress in a large textile mill and Rosa was able to get an advance from her new employer, allowing her to rent a room in a tenement building on Mulberry St.

Twenty-eight Mulberry St. was a five story walk up. Rosa's room was on the fourth floor. The tenements on Mulberry St. were filled with poor immigrants, mostly from the southern portion of Italy, Sicily and the Mezzogiorno. There were also many immigrants from other parts of Europe and even Asia. The streets were crowded, noisy and full of bread peddlers, vegetable vendors and merchants selling everything from hats to rugs. The Lower East Side, where Rosa now called home, was the most densely populated area on the globe.

"Mulberry Street" had come to be synonymous with slum, but there were things Rosa liked about Mulberry Street too. The comfort of hearing a familiar dialect and the celebrations that marked the passing of life; weddings, baptismals, funerals and the feasts of the saints warmed Rosa's heart and made her feel a part of a community. Like Berta, Rosa had also made friends. Rosa met Gitta Lachman at the market. She and her husband, Yekl and their three small children lived on nearby Hester Street. They came from Hungary. Her husband was a tailor and it was through him, at Gitta's urging that Rosa had been hired as a seamstress by one of Yekl's associates.

Rosa was a petite woman that looked much younger than her thirty years. She wasn't beautiful but she wasn't unattractive either. Her large hazel-brown eyes were striking and rimmed with thick dark lashes, balancing out her slightly prominent nose. Rosa had full lips and was blessed with flawless olive skin. It had been more than two years since her husband's death and over three since she had seen him, but Rosa still thought about her late husband, Gaston, every day and missed him deeply. He was the only man she had ever been intimate with. Rosa could not even imagine being with anyone else or loving anybody the way she loved Gaston.

The women Rosa knew at the textile mill complained that potential suitors were scarce. Thousands of young men had been sent off to fight the Great War. President Wilson called it the war to end all wars and it was finally over, with America and the Allied forces emerging victorious. The men were returning now, but Rosa wasn't looking for romance. She dreamt about Gaston. The dreams were always vivid. Sometimes they would be happy dreams; dreams of making love in a sweet smelling meadow on a warm breezy day. Sometimes the dreams were not happy and they made Rosa feel frantic and confused. She had one recurrent dream of running after Gaston as he walked slowly down a nondescript street.

"Gaston! Gaston! Please, Gaston, wait!" Rosa screamed in her dream, but Gaston never would turn around and Rosa could never catch up to him and she would wake in a cold sweat, twisted up in the bedding.

CHAPTER FIVE

Patrick walked past Leo Astor and Leo Lenox, the massive library lions that flanked the grand steps leading into the New York Public Library, almost every day. Most days when the librarian, Mrs. Wallace, was working she brought an extra lunch and ate with Patrick. Mrs. Wallace introduced him to all the great authors: his favorites were Horatio Alger, Mark Twain and James Fennimore Cooper. Patrick loved to learn and Mrs. Wallace was happy to teach him.

New York City was Patrick's oyster. He couldn't imagine being cooped up in an orphanage but he knew Chevonne was safe at Sacred Heart. The nuns at the orphanage were kind to him when he came to visit and although it was a girl's orphanage, occasionally clothes appropriate for a boy would be donated, and the nuns would be sure to pass them on to Patrick. He knew too, that the nuns would usually offer him a snack or even a meal when he was there. Patrick was energetic, optimistic and persuasive. He had a way of making people feel special. Even the nuns weren't immune to his charm.

The O'Farrell children received letters from their father at least once a month. He was a patient at Riverside Hospital. It was easy to see where the children got their good humor and positive outlook from. Mr. O'Farrell's letters were usually full of amusing anecdotes. He often wrote poetry and funny limericks. Some of his letters were brief and some were lengthy but they were always cheerful. He praised his children for their bravery and intelligence and managed to offer them guidance and advice without sounding didactic.

Tom O'Farrell was a devout Catholic, and though he heaped praise on his children, he often reminded Chevonne and Patrick that they were blessed with these attributes so that they could do God's work. He told them that he hoped they would both find noble vocations that would allow them to relieve the suffering of those less fortunate. Berta was privy to these wonderful letters because Patrick read them out loud to Chevonne, and Chevonne and Berta were almost always together.

Initially, when Patrick came to Sacred Heart the nuns would give him Mr. O'Farrell's letters because Chevonne was just starting to read when she came to the orphanage and the content of her father's letters was too complex for her to decipher. Eventually, Chevonne learned to read just as well as Patrick but she would never open one her father's letters until Patrick came to visit. It wasn't long before Berta understood and spoke English perfectly and she would become just as excited as Chevonne and Patrick when a letter came.

> *My Dear Children,*
> *I hope this letter finds you well and full of joy and wonder. As I write, I am basking in the last glorious, golden rays of the afternoon sun. The breeze is warm and gentle and I am grateful... I am especially grateful for you; Chevonne and Patrick. The Lord has blessed you each with keen minds and sturdy bodies to do His work. You are my inspiration. I have just an hour ago finished a delicious meal. And as they say, when a man's stomach is full it makes no difference whether he is rich or poor. I look forward to a restful sleep and will meet you in my dreams tonight... I see the ocean o' the waves and my children upon their faces I will gaze. The sea be calm the sand be warm and all day long we'll sing our songs.*
> *I love you with all my heart. God bless you and keep you.*
> *Dad*

Mr. O'Farrell's cheerful description of the fresh air, sunshine and healthy living he was enjoying at the tuberculosis sanatorium was fallacious and for the benefit of his children and their peace of mind. In truth, Riverside Hospital was secluded on North Brother Island in the East River, between the Bronx and Riker's Island. It was notorious for its poor sanitation and overcrowding. Other victims of infectious diseases such as smallpox, polio and typhoid were also treated there. Medical equipment was in short supply and not always cleaned properly between frequent uses.

For the upper class, fresh air, sunshine and good nutrition was deemed curative for tuberculosis, and it was provided for those who could afford lodging in such sanatoriums. For the poor, people like Tom O'Farrell and the shanty Irish, sanatoriums were more prison-like and the conditions were deplorable. Despite this, he would not burden his children with these revelations. He was determined to give them reassurance and hope and to survive to see them again.

Tom O'Farrell was no stranger to heartache. He had suffered the loss of his wife and their infant sons. However, the day he had to send Chevonne and Patrick away to live with a distant cousin of his late wife after becoming ill with consumption was gut-wrenching. Now over a year had gone by and he wasn't sure he'd ever see their faces again. Every day he fought valiantly against the demons of sickness and the despair and vowed to walk out of the sanatorium a cured man. He prayed every day that God would keep his children safe and that he would be reunited with them one day.

That conviction gave Tom O'Farrell the strength to fight on.

CHAPTER SIX

*F*ive year old Margo was brought to the Sacred Heart Orphan Asylum on a hot, balmy September afternoon in 1918. Sister Angelina noticed that the little girl felt warm. There were tiny beads of sweat on her forehead and upper lip. *The poor child is exhausted*, thought Sister Angelina. Margo was pale and her breathing came in short, raspy wheezes. The Sister thought that she might have a touch of asthma, a psychosomatic illness in her opinion. *Surely the wheezes are a suppressed cry for her mother*, thought the elderly nun.

"Well Margo, it looks like you'd do well with a little nap before dinner."

Margo said nothing but nodded her head slightly. Sister Angelina poured Margo a small glass of water but Margo did not lift her hand to take the cup. The Sister held the glass to the little girl's lips. Margo took a few small sips then turned her head away to cough. She took Margo gently by the hand, and walked her over to one of the cots in the room adjacent to the office where sick children could be tended to while the nuns also saw to the administrative tasks of the orphanage.

She covered the exhausted child with a light blanket and went back to her paperwork. A few hours later Sister Angelina was interrupted by one of the fourth graders in Sister Mary Agnes' class.

"Excuse me, Sister?"

"Yes Jacqueline, what can I do for you, child?"

"Sister Mary Agnes asked me to get some rags and vinegar to clean the black board."

The Sister let out a weary sigh, "I'll need to go to the kitchen for them. They're preparing dinner and I don't want you to be underfoot. Wait right here Jacqueline." Sister Angelina got up from behind the desk and left the office to retrieve the needed supplies.

Jacqueline could hear a strange noise coming from the small room next to the office and peeked in to see what it was. She saw a small girl lying on one of the cots covered with a white cotton blanket. The noise she heard was the sound of the girl's weak cough interrupted only by her wheezing. Jacqueline knew the Sister would not want her to bother the little girl, so she waited and watched the Sister walk down the dimly lit corridor until she turned the corner. Jacqueline felt like it took forever. The Sister's gait was slow thanks to the ravages of old age and arthritis. As soon as the Sister was out of sight Jacqueline ventured into the infirmary and sat on the edge of the cot.

The little girl's face was flushed and her skin gleamed with perspiration. Jacqueline instinctively put a hand to Margo's forehead in an attempt to provide comfort. Margo's eyes opened, but just partially as she struggled to bring Jacqueline's face into focus.

"Hello, my name is Jacqueline. I'm sorry to wake you. Are you very sick?"

Margo responded with a feeble attempt to form words. Jacqueline put her ear up to Margo's mouth in the hope that she would be able to hear what the little girl was trying to say. It was no use. What came out were unintelligible whispers and an odd gurgling sound. Jacqueline turned her head away from Margo's ear and stared at her mouth. But the sick little girl had fallen silent. Her lips had taken on a bluish hue.

"Jacqueline! Please leave that child alone," Sister Angelina admonished in a loud whisper.

Jacqueline was momentarily startled but too perplexed to simply leave. "What's wrong with her?" Jacqueline asked with genuine concern.

"She's just exhausted. She'll be fine once she gets some rest and has some food in her stomach." But as Sister got closer to the cot where Margo laid, her expression changed. What she saw alarmed her and she knew that something was terribly wrong with Margo.

The sick little girl's complexion had become dusky and her breaths came in uneven, ragged heaves. Jacqueline could see that Sister Angelina was shocked.

"Dear Lord, have mercy. Jacqueline, go find Mother Superior and tell her we need the doctor to come right away."

Jacqueline ran as fast as she could to find the Mother Superior. Sister Angelina knelt next to Margo with her rosary entwined in her clasped hands and began to pray. Mother Superior was in the rectory. Jacqueline was panting from her sprint. It took a moment to catch her breath enough to tell her what was wrong.

"She, she can't breathe. Sister Angelina said get the doctor."

"Sister Angelina can't breathe?" Mother Superior asked.

"No, no, the girl can't. The new girl in the infirmary can't breathe!"

What Mother Superior learned when she contacted the doctor was truly frightening. The doctor refused to come to help the little girl.

"There is nothing I can do for the child. But you must keep her away from the others. Anyone who has had close contact with the sick child should be quarantined and observed for symptoms. It may be Spanish flu and it is highly contagious and often deadly," the doctor explained. Mother Superior hung up the phone and sat for moment trying to digest the words the doctor had just spoken.

Sister Angelina had become so immersed in prayer as she knelt next to Margo's cot that she hadn't noticed that the child had not moved or breathed in more than five minutes. The elderly nun completed her prayer for the little girl with the sign of the cross and opened her eyes hoping for a miracle. Instead, she was horrified.

Margo's face was a hideous purple. Gravity had pushed a trickle of blood from the corner of her mouth over her cheek and down her neck. The child's eyes were half open and staring unseeingly straight ahead. Sister Angelina gasped. She had tended to many sick people in her eighty-one years but she'd never see death come so suddenly and brutally.

Upon hearing of Margo's death, Mother Superior advised Sister Angelina to quarantine herself in her room. She kept Jacqueline, the girl who had sat on Margo's bed, away from the other girls until she could be sure that she had not been infected. Unfortunately, little more than twenty-four hours after Jacqueline had run to tell Mother Superior of the sick little girl's illness, she herself became suddenly and gravely ill. Mother Superior tended to Jacqueline for two days before she died in the nun's arms just after the sun came up on a muggy Friday morning.

As the days passed the terrifying nature of the deadly disease became apparent. Sickness had begun to spread throughout the crowded city. Classes at Sacred Heart Orphan Asylum were cancelled for days. The older nuns monitored the children carefully, while the younger able bodied nuns scrubbed the entire orphanage and convent furiously with a diluted bleach solution, until their hands were red and raw. Mattresses were brought out to the rectory courtyard to be disinfected by the sunlight and every piece of bedding and every garment was laundered in the hot water and hung outside.

The nuns became even more meticulous about hand washing and clean fingernails. They enforced strict coughing etiquette. The slogan, "Cover up each cough and sneeze, if you don't you'll spread disease" was one all the girls would hear regularly for months. The nuns instructed the girls never to drink or eat after anyone and to keep their hands away from their faces. The nuns maintain their calm demeanor so as not to frighten the children though they were fully aware of the magnitude of the disaster.

"There is a rumor that Archbishop Farley fell ill and died of the influenza. There was no doctor to attend to him," Sister Angelina whispered to Sister Serafina in the hallway.

"Doctors are literally being accosted in the streets by desperate parents pleading for help. I've been reading the newspapers. Public gatherings are being cancelled, even church services. The morgues are overflowing and bodies are beginning to rot in the hospitals. All the hospitals are horribly overcrowded. I heard they're even releasing convicts under supervision to dig graves," Sister Serafina whispered back, in alarm.

One day Sister Angelina told the girls not to look out the windows, but wouldn't say why. Berta and Chevonne abided, for a while at least; but eventually curiosity got the best of them. They got up early one Sunday morning and looked down onto the street. There were three narrow wooden boxes, about six feet long and a few feet wide, lined up on the side of the street. There were two young boys playing on them, jumping from one to other. They thought it odd, but it satisfied their curiosity for a short time. A few weeks later they decided to look out the window again.

They counted seven bodies. There were two young women, a young man, and four children that looked to be between the ages of three and ten. They were all placed face down in the gutter with their arms at their sides.

"Why are those people sleeping in the street, Berta?" Chevonne asked.

"I don't think they're sleeping, Chevonne. I think they got sick from the Spanish flu." Berta and Chevonne looked at one another and back down at the bodies and said nothing more. They didn't dare tell anyone else for fear they'd get in trouble for disobeying Sister Angelina.

Not long afterward, Berta overheard the Sisters lamenting the scarcity of caskets as they too looked out the window.

"They can't make caskets fast enough, and then of course so many people can't afford them. I never thought I'd see such a grim sight in my life. Horse-drawn wagons with corpses piled on top of each other. They're bringing the dead to mass graves. They're digging huge holes with steam shovels, God help us," Sister Mary Agnes said, sounding utterly dejected.

"Father said that the larger hospitals in the city have had upwards of three hundred casualties a day; very few elderly people though. This hideous Spanish flu prefers to kill the young and healthy. Sometimes it feels like the end of the world," Sister Serafina added, as she stared down at the street.

CHAPTER SEVEN

*T*he Spanish flu ran rampant through the city, and the rest of the world for that matter, and it was deadly. Rosa, like so many others, fell desperately ill but managed to survive and make a full recovery. Visitation restrictions at Sacred Heart Orphanage went into effect in the summer of 1918. Eventually Rosa was allowed to see Berta but they had to remain at least five feet away from each other and no gifts could be exchanged.

Full visitation at the orphanage didn't resume until February of 1920.

Rosa thought about how much had changed in America since she and her daughter had arrived at Ellis Island. The Temperance movement was in full swing. Prohibition had begun and was a catalyst for an alarming rise in organized crime. The sale or consumption of liquor was prohibited, although it seemed as if secret clubs where alcohol was sold, called "speakeasies," had sprung up everywhere overnight. There was no shortage of them in the poverty ridden streets of Five Points.

Women had finally won the right to vote, the first radio news programs were broadcast, and cars were beginning to replace the horse and buggy as a mode of transportation. It was an exciting time, but for poor immigrants life was still difficult. Rosa was working long hours in the textile mill. The work was tedious and exhausting. She was barely making enough to buy food and pay for the small room she rented in one of the crowded tenements on Mulberry Street. She shared a bathroom on the floor below with three families. Leaking pipes, rodents and the smell of garbage were an everyday part of life.

Rosa carried her dirty laundry and small bar of lye soap to the sink in the hallway. When she finished washing and ringing them out she took them to the back of the building where there was a small rickety porch with a clothes line that was strung across the alleyway to another identical rickety porch. Hanging her clothes on the clothes line made Rosa nervous. It was four stories up and she'd heard stories of similar porches collapsing due to years of neglect or structural defects.

Rosa stood looking out at all the other porches that lined the back of the tenement buildings. She wondered about the lives of all the poor people who hung their modest garments out to dry like she did. Life in America was nothing like Rosa thought it would be. It was so hard. She couldn't remember the last time she had laughed, and aside from her visits to see Berta, there didn't seem much to look forward to; at least not until she met Vinny Capozza.

It was a hot, sticky summer morning. Rosa had a rare day off and decided to go to the Feast of Saint Rosalia in Bensonhurst. Saint Rosalia lived in the Twelfth Century and was the patron saint of Sicily. Rosa prayed to Saint Rosalia frequently and although the feast was a religious event it was also festive. Rosa thought paying homage the Saint Rosalia might improve her fortune and she needed all the help she could get. She missed Italy and loved the sounds and smells of the Italian festivals. She got off the trolley at 67th Street. The avenue was alive with the sound of music and the delicious aroma of food. Rosa walked slowly through the streets taking in all the sights and smells. The festival stretched over four blocks.

Rosa stopped to watch a zeppoli vendor drop small pieces of dough into a pot of boiling oil. Her mouth watered as she watched the vendor lift the pieces of dough from the oil and sprinkle them with sugar.
"Hey doll, you got a name?"
Rosa looked up to see a handsome, well dressed young man.
"I'm Vincenzo Cappozza, my friends call me Vinny."
Rosa looked away and said nothing.
Vinny laughed and with his heavy Brooklyn accent said, "What's a matta? I ain't gonna bite ya."
Rosa glanced up to look at Vinny's face and quickly looked back down. "My name is Rosa."
Vinny smiled, "Rosa, eh. That's a nice name. Were ya named after the Saint Rosalia?"
"I don't know. I mean, I don't think so." Rosa said feeling self-conscience and silly.

It was the beginning of a whirlwind romance.

Vinny treated Rosa like a princess. Rosa had had a very limited and dreary experience in New York City. Outside of her visits to see Berta, Rosa's world had been a small one. It was rare that she ventured far from Five Points. Most days Rosa walked only to the textile mill she worked at on Broome Street and back to her room in the dilapidated tenement on Mulberry Street. Vinny showed her a new world, a world full of excitement and wonder. He took her to Coney Island and Jones Beach and to the Club De Luxe in Harlem. Rosa had never met anyone like Vinny. He was self-assured, cocky even.

Up until Rosa met Vinny, her life in America had revolved around simply surviving. She never had money to spend on luxuries like amusement park rides or cocktails at a nightclub. Vinny lived a life that was very different from Rosa's. He lived a comfortable life where there was money for flashy clothes, and entertainment and he was happy to show Rosa the finer things in life. Rosa wasn't just impressed; she was awestruck at the decadence of it all. Vinny was bigger than life and never missed an opportunity to flaunt his good fortune.

His parents were eager for him to marry. They looked forward to doting over a house full of grandchildren. When Vinny told his parents about Rosa they were disappointed. She was too old as far as they were concerned and the fact that she had already been married and had a child was upsetting to them. They had envisioned their son marrying someone young and pure.

Vinny announced to his parents at dinner over his mother's pasta fazool that he wanted to marry Rosa. "You know that girl Rosa I told you about? Well, I'm crazy about her and I'm gonna ask her to marry me."

The clank of his father's silverware hitting the dish seemed to echo in the ensuing silence. Vinny was nervous. His father had a temper but he mustered his courage and went on. "I think you'd like her. I think you'd like her a lot, Pop. She's from the old country and she's a good girl."

Vinny's mother looked uneasily at her husband anticipating an outburst. In rapid Italian, while still focused on cutting up the food on his plate, Vinny's father said, "You're not marrying that woman. What about Lucia? She's a nice girl and she comes from a good family. You can marry her."

"Pop, Lucia is a spoiled brat. I'd rather die than marry her," Vinny whined.

"Fine, then you can marry Maria Cipriano." Vinny's father said with a finality that was intended to resolve the issue and end the conversation.

"Maria is as dumb as a brick and she's not even eighteen yet." Vinny protested.

Vinny's father inhaled deeply and exhaled slowly in an effort to maintain his temper. He put his fork and knife gently on the edge of his plate. He looked squarely at Vinny and said in a tone that was soft enough to make Vinny have to lean forward to hear his father's words.

"Vinny, this woman Rosa is a widow. She's had a child. She's had to make her way in this city alone. Her husband was killed in a mining accident and her daughter is in an orphanage. She spends her days working for peanuts and lives in squalor. It's all very tragic but you cannot throw your life away because you feel sorry for her. There are beautiful Italian girls whose families own businesses and who are untainted by another man."

Vinny knew better than to challenge his father any further. But his father's words did not discourage him. He was determined to rescue Rosa. He was her knight in shining armor and he knew that she would always be grateful to him. He could take her away from the slums of Five Points and keep her safe and she would be a devoted wife.

Rosa felt flattered by the attention that Vinny showered on her. He was a fairly attractive young man and he was particular about his appearance. Vinny's hair was always heavily greased with tonic and he was impeccably dressed anytime he left the house. Appearances were important to Vinny. He was born in America shortly after his parents came to New York from Italy. Like many immigrants, Vinny's parents were poor when they arrived and worked extremely hard to make a good life for themselves and their only child in the new country.

The Capozzas lived in a narrow three story brick house on 86th street in Bensonhurst. Vinny pronounced it "Bensonhoist." The family business was on the first floor at street level where a green awning read "Capozza's Bakery." There was a very tiny back yard enclosed by a wrought-iron fence with a small vegetable garden that Vinny's mother tended to meticulously. It was a modest home but compared to the tenements on Mulberry Street it was a palace. Cappozza's bakery was known as one of the best in the city. It was a lucrative business and Vinny's father was considering expanding.

Vinny was paid handsomely for the long hours he spent working at the family bakery but when he had free time he enjoyed rubbing elbows with a rough crowd. Vinny liked to fancy himself as a tough guy. In reality he had acquaintances that were notorious mobsters but Vinny himself only ran in the very periphery of those circles. Vinny could be charming and ingratiating, yet just below the surface of his jovial facade was a man whose fragile ego could not tolerate even a minor slight.

Vinny liked to drink and he was a regular at a few of the neighborhood bars and speakeasies. He was quick with a joke and generous when it came to buying drinks. Most nights he bought more drinks than he could comfortably afford. The more Vinny drank, the more generous he became.

Many of Vinny's friends from the neighborhood had been sent overseas to fight in WWI. The ones who survived had come home to a hero's welcome and it made Vinny envious. Vinny had registered for the draft in June of 1917 at the age of twenty four. He had envisioned himself performing acts of incredible bravery and coming home a war hero too but he was rejected by all branches of the military due to his flat feet. He was tall and burley, and aside from his flat feet, he was the picture of health. He felt embarrassed about the whole thing and hated explaining to people why he hadn't gone overseas to fight alongside all the other young men from the neighborhood.

So Vinny poured himself into his work at the bakery and tried to compensate for his shortcomings in other ways.

CHAPTER EIGHT

The Spanish flu epidemic disappeared in the latter part of 1920, as mysteriously and quickly as it had appeared. Only two deaths at the orphanage were attributed to it; Margo and Jacqueline. Neither Sister Angelina nor Mother Superior became ill. The Spanish flu found the majority of its victims in the young and healthy and made the casualties of the Great War pale in comparison. It seemed to Berta and the other girls at the orphanage, that God Himself had imbued Sister Angelina and Mother Superior with a superhuman ability to thwart the deadly disease. After ten days of confinement with only relatively mild symptoms, both nuns had returned to the business of running Sacred Heart Orphan Asylum.

Finally, life at the orphanage had gone back to normal. The girls who lived at Sacred Heart went into the church after lunch every day and said their prayers with the Sisters. On Sunday they went to morning mass with all the other parishioners. The nuns watched the girls like hawks during the mass. Anyone who dared to misbehave would be reprimanded by the Sisters afterward in catechism class. The entire mass was in Latin and neither Berta nor Chevonne really understood what was being said.

Chevonne was in the habit of whispering to Berta during church; a habit that didn't go unnoticed by Sister Mary Agnes.

"Chevonne O'Farrell, I'd like you to explain to the class why you thought it necessary to disrupt Father Demo's sermon with your yammering," Sister Mary Agnes said sternly.

Chevonne's plump cheeks went from light pink to red. She looked sheepish and lowered her head slightly but said nothing.

"Well Chevonne, we're waiting. Explain to the class why it's important for people to be quiet in church," Sister Mary Agnes commanded.

There was an uncomfortable silence.

Chevonne finally managed to stammer a response. "It's important to be quiet because... um, because..., because... people are sleeping?"

There was muffled giggling from the older girls. Sister looked heavenward and let out an exasperated sigh, "Lord have mercy."

Berta and Chevonne spent more than few a hours during their time at the orphanage peeling potatoes, scrubbing floors and writing "I will not talk in church or class" on a blackboard but despite being disciplined for occasional transgressions, Berta's life at Sacred Heart Orphan Asylum was a happy one. The older she got the easier it became to follow the rules. Berta still missed her mother and looked forward to seeing her when she came to visit, but Berta had grown fond of the others girls and the nuns. In many ways they had become like family to her. She was never lonely.

It was hard to imagine what life would be like outside of the orphanage but Berta would soon find out.

CHAPTER NINE

$\mathcal{R}$osa was reserved and shy. She worked hard and went to mass every Sunday and now it seemed that her prayers had been answered. Vinny Capozza was in love with her and had asked her to marry him. She had told Vinny all about her past. She told him about the harrowing voyage from Italy to Ellis Island and how she had had to leave Berta in an orphanage. She told Vinny how frightening it was walking the streets of New York City not knowing where her next meal would come from or where she would sleep at night. Vinny promised that he would always take care of her and that she would never have to worry about those kinds of things again. Rosa told herself that she loved Vinny but sometimes she wasn't sure if she loved him or loved the idea of having someone to take care of her so that she wouldn't have to spend the rest of life toiling in a textile mill.

Vinny treated Rosa with the utmost respect. He thought of her as a delicate fawn that had been abandoned in a forest full of predators. Of course, he knew that she was not a virgin but he would not consider making an improper advance. Rosa was sweet and innocent and she would be his wife soon. Vinny had slept with many women. He lost his virginity at the age of fifteen in a brothel in Queens and used prostitutes to satisfy his needs on a weekly basis. Vinny was a regular at a brothel in the Majestic Apartments on Central Park West where the Madame, Polly Adler, knew him by name and made sure the girls treated him right. Polly's girls knew that Vinny liked to be praised for his sexual prowess, but in reality, he was a selfish lover whose idea of sex was skewed by his lack of experience with any woman except for the ones he paid.

Rosa and Vinny dated for almost a year. Vinny was on his best behavior where Rosa was concerned. He always told her how beautiful she was and brought her flowers, chocolates and thoughtful little gifts. They went for long walks and talked about their hopes and dreams for the future. Rosa wanted nothing more than to be a good wife and mother. She longed to have a home with a kitchen where she could cook wonderful meals. She smiled at the thought of how happy they would all be. Rosa envisioned Vinny being a kind, affectionate father to Berta and the children they planned to have together. She imagined tucking their freshly bathed babies in bed at night where they would always be safe, well fed and loved.

Vinny's parents said nothing more about his relationship with Rosa, and Vinny told them nothing more. He knew his parents well enough to know that pressing them on the issue would be futile. He hated fighting with his parents, especially his father because they spent every day with each other at the bakery. The truth was that it was Vinny's nature to take the easy way out of any predicament. He was content to let his parents believe that he was only dating woman casually and that he was too busy working and spending time with his buddies to develop any serious relationship.

Occasionally his mother would complain in her broken English, "Vinny you getting too old. You need to find a wife. When you bring a nice girl home?"

"Ma, you know how busy we are in the bakery. I ain't got time to chase girls right now. Pop wants to expand the business and he works me like dog. He wants a Capozza's Bakery on every corner of New York City ya know."

But Vinny knew what his parents really wanted.

They wanted grandchildren. His parents had always planned on having a large family, but after Vinny was born, his mother was never able to carry another child to term. The doctors didn't know why. It left a void in their lives, and not only in his parent's lives, but in his as well. Vinny remembered all the times his mother cried because she miscarried and never forgot the sadness on his father's face. Vinny felt sad about it too. All the other kids he grew up with came from huge families and some of them had eight or nine siblings. Their homes were hectic, but filled with laugher and spirited commotion.

Vinny longed for siblings and wanted more than anything to have a big noisy family. But it never happened. He was lonely growing up. His parents were indulgent when it came to providing material things. Some might even say he was spoiled, but they could be demanding, controlling and quite strict at the same time. They had high expectations where Vinny was concerned and it made Vinny feel pressured and stifled at times.

Vinny understood that he was their life. They saw their future in him and he knew that he and the bakery were his parent's legacy.

Vinny would have liked to have a large, traditional Italian wedding, but of course, that would be impossible. Rosa had no family except for her daughter and Vinny had no intention of telling his parents about the impending nuptials. He decided it would be better if they eloped. His parents would come around, he just knew it. They'd have to if they wanted to get their hands on their first grandchild and Vinny believed that once they got to know Rosa they would love her too. Everything would work out just fine and they would be one big happy family.

Vinny wanted as many children as Rosa could give him. His friend Joey's mother, had twins at the age of forty three. Rosa was still fairly young; in her early thirties. He figured she had at least a decade to bear children. According to Vinny's calculations, that meant roughly five to six Capozza babies.

Vinny planned to propose at the Feast of Santa Rosalia at the spot they had met exactly one year before. He didn't need to buy Rosa an engagement ring becuase Vinny wanted to give Rosa a ring that had been in his mother's family for generations. It was gold and had a signet of two clasped hands. It was called a fede ring; "fede", in Italian, meaning, "a pledge of love." Vinny's mother kept it in a small green velvet pouch closed by a pull string. It had been in the right hand draw of the credenza in the living room for as long as Vinny could remember. Vinny's mother took it out one day when he was in high school and showed it to him and explained that it had been given to her great-great grandmother as an engagement ring. His mother told him that when the time came Vinny would give it to the woman he intended to marry.

He was torn about taking the ring without telling his parents. He told himself that the day would come when his mother would be pleased that Rosa was wearing it. Eventually, she would be glad that he had kept tradition and presented it to his wife-to-be when he asked for her hand in marriage.

On the day of the Feast of Saint Rosalia the sky was gray and overcast. A fine mist of rain fell intermittently during the afternoon. As they stood in front of the zeppoli vendor, just as they had the year before, Vinny put his hand in the pocket of his suit jacket and took out the green velvet pouch. He looked pensive. Rosa was perplexed and looked down at the green pouch. The rain came down a bit harder.

Vinny's hands shook slightly as he fumbled nervously to loosen the drawstring of the pouch. He reached in and took out the ring, the fede that his great-great-great grandfather had given his wife over one hundred years ago.

Rosa stood completely still not fully understanding what Vinny was doing until he bent down on one knee. He looked up at Rosa for a moment and took her hand in his. Vinny said nothing for what seemed to Rosa like a long time. She was becoming uncomfortable because a small crowd had begun to gather around them.

Finally, Vinny said, loud enough for the dozen or so on-lookers to hear, "Rosa, will you marry me?"

Rosa, burst into tears and brought a hand up to cover her mouth and nodded until she could find her voice. She laughed, "Yes, Vinny, yes! Of course I will marry you."

The crowd erupted in applause. At that moment there was a sudden torrential down pour.

Everyone including Rosa and Vinny ran for cover. Vinny hadn't even had a chance to get the ring on Rosa's finger. They took shelter in the doorway of nearby office building. Vinny took Rosa's hand again and slipped the ring on her delicate finger. The ring was a bit loose but Rosa stared at the gold signet ring in awe.

"It's beautiful Vinny."

"It's a little big, eh?"

"Not too bad. I'll have to be careful that it doesn't fall off though."

"It won't be too big for long," Vinny grinned broadly at Rosa.

"What do you mean?"

"Well, you know, women when they're with child usually put on a few pounds. It should fit just right before you know it."

Rosa laughed. "You sound like you in a rush Vinny."

"Yeah, I'm in a rush alright."

Vinny sublet a comfortable two bedroom apartment on 81st Street, not far from his parent's house. The regular tenants wouldn't be back for another eight months. The apartment was nothing special but it was clean and came furnished. The kitchen had a breakfast nook and a built in ironing board that came down out of the wall from behind what looked like a cabinet door. The ice box was on the opposite wall next to the sink. The living room got plenty of sun and there was even a small fireplace. The bigger of the two bedrooms had a good sized armoire, a bureau and two twin beds with a nightstand between them. The other bedroom had one twin bed, a bureau and a small desk. It wasn't fancy but it was all they needed for now.

Rosa spoke of Vinny occasionally during her visits with Berta but never offered much detail. Rosa referred to Vinny as her "special friend" and told Berta that he was "a very nice man". Somehow, Berta sensed that she ought not to ask too many questions about her mother's "special friend". Her mother talked of other friends more openly, like Gitta Lachman. Mrs. Lachman made special bread for Rosa to take with her whenever she went to see Berta. Berta looked forward to it and would give it to one of the Sisters to divide up for everyone at the next meal.

Rosa told Berta about all the women in the textile mill where she worked. Berta never tired of hearing about the lives of the women that worked there. Rosa also talked about some of the people that lived in the tenement building on Mulberry Street and how lovely some of them could be and how awful others were. But Berta knew very little about the man her mother had been dating for the past year.

One day Berta's mother explained to her that she and Vinny were planning to marry and that they were all going to live together in a lovely apartment in Bensonhurst. Berta would even have her own room. Her mother assured her that she would make many new friends when she went to school. Berta knew that she would miss all the friends she made at the orphanage but she would especially miss Chevonne. She was like a sister to Berta and Berta worried about her and Patrick and what would become of them if their father didn't get better.

Chevonne and Berta vowed to write each other often and they both cried the day Berta's mother came to take her from the orphanage.

CHAPTER TEN

Vinny and Rosa were married in the Church of St. Teresa of Avila on Classon Avenue in Brooklyn on a Saturday afternoon in October of 1921. Rosa wanted Berta to be there too, but Vinny thought it would be too hectic and convinced Rosa to take Berta out of the orphanage after they'd had a few days alone together as man and wife. Rosa wore a beautiful dropped waist sleeveless pale pink satin and lace dress that came to just below her knees with a hat to match. Gitta made it for Rosa to wear on her wedding day.

It was a short ceremony with just Gitta and Yekl Lachman as witnesses. It wasn't the first time that Father Donahue presided over hasty nuptials at the back of the church. He asked few questions and happily accepted a generous offering from Vinny for his trouble. Rosa never expected that she would marry again and she considered herself blessed. Yet she couldn't help but remember the day she married Gaston in a little village in Italy. She remembered how utterly exuberant she felt. She couldn't imagine living life without Gaston. Nearly one hundred people, friends and family, were there on that wonderful day with them. The celebration lasted almost two days and was the talk of the village for months. Rosa told herself that the twinge of sadness she felt standing in an enormous church in Brooklyn marrying Vinny Capozza wasn't because she didn't love him the way a wife should love a husband. No, that wasn't it. It was because she was no longer a naïve nineteen year old girl. She'd seen too much and now she knew how cruel and dreadful life could be sometimes and simply didn't trust it anymore.

Vinny never really thought much about what his wedding day would be like. He wished his parents could have been there. In his late twenties, Vinny was the last of his friends to get married and had been to more than a few big Italian weddings. He felt a little disheartened that their wedding didn't include any of the traditional festivities. But Vinny looked to the future and vowed to himself that he would make-up for the simple wedding they'd had. The Capozza family would have the most elaborate, opulent baptismal for their first born Bensonhurst had ever seen. They'd invite the entire neighborhood to the church and celebrate afterward at Grand Prospect Hall. Even if it meant having to work twenty hours a day at the bakery, it would be worth it.

Rosa, Vinny, Gitta and Yekl walked out of the church and into the fading afternoon sun. Vinny turned to Gitta and Yekl and said, "Mr. and Mrs. Lachman, Mr. and Mrs. Capozza request the honor of you presence at dinner tonight."

Vinny had arranged for a friend to pick them up in front of the church in a brand new Dodge Brother's Touring car. It was the first time that Rosa or the Lachman's had been in a car and they were excited beyond words. Vinny chuckled, "All right now, pick your jaws up off the sidewalk and hop in."

Gitta and Yekl sat in the back seat while Rosa sat on Vinny's lap in the passenger's side in the front seat.

"Vinny, we'd love to join the two of you for dinner but we have to get back to the children," Gitta explained.

He turned to the driver of the car. "We're gonna bring our friends home to Hester Street, Eddy."

They pulled up in front of the Lachman's apartment building. Rosa hopped off Vinny's lap and climbed down out of the car. She gave Gitta a hug and smiled at Yekl,

"I'm so glad you two could be with us today."

Vinny got out of the car and shook Yekl's hand. "We really appreciate you and Gitta standing up for us," he said with genuine sincerity.

"We wouldn't have missed it for the world, Vincenzo," Yekl told him.

Gitta and Yekl walked up the steps, stopping to turn on the landing as they waved to Rosa and Vinny before opening the door to the brownstone. "Mazel Tov!" they yelled. Vinny and Rosa waved from the back seat. Eddy honked the horn as they drove away.

"You know we've got big plans tonight Mrs. Capozza. I'm going to take you to a very special place," Vinny said as he put his arm around her. He yelled out to the driver. "Hey Eddy; take us to 142nd Street and Lenox Avenue." The Marquee was lit up with big yellow bulbs that read "Club De Luxe." Vinny helped Rosa out of the car and they walk in to the nightclub arm in arm. In the year it had been open Vinny had become a regular. The club was owned by heavy weight boxing champion Jack

Johnson and it was the place to be. On most nights you could find any number of celebrities, musicians, high society folks and high rollers like Owey Madden and Dutch Shultz. Rosa had no idea that it was a speakeasy. She'd never been in one but she'd heard about them.

A haze of cigar and cigarette smoke hung in the air. The room was dimly lit with elegant crystal chandeliers and small tiffany lamps that sat in the middle of each table. There were at least a few dozen round tables seating six to eight, all of them covered with crisp white table clothes. The chairs were decorated with fancy white satin covers with big bows on the back. There were enormous vases about the room filled with fresh flowers. "All by Myself" by Irving Berlin was being sung by a handsome colored man in front of an orchestra of nine men.

The Club De Luxe was crowded with men sporting smart looking suits and fedoras tilted to one side. The women were heavily made-up and dressed in true flapper fashion with colorful outfits that were impeccably coordinated and accessorized with expensive jewelry. The room was raucous with clever banter, laugher and music. The alcohol flowed freely despite prohibition. Vinny ordered a bottle of champagne. "We'll take a bottle of the best bubbly you got and keep'em comin doll. We're celebrating for a crowd," he told the cocktail waitress.

Rosa imagined that this was how very rich people spent their time. She felt as if she were in a dream and wasn't quite sure how to behave. The alcohol helped though. It didn't take long for the champagne to relieve her of her inhibitions. They left the club sometime after midnight, both having drunk too much. All Rosa could remember after leaving the club was the two of them staggering out to the car. Vinny gave Eddy the address of the new apartment. Rosa thought she must have dozed off during the ride home because she remembered nothing of it. She had a fuzzy memory of Vinny carrying her as he stumbled into their bedroom. He dropped her on one of the twin beds and fell, fully clothed, beside her. The last thing she remembered was the sound of Vinny snoring.

Rosa woke before the sun came up. She was disoriented for a minute and not quite sure where she was. She soon got her bearings but it didn't alleviate the vague sense of dread and panic she felt. Her heart was racing and her head was pounding. She didn't know why she felt that way. She had so much to be thankful for. She was a newlywed and she would never have to step foot in the textile mill again. The days of fending for herself in the tenements of Five Points were over. But best of all she could take Berta out of the orphanage.

Rosa slipped gingerly out from underneath Vinny's arm. He showed no sign of waking. The room was dark. She felt her way to the bedroom door. The sun was just beginning to rise and gave off enough light in the living room for her to make sense of her surroundings. She found the bathroom and turned the faucet on. She splashed cold water on her face and rinsed her mouth out. She felt mildly nauseous. Rosa ran the faucet and cupped her hands together and quickly brought mouthfuls of the cool water up to her lips. Once her thirst was satisfied she decided to explore the apartment. She looked around the kitchen in amazement. There was an oven and an icebox and a sink with running water and counter space to prepare food. It was lovely.

Rosa had given Vinny all her belongings to take to the apartment the day before they married. Everything she owned fit into a burlap Hunt & Behrans feed bag. Rosa found the bag in the corner of the living room. She emptied it out on the couch and picked out her toothbrush and nightgown. After getting changed she went back into the bedroom. Vinny was still passed out on the bed. Rosa went to the other bed and pulled back the covers and got in. She was asleep within minutes and didn't wake up until noon when she heard the church bells of Our Lady of Guadalupe ringing.

It was a Sunday morning. She had missed mass for the first time in years and Vinny was gone.

CHAPTER ELEVEN

$\mathcal{V}$inny woke at six a.m. and rushed to get to the bakery. He was as hung over has he'd ever been and he dreaded the long day ahead. Vinny's father was a stickler for punctuality and he was already late. Vinny rushed into the bakery looking disheveled. "What the hell happened to you? You look like crap! Where the hell have you been? I've been busting my ass all morning. Look at you. What's the matter with you?" Vinny's father bellowed in Italian without any concern for the spectacle he was causing. He gave Vinny a hard whack on the back of the head. Vinny flinched. The customers seemed not to be the least bit bothered by the scene. They were interested in getting their Sunday baked goods. Vinny's arrival just meant that there was more help and the line would move faster now.

It was the end of a long day and Vinny was so exhausted he could hardly keep his eyes open. He took off his apron after cleaning up the shop and went upstairs. His mother was tossing the caponata while the panella was frying in a pan on the stove. The smell of the food made his mouth water. The table was set. "Vinny go wash up, dinner will be ready soon." He thought about Rosa and how he tried to wake her before he left to tell her that he had to go to the bakery. All he could get out of her was a groan. He planned on telling his parents that he had eloped but today didn't seem like a good day to do it. He knew they'd be upset and he just didn't have the energy to deal with it. He'd have to wait until he had a good night sleep and a clear head to break the news to them.

Vinny's father was quiet at the dinner table. Vinny knew he was still angry. His mother broke the silence, "Vinny, where were you last night? You didn't come home. Your father and I worry."

"I was out with friends Ma." Vinny said without making eye contact with his mother. Vinny's father scoffed, "Friends? You mean those thugs

and crooks and whores? Those are your friends Vinny? Those kinds of
people are no good. I told you, you're going to end up getting in trouble
associating with people like that. I don't want any part of that kind of
thing and I don't want you involved with them."

"Pop, it's no big deal." Vinny's father shot back, "Yeah, no big deal my
foot!"

Vinny finished eating and went to his room to lie down. He closed his
eyes telling himself he would rest for an hour or so and go back to the
apartment. He wasn't sure what he would tell his parents when they asked
where he was going. Vinny fell asleep thinking about it and woke up eight
hours later in his bed. He considered telling his father that he had to run
an errand so that he could make a quick dash to the apartment to check
on Rosa but he didn't dare. It would invite questions Vinny wasn't
prepared to answer and leave his father shorthanded again during the
morning rush. His father would be irate. He just had to hope that Rosa
would understand. He planned to tell his parents that he was meeting
friends for dinner after work so that he could go back to the apartment to
see Rosa.

When Rosa woke to find Vinny gone she assumed that he went to the
bakery but didn't recall him saying goodbye. She felt abandoned but told
herself she was being childish; after all Vinny had to make a living to
support her and Berta. He'd be home after work and they could talk about
his day and relax in the privacy of their own apartment. Rosa's stomach
grumbled. She went into the kitchen looking for something to eat. All she
could find was a half loaf of bread and a few slices of provolone cheese
wrapped in wax paper in one of the cupboards. The bread was stale but
not moldy and the cheese was greasy. She sat at the kitchen table and ate
most of the bread and a few bites of cheese and wrapped them back up.
She didn't know what to think when Vinny didn't come home that
evening. She felt like the walls of the apartment were closing in on her. It
was nearly seven o'clock at night. Surely he would be home any minute.
It was plenty of time to close the bakery, clean up and walk back to the
apartment. Rosa paced and fidgeted and waited and waited. There was
nothing to do but wait. Finally she went to bed.

Rosa tossed and turned all night waking every hour or so to look over
at the other bed to see if Vinny had come home. She watched the sun come
up from the living room window; a great orange orb that rose slowly into
the sky, hour by hour the sun rose higher and higher and then it began to
sink again. Another day had passed and it was nearly dusk. Vinny still

wasn't home. Rosa ate the rest of the bread and cheese and decided to walk to the bakery to find out what had happened to her husband.

Rosa had never been to the bakery but Vinny talked about it so much she felt like she knew it just as well as if she bought a cannoli there every morning. It was on 86th Street so she walked in the general direction. Rosa estimated that the bakery was about five or six blocks away. It was dark when she got there. The light of the full moon shone brightly and she could read the name on the green awning- Capozza's Bakery. Rosa giggled; it wasn't until that very moment that she realized her married name was Rosa Capozza.

The lights were off in the bakery except for one in the very back by the ovens. Rosa could see a tall man with thick gray hair and a mustache; he looked to be in his early sixties. Rosa banged on the door with her open palm. The man looked up and walked toward the door. "We closed. Come in the morning when everything fresh made." the man yelled through the glass at Rosa. "I'm looking for Vinny; Vinny Capozza." Rosa yelled back.

The man opened the door. Rosa took a few steps into the bakery. The man looked Rosa over and scowled. "What you want with Vinny?" Rosa was angry that she had been left in the apartment like a dog and now she was furious to be spoken to as if she were a shifty solicitor. "I'd like to speak with Vinny." Rosa said tersely. The man said nothing for a moment and looked at her suspiciously, "Wait here." he ordered.

A few moments later Vinny came walking slowly out of the back room. He looked frightened. "What are you doing here?" Vinny whispered. "What do you mean..." Rosa shot back. Vinny cut her off, "Shhhh. Rosa calm down. I'm sorry. I couldn't leave; the bakery was too busy."
"Well now the bakery is not busy and it's time to come home." Rosa said flatly. "Look Rosa, I...well...I...ya see...I..."
"What is it Vinny? What are you trying to say?" Rosa said impatiently.
"I haven't had a chance to tell them." Vinny said sheepishly. Rosa stared at Vinny in stunned silence. "They don't know that we got married?"
"I was going to tell them but..." They were interrupted by the man who came to the door to let Rosa in.

"Vinny, there's still work to do." The man said brusquely."
"Okay Pop, I'll be right there."

"That's your father?" Rosa asked. "Yeah.", Vinny was clearly uncomfortable and gave no indication that he was going to introduce her to his father. "Vinny, when are you going to tell them?"

Vinny looked over his shoulder nervously and whispered, "Soon, I'm going to tell them soon. Please Rosa, it's been a long day; this is not the right time..." Vinny's father's booming voice came from the back room, "Vinny! Let's go we need to finish up; your mother will have dinner ready soon." Vinny took another nervous glance over his shoulder and whispered, "Listen Rosa, I'll be done in a minute. I'll tell them we're going to go for a walk. Just wait here."

Vinny went to the back room to help his father clean the bread racks. "Who is that girl Vinny?" Vinny lost his nerve. Things weren't happening the way he had planned. "She's a friend Pop."

"A friend", his father said cynically. "Well why's your friend here at seven-thirty at night?" Vinny's father asked, emphasizing the word friend sarcastically. "Pop, I'm tired. Can we talk about it later?" Vinny's mother appeared in the doorway to the back entrance. "Enough work for today; dinner is ready." Vinny's mother was annoyed that the meal she lovingly prepared was getting cold.

"Um, Ma, I'm going for a walk. I'm not going to eat."

"What? What do you mean you going for a walk? Dinner is ready. You go for a walk after."

"Ma, I'll eat later. I have a friend waiting for me." Vinny's mother could see a plainly dressed woman of slight build standing inside the bakery by the front door.

Vinny's father rolled his eyes, "Yeah, a friend. I bet she's a good friend too." Vinny's mother ignored the implication that the woman waiting for Vinny was loose.

"Vinny go get your friend. We have plenty and it's getting cold."

"Ma, I don't think..." His mother interrupted him loudly and said with exasperation, "Vinny, I've been cooking in that hot kitchen for hours. You go get your friend now!" Vinny's father shook his head in disgust. He knew that as much as he disapproved of the kind of women Vinny liked to spend his time with he would have to sit though dinner with this one whether he liked it or not. He knew his wife well enough to know when arguing was futile. "You heard your mother. Go!" Vinny's father, Salvatore, ordered.

Vinny had to fight the urge to run. He walked over to Rosa and purposely stood in front of her with his back to his parent's in order to obscure their vision. Vinny didn't invite Rosa to dinner as his mother had instructed him. Instead he said, "Rosa, I'm going to tell my parents that you have an engagement you need to get to. I'll meet you back at the apartment in twenty minutes."

"You'll do no such thing; your mother has invited me to dinner. I heard her quite clearly. I'm starving because you left me in that apartment with nothing but a crust of bread and a hunk of cheese for almost two days." Rosa hissed.

"Rosa please, Vinny pleaded, they'll hear you."

Rosa leaned so that she could look around Vinny and see his parents. She waved and yelled, "Bonjurneo!" and gave them a big, broad, albeit phony, smile.

Vinny's mother, Anna, didn't smile back. She was a plump woman with a pleasant face but she was obviously aggravated with the delay and made no effort to hide it. She gestured with both arms, "Come on!" she yelled. Rosa walked toward Vinny's parents and he walked behind Rosa. They followed his parents up the narrow stairway to their apartment on the second floor. The table was set for three. Vinny's mother quickly put another place setting down and said to Rosa, "Here sit." Rosa did as she was told. Nobody spoke. Vinny and Salvatore pulled out their chairs and sat. Vinny looked as if he was going to throw up. Salvatore eyed his son and then brought his gaze over to Rosa and back to Vinny again. Vinny's mother placed the large pan of manicotti on the table next to the antipasto. It smelled wonderful. She sat down and put her napkin in her lap. They all followed suit. "Eat!" Vinny's mother, Anna demanded.

Rosa was ravenous and was enjoying the meal so much that she nearly forgot about their predicament. They made small talk, although Salvatore said very little, Vinny's mother was gracious. For a while it seemed as if Vinny had relaxed too. They were all chuckling over a funny anecdote Vinny told about an old woman who came into the bakery to order a birthday cake. Suddenly his mother's face fell and she stopped laughing abruptly. Her eyes were fixed on the gold signet ring on Rosa's left ring finger.

CHAPTER TWELVE

Vinny's mother was rendered speechless at the sight of her great-great grandmother's wedding ring on the hand of the strange woman at the dinner table.

His father looked at his wife with concern. "What's the matter? You look like you seen a ghost."

"Nothing, nothing the matter... I...I...I forgot to put bread on the table."

Salvatore shrugged nonchalantly as if to say, "so what" and seemed a little vexed by his wife's sudden mood change. Both Vinny and Rosa knew exactly what startled his mother. Vinny broke out in a cold sweat and had to focus on trying not to hyperventilate. Rosa felt as if she'd just been punched in the stomach. Vinny's father was oblivious as he concentrated exclusively on devouring his manicotti.

Anna Capozza seemed to have no intention of letting her husband know that she had just found out that their only son had gotten married behind their back to a woman neither one of them had ever laid eyes on before. Rosa politely thanked Vinny's parents for dinner. Vinny wiped his mouth with his napkin, put it on the table and stood up. "I'm going to walk Rosa home," he announced. His mother had her back to them washing dishes in the sink. She didn't turn around or speak. Vinny's father was already engrossed in reading the paper. Without looking at them he put his hand up and said, "Goodbye; and Vinny- don't be late tomorrow."

Vinny walked over to his mother. He put his arm around her and kissed her cheek. It was wet from the tears that were silently streaming down her face. Seeing his mother cry was almost physically painful for Vinny and the truth was he felt like crying too.

"Ma..." Vinny began.

His mother interrupted him, "Go Vinny. Just go."

Vinny and Rosa walked back to their apartment in silence. The enormous butter yellow full moon bathed everything in a warm glow. The air was cool and dry but neither Vinny nor Rosa could appreciate the magnificence of the night sky. Rosa was on the verge of tears and Vinny was angry. He could taste the saltiness of his mother's tears on his lips from when he kissed her cheek. He knew he had hurt her deeply. His father would be enraged when he found out and Vinny dreaded being at the receiving end of his father's fury.

When they got back to the apartment neither Rosa nor Vinny spoke. Rosa was torn between feeling badly that she'd put Vinny on the spot and being disgusted that her husband wasn't man enough to tell his parents that he had gotten married. Rosa followed Vinny into their bedroom. She sat on the edge of one of the twin beds and waited for Vinny to say something. She wanted Vinny to apologize for leaving her in the apartment the way he did. She wanted him to apologize for denying her to his parents. But no apology came.

Vinny remained quiet while he stood facing the wall with his back to Rosa. He slowly unbuttoned his shirt and took it off and tossed it on the foot of the bed. Vinny took his wallet out of his pants pocket and opened it. He pulled out some bills and put them on the night stand and said, flatly without turning around to look at Rosa; "There's money to buy food." Vinny undid his belt and let his pants drop to the floor in order to step out of them. He bent over and picked them up, folding them before setting them next to his shirt. For a moment Rosa thought Vinny was going to say something. Still facing the wall wearing only his boxer shorts and a white tank t-shirt Vinny put his hands on his hips. "Rosa, I..."
He stopped and shook his head, letting out a defeated sigh. Vinny got into bed and turned on his side, facing the wall, and pulled the covers up over his shoulder.

Rosa was exhausted. She felt miserable and dejected. For a long while she sat on the edge of the bed opposite Vinny and simply stared at his shrouded figure under the covers. After ten minutes or so, Rosa finally mustered the energy to get ready for bed. She went to the bureau and quietly opened the draw and took out her nightgown. Vinny had fallen asleep and rolled onto his back. His eyes were closed, his chest rose and fell in soft, even breaths. Rosa studied Vinny's features. He was usually impeccably groomed but Rosa noticed that he needed a shave. His hair was mussed from being pressed on the pillow. He seemed like a completely different person from the Vinny she knew. The boisterous, gregarious man who seemed so tough and self-assured was gone, and instead, he looked vulnerable, almost timorous.

Rosa went into the bathroom to undress. She slipped her nightgown over her naked body and looked in the mirror. The nightgown was made of lilac cotton and Rosa could easily see the outline of her nipples and the tuft of her pubic hair under the thin material. She hoped Vinny wouldn't wake up. Her face burned with embarrassment at the thought of him seeing her unclothed. Rosa had to remind herself that Vinny was her husband now and she was a grown woman who'd already had a child. She knew what marital intimacy was. Nonetheless, Rosa couldn't help but feel deeply self-conscious. She opened the bathroom door slowly and peeked out to make sure Vinny was still in bed and tip-toed across the floor to the twin bed on the other side of the room. She slid quietly under the sheets. Rosa lay in bed thinking about everything that had happened and cried herself to sleep.

Vinny had set the alarm clock for 5 a.m. He turned, reaching over in the dark and fumbled to shut it off. He laid awake with his eyes shut thinking about how he would tell his father about Rosa. He rubbed his eyes as he yawned and stretched and then reached down in his boxer shorts. He felt the hardness of his morning erection. Vinny rolled out of bed and went over to Rosa. He looked down on her and brushed her hair out of her face.
"Rosa," he whispered. When she didn't wake, Vinny pulled the covers back just enough so that he could wiggle in next to her in the twin bed. He put his arms around her and kissed the back of her head. Her hair smelled clean and it was soft and warm on his face. He cupped one of her breasts with his hand and rubbed himself up against her buttock.

Rosa woke to Vinny's rapid, hot breathing in her ear. She feigned sleep while Vinny slid his hand under her nightgown and felt her bare breasts. He pushed her nightgown up and entered her from behind. Rosa squeezed her eyes shut tightly and held her breath. After a dozen or so short thrusts Vinny let out a low groan. Rosa felt Vinny's body relax and noticed that his breathing had slowed. "Good morning beautiful," Vinny murmured. The room was still dark.

Vinny got up and turned on the lamp on the nightstand. Rosa brought a hand up to her eyes to shield them from the brightness. "Sorry doll. I'll be outta here in no time and you can go back to sleep. It's real busy at the bakery. I might have to stay over and take a short nap at the folks to get everything done. We got a big job to cater and it's all hands on deck at Capozza's Bakery," Vinny said as he pulled on his pants and fastened his belt buckle. Rosa didn't know what to say. She couldn't believe he was actually telling her that he wasn't planning on coming home again.

Rosa didn't have the energy to argue with him. Instead she said, "I'm going to pick up Berta today." Her voice was hoarse from the early morning hour. Vinny was in a much better mood than he was the night before. He sounded relaxed and happy. "Yeah, that's swell honey." He picked his wallet up off the nightstand and pulled out a twenty dollar bill. "Why don't you girls do a little shopping or go see a movie? I think it'd be nice for you two to take a few days to get reacquainted. Get her a little welcome home present too will ya?" Vinny tossed another bill on the nightstand.

"Thank you, Vinny." Rosa appreciated Vinny's generosity but she felt as if he was trying to make amends for leaving her stranded in the apartment and humiliating her at his parent's the night before. Rosa thought Vinny's suggestion that she and Berta take a "few days to get reacquainted" was a bit convenient too. Vinny could sleep at his parents and not have to explain that he needed to go home to his wife. Rosa suspected that Vinny simply couldn't bring himself to tell his father that he had married her.

Vinny bent over and kissed Rosa's cheek before leaving for work. "See ya later gorgeous," he said sweetly. Rosa waited for Vinny to leave before she got out of bed. The insides of her thighs were wet and sticky from Vinny. Rosa remembered the last time she had had sex. It was the night before Gaston left for America. They made love for hours. They talked and laughed and ate in bed then made love again. But that was years ago and Gaston was dead and nothing would ever change that. She and Berta would have to survive the best they could. Rosa was married to another man now. But Berta was a constant reminder of her late husband. She had Gaston's eyes and it would only be a few hours before she would see them again in her daughter's face. She smiled at the thought.

Rosa went into the bathroom. She sat on the toilet and urinated. When she was finished she wiped the ejaculate from her perineum and tried to remember the last time she had had her period. It had been a long time since she had reason to pay much attention to it. She guessed that it had been a few weeks ago. Rosa thought about the prospect of getting pregnant again. She knew Vinny would be thrilled. Rosa got herself ready for the day and made the beds and straightened up. She couldn't wait for Berta to see the apartment.

Before she left, Rosa took the money from the nightstand. Vinny had left twenty-five dollars; more money than she'd seen at one time in her entire life. Outside, Rosa walked down to the corner store to buy as many groceries as she could carry. As she was shopping, she saw a doll and thought Berta would love it. The doll's name was Raggedy Ann. Rosa bought it and put Raggedy Ann on top of the groceries in the bag.

Finally, the day had come when Rosa could take Berta out of Sacred Heart Orphan Asylum.

CHAPTER THIRTEEN

Rosa came to get Berta from the orphanage a week before her eleventh birthday. Berta tried to imagine what it would be like living in an apartment and being a real family with a mother and a father. She imagined that Vinny would be like Chevonne and Patrick's father, loving and funny and wise... except that he would be well and very handsome. Berta had never met Vinny and asked her mother why Vinny never came with her to visit. Rosa told her that he and his parents owned a very busy bakery and Vinny had to be there during the day to take care of all the customers.

At the orphanage the older girls were to look after the younger girls and show them how to make their beds and do their chores. In the evenings after dinner Berta would also help the younger girls with their school work. Sometimes they would just sit together and play jacks or color.

The night before Berta left she sat on the floor next to a little girl that had arrived a month before. Her name was Dorothy and she was only four.

"I'm going to be leaving the orphanage tomorrow, Dorothy. Do you think you could draw a picture for me? I'd like to take it with me to remind me of you," Berta asked.

"Where are you going, Berta?" Dorothy asked.

"I'm going to live with my mother and her new husband."

They were both quiet for a few moments. "My mother went to be with God. Do you think she will come to get me soon too?" Dorothy questioned.

Berta didn't want to have to explain that "being with God" was a euphemism for dead, and that like her father, dead people never come back. Instead, Berta smiled and hugged Dorothy.

"I know that I will miss you Dorothy, but I also know that you will make a lot of wonderful friends here and I think you will be very happy."

For a moment Dorothy looked dreamily at the blank piece of paper in front of her, then picked up a crayon and began to draw diligently. Concentrating intensely, Dorothy held her tongue in the left corner of mouth as she worked on the paper.

Berta leaned closer for a better look. "What are you drawing Dorothy?"

"I'm drawing God," Dorothy said without looking up.

"But nobody knows what God looks like, Dorothy."

"They will in a minute," the little girl replied confidently.

Berta smiled and waited patiently for Dorothy to finish her drawing.

She handed Berta the drawing. "Here, Berta. Now when you leave here you'll be with God too," the little girl assured her.

Berta finished saying her tearful goodbyes and left the orphanage with her mother. It felt strange to be out of her uniform on a school day. Sister Mary Agnes brought her a light blue, button down shirt and a brown skirt the night before, clothes that had been donated, while Berta's uniform would be washed and pressed for another girl to wear.

It took two trains and a long walk to get to the apartment but Berta was excited to see her new home and Rosa was excited to show it to her.

Berta's room was just big enough for a dresser, a nightstand, a small desk and a twin bed. The walls were bare and there was a full length mirror fastened to the back of her bedroom door. Berta picked up the Raggedy Ann doll from her bed and lay on top of the pale yellow chenille bedspread. She held the doll up in front of her and examined its red triangle nose and red yarn hair. She wondered who the doll belonged to.

"Do you like it? It's a present from Vinny," Rosa beamed as she stood in the doorway.

But Berta didn't feel excited about the doll. She was too nervous about meeting the man who'd bought it for her. "Yes, that was very nice of him, Mama," Berta said politely, still staring at Raggedy Ann and imagining what she would say to her new step-father when they finally met.

Berta got off the bed, still holding the doll and walked over to the window. She pulled back the white lace curtains and looked down on the street. She could see a hopscotch course drawn in chalk on the sidewalk.

"Are there any girls my age in the building Mama? I see someone was playing potsy."

Her mother went to the window and looked down. "I see. Well, I don't know Berta. I've only been here for a few days myself. Come on sweetie, I'll show you the rest of the apartment."

Rosa led Berta into the kitchen. The walls were painted a light mint green, there were red and white gingham curtains on the windows and a small breakfast nook in the corner.

"Mama, you have a kitchen to cook in," Berta said sounding amazed.

"Well Berta, what do you think?"

It was a lot for Berta to take in. It felt unreal. For a minute she thought it might be a dream and that she would wake up like she had for years, in her bed at the Sacred Heart Orphan Asylum.

"When will Vinny be home?" Berta asked.

"Well, he thought it would be best if we had a chance to visit alone together for a little while. He's staying at his parents for a few days. The bakery is awfully busy and his father needs his help to run it."

Berta could tell by the sound of Rosa's voice that there was something wrong. She noticed that her mother started to fidget and looked away from her anytime she brought up the subject of Vinny.

"What is he like Mama?" Berta asked as they sat at the breakfast nook sipping their tea.

"Vinny? Well, he likes to have fun but he works very hard. He loves children and he'd like for us to have a baby soon. Would you like a brother or sister, Berta?"

She didn't respond right away and seemed to be in deep thought. "I don't know, Mama. I'm not sure. I think a baby could be a lot of work for you."

Rosa laughed, "Yes, babies can be a lot of work. You were, but definitely worth it."

Berta smiled.

The next day Rosa and Berta went to visit the Lachman's apartment. Gitta Lachman was a small woman with slightly buck teeth and a big warm smile. Her soft brown eyes crinkled up when she laughed and Gitta loved to laugh. She had been a good friend to Rosa. Berta had heard so much about the Lachmans that she felt as if she too had known them for years.

Their apartment was on Hester Street on the second floor of a brownstone building. From the hallway Berta and Rosa could smell Gitta's cooking. Rosa knocked on the door. "Come in!" Gitta yelled. Gitta stood in front of the stove stirring a big pot of matzah ball soup. Gitta wore a flowered apron over her long sleeved dress and had a brown mitpachat scarf on her head. She screamed in surprise when she saw Berta. "Berta! Oh Berta, you're finally here!" Gitta quickly took the wooden spoon out of the soup pot and put it down on the counter before wiping her hands on her apron. She ran toward Berta and gave her a tight hug and a kiss on the cheek.

"Your mother talked about you every day Berta! She missed you and I'm sure you missed her too. You must be so happy to be home." Before Berta could answer Gitta yelled over her shoulder, "Yekl! Yekl! Rosa and Berta are here!"

Yekl came into the living room where they all stood. He smiled when he saw them. "Well there you are! Shalom!" He walked over to Berta and put his arm around her and kissed the side of her head. Yekl held their four year old, Sylvia, on his hip with the other arm.

"Berta, this is Sylvia. She's just up from her nap." Sylvia, with her thumb in her mouth, buried her face in her father's shoulder.

"Dinner will be ready soon Yekl," Gitta announced. "Will you wake Yetta and David?"

Yekl turned to Sylvia and said, "Come on sleepyhead, let's go wake up your brother and sister."

The living room and kitchen were one big room separated by a wide doorway with pocket doors that had been pushed back into the walls. The golden, late afternoon sun filtered through the wide slats of the metal venetian blinds. The big oak gate leg table was set for six. Two of the chairs had stacks of books on the seats for Sylvia and Yetta to sit on so that they could reach the table. There was a wooden high chair for two year old David. A large, steaming noodle casserole sat in the middle of the table.

Berta felt happy and loved sitting at the table with her mother and the Lachmans. They told stories and laughed and ate. The food was delicious. She watched as Gitta and Yekl managed their children. The youngest, David repeatedly banged his spoon on the highchair tray and babbled happily. Gitta and Yekl ignored the racket and everyone just spoke a little louder. Six year old Yetta was refusing to eat. She sat with her arms folded in front of her and pouted.

"Yetta, be a good little girl and eat your dinner before it gets cold," Yekl cajoled.

"No," Yetta said emphatically. Gitta said something to Yetta in Yiddish and Yetta responded. "Sylvia broke my new doll!" Yetta cried.

"Sylvia, why would you do such a thing?" Yekl asked the four year old. Sylvia put her head down and said nothing. Yetta sat next to Sylvia. Unable to contain her fury any longer, Yetta raised her arm and with an open hand hit her sister on the top of the head. Sylvia wailed.

Yekl stood up calmly and picked Yetta up off of the chair. He carried her into the living room and sat her on the couch. He spoke too quietly for anyone but Yetta to hear him. Meanwhile, Gitta comforted Sylvia. Several minutes later, Yekl came back to the table and sat down and joined in the conversation, leaving Yetta sitting on the couch, pouting, for the duration of the meal. Berta wondered if she would have little sisters one day like Sylvia and Yetta, or a little brother like David. She wondered if Vinny would be kind and affectionate like Yekl. She could barely remember her real father. Her idea of what a father was supposed to be had come entirely from the letters that Chevonne and Patrick received from their father and by watching Yekl with his children. She thought it would be nice to have a father.

Berta and Rosa left the Lachman's with full stomachs and in high spirits and took the train back to the apartment in Bensonhurst. Berta got ready for bed thinking about all the girls at the orphanage and feeling a little sad that most of them would never see their mother or father again. She missed Chevonne terribly. Berta got ready for bed and went out into the living room to say goodnight to her mother. Rosa sat on the sofa reading the New York Tribune, or at least what she was able to read in English.

"Goodnight Mama." Berta went to her mother and kissed her on the cheek.

Rosa hugged Berta tight, "Goodnight. Maybe tomorrow we can read the paper together. I think you probably read English better than I do now." laughed Rosa.

The next morning, Berta awoke early in her quiet little bedroom in Bensonhurst. It seemed strange not to hear the chatter of a dozen other girls and the opening and closing of closet doors and the rustling sheets of hastily made beds. The sun was shining brightly and the lace curtains in her window lifted with the gentle breeze that blew softly into her room. It was a brisk, clear fall day. Berta felt like the luckiest girl in the world to have her mother just steps away. She got out of bed and went into the other bedroom where her mother was still sleeping soundly and crawled in next to her and fell back to sleep.

Berta awoke to the sound of her mother humming while she poached eggs on the stove for their breakfast. She went into to the kitchen.

"Well, good morning. Did you sleep well?" Berta's mother asked.

Berta smiled sleepily and nodded.

"Good. Are you hungry?"

"Not that much. What are we going to do today, Mama?"

Rosa grinned and said, "It's a surprise."

Berta thought for sure that the surprise was going to be going the bakery to meet Vinny and his parents. Berta imagined that they might have a little party and that there would be cake and cookies.

"What is it mama?" Berta asked excitedly. "What's the surprise? Are we going to go to the bakery?" Berta was nearly jumping up and down with eager anticipation.

Rosa's expression changed suddenly but she regained her composure quickly. She smiled stiffly. "Oh no, Berta we'd just be in the way. The surprise is much better than a visit to a bakery," she said, sounding a bit defensive.

Berta tried not to look too disappointed. *It's not just a bakery... it's our bakery. It's my step-father's bakery.*

Rosa changed the subject. "I think we ought to clean up the breakfast dishes and get dressed, don't you?" her mother said with a forced cheerfulness.

Berta wore the same clothes she left Sacred Heart Orphan Asylum in.

"Mama, is this okay to wear?"

Her mother glanced over her shoulder as she wiped down the kitchen counter. "That looks lovely," Rosa replied. Rosa had had her hair cut at Vinny's urging a few months before the wedding but Berta preferred her mother's hair long. She remembered back to when she was a very little girl and how she would watch as her mother sat on the small chair in front of the vanity mirror with her head tilted to one side to brush her shiny, thick waist length hair. Her mother's dark brown hair was cut in a short bob now.

Rosa pulled a beige hand crocheted cloche hat over her sleek haircut before they left the apartment. Berta thought her mother had become quite avant-garde since she started seeing Vinny, but the truth was that she missed the way her mother used to look. Berta couldn't help but notice that her mother was preoccupied and tense. Rosa surely thought that as a child, Berta wouldn't understand. All Berta knew was that her mother was keeping something from her, pretending that everything was alright when it really wasn't. She doubted that her mother would confide in her, even if she asked and Berta was right, so she focused on enjoying the day and hoped that Rosa would forget about whatever was bothering her, at least for a little while.

"So, are you going to tell me mama? Where are we going?"

Rosa laughed a genuine laugh and said, "It's really driving you crazy isn't it? You'll see." Berta noticed that her mother's bad mood was starting to lift a bit and felt relieved. The two strolled leisurely down the sidewalk holding hands and taking in the scenery. They took the train into Manhattan and walked about four blocks from the last stop on 7th Avenue to Broadway. Broadway and Times Square were crowded with people. There were playhouses, theatres, restaurants and shops of all kinds.

There were big signs everywhere. Berta heard that they lit up and made it seem as if it were daytime in the middle of the night. There was a marquee that read "Marilyn Miller in Sally." There were gigantic electric signs and huge colorful billboards advertising just about anything you could think of from cold cream to Coca Cola.

Finally, Rosa stopped walking and looked up. Smiling, she announced, "Well, we're here." They stood in front of 1645 Broadway; the Capital Theatre. Berta was speechless. The Capital Theatre was enormous and elegant and Berta could hardly believe that she and her mother were actually going to walk in the doors and sit in one of the deep yellow upholstered seats and watch Dorothy Gish in "The Country Flapper." Berta had never seen a movie.

They were early. Rosa bought the tickets and the usher showed them to their seats. They sat and watched the crowd fill up the rows. The room darkened and the heavy red velvet curtains separated and the music began. Berta read the title cards effortlessly. She wasn't sure if her mother was able to read much of what was on the screen, but it didn't seem to matter. They both laughed uproariously at the pantomimes and antics of the actors. The crowd clapped and cheered at the end of the movie and the lights went on and the curtains closed.

Berta and her mother walked out of the matinee, arm in arm, and walked down Broadway toward Herald Square.

"Well I think it's time we bought you some clothes Berta," Rosa told her.

Berta hadn't thought much about clothes because at the orphanage all the girls wore uniforms. All their undergarments, night gowns, socks, shoes and coats were usually second hand from donations. Wearing something that nobody had worn before her was novel.

"Really Mama, do you mean we're going to buy new clothes?"

Rosa laughed at the look of awe on Berta's face. "Come on, Macy's isn't far. It'll be a nice walk. We should have at least an hour to shop before they close."

They bought three skirts, three blouses, four pairs of socks, a gray tweed coat and a new pair of black patent leather Mary Jane shoes. Berta felt like a princess. She and Rosa carried the shopping bags happily to the train stop. It was getting dark and they looked forward to getting washed up and ready for a light dinner and an early bedtime. Berta thought it was definitely one of the most amazing days of her life and she couldn't wait to write to Chevonne and Patrick to tell them all about it. The only thing that could have made the day better was if Chevonne could have been with her too.

They got to the door of the apartment. Rosa set the bags down and turned the doorknob. But before she could open the door, Rosa and Berta were startled by a loud crash that came from inside the apartment.

CHAPTER FOURTEEN

Rosa and Berta stood frozen in fear for a few moments before Rosa cautiously pushed the apartment door open. Then they heard a man's voice singing... "I ain't got nobody...I'll sing you love songs honey all the time..." Berta stood nervously behind Rosa holding a shopping bag in each hand. Rosa could see nothing in the living room.

"Hello!" Rosa yelled into the apartment. She heard the sound of a man laughing. "Hello, who's there?" Rosa called out again. Vinny wasn't supposed to be home until the next evening. "Vinny, is that you?" Rosa hollered, still standing in the doorway.

"Well, who the hell did you think it would be?" Vinny shouted back from the bedroom. Vinny's words were nearly unintelligible because of his slurring.

Berta looked at her mother's expression. She could see the trepidation on her face. They walked slowly into the apartment. Rosa put the bags down and turned to her daughter. "Stay right here. I'm going to go see what's wrong with Vinny..."

Berta sat on the couch wondering what was happening in the bedroom and why her mother looked so scared. Then Berta heard Vinny's booming voice.

"Well, looks like you and the kid had a nice day! Wish I could say the same for myself..." Vinny laughed, but it wasn't a happy laugh. It sounded more like contemptuous mirth. The bedroom door was more than half way open but Berta couldn't see her mother or Vinny from where she sat on the couch until she leaned forward just right. She could see Vinny through the crack where the door hinges met the doorjamb. He was on the floor on his back.

"I did what you wanted Rosa. I broke the news to my father and told him that I had married a widow with a kid," Vinny slurred. Berta could hear that her mother had said something but couldn't quite make out what it was.

Her mother's voice became louder. "Vinny get up." Rosa urged in panicked whisper. Berta could see her mother's hands pulling on the back of Vinny's shirt. "Get up off the floor. Berta's in the living room and I don't want her to see you like this. And for heaven's sake, keep your voice down." Rosa implored.

Vinny attempted to get up by rolling over on his stomach and pushing himself up with great effort on his hands and knees. His heavily greased hair hung in front of his face.

"Well, aren't you the fancy one, you don't want your precious daughter to see her new daddy like what, Rosa? Drunk? Ya mean drunk, right? You two would be out on the street if it weren't for me!" Vinny roared while still on his hands and knees, his head hanging down.

The milk glass lamp had shattered on the bedroom floor.

Please, Vinny get up. You'll cut yourself..."

Vinny reached up and put a hand on the edge of the bed, pulling himself up to crawl on top of it.

"So why don't ya ask me how things went at home Rosa? Ask me how they took it. Go ahead; ask me." He chided; his words thick with liquor. Rosa didn't respond. "Crappy, that's how. I've been disowned ya know. The old man even fired me." Vinny's words trailed off as he lay on the bed. Slowly, his eyelids began to droop and he fell silent.

Rosa hoped that he was passing out. Finally, Vinny began to snore. She went back out into the living room where Berta sat on the couch looking frightened.

"It's alright Berta, don't worry. Vinny's just had a hard day today. He'll be okay soon."

Rosa no sooner got the words out of her mouth when Vinny bellowed, "Rosa!"

She walked hurriedly back into the bedroom. Berta stayed on the couch as her mother had instructed until she heard Rosa yell. "Stop it Vinny; stop it right now!"

Berta got up and went to the doorway of the bedroom and saw Vinny lying on the bed. Her mother was trying to pry Vinny's hands off of her arm but she wasn't strong enough. Vinny pulled her mother down on top of him. "Let go of me!" Rosa hissed as she twisted her body to get free.

Berta was stunned. All she could get out of her mouth was, "Mama!"

Vinny let go and Rosa stood up quickly and straightened her clothing. She looked upset and embarrassed. After a few awkward moments she said, "I'm going to go make us all something to eat," and walked out of the room. Berta stood frozen in the doorway staring at Vinny.

"Come on Berta, you can help me in the kitchen." Berta followed Rosa in to the kitchen and watched her mother make three egg salad sandwiches. She poured two glasses of milk, setting them on the table at the breakfast nook before bringing over the plate of sandwiches.

"Is Vinny sick?" Berta asked after sitting silently at the table for ten minutes or so.

"No, Vinny isn't sick, Berta. But I bet he'll be plenty sick when he wakes up tomorrow." Berta could tell her mother was angry and disgusted. Berta finished her sandwich and asked to be excused. She went into the bathroom and got ready for bed while her mother cleaned up the dinner dishes. When Rosa was done she went into Berta's room and sat on the edge of Berta's bed.

"Every night for years I wished I could sit at your bedside and give you a kiss good night and tuck you in. We had a wonderful time today at the movies and shopping, didn't we? I'm sorry things didn't go as well when we got home." Rosa bent over and kissed Berta's forehead. "Goodnight."

Her mother stood up and turned off the light as she left the room, leaving the door three quarters of the way shut behind her.

It seemed to Berta that so much had happened since she left the orphanage that morning. It almost seemed like a lifetime ago. Of course, it was a much different life. Berta wasn't yet sure if it was going to be the life she had imagined or something very different. She never imagined that her new father would be like Vinny. Vinny didn't seem wise or funny like Mr. O'Farrell, or kind and loving like Yekl. Berta thought about Vinny's angry words and fell asleep wondering if Vinny would throw them out one day soon. She would have to be careful not to upset him. The thought of being thrown out on the street frightened her and Berta thought it probably frightened her mother too.

Rosa went back into the bedroom where Vinny lay on the bed passed out. She swept up the glass pieces from the broken lamp that had shattered all over the floor. Vinny woke momentarily at the sound of the broken glass being swept into the dust pan. He opened his eyes and squinted over at the clock.

It was almost ten at night.

"You need to eat something, Vinny. There's an egg salad sandwich in the ice box for you," Rosa said tersely. Vinny rolled over and went back to sleep.

Vinny looked rough when he awoke the next morning. He was clearly suffering the aftermath of all the beer and whiskey sours he'd consumed the night before. After the explosive scene at his parent's house he had met up with his buddy, Eddy Belachi and they went out. He told Eddy what had happened. When Vinny asked Eddy to drive the car on the day he and Rosa married, Eddy said he'd be honored to do it. He also told Vinny that he didn't think his parents were going to take it very well when they found out that he had eloped. Eddy was right.

Vinny and Eddy had been friends since they were kids. They grew up together. Eddy knew the Capozza family well.

"What are ya gonna do for work now?" Eddy asked him. Vinny was a guy who liked to live in high style but he hadn't even thought of that yet. He was never good at saving money and his father had cut him off abruptly. Now he had a wife and child to support on top of it. He had a vague recollection that Eddy had told him about a so-called "career opportunity" that "might interest a guy who needed a job in a hurry." He couldn't remember the particulars. One drink turned into a few dozen drinks as Vinny and Eddy went from one club to another. Vinny had gotten so tanked that he couldn't even remember coming back to the apartment or anything else that had happened afterward. He woke up on top of the covers in his street clothes. Rosa's bed was empty and unmade.

Vinny got up and went into the bathroom. The throbbing pain in his head was excruciating. His stomach was churning and his mouth was so dry it felt like it was full of saw dust. He walked slowly out of the bathroom, through the living room and into the kitchen. It was as if a small explosion went off in his head with each step he took. Rosa and Berta sat at the breakfast nook eating tomato soup and grilled cheese sandwiches. It was noontime. He didn't acknowledge Berta or Rosa. He opened the door to the ice box and pulled out a bottle of milk and stood guzzling it. When it was half empty he put it back and wiped his mouth on his sleeve. He took the loaf of bread off of the kitchen counter, pulled it out of the wax paper, ripped a large piece off and ate it in giant, ravenous bites. When he was done he tossed the bread back on the counter and went back to bed.

Berta and Rosa watched as Vinny walked out of the kitchen. Berta thought Vinny's behavior was disgusting but she said nothing to Rosa. Instead, she waited for her mother to react. Rosa continued to eat her lunch as if nothing had happened.

"I think it would be a good idea for us to take a walk to your new school. It's not far from here at all," Rosa said casually. Berta thought her mother's response, or lack thereof, was peculiar, considering how blatantly rude Vinny had been.

"Is Vinny going to go to the bakery today Mama?" Berta asked hoping that the answer was "yes."

Rosa thought for a minute. "I'm not really sure Berta," she said.

Rosa and Berta finished lunch and walked to PS 128, the school Berta would be attending. She was supposed to start sixth grade but the Sisters at Sacred Heart Orphanage had told Rosa that it would be best if Berta were placed in the seventh grade. Berta didn't really care if she was put in the sixth or the seventh grade. She just hoped that she would meet some nice girls her age to play with. Berta had already written a letter to Chevonne and she couldn't wait to mail it off.

"Mama, I have a letter I need to send to Chevonne," Berta informed her mother.

"We'll see the postman on the way to your new school. He's usually making his route this time of day. We'll give it to him. I'm sure you'll be getting a letter from Chevonne any day now too."

"Their father is going to be getting out of the tuberculosis sanatorium soon. When he does, he's going to go get Chevonne and Patrick. Chevonne thinks they'll probably get a bungalow in Gerritsen Beach and go to Resurrection Elementary School. They won't be far away at all and we'll be able to visit." Berta said excitedly.

Rosa hoped that that was true. "That would be wonderful for them," Rosa responded, trying to match Berta's optimistic tone.

Within the week Berta received a letter from Chevonne. It was written the day after Berta left the orphanage. Berta came home from school to find the envelope with Chevonne's neat handwriting on it addressed to "Miss Roberta DeLuca." She was ecstatic.

"Mama, Mama!" Berta yelled.

Her mother came out of the kitchen wearing an apron spotted with flour. "Mama, look, it's a letter from Chevonne!"

Rosa laughed. "Yes, it came today. I put it on your bed." Berta held the letter in her hand and stared at her name on the envelope and smiled. 'Well, aren't you going to open it?" Rosa asked, amused by Berta's look of astonishment. Berta opened the letter carefully. There were two pages with writing on both sides. As Berta began to read, the expression of elation on her face faded.

"Berta, what's the matter? Is everything okay?" Rosa asked.

Berta didn't respond. She was so absorbed in reading the letter that her mother's words didn't yet register. She was visibly shaken. Finally, she looked up. "No Mama, everything isn't alright."

CHAPTER FIFTEEN

Vinny wasn't home much and he didn't go to the bakery anymore. Instead, he went out at night to meet "friends" at various clubs. Eddy Belachi was a bouncer at one of the speakeasies in Harlem. Rosa knew that Vinny's father had cut his income off abruptly and that Vinny was in need of employment. Vinny told Rosa that Eddy had "a few things lined up" for him. When Rosa pressed Vinny on details he was evasive. "Let's just say this particular job has to do with public relations," he told her and chuckled to himself as if there were some inside joke that she wasn't privy too.

Vinny had never had a job outside of the bakery and Rosa couldn't imagine what kind of job Vinny would end up with. It didn't look like Vinny's father and mother were ever going to warm up to the idea that Vinny had married a woman they didn't approve of behind their backs. Vinny still thought that they would soften up once Rosa got pregnant, but until then, he had to figure out how to make a buck.

Eddy was definitely connected and there were all sorts of "odd jobs" Eddy would be willing to include him in. Vinny came home late most nights, at three or four in the morning and most of the time he'd been drinking. Whenever Rosa questioned Vinny about his whereabouts he became belligerent.

"Get off my back Rosa! I pay the bills around here, not you. This is business Rosa and you need to respect that," Vinny would growl.

Rosa didn't dare challenge Vinny any further. It wasn't worth the aftermath.

When Vinny came home in the wee hours he was usually inebriated. Most of the time, he was pleasantly sloshed and would go into the kitchen and cook a big breakfast for himself. Sometimes he even baked cakes. He whistled and sang while he cooked. When he was done eating he left the mess for Rosa to clean up. At least a few nights a week Vinny went to Rosa for sex when he came in from the clubs.

Their sex was perfunctory and devoid of passion or tenderness. Vinny would come into the dark room and take off his pants and boxer shorts. He'd let them fall to the floor and step out of them, though he kept his shirt and undershirt on. If Rosa was lying on her back Vinny would simply lay on top of her, push up her nightgown, spread her legs and enter her. Usually he was finished in a minute or two. Rosa never said anything during coitus. She was just glad it didn't take long and that Vinny got up and went out into the kitchen afterward so she could fall back to sleep.

It wasn't long before Rosa figured out what Vinny did for a living. Eddy Belachi was a member of the Five Points Gang. The gang was involved in extortion, armed robbery, gambling and prostitution. Eddy knew that Vinny had been nothing more than an empty suit when it came to the gang's activities but now that Vinny was hard up for cash, Eddy had an easier time of getting his buddy involved in what he referred to as the "business end of things."

Vinny thought it was funny to tell people he was in "public relations." It was a term Eddy used regularly. Rosa didn't know for sure what kind of "services" her husband was providing to the Five Points Gang, but she suspected from the few conversations she'd overheard between Vinny and Eddy that collecting debts was one of Vinny's jobs.

Vinny usually didn't get out of bed until late in the afternoon. Most days when Berta came home from school he would be sitting in the kitchen smoking cigarettes, drinking coffee and reading the newspaper. If it was warm out he sat at the table bare-chested. He was burly and stood about five foot nine. He had thick black hair on his shoulders, back and chest. Berta was repulsed by the sight.

She got home from school and stuck her head in the kitchen doorway. "Hello, I'm home!" Berta yelled. Her mother was sitting across from Vinny shelling peas. Vinny had the New York World newspaper out on the table and was absorbed in an expos'e about the Ku Klux Klan. Berta watched as he spread a large dollop of butter on a Kaiser roll and took a big bite. He continued to read the paper without looking up.
"Hello, Berta. How was everything at school?" her mother asked.
"Alright, I suppose," Berta answered.

When Berta went into her bedroom she found another letter from Chevonne on her nightstand. She hadn't heard anything from her in over two weeks and was anxious to find out what had happened. She couldn't stop thinking about what Chevonne had written in her last letter because it seemed impossible. Chevonne and Patrick had received a letter from one of the nurses who worked at the Riverside Hospital where their father lived for years with the other patients suffering from quarantinable diseases. Berta's knees had become weak as she read the words on the pages of Chevonne's last letter. The revelation took her breath away.

Tom O'Farrell had died almost a year ago, unbeknownst to Chevonne and Patrick. The letters that they had been getting, one received just weeks earlier, full of hope and encouragement had been sent posthumously. In reality they were being mailed off, two or so a month, by one of the nurses Mr. O'Farrell had befriended during his lengthy stay there. At least two dozen of their father's letters had been sent to Cheveonne and Patrick after he had succumbed to tuberculosis, all lovingly written by a dying man desperate to provide comfort, strength and guidance to his children for as long as he could.

The nurse herself wrote a letter and included it with the last letter their father was able to write on his own. She apologized for the ruse and explained that she had felt torn about the deception but felt obligated to fulfill Tom O'Farrell's last wish. She told Chevonne and Patrick that she never met a man who loved his children as much as their father loved them and how proud he was of them both. The thought of it all brought Berta to tears.

She hoped that the new letter she was about to open would bear some good news. Naturally, Chevonne and Patrick were stunned and devastated to learn that their father had been dead for nearly a year. Their father's letters had sustained them in so many ways. Patrick was insightful enough to understand that the letters were not just an attempt by his father to reassure them that everything would be alright, but also wishful thinking on his father's part. Tom O'Farrell had a propensity for optimism that some might have said bordered on a complete refusal to accept reality.

Patrick took the nurse's letter to the library where he often went to study and have lunch with Mrs. Wallace. He took the letter out and handed it to Mrs. Wallace without saying anything. She looked up puzzled by the blank expression on Patrick's face and took the letters from him.

She read it quietly. After a few moments tears welled up in her eyes and spilled over on to her cheeks.

"Oh Patrick, I am so sorry for you and your sister." She reached into her sweater pocket and pulled out a peach linen handkerchief and wiped the tears from her eyes. Mrs. Wallace had never seen Patrick cry in all the years she had known him. He'd come in to the library, hungry, bruised from fights or exhausted from being out in the elements selling papers and shining shoes and she'd never seen him be anything but brave and cheerful. He had had to grow up fast, and at the age of thirteen, he'd endured more hardship and loss than most adults would in an entire lifetime. But Patrick did not hide his sorrow from Mrs. Wallace that day. He stood in front of her desk in the library and watched as she read the words on the pages. He said nothing. He looked completely desolate and defeated.

Mrs. Wallace walked around the table to Patrick and put her arms around him. He sobbed for the first time since reading the letters.

Katherine Wallace and her husband lived a comfortable life on the Upper East Side of New York City. Both came from well-to-do families, although neither felt the need to be ostentatious about their affluence. They lived at the corner of East 68th and Fifth Avenue. Mrs. Wallace's family had made their money in real estate and construction. Her brothers still operated the largest construction company in the city. The Wallace's lived on the 5th floor of the building.

The apartment was spacious enough to house a grand piano in the living room and when the Wallace's entertained, which was usually only for charity and fund raising purposes, the apartment could easily accommodate fifty guests and ten domestics. There were six large bedrooms, a study, a large galley kitchen, a dining room with a table big enough to seat twenty with a massive crystal chandelier that hung over it. The ceiling rose sixteen feet with spectacular crown moldings. Katherine Wallace couldn't have cared less about the particulars of decorating and so it was left to professionals to adorn the residence in the latest Parisian decor.

Every morning and every evening a uniformed doorman greeted the prominent residents of the exclusive Fifth Avenue address. The Wallace's had been quietly dwelling there for the past decade and a half. The doormen wore white gloves and top hats and stood outside under the long burgundy awning that led into the meticulously appointed marble floored foyer.

The Wallace's had decided before they married that they would not have children. Both Katherine Wallace and her husband had been raised by governesses and nannies until they were old enough to be sent off to boarding school in Europe. They didn't see the point of bringing children into the world for virtual strangers to raise. They enjoyed travel, the arts and the company of clever adults, like notable literary greats and world renowned scientists and educators. Becoming parents wasn't ever a consideration for either of them. Children just wouldn't have fit their lifestyle.

For nearly three years, since she'd met Patrick O'Farrell, Katherine had her cook pack two lunches, one for her and one for Patrick. Patrick had slowly but surely became such an important part of her life that she felt anxious and out of sorts on days that he didn't come to the library. She worried about him and missed him. It nearly ripped her heart out to see him cry. The day Patrick brought the letters into the library for Katherine to read he told her he was considering taking his sister out of the orphanage. She was getting to the age where she might have to be put out anyway. He thought maybe they should get on an orphan train. Perhaps they would find a decent family to take them in out west.

"Patrick, you mustn't do that," warned Mrs. Wallace. There was panic in her voice. Patrick didn't know what to think, he was numb.

"Chevonne is ten years old. She deserves a chance to have a home and family. I can't expect her to live on the streets of New York City with me," Patrick replied sagely.

"No, Patrick of course you can't. You're right. I have an idea though. I want you to come back tomorrow so we can discuss it." Mrs. Wallace looked intensely into Patrick's eyes to make sure he understood her directive. He seemed dazed and spent. Patrick nodded and they sat as they always did next to one another at one of the large library tables. Mrs. Wallace put her arm around Patrick and rubbed his back briefly in an effort to console him. They sat in silence for a good part of the afternoon reading.

Patrick O'Farrell knew nothing of Katherine Wallace except that she was the kind lady in the library who appreciated his intellectual curiosity and enjoyed cultivating it. Their love of learning and literature was a mutual interest and Katherine couldn't help but admire Patrick for his incredible strength of character. He was both courageous and compassionate and she knew that he trusted her and was genuinely fond of her. It seemed to Katherine that their souls just somehow knew each other immediately.

Katherine couldn't explain her urge to protect and nurture Patrick. All she knew was that she couldn't suppress it, or turn it off at will. She knew she couldn't bear the thought of never seeing Patrick again and she knew that she would have to go home to her husband that evening and discuss the prospect of adopting two children.

It wasn't a conversation she looked forward to, considering Arthur's sentiments on the rearing of children, no less an orphaned Irish street urchin and his little sister.

CHAPTER SIXTEEN

Berta was the new kid in the fifth grade class at PS128. All the other kids seemed to know each other from kindergarten and some of the kids were even related to one another in some way. Berta felt like an outsider and it wasn't a good feeling. One day during recess a classmate asked Berta where she used to go to school. "Sacred Heart Orphan Asylum," she said, feeling uncomfortable about revealing this information to a potential friend.

"You were an orphan? Did you get adopted?" Sophia Fabiano asked with a look of astonishment on her face. Sophia's two favorite books, Pollyanna and Anne of Green Gables, were about orphans.

"Well no, not really" Berta answered, somewhat puzzled by Sophia's intense interest. "My mother and I came here from Italy when my real father died. She couldn't take care of me so she brought me to the orphanage," Berta explained.

Sophia was clearly intrigued. A few days later she invited Berta to her house for dinner. Berta couldn't wait to get home to ask her mother if she could go.

When she got home she ran into the kitchen. "Mama! Can I go to Sophia Fabiano's house for dinner tomorrow after school?"

Before Rosa could respond Vinny interrupted. "How about saying hello first?" Vinny was clearly annoyed.

Berta felt demeaned at his harsh tone. "Oh. Hello..." Berta said timidly. Vinny said nothing but gave Berta a dirty look and went back to reading the newspaper.

"How was school?" Rosa asked.

Vinny interjected again. "Hey kid hand me the orange juice from the icebox, will ya?"

She put her school books down on the counter and opened the icebox. She took out the juice and handed it to Vinny. "Thanks kid," Vinny said without looking up from the paper.

Vinny rarely called Berta by name and she suspected it was because he hadn't yet committed it to memory.

"Can I go Mama?" Berta asked. "She only lives on the next block over. We walked home together from school until we got to 23rd Street. Can I go?"

Rosa continued to iron, "We'll see Berta."

"Mama, please? She's really very nice. Her parents said she was allowed to have one friend over for dinner tomorrow night and she picked me. Please, please…?"

Vinny looked up from his newspaper and glared at Berta. "Hey! You heard your mother. She'll think about it, now that's enough," Vinny snarled.

Berta didn't dare protest. She just looked at her mother. Rosa said nothing and looked back down at the shirt she was ironing. Feeling dejected, Berta picked up her school books from the counter and went to her room.

Vinny left the apartment around six o'clock like usual. Berta was relieved. Vinny was crass and hostile. Berta tried her best to stay clear of him. Vinny never talked to Berta, he talked at her. They had never had a conversation.

"Goodnight. Good morning. Shut the door. Pass the salt. Where's your mother?" Just the most cursory of communications were all Vinny would engage in when it came to Berta. But Berta knew that Vinny was capable of being pleasant. Sometimes, Vinny had his friends over. They would sit around a card table in the living room and play poker. Vinny was a gracious host even to the point of being obsequious. It seemed to Berta that Vinny was trying too hard to ingratiate himself with them. She could hear most of the conversations that went on. To her it seemed that the men that came to play cards treated Vinny as if he were nothing but a gopher.

"Vinny, what the hell kind of card game you got going on here? For cripes sake, are you trying to starve us?"

"Oh, geez Joey, sorry about that! Let me get you something to eat." Then Vinny would yell toward the bedroom: "Rosa! Rosa!" and Rosa would scurry, dutifully into the living room. "The boys here need food. Why don't ya make some of them deviled eggs, and while we're waiting for them, bring out some pretzels. You guys ready for some more beer?" Vinny was like a different person. He smiled easily and listened politely when the other men spoke. He was normally brooding and irritable when nobody but Berta and Rosa were around.

Vinny had gone out for the night and it was just Berta and her mother in the kitchen sitting at the table eating their sandwiches. "Mama, can I go to Sophia's?" Rosa finished chewing the bite of peanut butter and jelly she'd just taken.

"Alright Berta, but you shouldn't stay too long afterward, it's not polite."

Berta clapped her hands in delight. "Oh don't worry Mama. I'll use my best manners. Thank you!" Berta hopped off the kitchen chair and hugged Rosa. They finished the dishes and went into the living room to listen to the new radio Vinny brought home the week before. Rosa tuned the radio to 77WABC; the announcer exclaimed, "Lopez speaking!"

Berta walked home with Sophia afterschool the next day. Sophia had an older sister and two younger brothers. They lived in an apartment not much bigger than the one Berta lived in. It was crowded. Toys were strewn across the floor in the living room: blocks, dominos, crayons and paper, dolls and doll clothes. There was a sewing machine in the corner of the room and a big wicker basket with pin cushions, scissors, spools of thread, lots of bright colored scrap material and patterns sat on a table next to it.

The victrola in the living room played Alberta Hunter's "He's A Darn Good Man." Sun streamed in through the large bow windows where lush English ivy grew in hanging planters. Sophia's brothers, who both looked to be between seven and eight, were rolling around on the floor pulling each other's hair.

Mrs. Fabiano yelled in. "Boys stop it this instant, or you'll go to bed without supper!"

They released each other and scowled at one another for a moment. One of the boys stuck his tongue out at the other and the other boy immediately returned the gesture.

Mrs. Fabiano turned to look at Berta and smiled. "Well hello there! Sophia's told me a lot about you Berta. It's nice to meet you."

Berta smiled back and said, "Thank you for inviting me to dinner."

Sophia's mother laughed. "Don't thank me yet Berta, you haven't tasted my cooking."

Sophia laughed. "Mom, you're a great cook!"

Mrs. Fabiano smiled. "Well thank you. Papa won't be home for a few more hours, so dinner will be a little late. Would you girls like a snack to tide you over?"

"What can we have mom?"

"Hmmm, let's see, how about an orange...or maybe some Animal Crackers and milk?"

Sophia turned to Berta. "Which one do you want?"

"May I have the Animal Crackers?"

"Why you certainly may, Berta."

"Me too," Sophia chimed in. Mrs. Fabiano poured two glasses of milk and placed them and a plate of the small cookies on the table.

After Berta and Sophia devoured the cookies they went into the bedroom that Sophia shared with her older sister Mildred. "You two will have to be quiet, I'm studying," Mildred said haughtily as she lay in the bed with a magazine in front of her face.

Sophia furrowed her eyebrows and walked closer to Mildred in order to get a better look at what she was reading. "You're not studying. You borrowed another one of those magazines from Celeste. Mom said you weren't allowed to read them. I'm telling!" Sophia started toward the door.

"Wait! Okay, okay! I'll let you read it when I'm done," Mildred said in an attempt to coerce them into staying quiet about her reading material.

Sophia tapped her chin with her index finger and looked up as if pondering her options. "What do you think Berta?"

Berta was practically drooling at the thought of reading Photoplay magazine. "Can we read it before dinner?" Berta asked excitedly.

Mildred let out a sigh and rolled her eyes, "Alright you pests, but only for fifteen minutes; deal?"

The girls looked at each other and responded in chorus; "Deal!"

Berta and Sophia had just about finished pouring over all the pictures of the starlets in the magazine when they heard peals of laughter and screaming. "Papa's home!" Sophia shouted, as she bounded out of the room to greet her father at the door.

Her brothers, Carlo and Giuseppe, hung on their father's leg, one on each side. "Have you been good boys today?" Mr. Fabiano asked in a heavy Italian accent. He reached down and tousled their hair. Both boys looked up and grinned, nodding. Mr. Fabiano reached in his pocket and pulled out two pieces of black licorice and gave one to each boy. The boys then ran off to play. Sophia ran up and hugged her father. "Hello Papa!"

Mr. Fabiano was a tall man. Sophia only came up to just above his waist. He gave her a tight hug and said, "There is my little chiaccheirona. Who is you friend, Sophia?"

Berta knew that chiaccheirona meant chatterbox in Italian and thought it was fitting for Sophia.

"This is my new friend. Her name is Berta. She used to live in an orphanage," Sophia announced.

"Well Berta, it's an honor to have you as our guest," Mr. Fabiano said, as he gently shook Berta's hand.

"Thank you." Berta said blushing.

Mr. Fabiano went into the kitchen and snuck up behind his wife, who was at the kitchen counter preparing dinner. He kissed her on the neck. She turned and gave him a smile. "What's for dinner?" Mr. Fabiano asked.

"Go get washed up and by the time you're done it will be on the table," she replied. Mrs. Fabiano called for Sophia and Mildred from the kitchen. "Girls! Come and help set the table!"

When they were done setting the table Sophia took it upon herself to run out into the living room and yell, "Dinner's ready!"

Mr. Fabiano sliced the roast pork while Mrs. Fabiano put mashed potatoes and peas on the boy's plates and handed the bowls to Mildred and Sophia to be passed around the table. Once everyone was settled the family bowed their heads while Mr. Fabiano said a prayer of thanks. The second the prayer was over Giuseppe blurted, "That Babe Ruth is something else, isn't he Papa? I bet the Red Sox wish they never traded him!"

Mr. Fabiano laughed. "It's funny you should bring up baseball. It just so happens that I have three tickets to a baseball game Wednesday. Do you know anybody who would like to go see a game?" he asked.

Carlo and Giuseppe sat in utter amazement and stared at their father. Finally Carlo said, "Papa, do you mean you have tickets to the World Series?"

"Yes, I believe it is the seventh game," Mr. Fabiano said nonchalantly. "But you two probably have better things to do with your time than go to a boring old baseball game."

After a few seconds their father's disclosure registered, Carlo and Giuseppe sprung up out of their seats and jumped up and down and screamed, "We're going to the game! We're going to the game! World Series here we come!"

When there was a lull in the dinner conversation Mr. Fabiano looked at Sophia and said, "Sophia, your teacher, Miss Cohen came into the grocery store today. She say you talk too much and you not studying you spelling words. Papa is not happy about this at all. I told you last week if you no be a good girl in school you gonna get a spanking. How many spanks you think you should get?"

"None," Sophia said, obviously vexed by the accusation but not denying it.

"Carlo, how many spanks you think Sophia should get?"

"One hundred!" Sophia's little brother offered enthusiastically.

"One hundred, eh?" Mr. Fabiano nodded in the affirmative as if giving the suggestion serious consideration. After a moment of pretending he was in deep thought, he said, "No, no that's too many. My hand will get sore."

Mildred giggled and Mrs. Fabiano was smiling, but Sophia was not enjoying the conversation and didn't appreciate being teased.

After dinner the three girls washed and dried the dishes and put them away. Sophia hoped that her father would forget about the spanking, but as the girls went to leave the kitchen Mr. Fabiano said to Sophia, "Sophia, you forgetting something?"

"No," Sophia said, with just a hint of impertinence.

"Come here Sophia." Mr. Fabiano said sternly.

"I'll be there in a minute," Sophia said to Berta. Mildred and Berta went to back to the bedroom.   "So, how many spanks you think you should get?"

"One," Sophia said confidently.

"One? I think three." Mr. Fabiano responded.

"No, one," Sophia said insistently.

"Okay then, two," Mr. Fabiano said with exaggerated seriousness. He was trying to conceal his amusement with Sophia's attempts at negotiating her punishment.

Sophia decided that she was better off taking two spanks than wasting any more time debating the subject. She wanted to get back to Mildred's borrowed Photoplay magazine. "Okay, two," Sophia agreed.

Mr. Fabiano pulled the chair out from the table and sat down. He patted his leg and Sophia bent over his lap. He raised his hand and brought it down hard on Sophia's buttocks and repeated the motion. Sophia hopped off her father's lap and stood up straight and rubbed her back side. It stung.

"Now remember, you a smart girl Sophia. But no matter how smart you are you can no learn unless you listen and you can only listen when you not talking." Sophia rubbed her buttock and pouted. Mr. Fabiano gave Sophia a kiss on the top of her head and said, "Papa love you and want you do good in school. Now go play with you friend."

CHAPTER SEVENTEEN

*O*ver a year had gone by since Vinny and Rosa married and the Capozza's and their son remained estranged. For a few days each month Rosa would notice that her breasts felt tender and sore. She remembered them feeling that way when she became pregnant with Berta. Rosa would become convinced that she was pregnant, only to end up being deeply disappointed.

She knew Vinny was frustrated and upset at their failure, or to be more precise, her failure to get pregnant, according to Vinny. Rosa wanted a baby because she knew how much Vinny wanted one and she, like Vinny, thought that his parents would come to accept her and Berta once they found out that a grandchild was on the way. But month after month Rosa's period came. Sometimes when Vinny was drunk he would say mean things.

"You aint ever gonna get pregnant cause you're too damn old," he would rant. "I shoulda listened to my old man. What good are ya?"

Rosa felt humiliated and worthless.

Vinny slept most of the day and went out at night "on account of business," he would tell Rosa. But Rosa suspected that Vinny had no problem mixing business with pleasure. More than a few times Rosa found lipstick smears on Vinny's shirts and he often came home smelling like another woman's perfume. At first Rosa was angry and demanded answers; Vinny would lie, and Rosa would believe him, but not because his lies were so convincing. Rosa believed Vinny because she wanted to believe him and the truth was she wasn't in the position to do anything about Vinny's infidelity.

Rosa was completely dependent on Vinny and the few times Rosa broached the subject of getting a job Vinny forbade it. "No wife of mine

is gonna scrub floors and clean toilets in someone else's house, dammit!"
Then she suggested that she might be able to find work in a shop, ladies
apparel or something of that nature. Vinny laughed, "Ladies apparel?
What do you know about ladies apparel? Look at you. I haven't seen you
out of your housecoat in three days."

It was a snide thing to say but it was true. Rosa spent her days tidying
up the apartment and listening to musical variety radio shows. She didn't
go anywhere except the market and occasionally to visit Gitta. Once in a
while Rosa and Berta would go see a movie.The truth was that Rosa felt
isolated and lonelier than she ever had. Vinny's life didn't include her
outside of household duties. He expected to come home to a clean home.
He expected that Rosa would make sure his clothes were freshly
laundered and pressed and that there was food in the icebox. He expected
that she would be available to satisfy his needs when he came home late
from the clubs.

They didn't engage in conversations unless Vinny wanted to gripe about
his "associates", but even that was a one-sided conversation. He wasn't
looking to hear Rosa's thoughts or advice. It was as if Vinny was just
thinking out loud, mulling over whatever dealings his "job" required. It
sounded like Vinny had graduated from collecting debts from small time
gamblers to more dangerous endeavors. Rosa noticed that he had started
to carry a gun.

Vinny was on edge all the time and complained that his friend Eddy was
"messing with the wrong people." He spouted off about a civil war going
on in the Morello crime family and how there was no way to tell who was
going to come out on top; Rocco Velanti or Joe Masseria. His friend Eddy
was in the thick of it and wanted Vinny to go with him to the curbside
liquor exchange near Grande and Elizabeth Streets in Manhattan. It
wasn't far from the police station but bootleggers met openly there to
swap or sell their surplus liquor. Vinny was reluctant, but there was decent
money to be made and so he went with Eddy.

What Eddy didn't mention was that Joe Masseria had planned to
ambush Rocco Velanti at the liquor exchange and wanted a little back up.
Eddy volunteered his services and those of his buddy, Vinny Capozza.
Vinny never pulled his gun. It all happened too fast. He had no idea
what was going on and so he dove for cover behind a crate of whiskey
when the shooting started. Bullets were flying everywhere. Eddy was
wearing a trench coat, which had seemed odd to Vinny when Eddy picked

him up. It was warm out. But Vinny soon understood Eddy's choice of attire.

When Eddy thought he had a clear shot at Rocco Velanti he pulled a sawed off shot gun from the bulky black coat and started blasting away. Shots ricocheted off of several crates and liquor poured from the holes the bullets made. Joe Masseria pulled a shot gun out of one of the crates and started firing. Amazingly, Rocco Velanti escaped unharmed.

Vinny was shaken. He thought for sure that he had heard a few bullets whistle past his ear. But, what was more distressing was the fact that Rocco Velanti would tie him to Eddy, and Vinny would be sure to end up on Velanti's hit list. Rocco Velanti was suspected in the murders of at least twenty people and he was considered one of the best gunmen in New York City. Rocco wanted control of the Manhattan Mafia and as far as Rocco could tell, Joe Masseria, "the Boss" was the only one standing in his way. Now Vinny had to worry that he was on Rocco's "to do" list and lived in fear that he would be ambushed and murdered in cold blood on the street like so many other gang members. Vinny was terrified.

"Jesus Christ Eddy, why didn't ya tell me what the hell was gonna happen?"

"I figured you wouldn't show if I did," Eddy laughed, as if he had just played a clever practical joke.

"You're Goddamn right I wouldn't have, Eddy. Rocco Velanti is nobody you want to be making an enemy out of."

"Rocco's not gonna be a problem for long. We're gonna put him on the spot soon enough."

Vinny felt like there was a target on his back now. He had to make sure he changed his routine. He knew how the gangs operated enough to know that they spent a lot of time watching their prey and lying in wait until they could gun them down when they least expected it.

Vinny was seething with anger. He wanted to punch Eddy in the face for dragging him into the middle of the Morello crime family's civil war but Vinny knew he was in too deep to back out now, and that's exactly what Eddy wanted. Vinny would never be able to go back to his quiet life at Capozza's Bakery. If his father ever did let him come back to work at the bakery Vinny would still need the protection of the Five Points Gang. He was beholden to them now and needed their protection.

Things hadn't turned out the way Vinny thought they would when he married Rosa. His parents had all but disowned him and Rosa was usually apathetic. Her eyes would be swollen from crying, and when Vinny asked her what she was blathering about, Rosa would say, "nothing, never mind." He'd taken her out of the slums of Mulberry Street and given her and her daughter a decent place to live and all she did was sit around with a long face feeling sorry for herself.

Rosa didn't find much comfort in Berta either. Berta wasn't the dependent six year old little girl she was when Rosa brought her to the orphanage. She was twelve now and she was interested in spending time with her friends. Berta usually made plans to spend time with classmates after school and if Rosa refused to allow her to play with her friends after school or on the weekend, Berta would sulk and shun her by spending most of her time in her room and giving Rosa the cold shoulder during meals.

Rosa felt rejected by her daughter's preoccupation with her friends and that rejection made her angry. Sometimes Rosa would complain to Vinny about her.

"Sounds like she needs a good kick in the ass to me; you oughta send that ungrateful brat back to the orphanage," Vinny would say, his words laden with antipathy. In Vinny's mind, Berta was the reason for Rosa's seemingly perpetual glum mood and Vinny was fed up with coming home to Rosa's moroseness. But Vinny had bigger things to worry about than his wife's sullen mood. Word on the street was that Rocco Velanti was out to knock off Joe Masseria, retaliation for Masseria's assassination attempt on Valenti at the liquor exchange.

Vinny had hoped he could keep a low profile long enough for the whole mess to blow over but that didn't happen. Instead, he ended up with his name plastered all over the newspapers.

CHAPTER EIGHTEEN

*I*t was a sticky August afternoon. It had been three months since the incident at the liquor exchange. Eddy and Vinny were sitting on Joe Masseria's sofa smoking cigars and discussing the details of an extortion scheme they wanted the go ahead for. At the close of the meeting the three men decided to go out for a celebratory lunch. Eddy was the first one to step out of the apartment building onto 2nd Avenue. They were met with a hail of bullets.

A Hudson Cruiser was parked at the curb. Eddy could see that there was a man sitting in the driver's seat as well as a man in the back seat. Both wore their hats tipped low over their foreheads to hide their faces. The man sitting in the passenger seat firing shots from a .45 had jumped out and ran after Joe and Vinny when they dashed into Heiney's Millinery shop a few doors down. Eddy pulled his gun, a nine shooter pistol, from inside his suit jacket.

The man in the backseat of the car had gotten out and was standing on the car's wide sideboard, using the car as a shield, and shooting over the top of the car at Eddy. Eddy was on the sidewalk in front of the apartment building about fifteen feet from the car. He stood perfectly still with his arms extended holding the gun with two steady hands. He cocked his head slightly to the side and closed one eye to look through the sight, methodically squeezed off one round after another. Through all the gun fire exchange Eddy didn't flinch, he just kept shooting.

The Cruiser sped away toward the Bowery. Eddy watched the guy riding on the sideboard fall off onto the street as the car rounded the corner. A mob swarmed around his dead, bullet riddled body. The car kept going, and according to the newspapers the next morning, the driver stuck his gun out the window of the car and tried to shoot his way through dozens of laborers who were milling in the street after a large garment industry union meeting had adjourned. They didn't move fast enough and the driver plowed into the crowd of workers, hitting six people and killing two of them. He was eventually stopped and pulled out of the car by the irate throng, and beaten.

The front window of the millinery shop had been almost completely blown out by gun fire. Eddy found Joe and Vinny along with the store clerk crouched down behind the sales counter. He pointed the gun at the store clerk and said, "You don't know nothin and ya didn't see nothin, understand?"

The store clerk's eyes were wide as saucers and he nodded his head nervously. Joe's straw hat had two bullet holes in it. The gunman had obviously run out the back of the store. "Come on let's go," Eddy said to Vinny and Joe.

The three men walked swiftly back to Masseria's apartment. Joe and Vinny seemed to be shell shocked. "Joe, go lie down." Eddy instructed.

Joe went into his bedroom and got in the bed, leaving his shoes and hat on. Vinny walked over to the small table in the living room stocked with assorted liquor. He poured himself a large glass of Kentucky whiskey, his hands shaking visibly. He guzzled it greedily, spilling some down the sides of his mouth.

It wasn't until then that Eddy noticed that he'd been hit in the upper thigh and was bleeding. He rifled through Joe's medicine cabinet to find bandages or antiseptic, but to no avail. He cleaned the wound with soap and water and held a towel over the bullet hole. "Vinny, bring me some vodka," Eddy yelled out from the bathroom.

Vinny brought the bottle in and saw Eddy holding the bloody towel at the top of his thigh. "Jesus, Eddy, what happened? Did ya get hit?"

Eddy shot Vinny a disgusted look. "No Vinny, I didn't get hit. I'm on my God damn menstrual cycle. What the hell does it look like?"

Eddy grabbed the bottle of vodka out of Vinny's hand and took the towel away from his leg to pour the alcohol over the wound. He winced, gritted his teeth and grunted. He placed the towel over the area again and applied pressure. Vinny stood with his mouth hanging slack watching. "Hey, nurse Capozza," Eddy said mockingly. "Rip those in half."

He pointed to the towels hanging on the rack. Vinny did as he was told. Eddy tied the towels firmly around his thigh and pulled up his pants. "Pour me a glass of scotch will ya?"

Vinny went back out to the living room while Eddy washed his hands.

As Vinny started to open the bottle of scotch he was startled by a loud boom. It was the apartment door being kicked in. Police and detectives swarmed the place. An officer quickly grabbed Vinny and frisked him, relieving him of his revolver.

"Have a seat, Slick," the police officer said as he gave him a hard shove toward the couch. The officer held a gun on Vinny while the others searched the rest of the apartment. They found Joe, still lying in bed. They all knew the infamous mob boss, Joe Masseria. Joe was a notorious gangster and in some circles a bit of a celebrity. "So Joe, ya wanna give us the skinny on what's going on?" the detective asked cordially. We heard you were involved in a shootout, oh, about twenty minutes or so ago," he said, calmly looking down at his wrist watch. "Looks like a few of Rocco Valenti's guys were planning on filling you full of lead today."

Joe had recovered from the shock of the ordeal enough to say, "I don't know what the hell you're talkin about. We've been sittin here all afternoon mindin our own business."

The detective leaned over and plucked Joe's hat off of his head and examined it. "Is that right…Well, it looks like you got one hell of a moth problem, Joe," he said as he fingered the holes in Masseria's hat.

Vinny and Joe were taken downtown and questioned but they were released for lack of evidence. Eddy was never found.

Eddy dove head first into the garbage chute outside of the bathroom in the hallway when he heard the commotion. Eddy landed in the basement and found his way to a doctor, whose services he used for the kinds of injuries that might raise questions anywhere else. The bullet that hit Eddy's leg managed to miss any major arteries and eventually healed, leaving a thick, silvery white, nickel sized scar on the inside of his upper thigh.

Eddy limped out to the newsstand the next morning. The New York Tribune and the Brooklyn Eagle both ran stories about the shooting. The reporter must have been on Joe's payroll because he made Joe sound like a real tough guy. It elevated Messeria and gained him even more respect. Thanks to the incident, Joe became known as "the man that could dodge bullets."

Eddy chuckled to himself and shook his head. If they only knew that Joe was cowering behind the sales counter with Vinny and the store clerk like a scared little girl waiting for someone to rescue him. The reporter named Vinny too, and aptly described Vinny as one of Joe Masseria's goons. There was no mention of Eddy and that was just fine with him.

CHAPTER NINETEEN

The previous tenants had decided not to return to the apartment that Vinny sublet shortly before he and Rosa married. He was relieved. Vinny didn't want to deal with all the upheaval that a move would involve, and with just the three of them, the apartment was fine for the time being.

Berta did her best to stay out of the way. Vinny had begun to spend a lot more time at the apartment over the past few months. He was anxious, like a caged animal at times. He paced a lot and wouldn't allow them to have the shades up. Berta didn't understand why.

One day she mustered the nerve to ask. "Vinny, how come we can't ever have the shades up anymore?" Berta asked.

"Never mind why, just do what you're told," Vinny said, sounding aggravated as he pulled a shade back slightly and peered out of the window. His eyes quickly scanned the street below.

The apartment was dark and dreary and Vinny was always tense. He and Rosa were more miserable than ever. Rosa had become indolent, both physically and intellectually. She seemed to lack her own perspective on just about everything and Vinny's inimical presence had a way of sucking the oxygen out of the room whenever he was around. Berta tried to find ways to cheer her mother up but most of the time she was unsuccessful. After a while she stopped trying because it was exhausting and futile. The only time Berta saw Rosa make an attempt to be cheerful was when they were in public. Once at home, her mother indulged herself in sour moods and crying jags.

Sometimes Rosa said things that made Berta worry all day or for weeks even. "I just wish I could run away," her mother would sob as she sat slumped on the couch before Berta left for school in the morning. Berta often went to school upset and would find it hard to concentrate on her subjects for fear that she would come home and find that her mother had left her behind. The teachers complained that Berta wasn't working up to her potential and that she seemed distracted.

When Berta lived at the orphanage she had imagined what Christmas would be like when she had a real family to celebrate it with. Even though the children didn't receive toys or gifts other than perhaps a pair of used gloves or something of practical use, the Christmas season was a festive time at the orphanage. The girls worked on hand made decorations and sang songs. Sister Serafina had the most beautiful voice Berta had ever heard. She sounded just like Elsie Baker when she sang 'Silent Night, Holy Night.' The girls, with the help of the nuns, put on plays.

Chevonne played Tiny Tim in 'A Christmas Carol' one year. They fashioned costumes out of old clothes and their imaginations. Berta helped Chevonne with her lines. Chevonne was a natural actress. Christmas had been a magical time, but more than anything, it was a hopeful time. There was no talk of Santa or presents under a tree. No, the gift that the nuns rejoiced in and taught the girls to rejoice in was that Jesus was born. That was enough of a present.

The holidays in the apartment in Bensonhurst weren't anything like what Berta had imagined. Vinny refused to allow a real tree in the apartment. He said that they were "a goddamned pain in the ass mess."
Instead, Vinny bought a feather tree from Abraham & Strauss and lugged it all the way home from Fulton Street. It was made of green dyed goose feathers attached to wire branches wrapped around a dowel. There were fake red berries at the tips of the branches where small candles could be secured. It stood over six feet high in its red metal stand.

Berta thought the artificial tree was ugly, but decorated it anyway with strung popcorn and gumdrops. She hung some of her paper dolls on it too. Rosa sipped her tea and watched Berta decorate the tree. She smiled feebly. "I just don't have much Christmas spirit this year," her mother sighed. Vinny sat back in the wing chair in the living room and swigged from a clear bottle with a painted label that read "Rheingold Beer."
"Whoever started the tradition of draggin a live tree into the house to celebrate Christmas was a stupid son of a bitch... Oughta have their head bashed in," Vinny grumbled as he took a long drag off of his cigarette and eyeballed the feather tree. He was clearly pleased with his purchase.

Berta didn't expect presents on Christmas. She didn't believe in Santa Claus and her mother fretted about money. Vinny could be generous but usually it was only after he'd had a few drinks, and due to the nature of his employment, his income wasn't exactly steady. She got the distinct impression that she was a financial burden Vinny would rather not have had. It seemed that he resented her for it. Rosa, at least, earned her keep by cleaning and cooking and such.

On Christmas morning there were four gifts under the feather tree.

They were wrapped haphazardly. Two of the gifts had "Birta" written on the wrapping paper and two had "Rosa" written on them. They were from Vinny.

Rosa and Berta got up Christmas morning and ate breakfast. They waited for Vinny to come out of the bedroom. He woke at one o'clock in the afternoon and sat down on the couch next to the end table and squinted. He brought a hand up over his brow to shield his eyes from the light and watched Berta and Rosa open their gifts. Berta suspected that Vinny might have been a little bit hung over.

Berta opened her gifts first. Vinny bought her a bisque kewpie doll and a comic book; "The Adventures of Mutt and Jeff." "

I love them! Thank you Vinny," Berta said smiling.

Rosa opened her gifts next and brightened when she saw the perfume. It was called "Mitsouko" and was named after the heroine in a book she had read called LaBataille. Rosa looked overjoyed and surprised, "How did you know about this perfume?"

"I got eyes and ears ya know," Vinny said, sounding almost self-conscious. "Okay, let's go, open the last present," Vinny urged. It was a silk, navy blue nightgown.

"Oh Vinny, its lovely... Thank you." Rosa stood up from where she sat on the floor and walked over to Vinny and kissed his cheek. "I have something for you too," Rosa said, as if she were about to reveal a secret. She opened the drawer of the end table and took out a small neatly wrapped box.

"What is it?" Vinny asked.

"Open it! It's your Christmas present."

Vinny looked suspiciously at Rosa and pulled the wrapping paper away from the box and opened it. He stared down at the wristwatch, expressionless. Without looking up he said to Rosa, "Where did you get this?"

"I bought it at Gimbals. Why?" Rosa asked sounding perplexed.

"You bought it?" Vinny said, still staring at the watch.

"Yes, Vinny, I bought it. Why? What's the matter?" Rosa bent her head down slightly to try to read Vinny's expression as he sat staring into the box.

"You didn't buy it Rosa." Vinny said flatly.

"What do you mean? Of course I bought it. I have the receipt," Rosa explained, still not understanding what Vinny was talking about.

"Where'd you get the money to buy it?" Vinny asked, now looking squarely at Rosa.

"Well... I.... I saved a little here and there from the grocery money," Rosa said with a nervous laugh.

"So, let me make sure I understand this right. You bought me a watch with my own money?" Vinny said, not trying to hide his seething anger.

Rosa looked down, as if deeply ashamed and began fidgeting with a button on the cuff of her blouse. "I'm sorry Vinny. I thought it would be a nice surprise." She was afraid to even look up at Vinny's face.

"If I wanted a goddamn watch, I would have bought one," Vinny spat. He tossed the box with the watch in it on the couch and walked into the kitchen.

Rosa said nothing to Berta, who sat stunned on the floor next to the Christmas tree and picked the box up off the couch and went to the bedroom, shutting the door quietly behind her. Berta looked down at the kewpie doll's side glancing eyes and red rose bud mouth and wished she were somewhere else. She envisioned what the girls at the orphanage were doing.

Berta was startled out of her daydream by a loud racket coming from the kitchen. It sounded like pots and pans being thrown about. Then she heard Vinny's booming, rage filled roar, "Son of a bitch! Who the hell did this!"

Vinny came storming out of the kitchen toward Berta; she sat on the floor next to the Christmas tree, frozen in terror.

CHAPTER TWENTY

Vinny reached down and grabbed Berta's arm and hauled her away from the feather tree and into the kitchen. His face was taut with fury, "Did you do that!" he screamed, as he pointed to the side of the cake he had made the night before.

Berta had swiped her finger at the base of it to taste the frosting. She was hungry and before she even realized it she had eaten more of the frosting than she intended. She tried to smooth the icing over but it only made it worse. Now it was obvious that the icing had been disturbed. Berta was too terrified to even form words.

"Did you do that!" Vinny yelled at the top of his lungs. His face was red, his neck veins bulged and spittle flew out of his mouth as he screamed. Berta never realized that it was possible to be as frightened as she was at that moment.

Her eyes were wide with horror. She shook her head "no" in an almost tremulous motion, unable to form the word. Vinny fixed his eyes on Berta and unbuckled his belt. "Don't you lie to me! You hear me... You don't lie!"

Berta felt as if she'd never take another breath again. Her stomach was in a knot. She felt slightly dizzy. "Please no, don't Vinny, please," Berta begged.

Vinny removed his belt and the expression on his face went from one of utter rage to a smug satisfaction at hearing Berta beg him to stop his assault. Vinny took his black leather belt off and folded it in half, and with one hand grasping each end, he brought the ends of the belt together and then pulled them apart hard and fast. The leather made a cracking sound on contact.

It was an awful sound. Berta imagined that that was what it would sound like when the leather belt hit her flesh. Vinny stepped toward her with a look of sheer hatred in his eyes and raised the belt up over his head.

Berta ran out of the kitchen. Vinny followed and caught her before she could run out of the apartment. He grabbed her and pushed her face first into the wall and continued screaming. "Don't you ever, ever do that again! You hear me!" His bellowing was so loud that there was no doubt that every tenant in the building could hear him.

Rosa had come out of the bedroom. She stood watching Vinny whip Berta. She folded her arms in front of her and looked uneasy, but made no attempt to stop him.

"Please, no, don't please!" Berta cried. Vinny's belt hit the back of Berta's legs and buttock. At some point Berta had heard her cries as if they were coming from someone else in the distance. The fear and panic was so profound that it gripped Berta and took over her body entirely. She felt the warmth of her own urine stream down her spindly legs.

"Now get outta here," Vinny said with disgust when he was done whipping her.

Berta was dazed; she walked slowly into her bedroom. She pulled off her wet underpants and got undressed. She put on her nightgown and crawled into bed. She was numb. After a while Rosa came into the room and crouched at the side of the bed.

"I hate him." Berta whispered, still shaking.

"Don't talk like that. You shouldn't say that. You don't hate anybody." Rosa admonished. "The important thing is that you understand what you did wrong." Rosa said calmly. Berta didn't speak. The tears burned in her eyes and she felt hopeless.

"Oh, Berta, he didn't hurt you that bad," Rosa said as if Berta's response to Vinny's vicious attack were a silly overreaction. "Goodnight Berta," her mother said coldly before she stood up and walked out of the room.

It wasn't the last attack that Berta would suffer at the hands of her stepfather. Vinny could find nearly any reason to vent his rage out on Berta. It didn't matter if he was drunk or sober. If she got too much water on the bathroom floor while washing up, or if she was late coming home from a friends, or if the tone of her voice didn't convey enough deference, Vinny could find a reason to vent all the disappointment, frustration and bitterness that festered inside him out on Berta without consequence.

Berta knew Vinny didn't hate her. Vinny didn't care enough about her to hate her and Berta understood that. Even as a child Berta understood on some level that true hate is reserved for people who have power over

85

them; Berta was powerless. As far as Vinny was concerned, Berta was completely inconsequential.

Berta's mother never intervened during any of Vinny's violent outbursts or tirades. Rosa seemed to cope with Vinny's abuse by pretending that his behavior was normal. She receded into her own world of radio shows and romance novels and alternated between sitting in the kitchen on the verge of tears overwhelmed at the prospect of having to wash the breakfast dishes to cleaning the apartment obsessively. Berta couldn't go to Rosa like most children go to their mothers for comfort. Rosa was too emotionally fragile to cope with anything more than her own struggles. Instead, Berta looked for a reprieve from the fear and anxiety she lived with at home by spending as much time as possible with her friends and their families.

The times that Berta spent with her friends growing up were happy times, but there was no doubt that there were two Berta DeLuca's now: the old Berta and the new Berta. There was the Berta that had woken up most every morning feeling joyful and optimistic, looking forward to the day because she expected good things to happen. That girl was gone now. The new Berta woke most every morning with a vague sense of dread wondering what horrible thing might happen that day. She understood now that even for a minor infraction she could have her dignity ripped away, her security threatened and her spirit broken.

In the bleakness of the apartment in Bensonhurst, Berta learned to deny her feelings because she wasn't entitled to them. She learned that she could be mistreated and not have the right to be angry. The people that were supposed to love and care for her all but told her so, and she had no reason not to believe them.

Berta turned on her side in bed to get off of her sore buttock and noticed an envelope on her nightstand. It was a letter from Chevonne. Her mother must have put it there the day before and forgot to mention it. Berta brightened and opened the envelope eager to hear about all she had missed at Sacred Heart. Instead, Chevonne had written to tell her that she was no longer living at the orphanage.

CHAPTER TWENTY-ONE

*K*atherine Wallace and her husband Arthur were kindred spirits. They understood each other and had grown used to each other's peccadilloes and eccentricities. Their sixteen year marriage was indeed a happy one. Since their wedding day, they'd never spent even one night apart from one another. They were inseparable and if there were one word that could describe their relationship, it was comfortable.

They led a charmed life. Both were quiet and cerebral by nature and appreciated solitude and order. Children would certainly change that. As strong as their marriage was, Katherine knew it was about to be tested.

Katherine rehearsed how she would tell her husband that Patrick and his sister Chevonne would be coming to live with them. She stood in the study of their home facing the bookcases and talking out loud, practicing what she might say. "Arthur I have something very important to tell you and I don't want you to say a word until I'm done..." Katherine announced boldly to the new set of Harmsworth's Universal Encyclopedias in front of her.

"No, no. Too pushy," Katherine muttered to herself.

She attempted again. "Arthur, darling, I have wonderful news... You're going to be a father." Katherine burst out laughing at the thought of her husband's expression in response to such a proclamation.

Katherine was interrupted by one of the maids. "Madame, dinner is served."

"Thank you Colette."

Katherine had arranged for the cook to make Arthur's favorite meal: lamb chops with mint jelly, roasted red potatoes and asparagus. She told the cook to make sure he stalled long enough for Arthur to drink at least two glasses of wine before dinner was brought out. She wore one of

Arthur's favorite dresses and refreshed her perfume and lipstick before coming to the table.

Arthur was already sitting at the table when she arrived in the dining room. The victrola played softly in the background. The smell of lilacs and orchids from the flower bouquet on the table was intoxicating and the candles set the room in a warm glow. Katherine decided on the walk from the study to the dining room, that telling Arthur they would be taking in two orphans in the next few days would simply be too much of a shock for him. She decided on a different tact.

Katherine approached the table and bent down and kissed her husband on the mouth. She sat down and summoned the butler. "Bertram, would you please bring us a bottle of wine? A Grand Cru would be lovely." She turned to her husband and reached over, softly stroking his cheek with the back of her hand. "I missed you," she said with a coy smile. Arthur grinned devilishly. "I missed you too. It's been over six hours since we've seen one another and you look even more beautiful than the last time I saw you. I love that dress on you... Of course, I love it off of you even more."

Katherine giggled. "Shhh, Arthur, Bertram will hear you."

Her husband laughed, "I'm sure Bertram's heard a lot worse in his day. I bet the old chap's even gotten lucky a time or two."

She laughed. "You're awful."

Bertram arrived with two glasses of wine on a silver tray and set them down gently on the table in front of them. "Thank you, Bertram," Arthur nodded. "I was speaking with the Chamberlains today. I ran in to them at the Metropolitan Club. They're going to the Opera in Monte Carlo on the first of April. "Amadis" is making its debut. I think it would be a wonderful little get away for us Katherine. What do you think?"

Katherine smiled, "I think that sounds stupendous. I'll mark it on the calendar and arrange for a suite at the Hotel de Paris."

They sat contently sipping their wine and listening to Ralph Vaughan William's London Symphony. "We may be having house guests for a few days, Arthur." Katherine began casually.

"Please tell me your cousin Evelyn and her poodles, Yip and Yap, aren't coming to stay," Arthur said dryly.

"I don't believe her poodles are named Yip and Yap," she said, laughing. "But I have to agree those names would be fitting. No, no, that's not it. Darling, you remember that boy I told you about, the one that comes to the library?" Katherine continued nonchalantly as they were getting near the end of their second glass of wine.

"Yes, I remember," Arthur said.

"You remember how his father was on North Brother Island in Riverside Hospital recuperating from tuberculosis?"

"Awful thing, yes I remember. What about him?"

Katherine sighed and took the last few sips of her wine. "Well, it's all quite sad. Patrick and his sister just got word their father died over a year ago."

"A year ago...?" Arthur sounded surprised and confused. "I thought you told me last month that Patrick and his sister were going to move to Garritsen Beach with their father when he got out of Riverside Hospital. It sounded as if he were on the mend."

"Unfortunately, that wasn't the case. It's a long story, so I won't bore you with the details. Anyway, they're planning on getting on an orphan train. You've heard of them, haven't you Arthur?" Katherine asked.

Katherine had no intention of ever letting Patrick and his sister get on an orphan train. Her plan was to stall their departure so that Arthur would have a chance to get used to them and to see that they weren't the filthy little hoodlums he'd imagined them to be. Arthur finished his wine and picked the bell up from the table to ring for dinner to be brought out. He then went on to answer Katherine's question.

"Why, of course I've heard of the orphan trains. We just made another sizable donation to the New York Foundling Hospital. They've done a wonderful job of organizing the effort. It's a massive undertaking, you know. Thousands of abandoned and orphaned children have found homes on farms where they can receive a wholesome upbringing."

"Exactly dear, I'm excited for Patrick and his little sister," Katherine said happily. She could be quite an actress when she set her mind to it. "He's such a sweet boy. They're planning on taking an orphan train to Michigan. But there's a small problem; it won't be leaving until early next week and as things turned out, Patrick will have to take his sister from the orphanage tomorrow. They'll be staying with us for a few days before they leave."

Katherine Wallace wasn't in the habit of lying to her husband. She felt a twinge of guilt but she knew her husband well enough to know that if there was any hope of Arthur agreeing to take Patrick and Chevonne into their home he'd need time to adjust to the idea. Arthur was a decent man and he was a compassionate man but he was very set in his ways. And there was something else that made the situation even more difficult.

Arthur wasn't exactly objective when it came to the Irish. He came from a long line of English blue bloods and the history between the English and the Irish had been a contentious one, to say the least.

"Katherine, I'm sure that won't be necessary. There must be somewhere they can go until the day their train arrives. For heaven's sake, they're probably teeming with bed bugs and body lice. They'll likely rob us blind too before they leave. I don't think it's wise to have them in our home, there's no telling what mischief they'll get into."

Katherine laughed. "Oh Arthur, don't be so dramatic. They're just children. Don't worry, I'll make sure they're both properly cleaned up and supervised. I've grown a bit fond of Patrick, and I know how worried he is over the prospect of trying to survive on the streets with his little sister before they can get on the train. It'll only be for a few days."

"I'm not at all happy about this Katherine and the idea of listening to an Irish brogue in my own home makes my stomach queasy. My heart goes out to all the children who are homeless and destitute but we give generously to the charities that look after them so that we don't have to take street urchins into our own home," Arthur said resolutely.

She chuckled. "Well, for your information Mr. Wallace, neither child has a brogue. Their grandparents came over during the potato famine and they were both born and brought up in Roxbury Massachusetts before their father fell ill. They'll be here tomorrow."

"Indeed," Arthur said with a sardonic look on his face, realizing he'd lost the argument.

Katherine and Arthur enjoyed their meal and the rest of the evening without bringing up the subject of Patrick and Chevonne again.

The next morning Katherine got up early. She was excited. She couldn't wait to get to the library to meet Patrick. They had planned on meeting late in the afternoon and Katherine wanted to surprise him by having his sister waiting for him with her. Katherine called down to the lobby and asked for their chauffeur.

"Good morning Edgar! I'd like you to bring the car around. We'll be going to Sacred Heart Orphan Asylum."

They arrived at the orphanage at nine o'clock in the morning. Katherine had had her secretary call the orphanage to explain the situation a few days earlier. Sister Angelina told Chevonne the night before that Mrs. Wallace would be arriving to collect her in the morning. Chevonne had heard so much about Mrs. Wallace from Patrick over the past few years and had imagined what she would be like. She pictured a dowdy woman with glasses that rested at the end of her nose.

"This shouldn't take long Edgar," Katherine said to the chauffeur as he held the car door open for her. She slid off the car seat and walked up the steps to the rectory. The door opened before Katherine reached it. Two nuns in habits stood in the doorway.

"Good morning Mrs. Wallace," the older nun said with a welcoming smile. The younger nun nodded politely.

"Good morning Sisters," Katherine replied.

"Please come this way," the younger nun said as she motioned toward the office at the end of the corridor. Katherine followed the older nun, the younger trailing behind them.

"Mother Superior, Mrs. Wallace is here."

The elderly nun stood up from behind her desk and walked over to Katherine, extending her hand in greeting. "It's a pleasure to meet you Mrs. Wallace. Thank you so much for your generous donation to the orphanage. We're planning on buying new uniforms for all the girls and repairing the roof."

"My husband and I are grateful for the work you do here Sister. We're happy to help." Katherine was eager to meet Chevonne. She'd heard about her from Patrick, of course, but had never met her.

"Sister Serafina, would you please go and get Chevonne O'Farrell." Mother Superior instructed the young nun.

"Of course," Sister Serafina replied and left the office.

Katherine sat making polite small talk but she could hardly concentrate on the conversation. She felt inexplicably nervous. Ten minutes seemed like an hour. Finally, Sister Serafina walked into the office with Chevonne. Immediately, Katherine could feel her heart swell. She thought Chevonne was one of the most beautiful young girls she'd ever seen. Tears welled up in Katherine's eyes. She felt a bit foolish but she couldn't help it. She'd never met the girl before in her life but she knew Chevonne was her child just as much as Patrick was and she was overcome with emotion.

Katherine fought back the tears and smiled. "Hello Chevonne, I'm so happy to finally meet you. Patrick has told me so much about you."

Chevonne smiled shyly. "Hello Mrs. Wallace. Patrick has told me a lot about you too, except he didn't tell me that you looked like a princess," Chevonne said, sounding awed.

Katherine laughed. "I think you look like a princess too." Chevonne beamed at the compliment.

"I'm afraid we don't have a lot of time. We're going to be meeting Patrick at the library at two o'clock. Does she have anything we need to bring with us?" Katherine asked, turning to Mother Superior.

"No, I don't believe so. She's long grown out of the clothes she arrived in."

"Chevonne, are you ready to go?" Katherine asked. Chevonne nodded. Katherine noticed that Sister Serafina was teary eyed. Chevonne walked over to her and gave her a hug. "I'll miss you Sister," Chevonne said, looking up at the young nun.

"I'll miss you too, Chevonne."

Katherine took Chevonne's hand and they walked down the corridor and out into the cool morning air.

Chevonne wore an olive green jumper that was obviously too big for her and a cream colored blouse that was frayed at the cuffs. Katherine looked down and noticed that Chevonne was wearing boy's shoes. They were brown leather and her gray wool socks drooped at her ankles. "Chevonne, are you cold? Katherine asked.

"No, not really," Chevonne replied. Edgar stood by the car waiting for them and opened the backdoor of the Rolls Royce. He took Chevonne's hand and helped her into the back seat. Katherine was next.

"Whose car is this?" Chevonne asked Katherine once they were settled into the car.

"It's mine," Katherine answered.

"Are you rich?" Chevonne asked causing Katherine to chuckle. She was used to the pretentiousness and posturing of adults. Chevonne's innocent candor was a breath of fresh air. "Do you want the short answer or the philosophical answer? " Katherine asked.

"The short one please," Chevonne said without hesitation.

"Yes, I'm rich," Katherine said.

"Is it fun?" Chevonne asked.

"Yes, it's a lot of fun," Katherine replied. Chevonne looked delighted at the answer.

"Edgar, take us to Fifth Avenue please. Stop at Bergdorf's first." Katherine looked over at Chevonne. Chevonne looked as if she were thoroughly enjoying the scenery as they rode down Fifth Avenue. She looked completely content.

For the next few hours Katherine and Chevonne shopped for everything a little girl could want in the way of the latest couture. Katherine bought Chevonne seven new dresses with matching lace trimmed ankle socks and three pairs of T-strap patent leather shoes. They bought big satin ribbons for Chevonne's hair, one to go with each outfit. The last store they went to was Lord and Taylor.

Katherine had Chevonne wear the outfit right out of the store and gave Chevonne's old clothes to the store clerk to be thrown out. They were nearly to the car when Chevonne asked where her olive green jumper was. "I gave your old clothes to the store clerk to throw out," Katherine told her.

Chevonne immediately turned and ran back into the store. "Chevonne, where are you going?" Katherine yelled after her. But Chevonne didn't answer. She ran so fast she was nearly out of sight before Katherine had a chance to go after her.

CHAPTER TWENTY-TWO

$\mathcal{A}$ nother year had passed. It was 1924 and Berta and anyone else who knew her mother knew something wasn't right.

Rosa wasn't sure what was wrong with her either. She had found it increasingly difficult to organize her thoughts. It was hard to initiate tasks. Everything had become a chore. Making meals, doing laundry, shopping could be a challenge. Rosa also noticed that at times it was difficult to form words. Sometimes her speech sounded slightly slurred and her balance was off. Vinny asked if she been "hitting the hooch" but she'd never been interested in drinking and she hadn't had any alcohol in months. She didn't know what was happening to her and she was frightened.

Rosa only really felt comfortable in the confines of the apartment. Venturing out was an ordeal. The last time she had gone any further than the corner market was when she went to visit her friend Gitta Lachman.

Gitta was concerned. "Rosa, what's wrong? You don't seem to be yourself. Are you feeling all right?" Gitta asked during their last visit.

"No, I'm not feeling well. I don't know what's wrong with me," Rosa said sounding tired.

"Have you been to the doctor? "Gitta asked.

"No, I'm not sure what he could do for me... Vinny says that it's all in my head and that I need to find something better to do with my time than listen to radio shows."

"Well, what do you think?" Gitta asked with concern.

"I don't know what to think," Rosa replied despondently.

"How is everything with you and Vinny?" Gitta asked, suspecting that Rosa's state of mind might have something to do with her unhappy marriage. She knew that things were not good between Rosa and Vinny. Rosa had complained that although she and Vinny had only been married for a relatively short time they had already become alienated from one another. Vinny blamed her for the state of his relationship with his parents, and in his mind, it was Rosa's failure to get pregnant that ruined everything and Vinny was bitter about it.

Rosa told Gitta that she suspected that Vinny was unfaithful and that it had gotten to the point where he didn't even bother to try to hide the tell-tale signs. Vinny was rarely home, and when he was, he was distant and angry toward both Rosa and Berta. Gitta worried about her friend and couldn't help but notice Rosa's slow deterioration. As they sat at Gitta's kitchen table during their visits, she noticed that Rosa had lost weight. She had dark circles under her eyes and complained that she couldn't sleep.

Rosa's melancholy seemed to be worsening. Gitta was also unnerved by Rosa's near constant fidgeting. "I feel like things are crawling on me," Rosa said as she scratched and rubbed her arms vigorously.

"Maybe you're so down in the dumps because you need to get out of the house more," Gitta offered, not knowing what else to say. Rosa was certainly isolated. There was a time that she wanted to get out of the house and work, but now she didn't feel as if she had the ability to anymore. She didn't believe that her thinking was coherent enough to learn a new skill.

Rosa had started to wear a cloche hat all the time. Her hair was thinning in spots and her scalp had a moth-eaten appearance. At one point she had reddish-pink splotches over her chest and the palms of her hands. Vinny said it was because she kept scratching herself.

"Rosa! Knock it off!" Vinny would yell when he saw her scratching her skin and pulling at the hair on her head, muttering, "Damn fleas."

"There ain't no damn fleas around here Rosa, now stop your fidgeting and change your clothes. You've been wearin those rags for three days and you're startin to stink," Vinny would complain.

Sometimes Rosa would go change her clothes, but other times she would just get up and go into a room by herself and continue to scratch and mutter. Berta drew her mother a bath at least once a week but sometimes her mother would refuse to get in because "the blood of Christ must be preserved for the righteous," or "all the babies should be washed first," or some other nonsensical excuse. Rosa complained of random aches and pains, particularly in her legs. Sometimes she cried because the pains were so sharp, almost like an electrical shock. Berta didn't know what to do. Vinny was hardly ever around, and neither she nor Mrs. Lachman could make Rosa go to the doctor.

The truth was that Berta barely recognized her mother anymore. When she spoke to her mother, Rosa looked at Berta as if she were speaking a foreign language. She seemed to have difficulty understanding the words that came out of Berta's mouth. Sometimes Berta would become so frustrated she would cry, "Mama, stop it! Please stop it!" Most of the time when Berta became exasperated with her mother and pleaded with her to stop her rambling or rocking or scratching, Rosa would just shuffle into her bedroom, or smile and stare off into space. Berta didn't bring anybody over to the house. There was no telling what her mother might do or say and Berta didn't want to be embarrassed in front of her friends. Only Vinny really knew the extent of her mother's decline.

Gitta used to come over once a month or so to see Rosa. It was hard to visit more frequently because she had nobody to watch the children. Making the trip from Hester Street to Bensonhurst was difficult unless Yekl was able to come with her, and he was usually working. It had been a while since Gitta visited. One afternoon Gitta asked a neighbor to watch her children so that she could go visit Rosa. Berta was in school and Rosa refused to open the door and let Gitta in. Gitta knew Rosa was home.

She could hear her laughing and mumbling to herself on the other side of the door.

CHAPTER TWENTY-THREE

Berta's new friend Sophia and her family made Berta feel safe and welcome in their home. Mrs. Fabiano taught Sophia and Berta to sew simple dresses. Mr. Fabiano was full of fun and took all the children to the drugstore for egg creams every Friday when he came home from work. He always invited Berta too if she was there. Sometimes he played stick ball with them and ringalevio. When the weather was nice, especially in the summer when the apartments were too hot, everyone would sit outside on their stoop. Mrs. Fabiano and some of the other women in the neighborhood set up folding chairs and card tables and played mahjong and pinochle.

Berta usually went to Sophia's house after school since it was on the way home. She ate dinner with the Fabianos a few times a week. She liked to pretend, at least in her head, that she was a member of their family. Sophia and Berta and some of the other girls in the neighborhood passed the time after school by playing potsy and skipping rope on the sidewalk in front of the apartment building. Often times Sophia's mother would yell out the window when she needed Sophia or her sister Mildred to go to the store.

"Sophia! I need soup greens for dinner. Will you girls run to the fruit store and get some?"

"Okay, Ma. Can we go for a walk around the block too?" Sophia yelled up to the window.

"Alright, but don't be late for dinner. Here, catch!" Mrs. Fabiano yelled down, as she leaned over the window sill and dropped a bunch of coins wrapped in a scrap of paper. Sophia cupped her hands together and caught the tiny, makeshift package.

Sophia and Berta skipped down the sidewalk for a minute when Sophia stopped and turned to look up at the window where her mother had just been leaning out.

"What are you doing?" Berta asked.

"I'm checking to make sure my mother isn't watching," Sophia said, still looking up at the window.

"Why?" Berta asked.

"Because we're not walking around the block; we're going to Gravesend Bay, that's why."

"Why are we going to Gravesend Bay?"

"You'll see," Sophia laughed and grabbed Berta's hand and they ran across the street, cut over to Cropsey Avenue and down 20th Street.

Sophia and Berta walked past Supper's Hotel and Shield's Pavilion and down to the dock. At the end of the pier stood two boys, Sophia waved and yelled, "Ah, gumbas!" Berta recognized the boys right away. It was Frankie Rossi and his older brother Marco. Frankie was in the same class as Berta and Sophia. Marco was a year ahead.

"I thought you two were gonna be here an hour ago," Marco said to Sophia, sounding slightly annoyed.

"Come on let's go," Marco motioned for them to follow him. They walked off the pier and down to the water, where there was a small skiff with two oars in it. Frankie pushed the small, flat-bottomed boat half way into the shallow water. Marco got in and picked up the oars.

"Okay, get in," Frankie told the girls.

Berta hesitated. "Oh, go ahead Berta, get in," Sophia said with a hint of impatience. Berta stepped into the boat gingerly and Sophia stepped in after her. They sat on the slat of wood that spanned the boat. It was just big enough for the two of them. Marco sat on the one at the other end of the boat and Frankie sat between them. The boat was barely big enough for the four of them.

Marco rowed out into the bay. After they were out a ways he said, "I think we're out far enough."

Frankie looked around. "Yeah, I don't see anybody."

"Well, alright already, Frankie. Take it out," Marco directed. Frankie reached into his front pocket and pulled out a cigarette and a match box.

Berta's eyes widened a bit and she looked at Sophia. Sophia shrugged her shoulders and smiled demurely. Frankie held the cigarette in his mouth and fumbled with the match box. He took one of the match sticks out and swiped its red tip across the side of the box where the sulfur strip was. Nothing happened. He tried again and still no flame appeared. Marco reached for the box and Frankie blocked his hand.

"Gimme the damn matchbox Frankie, you moron, you don't know what the hell you're doing."

"Get outta here Marco. I know what I'm doin'."

"No you don't," Marco said as he lunged for the matchbox. Frankie turned sharply and huddled over the matchbox and tried to light the cigarette again.

"Knock it off, Frankie! We only got three match sticks," Marco ordered.

"You knock it off Marco," Frankie responded angrily. Marco reached out deftly and swiped the cigarette out of Frankie's mouth. Frankie dove at Marco in an attempt to pry the cigarette from Marco's hand, but it was too drastic a shift in weight for the small boat to withstand. The skiff capsized.

The four of them were dumped into the water in the middle of Gravesend Bay, a good fifty yards from the shore. Frankie and Marco seemed to hardly notice as they continued to pummel each other.

"Hey! Hey! Cut it out!" Sophia yelled. She grabbed an oar and jabbed them with it. "Cut it out! We have to go. Get the boat!" she commanded.

Marco flipped the boat back over and managed to climb in. He pulled Sophia in and they both pulled Berta up into the skiff.

"Marco, you big dumb ass, show off!" Frankie yelled and began to swim to the shore.

Macro rowed the skiff back and pulled it up onto the sand. None of them spoke until they were out of the boat. Marco sat on the edge of the skiff with a sour look on his face and waited for Frankie to swim ashore.

"See ya later Marco," Sophia said blandly.

Berta gave a weak wave and they began to run, sopping wet; all the way home.

Sophia's mother would surely want to know how they got drenched.

"What are you going to tell your mother?" Berta asked Sophia nervously.

"Well, I'm certainly not going to tell her that we went out in a boat with two boys to try a cigarette and it flipped over when they started to fight over who was going to light it. Do you have any ideas?" Sophia asked.

Berta thought for minute, "No, not yet."

They were still soaked when they arrived at the Fabiano's apartment.

"What in the world happened to you two?" Mrs. Fabiano asked.

"Well, ya see, um... Well... it was a fire hydrant. Just as we were walking by, a car backed right into a hydrant and water gushed like a geyser."

"Well that's some bad luck. Did it happen before or after you bought the soup greens?" Mrs. Fabiano inquired.

It wasn't until that moment that either Berta or Sophia realized that they'd completely forgotten about going to the store. Sophia checked her pocket. The change that her mother had dropped from the window was gone. It must have fallen out when the boat tipped over. Mrs. Fabiano read the look on Sophia's face.

"You did go to the store didn't you?" she raised a skeptical eyebrow.

"I... I think it must have fallen out of my pocket when the water hit us," Sophia stammered.

Her mother put her hands on her hips, clearly irritated.

"You mean to tell me that you've been gone for over an hour and you just now realized that the money fell out of your pocket? What have you been doing all this time?"

Sophia stood looking dumbfounded.

Berta interrupted the silence.

"I have to go home now and change. My mother will be looking for me." She turned and gave Sophia a wary look. "Bye, Sophia."

Berta turned her head back to Mrs. Fabiano.

"Goodbye Mrs. Fabiano," Berta said with a hangdog expression on her face. She left feeling relived to be out of the line of questioning. Walking home, she figured the fire hydrant excuse would work just fine. Berta walked into the apartment and yelled, "I'm home!" and sprinted into her bedroom to change her clothes before her mother or Vinny could see her.

When she was finished changing her clothes she went into the kitchen. Vinny and Rosa were sitting at the kitchen table.

"Rosa, you gotta eat something. You're skin and bones." Vinny had cooked some pasta and was trying to get Rosa to eat and he was quickly losing patience.

"Go ahead eat it," Vinny demanded. Rosa heaved a sigh and shook her head. Vinny picked up a fork off the table and began to hit the side of Rosa's plate, making a loud, annoying ting, ting, ting sound and raised his voice. "Eat it!"

Vinny noticed Berta standing in the doorway of the kitchen, "Take care of her. I don't have time for this shit. She's acting like a goddamned fruit cake again," he said, clearly aggravated.

Berta rarely saw Vinny but she often heard him come in in the wee hours of the morning, drunk, after being out all night. Sometimes he didn't go to bed until after the sun came up, right before Berta got up for school. He usually left the house around five o'clock in the afternoon.

Once a week, he would leave money on the coffee table in the living room so that Rosa could pay the egg man and the milk man and buy groceries.

Vinny was waiting for his friend Eddy to pick him up. Berta's stepfather had always been a snappy dresser but his tastes had grown more sophisticated as his income grew. He was dressed meticulously in a tailor made suit. He smelled of expensive cologne and wore the best hand-made Italian shoes. His cuff links were made of black onyx with small inlaid diamonds and his nails were freshly manicured. Berta noticed that Vinny had plenty of money but he didn't really have a job. His job, as far as she could tell, was hanging around with Eddy and some other men who used to come to the apartment. Vinny hadn't had them over for a long time; not since Rosa had gotten too sick to play hostess.

The contrast between her mother's disheveled, withdrawn look and Vinny's exceedingly well groomed appearance was striking. Rosa never went out with Vinny. It seemed like Rosa was more like a housekeeper and lately not much of one, than a wife. Vinny paid the rent and all the household expenses, and sometimes when he was in a good mood and feeling generous he would give Rosa extra money so that she and Berta could go clothes shopping or to a movie. But they didn't seem like husband and wife. Berta never saw any display of affection between them.

A car horn honked outside. Vinny pulled the shade back just enough to see who it was. It was Eddy. Vinny grabbed his fedora hat and jaunted toward the door. "See ya, kid," he said to Berta, and left.

CHAPTER TWENTY-FOUR

*K*atherine turned toward the salesman who was carrying their packages. "Please take our boxes to the car," she instructed, before running off after Chevonne, who had inexplicably run back into Lord & Taylor after hearing that her old green jumper had been given to the sales woman to be thrown out.

Chevonne's face was flushed and she was winded after running.

"Do you still have my old clothes, Ma'am?" Chevonne panted.

"I put them in the trash in the back room," the saleswoman responded with a perplexed look. Chevonne ran into the back room past the "employee's only" sign, where she caught sight of a large galvanized steel trash can.

Katherine had just caught up to her. She watched Chevonne struggle to pull the lid off the large trash can. Chevonne peered into the trash can and reached in and pulled the olive jumper out. She put her hand in the side pocket and pulled out the tattered picture of her mother and examined it with a look of relief. Katherine was silent as she looked on, watching as Chevonne held the picture in her hand.

"I'm sorry Mrs. Wallace. I left something important in my pocket." Katherine looked down at the small picture in Chevonne's hand. It was of a forlorn looking girl in her late teens.

"That's my mother," Chevonne said, and looked at Katherine's face for a response.

"She's lovely. Is that the only picture you have of her?"

Chevonne nodded.

"You should have a safe place to keep it," Katherine said, with genuine concern.

"I used to keep it under my pillow at the orphanage," Chevonne said.

Katherine thought for a moment.

"Hmmm, I think I have an idea. Hold on to that picture. We'll need to make one more stop before lunch," she said.

They stopped at Fusaro's jewelry store and bought a platinum locket for Chevonne to put her mother's picture in. Katherine pulled Chevonne's ruffled Peter Pan collar out just a bit and dropped the locket inside her top. "There, now your mother will always be safe and close to your heart and you can pull the locket out and look at her anytime," Katherine said as she smiled at Chevonne.

"Thank you Mrs. Wallace," Chevonne replied earnestly, as she felt the locket under the material of her dress.

"Well Chevonne, I don't know about you, but I'm getting quite hungry. Edgar, take us to the Plaza, please." The car turned down Central Park South. "Isn't shopping fun?" Katherine asked, rhetorically.

Chevonne said nothing for a moment. "I think it's the most fun thing I've ever done," Chevonne answered solemnly, after giving the question serious thought.

Katherine laughed, "I think we're going to get along just fine Chevonne."

They soon arrived at the Plaza. Chevonne was fascinated by the splendor of the magnificent hotel. The marbled columns, grand mirrored doors and the enormous skylight were breath taking.

"Good afternoon Mrs. Wallace," the waiter greeted when he approached the table they had been seated at in the Palm Court. Katherine noticed that Chevonne was a bit overwhelmed. Chevonne looked around the room wide eyed. She hardly noticed the waiter. Katherine reached over and rubbed Chevonne's arm lightly, "It's beautiful here, isn't it?" Katherine said softly. Chevonne nodded.

"What would you like to eat?" Katherine asked.

Chevonne glanced briefly at the waiter and then spoke to Katherine, "May I have a peanut butter and jelly sandwich?" Chevonne asked bashfully.

"Of course you may. In fact, that sounds delicious." Katherine looked up at the waiter. "Make it two please, and two large glasses of cold milk."

"Excellent choice," the waiter responded, sounding impressed. He made a note on his order pad and left.

Katherine and Chevonne finished lunch and rode back to the Wallace's apartment. Under the long, burgundy awning stood two uniformed doormen who hurriedly approached the car and took the packages.

"Thank you Ronald. Please bring them up and give them to Colette. They'll be going into the south-facing guest room."

"Yes, Mrs. Wallace."

Katherine and Chevonne walked into the lobby of the East 68th Street apartment and took the elevator to the fifth floor. Chevonne was as awestruck at the opulence of the Wallace's apartment as she was at the Plaza Hotel. "Colette, have Patrick's clothes been delivered yet? I called Albert at Brooks Brothers yesterday and ordered a number of trousers, sweaters, shirts and such. I hope they'll fit."

"Yes, they're here Mrs. Wallace. I've prepared the guest rooms as you asked. The deliveries from Schwarz Toy Bazaar have arrived as well, Madame," Colette said in her heavy French accent.

"Wonderful!" Katherine exclaimed, clapping her hands together. "Chevonne, why don't you go with Colette? She'll help you get freshened up before we go to the library to get Patrick."

Colette took Chevonne into the spacious bathroom and turned the tub faucets on full force and sprinkled in baths salts and Ivory soap flakes. As she prepared the bath she spoke to Chevonne.

"Did you know, Miss Chevonne, that I was a beautician in my country?" Colette said.

"No, I didn't know that. I wish I had a haircut like Louise Brooks," Chevonne confided.

"Ah yes, the actress; I know who you mean. I think that haircut would look nice on you," Colette said while surveying Chevonne's light blond ringlets, pulling strands through her index and middle finger. Chevonne's hair came to below her shoulders and had been pulled back with a hair tie.

"Would you like me to give you a haircut?"

"Yes, I'd like that."

Colette took out a pair of sheers and cut Chevonne's hair expertly. Colette owned her own Salon on Rue de Vaugirard in Paris before the war forced her to flee France. Her customers waited weeks for an appointment with her. Chevonne looked in the mirror when Collette was done and gasped.

"I look like one of the girls in the fashion magazines!" Chevonne exclaimed.

"Yes you do. You look like you have just stepped out of La Gazette du Bon Ton," Colette told her, smiling. "We have to hurry now. Madame will be taking you to see your brother soon."

"Yes, she told me. Patrick will be so surprised when he sees me," Chevonne said gleefully.

Collette brought Chevonne back to Katherine as soon as they were done. Chevonne wore a large light blue satin ribbon in her hair. It matched her dress. "Mrs. Wallace, do you like my new hair-do?" Chevonne asked excitedly.

"Oh my, Chevonne! It certainly is chic. It looks fabulous." Katherine looked at Colette.

"I can see why your salon in Paris was so well-known. But Colette, the next time, please consult me before you cut Chevonne's hair."

"The next time? I am sorry Madame. Mr. Wallace told me that the children would only be staying for a few days," Colette explained.

Katherine hesitated for a moment and then changed the subject. She looked down at Chevonne and smiled.   "Let's go get your brother, shall we?"

Patrick expected that it would be a day like any other day at the library. He never tired of spending time there. It was his sanctuary. He was curious to hear what Mrs. Wallace's idea was. He imagined that she might suggest an apprenticeship for him or maybe she knew someone looking to hire a girl like Chevonne as a domestic. Patrick found Mrs. Wallace sitting at the library table they always sat at together. "Hello, Patrick," Mrs. Wallace said.

Patrick thought the expression on her face was strange. She seemed to be looking at him as if anticipating that he would do something remarkable at any moment. He couldn't help but think it was odd.

"Patrick, would you be a love and bring this book over to the girl at the last table in the blue dress?" Mrs. Wallace asked.

He took the book from Mrs. Wallace's hand and met her eyes and held them. "Are you feeling alright?" Patrick asked.

"Why yes, I'm feeling just fine," Katherine responded confidently.

He nodded slightly but still looked skeptical. He walked slowly toward the table where the girl sat. "Excuse me Miss, this book is..." Patrick stopped talking in mid-sentence when he realized that the young girl sitting at the table was his sister.

"Did you run away from the orphanage and become a child star?" he said, laughing.

Chevonne didn't miss a beat. "Of course I did. I just ducked in here to get away from the crowd that was following me. Why, Jackie Coogan asked me for my autograph just this morning," Chevonne stood up and curtsied.

Patrick stood back and smiled as he watched his sister preen.

"Actually, Mrs. Wallace came and got me. We drove in a beautiful car and went shopping and then we went to the Plaza Hotel for lunch and

then we went to her apartment and her maid who was a beautician..."
Chevonne chattered without taking a breath, eager to tell Patrick about all
her adventures since she left Sacred Heart Orphan Asylum that morning.

Mrs. Wallace interrupted. "You two will have plenty of time to catch
up," she assured them. Katherine turned to Patrick and apprised him of
her plan, at least as much as she thought he needed to know for the time
being. She knew Patrick was fiercely independent, and that if it wasn't for
his sister and his concern for her welfare, he would most likely have
turned down her offer.

"Patrick, I thought that you and Chevonne could stay with my husband
and me until you decided what to do."

Patrick looked stunned. For a moment he said nothing.

"I think that's very generous of you Mrs. Wallace. Are you sure we
won't be an imposition?" Patrick said, sounding a bit embarrassed.

"Of course not.; we're looking forward to it. Now let's go home and get
you settled in," Katherine said with a broad smile.

Patrick never imagined that Mrs. Wallace and her husband were as
affluent as they obviously were. Patrick had seen all the trappings of great
wealth. He shined the shoes of the wealthy business men on Wall Street
and sold them their papers. He listened to their shrewd observations about
politics, world finance and any other insights they might have been
interested in sharing with a lowly shoeshine boy. Patrick studied them
closely and he was keenly aware of the differences between the rich and
the poor. He knew that the difference between them wasn't just the
amount of money one had or didn't have. It was more than that.

The very wealthy carried themselves with an air of confidence and a
sense of entitlement that people of lesser means didn't possess. When they
spoke, they never sounded apologetic or questioning. They assumed that
people would simply do as they told them to. Patrick thought Mrs.
Wallace was the exception. She had never talked down to Patrick and was
always kind and compassionate without being patronizing. She treated
Patrick with respect and spoke to him as an intellectual equal.

Patrick stood mesmerized in the corner guest room of the Wallace's
apartment. There were clothes laid out for him to put on after his bath
and Mr. Wallace's barber had come to give Patrick a manicure and a
proper haircut. He suspected that the barber was also commissioned to
ensure that he didn't have a head full of lice.

He was amazed as he looked around the room and admired the expensive European furnishings, the thick Persian rugs and the artfully tailored drapes that hung on the massive windows that overlooked Fifth Avenue and East 68th Street. *So this is it*, Patrick thought. *This is how they live.*

Patrick put on the clothes that had been laid out for him on the bed. They fit perfectly. He looked in the mirror and laughed. He looked just like the rich boys that he watched come out of the New York Athletic Club on Central Park South. Patrick wondered what the farmers in Michigan would think when he and Chevonne got off of the train wearing their fancy new clothes. Patrick folded his old clothes and placed them in one of the dressers. He put his well-worn boots and treasured shoe shine kit under the bed.

There was a knock at the door. "Come in," Patrick said.

It was Bertram, "Dinner is served Master Patrick."

"Thank you, Bertram." Patrick went out to the dining room. Mr. Wallace was sitting at the head of the table and Chevonne sat to his right. He was laughing at something Chevonne had said. Patrick only heard his response.

"Well, Chevonne, that certainly is an interesting way to look at it." He laughed again. Chevonne looked amused as well. Mr. Wallace cleared his throat and regained his composure when he saw Patrick. He stood up from the table and extended his hand, "Hello Patrick, Arthur Wallace," he said as way of introduction. "It's a pleasure to meet you."

Patrick took Mr. Wallace's hand and shook it firmly, "Thank you sir. It's a pleasure to meet you as well. We appreciate your having us."

Arthur smiled and motioned for Patrick to sit. He remained standing and said, "Will Mrs. Wallace be joining us?"

"Yes, of course," Arthur responded. At that moment, Katherine Wallace appeared from the study and walked toward the table. Patrick pulled out her chair for her.

"Thank you Patrick," she said, as she gave her husband a sideways glance.

Arthur Wallace dealt in finance. He and his family owned one of the largest investment banks in the United States. Their holdings spanned the globe. Arthur's job required that he be extremely astute when it came to world events because of their effect on the markets and investment trends. Arthur was taken aback by the ease in which Patrick discussed finance and how events were likely to impact holdings. He had to admit that

Patrick seemed extraordinarily mature for his age and it was apparent that he was obviously quite bright.

Katherine was delighted at how well things were going. Arthur seemed to take a genuine liking to both of the children. He was certainly enjoying Chevonne's sense of humor and it was clear that he thought she was absolutely adorable.

She hummed as she got ready for bed that night.

"You're in a chipper mood, aren't you?" Arthur chuckled.

"I certainly am. So, how'd they taste?" Katherine asked her husband.

"How did what taste?"

"Your words," Katherine said with a knowing smile.

"Alright, they aren't the flea infested hooligans I expected. The truth is they were both quite impressive," Arthur admitted.

"Well, I'll be gracious and not say I told you so," Katherine said and smiled at Arthur, obviously pleased with herself.

"Thank you Katherine. You know how much I appreciate it when you make a point of telling me that you're not going to tell me you told me so, when you know you ought to. It's heart-warming, really," Arthur said sarcastically. Katherine laughed and kissed her husband on the cheek.

Arthur put on his robe and slippers and went to the kitchen. Every night, Bertram prepared Arthur a warm glass of milk and placed two tea biscuits on a dish. Arthur often sipped the milk and nibbled on the tea biscuits and reflected on his day. "So Bertram, what do you think of our little house guests?" Arthur asked his trusted butler.

"I think they're remarkably well-mannered, Sir," Bertram replied sincerely.

Patrick was exhausted but had decided he'd go to the kitchen to get a glass of water before turning in for the night. He stopped at the doorway of the kitchen when he heard voices.

"Yes, they certainly were well behaved. Katherine had them cleaned up nicely too, didn't she?" Patrick heard Mr. Wallace remark.

"Yes, Sir, she certainly did. They're handsome children too," Bertram commented.

"Indeed they are Bertram, but don't let that fool you. You can take the Irish out of the shanty but you can't take the shanty out of the Irish. You ought to keep a close eye on the silverware until they're gone," Arthur laughed.

To Patrick, Arthur Wallace's words felt like a cold slap in the face. He'd been on the streets fending for himself since he was eight years old. There were more nights than he could count that he fell asleep in an alleyway with his stomach rumbling from hunger but he had never stooped to stealing. He had earned every cent he put in his pocket. Patrick was livid, but more than that he was angry at himself for letting his guard down and believing that people like the Wallaces' were capable of feeling anything but some peculiar combination of contempt and pity toward people like him and his sister.

CHAPTER TWENTY-FIVE

*U*nlike Vinny's mother, who would become pregnant but miscarry, Rosa had not become pregnant at all. Vinny didn't think Rosa was in any condition to have a child anyway and it had been months since they'd been intimate. He had lost all hope of making amends with his parents at that point. It was bad enough that he married a woman they didn't approve of, but it was no secret that Vinny was deeply involved with the kind of people that his father referred to as "crooks" and "rotten thugs."

At nearly six feet tall, Eddy had a thin, wiry build. His straight white teeth seem slightly too big for his angular face. Eddy was the son of a brick layer and as far as he was concerned his old man had worked himself into an early grave making an honest living Eddy thought he was a chump for doing it too. His mother had walked out on him and his three younger brothers when Eddy was eight years old. She took off with a bartender never to be seen again. No, Eddy had no intention of following in his father's foot-steps; he loved being a wise guy.

Vinny was amazed at how his buddy took everything in stride. Between Eddy's gambling debts and his shady business deals, there had to be more than a few people who would have liked to introduce his head to a crow bar, but you'd have never known it. Eddy walked around glad-handing like he was running for mayor. He was fast gaining a reputation too. Eddy had shot Rocco Valenti to death not long after the shoot out in front of Joe Masseria's apartment. He had arranged a meeting with Rocco under the guise of calling a truce. He managed to convince Rocco that Joe had been shaken up enough to give up his position as the head of the Morello crime family and set up a meeting with Rocco Valenti and a few of Rocco's soldiers in a 12th Street restaurant. The meeting didn't last long.

In the first ten minutes, Rocco realized that it was a set up. Again, everyone went for their guns and bullets flew. Vinny shot one of Rocco's men before the guy even had a chance to pull out his gun. It was the first time Vinny had ever killed anybody, and though he'd never admit it, he felt sick to his stomach for days afterward. Eddy shot the other guy and Rocco ran out of the restaurant. Eddy gave chase and shot him dead in the street.

There were no witnesses of course. At least there were no witnesses that were willing to speak up, but Vinny was worried he'd be fingered.

"Eddy, you sure nobody's gonna put the fix on us? It was broad daylight."

"For Christ sake, Vinny, how many times I gotta tell ya to relax? Nobody's gonna blow the whistle, and if somebody does I guarantee you that they'll be dead long before anything goes to trial." Eddy was right. Neither of them was ever questioned by the police. Masseria, and the Morello crime family, thanks to Eddy, had effectively squashed a good deal of the competition.

Vinny was relieved that Rocco Valenti was out of the way but that wasn't the end of his worries. He stopped at the butcher shop a few times a week. "Hello Mr. Capozza. What can I get you today?" the butcher asked.

Vinny placed his order and waited.

"Oh, I almost forgot. A man came in today and asked me to give this to you. He said it was a special recipe, he thought you'd like it." The butcher turned and continued wrapping and cutting meat. Vinny opened the letter. It was handwritten. The letters had a peculiar left slant and there were a lot of misspelled words. The author of the letter explained that Vinny's father had refused to join the "Bensenhurst Business Association" and pay dues to ensure that nothing untoward happened to his bakery. The letter went on to say that if Vinny didn't pay two thousand dollars, which was to be put in the garbage pail in front of Vinny's apartment building; that "something very bad" would happen to Salvatore Capozza. The letter warned not to go to the police. It was signed "anonomis"

Vinny was stunned. He didn't know what to do, so he went to Eddy. Eddy examined the letter. "Well, the first thing is, you don't wanna go to the police because that'll for sure get the old man killed. Let me look into this a little further and see what I can do. Don't let it get to ya Vinny, I'll get it straightened out," Eddy said reassuringly as he folded the letter and slipped it into the inside pocket of his suit coat.

"Thanks Eddy, you're a pal. I owe ya," Vinny said sincerely.

"Aw forget about it. It's no big deal. What are friends for?" Eddy said with a warm smile.

In actuality, Eddy was the real author of the extortion letter. He knew Vinny would bring the letter to him looking for advice. Eddy told Vinny that through his connections he'd managed to get the "dues" cut in half. All Vinny had to do was give Eddy one thousand dollars and he'd take care of the pay off. Vinny was relieved and felt indebted to Eddy, and Eddy was a grand richer.

Eddy didn't extort money from people because he needed it. He extorted money, and stole and cheated for sport. It was a hobby he was passionate about and he excelled at it. Eddy had been involved in the rackets since he was a kid in some way or another and he had made more money than he knew what to do with. He could've gone into a legitimate business, or even retired all together and moved to some obscure paradise on another continent, but Eddy loved his work and he especially enjoyed showing Vinny the ropes.

Eddy was only a few years older than Vinny but it was obvious that his childhood friend had lived a sheltered life. Vinny was aghast at the brutality he witnessed. He tried to hide his shock and horror but he couldn't. While watching a few of the particularly nasty beatings, Vinny actually vomited. Eddy got a kick out of watching his reactions. Nothing surprised Eddy. He'd seen everything, but he looked forward to seeing it all again through the eyes of a novice.

Although Vinny had known Eddy most of his life, the truth was he didn't really know much about Eddy's personal life. When Eddy referred to "his girl Ruby" he was talking about his gun. He wasn't a bad looking guy and he got plenty of attention from the ladies when they were out in the speakeasies. Occasionally, he'd buy a flapper a drink or two, but that was only if she had a jealous boyfriend and Eddy was looking for an excuse to get into a scrap. Outside of that he never pursued any of them, even when getting lucky looked like a sure thing.

Eddy never spoke about any family. Vinny knew he had three younger brothers growing up but he never mentioned them except to say that he hadn't seen them in years. As far as Vinny could tell, he was the only friend Eddy had. On the outside, Eddy was outgoing and social. He had dozens of casual acquaintances and of course, "business associates." But that was just his exterior. On the inside Eddy was a lone wolf.

Eddy wouldn't even go in Polly Adler's brothel. He always waited outside in the car for Vinny. More than once Vinny tried to talk Eddy into coming in.

"Come on Eddy. Ya can't tell me a guy like you don't get a little lonely once in a while."

Eddy would sit with both hands on the steering wheel looking straight ahead and say, "No thanks Vinny, it's not my style."

Usually Vinny was out within twenty minutes. He'd hop back into the car and adjust his shirt tails and then take his comb out and run it through his well-oiled hair with one hand while simultaneously smoothing it with the other. Eddy would look over at Vinny with a mordant smirk, and say "Feel better?" and shake his head.

Eddy lived by himself. He brought his clothes to the Chinese laundry on the next block over from his apartment. He lived simply, to say the least. He rarely kept food in the refrigerator and ate almost all his meals out.

Most nights he met up with members of the gang. They made the rounds at all the best clubs and frequented a few dives too. Eddy still worked as a bouncer now and again just for kicks. He loved a good bar fight and besides; it was a good way to keep up "public relations."

He introduced Vinny to the lottery scam. It was a pretty straight forward game. The winner came up with the right four numbers and cashed in. The pot could be worth thousands except that it wouldn't be long before the winner lost every penny. Either they were mugged out-right, the money was extorted from them, or they made a bad "investment." One way or another the money went to the gang.

Eddy never felt bad about taking the money back from the lottery winners and he was happy to share his philosophy with his new protégé. "Don't lose any sleep over it, Vinny," Eddy imparted. "They're all just trying to get something for nothing, and the only way anyone gets something for nothing is if they're willing to steal it fair and square." The irony of the statement wasn't lost on him, but Vinny suspected that Eddy believed every word of what he said.

Besides running scams and other gang business, Eddy did have another passion. He loved cars and the faster the better. Eddy picked Vinny up one night in a 1923 Model A Duesenberg Roadster.

"So how do you like my new girl?" Eddy asked as his hand caressed the dashboard.

Vinny smiled excitedly. "She's a real looker, Eddy," he said as he examined all the gadgetry.

They drove over to the Cotton Club and had dinner and a few drinks. Eddy chewed his steak ravenously and told Vinny all about his latest acquisition. "That baby is made to run. Set me back seven G's and worth every penny. She got an inline eight cylinder engine with an overhead camshaft. She hits top speeds of 90 mph. Can ya believe that Vinny? 90 goddamn miles an hour, whoowee!" Eddy grinned. Vinny had never seen Eddy so animated.

"Finish up that drink Vinny, we're goin to the racetrack," Eddy said, still smiling broadly.

"Why? Ya wanna go to the Aqueduct and bet on a few horse races?" Vinny asked.

Eddy laughed. "Come on, you'll see."

They got into Eddy's new car. Eddy turned the car on to 77th Street, beaming with pride as he drove.

"You missed the turn for Ozone Park," Vinny pointed out.

"We ain't goin to the Aqueduct to bet on horses. You've heard of the Vanderbilts, right? Well, thanks to them rich fellas, there's a forty-five mile stretch of concrete tarmac from Queens goin all the way out to Lake Ronkonkoma called Long Island Motor Parkway. They built it special just to race their cars. Of course they don't race cars on it anymore, at least not officially, on account of all them spectators getting run over. But it's just sitting there waiting for us to take this honey out on it and see what she can do."

It was near dusk when Vinny and Eddy pulled up to the toll booth.

"That'll be one dollar, sir," the toll booth attendant told Eddy. Eddy reached in his front pant pocket and pulled out a large wad of cash.

"Why, that's a fine car you got there mister," the attendant said as he scanned the length of the Duesenberg with his eyes.

"Yeah, ain't she?" Eddy agreed and peeled a twenty dollar bill off of his bank roll. "Keep the change, pal."

The toll booth attendant looked down at the bill and started to say something. "I can't—" Eddy stepped on the gas and sped off before he could finish his sentence.

"Remind me to hold up that toll booth on the way back," Eddy said, laughing as he pulled away. Vinny laughed too, but he wasn't sure if Eddy was serious or not. The windows were down and the cool night air smelled sweet and fresh mixed with the smell of the new black leather, tufted car seat. Vinny held a cupped hand out the window to enjoy the odd sensation of the wind pushing against it. They were cruising at about forty miles per hour. The sun had set and the moon shone hazily through the intermittent clouds. The headlights lit up the concrete road enough to see the next banked turn.

Suddenly, Vinny noticed that Eddy had accelerated causing the Duesenberg to start to rattle. Eddy's eyes narrowed and he leaned forward slightly and tightened his grip on the wheel. Eddy glanced down quickly at the speedometer and then focused back on the road. The speedometer reading had crept up to 75 mph.

"Eddy, maybe you ought to slow her down a little..." Vinny suggested anxiously.

"Are you kiddin'? I'm gonna get my money's worth. How often do you have the chance to go ninety miles an hour? Lemme answer that for ya; never."

Vinny braced himself and focused on the road ahead. The rattling became louder and the car started to shake. There was an overpass coming up and the road curved slightly after it. Vinny looked over at the speedometer again. They were flying at 88 miles per hours. Vinny's eyes were fixed on the speedometer when he heard Eddy yell, "Fuck!" and slam on the breaks.

The tires squealed, the inertia pushed Vinny into the dashboard. Eddy's arms were locked out straight as he gripped the steering wheel. The Duesenberg started to spin and neither Vinny nor Eddy said a word. It all seemed surreal. It happened so fast and yet there was the bizarre sense that they were moving in slow motion. Vinny couldn't focus on anything outside of the car. It was all a blur. However, he did notice flickers of light from the corner of his eye. They were sparks.

It was the last thing he remembered.

CHAPTER TWENTY-SIX

If Patrick O'Farrell had one flaw, it was that he was extremely proud. He went back to his room and sat on the edge of the bed, furious over what he'd overheard Arthur Wallace say. He thought about what he and his sister should do. Patrick had planned to leave on one of the orphan trains with Chevonne on Wednesday. It was Friday, four days of being patronized and surveilled like criminals was four days too many in Patrick's opinion. Patrick awoke and put his old clothes on and took his shoe shine kit out from under the bed. It was only five thirty in the morning. He went to the desk in his room and wrote a note to Mrs. Wallace.

> Dear Mrs. Wallace,
> Chevonne and I would like to thank you and Mr. Wallace for your kindness. We've decided that it would be best if we left earlier that anticipated. We shall always remember you fondly.
> Sincerely,
> Patrick and Chevonne O'Farrell

Patrick took nothing but what he'd come with and went to wake Chevonne. She was sleeping soundly.

"Chevonne, wake up." Patrick whispered.

"What's the matter Patrick?" Chevonne asked sleepily.

"Nothing, it's just time to go." Patrick responded.

"Where are we going?" Chevonne said rubbing her eyes and stretching.

"To the trains, I'll explain everything later."

"What should I bring with me?"

"Get dressed and leave everything else here".

"When are we coming back?" Chevonne asked.

"We're not coming back." Chevonne looked as if she would cry.

Patrick could see she was upset. He put his arm around her and said,

"Don't worry Chevonne, everything will be okay. Maybe Mrs. Wallace can send you your dresses and things when we get to our new home."

"It's not the dresses, Patrick. I like Mr. and Mrs. Wallace very much and I think I'm going to miss them terribly."

"I'm sorry, Chevonne, but we have to go."

Chevonne picked out the fanciest dress she had and tied the matching satin ribbon around her head in a big bow. "Aren't we going to say goodbye to them, Patrick?"

"No, Chevonne. I left them a note." They left the apartment and headed to Grand Central Terminal.

Katherine laid in bed thinking about how everything was going just as she had planned. Arthur was already up. Katherine dressed for breakfast and went out to the parlor where they usually ate breakfast in the morning. Arthur sat reading the paper and sipping tea.

"Good morning Mrs. Wallace. You look radiant as usual."

Katherine kissed her husband on the cheek. "Good morning, Mr. Wallace. Aren't the children up yet? It's nearly nine o'clock."

"Apparently not," Arthur said as he took another sip of tea and continued reading.

Collette came into the room, "Good morning, Madame. What would you like for breakfast?"

"I'll just start with a cup of tea; Colette, could you go and wake the children?"

"Yes, Madame."

Katherine picked up the teapot and poured herself a cup. A short while later Colette came back with a distressed look on her face. She handed Katherine the note that she'd found on Patrick's bed. Katherine read it and looked up at Arthur with fury in her eyes. She felt betrayed and hurt.

"What did you say to him Arthur?"

"I'm sure I have no idea what you're talking about, Katherine," Arthur said sounding mildly offended.

"They're gone, Arthur!"

"What do you mean?"

"I mean, Patrick and Chevonne left early this morning." Katherine crumpled the note up in her fist and threw it down on the table. She grabbed her purse and hat and ran out of the apartment, leaving Arthur sitting dumbfounded in her wake.

She got down to the lobby, obviously harried.

"Get the car this instant. We're going to Grand Central," she ordered the doormen.

"But Mrs. Wallace, you gave the chauffer the day off and I don't know how to drive."

Katherine looked panic stricken and ran out into the street. There was a man sitting in a Model T a half a block away. She ran to the car. "Excuse me, sir. I'm in desperate need. Could you bring me to Grand Central Terminal?"

The elderly man in the car looked at Katherine curiously and said, "I've got an appointment to get to. I'm sorry I can't help." She reached into her purse and pulled out a wad of bills.

"Please, sir, I beg you, there must be at least fifty dollars here. Take it." Katherine grabbed the man's hand and pushed the money into his palm.

The man wrapped his fingers around the cash and said, "get in."

When they arrived, Katherine jumped out of the car and rushed into the terminal. Her eyes darted about wildly looking for Patrick and Chevonne. It was crowded. She ran past the line and up to the ticket booth.

"Hey lady, wait your turn!" a man yelled. Katherine ignored him.

The man selling the tickets looked annoyed. "Ma'am, ya gotta wait ya turn. Now go back and get in line."

"I'm sorry, I don't need a ticket. I just need to know if the orphan train has left."

"Lady, I aint got time to go over the train schedules with ya. We got trains packed with those poor kids goin' outta here all the time. They send them to Indiana, Michigan, Upstate New York; heck, some of them trains go all the way up to Canada. There's no tellin where they might end up."

Katherine felt as if her heart had been ripped out and it was all she could do to keep from collapsing. She walked over to one of the benches and sat down and with her face in her hands, began to sob.

Katherine didn't know what else to do but cry. Within minutes Katherine heard her husband's voice calling her.

"Katherine!" Arthur waved from the distance and walked briskly toward her. It wasn't until he got closer that he could see that her face was tear-streaked and her nose was red. He took out his handkerchief and handed it to her.

"What in the world has gotten into you? What's wrong?"

Katherine wiped her eyes and could barely speak she was so wracked with sorrow. "I lied to you Arthur. I didn't mean for this to happen, truly I didn't."

"Katherine, please tell me what you're talking about."

"The truth is I had no intention of allowing them to get on an orphan train. Not next week, not ever. I love them Arthur, and my heart is broken. It's so broken I don't think I'll ever be happy again." Katherine told Arthur through her tears.

If there was one thing Arthur Wallace couldn't tolerate, it was seeing his wife upset. He sat close to Katherine and put his arms around her and held her tight. "It's alright Katherine. Everything is going to be alright."

CHAPTER TWENTY-SEVEN

*T*here was nothing to do but hit the brakes and try to swerve around it. The large buck that had jumped onto the road had to have been a good three hundred pounds. Eddy saw the buck standing in the middle of the road as he came around the turn. There was hardly any time to react. The car went into a spin after Eddy slammed on the brakes. The Duesenberg hit the buck's hind quarters. The car continued to spin until it flipped over. It rolled, landing back on its tires about twenty five feet into the woods. Eddy had lost consciousness briefly. It was the crackling of the burning underbrush and the searing pain that radiated from his left shoulder down to his wrist that brought him to.

Eddy struggled to make sense of his surroundings. He was disoriented. Smoke began to fill the car and bright orange flames danced along the driver's side of the Duesenberg, licking at his closed window. He looked over at Vinny. He was slumped over. It was dark, but there was enough light from the fire to see that Vinny's hair was soaked with blood. He wasn't sure if Vinny was alive or not.

"Vinny, Vinny! Wake up!" Eddy yelled as he grabbed Vinny's shoulder with his right hand and shook him as hard as he could. Vinny didn't respond. Eddy knew he had to get out of the car and away from the flames and smoke but he couldn't get around Vinny's flaccid body.

Eddy leaned over Vinny and tried to open the passenger door. The handle was just out of his reach. He tried again but failed. The temperature in the car was stifling. Eddy turned and put his back up against the driver's side door and brought his legs up to his chest. He pushed Vinny toward the passenger door and then slid over on the seat and reached for the door handle again. This time he was successful and the door swung open. There wasn't enough room to crawl over Vinny so Eddy continued to push Vinny with his feet until Vinny's body fell out of the car, landing face down on the ground in a motionless heap. Eddy sat at the edge of the seat sweating profusely from exertion and the intense heat from the growing inferno. His legs hung out of the car and were planted on Vinny's back. He pushed off the door frame with his right hand and stood up. Vinny let out a loud groan. He stepped off of him and looked down in shock. Vinny was still alive.

Eddy's left arm felt like it was being crushed in a vice grip. It was hard to think of anything but the excruciating pain. He kicked Vinny's leg in an effort to rouse him. "Vinny!" Eddy yelled. Eddy buried his nose and mouth in the crook of his right arm to keep from inhaling the smoke and looked down at Vinny for a few moments trying to decide if he should pull him from the burning wreckage or not.

Finally, Eddy reached down and grabbed the back of Vinny's collar and began dragging him toward the road. He trudged up the slight incline that the Duesenberg had rolled down. He was half way to the shoulder of the road when his vision began to dim. Everything around him turned gray and then black. He staggered a few steps and passed out, still holding Vinny's collar in his fist.

A big cold drop of rain woke Eddy. It hit right in the middle of his forehead. Another followed and then another. Eddy opened his eyes and looked up at the quiet gray sky. An acrid fog hung in the air from the smoldering Duesenberg. It had been raining on and off through the night. Eddy and Vinny lay on the ground as the rain came down harder and eventually began pelting them in a frigid down pour. It was just barely light out.

Eddy estimated that it was about six o'clock in the morning. For early November, it was relatively warm. It was in the high forties but Eddy's teeth were chattering and his wet three piece black pin stripe suit clung to his slim frame. Eddy struggled to his feet, nearly passing out again from the pain in his injured arm. He reached over with his right arm and braced his left elbow hoping the pain would subside. That's when he noticed that a peculiar whitish stick-like protrusion had ripped through his suit coat at mid-arm. It was his humerus bone. He vomited at the realization.

Eddy staggered to the side of the road and sat for nearly two hours. Finally the rain stopped. A half hour later he saw a green Model S pickup truck driving toward him. He stepped into the road still supporting his left elbow with his right hand. The pickup stopped and Eddy stumbled over to the driver's side window.

"Take me to Bellevue, will ya?"

The two middle aged men in the pickup looked at one another and back at Eddy. "What are you doing out here in the middle of nowhere pal?"

"My car went off the road last night. It's over there," Eddy said, motioning with his head.

The man sitting in the passenger seat of the pickup truck turned to peer into the woods. The tangled Duesenberg was partially obscured by the foliage but what he could see plainly was Vinny, lying unconscious on his back in a mud puddle.

The man in the passenger's seat of the pickup truck reached over and patted the back of his hand on the driver's chest while keeping his eyes fixed on Vinny.

"Bud, look over there," he said pointing to where Vinny lay.

The driver stared at Vinny's still body and then looked at Eddy. "Is he alive?"

The truth was that Eddy didn't know. He was so focused on himself he never bothered to check on Vinny.

"Do I look like a God damn doctor? For Christ's sake my arm's half ripped off here," Eddy snapped.

"Get in the back," the man driving the pickup truck said tersely. Eddy managed to get up into the bed of the truck. He watched as the two men ran over to Vinny and knelt next to his body. One of the men took Vinny's legs and the other squatted down and hooked his forearms under Vinny's armpits. They lifted his portly body off the ground and carried him over to the bed of the pickup truck. They placed him at the edge and one the men got up into the bed of the truck and pulled Vinny's body in the rest of the way.

The driver looked at Eddy. "Your friend here is alive alright, barely, but he's alive."

Eddy said nothing but somehow he resented Vinny for making him look foolish in front of the two men.

The ride to Bellevue hospital in the back of the truck amid the tackle boxes and fishing poles was a long, cold one. When they arrived, three burly orderlies in white uniforms came out to the truck with a gurney. They pulled Vinny's unconscious body on to it and rolled him away. Meanwhile, an attractive young nurse stood by with a wheelchair for Eddy. He felt like his arm was on fire although he was still shivering from the cold.

"I'm Nurse Warren. What's your name?" the nurse asked.

"Eddy," he replied without expression.

"Eddy, what's your last name?" the nurse asked as she grasped Eddy's good arm in an attempt to help him down from the bed of the truck. Eddy pulled away. "I'm okay. It's Johnson, the name's Eddy Johnson."

"What's your friend's name?" the nurse asked as she pushed Eddy in through the hospital doors.

"Vinny Smith," Eddy said without hesitation.

Eddy was brought to an examining room.

"The doctor will be in to see you in a minute," Nurse Warren informed Eddy, and left. She came back a few minutes later with a syringe and an orderly holding a pair of large shears. "Mr. Johnson, I'm going to give you an injection that will relieve your pain. Once it starts to take affect we'll need to cut your jacket and shirt off of you. Stand up please."

He stood and the orderly unfastened Eddy's belt and unbuttoned his fly. The nurse stood behind Eddy and pulled the waist band of his pants past his buttock. Eddy felt a sharp stinging sensation as the nurse injected the medication.

The next thing Eddy remembered was waking up in a hospital bed with his left arm in traction.

"Nurse!" Eddy screamed.

A petite woman wearing a nurse's uniform and white cap over her salt and pepper hair came into the room. She had a pinched face that bore an expression of smug superiority. "Mr. Johnson, that kind of raucous isn't necessary. It's three o'clock in the morning. There's a bell right next to your bed. There are people sleeping, people like you who need their rest," she admonished. "Now what seems to be the problem?"

"The problem is I'm sitting in my own piss and I don't know how the hell I got into this bed and why my arm's tied to this contraption!" Eddy hollered. "Now get over here and cut me loose!"

"Mr. Johnson, you'll need to calm down before I can do anything for you." the nurse said flatly with her hands clasped primly together at her waist.

Eddy inhaled deeply and exhaled slowly. "Okay, I'm calm," Eddy said and squeezed his lips flat in an exaggerated closing of his mouth.

"That's better. You'll notice that you're in an eight bed ward. You'll have to make an effort to be considerate of the other patients. Now what do you want?" the nurse said coldly.

"I'd like a sip of water, ma'am," Eddy told her politely.

The nurse walked over to Eddy's nightstand and poured tepid water from a pitcher into a glass and handed it to Eddy. Eddy reached out, but not for the glass of water.

Eddy reached for the nurse's starched white collar with his right hand and twisted it with all his might. He smiled as he watched her eyes bulge and her face go from a ruddy pink to a beautiful light purple as he choked off the flow of blood to her brain. Her small hands held Eddy's wrist in a futile attempt to loosen his grip. Finally, her hands fell from his wrist and her arms hung slack at her sides. Eddy let go. She slid to the floor, a small white mound next to Eddy's bed. Eddy fell back exhausted. He shifted from side to side noting an uncomfortable lump at his right shoulder blade. He was annoyed with himself for not thinking to have the nurse adjust his pillows before he strangled her. Eddy closed his eyes and fell asleep wondering if Vinny was still alive or not.

CHAPTER TWENTY-EIGHT

Patrick and Chevonne boarded an orphan train the same morning they left the Wallace's. There were twenty-five to thirty children crowded onto the train ranging in ages from one to about fifteen years old. There was even an infant. A man in his thirties and a middle aged woman served as chaperones. The train was hot and smelled of sour milk and a diaper in need of changing. It was noisy. Children were laughing and crying and running about.

They were headed toward Pennsylvania. The last stop was Chicago. Patrick had gone to the New York Foundling Hospital to ask about the trains after finding out that his father had died. He wasn't excited about the prospect of living with strangers but he didn't see that there were many other options. The clerk at the Foundling Hospital wanted to know how old he and his sister were. He wanted to know what color hair and eyes Chevonne had and if either of them had any "defects." Patrick said they didn't.

"Where are your parents? He asked.

"They're both dead, sir."

The clerk looked him over; "Relatives? "

"No sir, none to speak of."

"Alright then, I'll send out your information. There'll be ministers and priests along the train routes that will get this information and they'll ask their parishioners if any of them can take you and your sister in. Sometimes they'll put up postings in the local stores."

"How long will that take?"

"It's hard to say. You can get on one of the trains and take your chances. The townspeople will come out and look you over. The trains usually go out of Grand Central pretty regular."

After what Patrick had overheard Arthur Wallace say, he thought it'd be best for him and his sister to take their chances. They rode for hours.

As night began to fall the train had quieted. Most of the children were asleep and the ones that were still awake seemed too tired to make any more fuss. Patrick listened to the rhythmic sounds of the train in motion and felt himself relaxing. He wondered what their new family would be like. Patrick imagined that he and Chevonne would have a mother and a father and maybe more siblings and they would live on a beautiful farm with dairy cows and chickens and crops, maybe even a horse.

Patrick fell asleep smiling thinking about how much fun it was going to be playing in the barn and jumping from the loft into huge piles of fresh hay. He woke to Chevonne patting his shoulder hard.

"Patrick, wake up; we're here."

Patrick struggled to come out of his deep sleep. It had been a long time since he'd slept so soundly.

"Patrick, wake up. We have to get off of the train." Chevonne said excitedly.

"Where are we?" Patrick asked.

"I don't know. I'm not sure." Chevonne said with a hint of anxiety in her voice.

"Let's go, let's go." The chaperones ordered. Patrick pulled his shoeshine kit out from under the seat.

"Leave that here. If you get picked you can come back for it," the chaperone said.

Patrick looked at him with a wary expression.

"My guess is you'll be getting right back on this train. Now let's go." The male chaperone said impatiently.

Patrick pushed the shoe shine kit back under the seat. The children walked single file off of the train. There were townspeople waiting at the platform. One of the chaperones held an infant in her arms and walked over to a waiting couple and handed the baby to the woman. The woman looked down at the baby and from her expression Patrick could tell she loved that baby just as if it were her own. Other children were united with new parents as well, but for most of the children, it was just an opportunity to stretch their legs and get some fresh air before getting back on the train.

They rode for another two hours before stopping at a rural train station in the middle of a large field in a small town in Pennsylvania. There was nothing around except for a hut-like structure and a bench long enough to seat four people. A crude stage had been erected on the opposite side of the tracks in the field. It stood about four feet high and was about eight feet in width and sixteen feet in length. It had make shift steps at each end, designed to allow people to get a good look at the children who had come off the orphan train.

Patrick could see that there were at least a dozen people waiting in front of the stage. There were horse drawn wagons and buggies and a Model T Ford Coupe as well. Patrick looked over the crowd at the potential parents. There were only three females among the group of people waiting: an elderly woman, a Negro girl that looked to be sixteen or so, and a woman holding a toddler.

There were two men in tan uniforms. They wore badges and had holsters with guns around their waists. They stood leaning up against the car. The rest were men that looked like hard working farmers.

"Alright children, leave your belongings on the train and walk out onto the platform," the male chaperone instructed loud enough for all the children to hear. Patrick and Chevonne walked out onto the platform. The high grass in the field swayed in the warm autumn breeze. The only structure that could be seen, besides the small hut, was a white church with a steeple in the distance.

The children were led over to the stage and paraded up on it, standing to face the onlookers. Small groups of siblings huddled together. The stage was crowded when all the children were on it. At the far right end of the staging was a teenage girl holding her nine month old sister. Her seven year old brother clung to her leg. Next to them stood a boy who looked to be about ten who was holding hands with his sisters. Both looked to be four or five. Patrick and Chevonne stood next to them. He placed his hands on Chevonne's shoulders and held her close to him.

An older boy, probably fifteen or so, and three younger boys, somewhere between the ages of seven and ten, stood close to one another. Patrick assumed they were related. They all looked alike with olive skin and thick dark, wavy hair. They were a rowdy bunch and had been horsing around a lot on the bus. They had to be spoken to by the chaperones a number of times for their antics.

Patrick looked out at the crowd and saw a rotund man with a large, red bulbous nose. He wore a plaid flannel shirt, overalls and a straw hat tilted back on his head. He stood stroking his long salt and peppered chest length beard as he eyed Chevonne. A sad looking Negro girl stood next to him.

The men wearing the tan uniforms and badges were the town sheriff and the sheriff's deputy. The sheriff walked up the stairs onto the stage with the children. The woman in the crowd with the toddler pointed to the teenage girl who was holding her baby sister of similar age.

"I'll be taking the little one Henry," the woman called up to the Sheriff. The Sheriff went to pull the child out of the girl's arms.

"What are you doing?" The teenage girl said to the sheriff. "You can't take our baby sister from us!" The girl held the child tight with both arms and turned away from the sheriff.

"Don't you want your little sister to have a good home? They're going to take good care of her," the sheriff cajoled and reached for the baby again. But the girl refused to let go and began pleading with the woman in the crowd.

"Please, please take us too! I can cook and clean and help with the babies. We won't be any bother, I swear! Please!"

The girl was becoming hysterical. Her little brother, still clinging to his older sister's leg, began crying loudly too. The sheriff's deputy came up on the stage and between the two of them wrenched the baby out of the girl's arms. The teenage girl started to scream.

"No! Please, please no!"

The sheriff took the small child and brought it over to the woman in the crowd. The woman then walked quickly over to a man standing next to a horse drawn carriage. He helped her into the carriage with the child and then got up into the driver's seat, took the reins and rode off. The children on the stage watched the spectacle in horror.

Patrick bent down and whispered in his sister's ear.

"Chevonne, listen to me." Patrick could feel Chevonne trembling. He forced himself to sound calm.

"I think that man with the beard is going to take you. When he does don't fight. Don't try to hold on to me. Stay calm and go with him; I have a plan."

Chevonne said nothing in response. She just nodded and continued to look terrified. The teenage girl and her little brother were brought back to the train by the chaperones after their baby sister had been taken away.

As Patrick had anticipated the bearded farmer yelled up to the Sheriff.

"Henry, I'm taking the blonde girl right there." He pointed to Chevonne.

"How about the boy, Earl?" the sheriff asked, hopeful that the farmer would take Patrick too and they could avoid another uproar.

"Nope; Henry, no room; just the girl," the farmer answered. The Sheriff and his assistant looked at one another and then looked warily at Patrick, bracing for a fight.

Patrick hugged Chevonne and said, "Go on Chevonne. Everything is going to be okay."

"Atta boy," the sheriff smiled and patted Patrick on the back. "Alright then honey, go on down the steps over there and meet yer new daddy," the sheriff said kindly to Chevonne as he ushered her toward the stairs at the left side of the stage. Chevonne looked at her brother nervously and walked slowly off the stage and down the stairs.

"Why ain't you a purty one," the farmer said, looking down at Chevonne with a salacious grin that exposed the few tobacco stained teeth he had left. Chevonne thought he smelled faintly of manure. The farmer reached toward Chevonne's face and with his dirty index finger and thumb pulled her top lip up.

"Let's get a look see at that mouth of yours." The farmer examined Chevonne's gums and teeth. "Them is some nice pearly whites ya got there," he said. Chevonne stood looking up at Patrick on the stage with pleading eyes hoping he would do something.

Patrick's blood was boiling and his jaw was clenched tight. Then another farmer spoke up. "Henry, I'm lookin for some boys to help me tend the farm. I'll take them two: the one right there in the blue shirt and the one next to him in the brown sweater," the old farmer ordered. He pointed to two of the four boys with the dark hair and olive skin.

The sheriff looked at the two boys and said, "Well, you heard him boys. Go on now."

The older boy turned and stomped hard on the sheriff's foot. Patrick actually thought he heard the sheriff's bones break.

"Jesus Christ! Son of a bitch!" the sheriff screamed and hopped around in a circle on one foot while he bent over and held the injured one in his hand. The sheriff's deputy grabbed one of the younger boys, who reacted by biting into the deputy's wrist so hard he must have hit and artery. Blood spurted out of the side of his mouth.

It was pandemonium, just as Patrick had anticipated, and that's when he made his move.

The bearded farmer had begun to walk with the Negro girl and Chevonne toward one of the horse drawn carriages. They were about thirty feet away. Patrick jumped off the stage and ran full bore toward the farmer and hit him with such force that the farmer's feet lifted off the ground at least six inches. His podgy frame landed with a heavy thud. The farmer lay still trying to recover his breath. The wind had been knocked out of him completely.

Patrick grabbed Chevonnes's hand and they ran toward a thickly wooded area about two hundred feet in the distance. "Run, Chevonne!" Patrick yelled.

Patrick was fast. Chevonne couldn't keep up and she was slowing them down. "Come on Chevonne!" Patrick encouraged.

Just then, they heard the sound of gun fire: one shot echoed behind them. Patrick hoped that it was the sheriff firing into the air but he didn't dare look back. They heard another shot.

Patrick considered stopping. He didn't think they could make it and was afraid they'd be shot.

Suddenly, Chevonne felt lighter and they were able to move much faster. It was an odd sensation. Patrick turned his head to look at Chevonne. The Negro girl had run up beside Chevonne and grabbed her other hand. Patrick and the Negro girl had virtually lifted Chevonne's small frame from the ground and the three of them sprinted for the woods.

The twigs and dried leaves snapped and crunched under their feet. They dodged tree limbs and jumped over logs. Patrick and Chevonne had no idea where they were. The Negro girl motioned for them to follow her. They ran deeper into the woods and finally came to a ravine.

"This way," the girl waved them on. They slid down an embankment that came to a precipice. The drop was over thirty feet. They took careful side steps along a ledge that eventually came to a shallow cave.

"In here," the girl said.

They all sat cross legged. There wasn't a lot of room. "What's your name?" Patrick asked the girl.

"My name is Ginny."

Patrick was too exhausted to say anything more than, "Thank you."

CHAPTER TWENTY-NINE

$\mathcal{B}$erta sat in the last class of the day at PS 128. The usual announcements over the PA system signaled the end of another school day. "If anyone has lost a bracelet and can identify it please come to the office…" came the crackled voice over the intercom.

Berta was planning on meeting Sophia and some of her other friends in front of the school. It was Friday and the girls were making plans for the weekend. Helen Demaio and Jeanine Russo were talking about going to the opening of the Coney Island boardwalk.

"I wish I could go. My parents never let me go anywhere," Sophia pouted. The two girls walked down 82nd Street in silence with Sophia sulking all the way home.

"I'm sick of my brothers and sister. You're so lucky that you don't have to put up with siblings. It must be nice not to have little snot-nosed monsters getting into your things or a sister that thinks she's the Queen of Sheba," Sophia complained.

Berta could never begin to explain how lonely it could be at her house. She just said, "It's not as great as you think."

Suddenly, Sophia perked up. "I have an idea! Let's go to your house for a change Berta!" It wasn't the first time Sophia suggested that they go to Berta's.

"Sophia, I told you; we can't go to my house, my mother's sick."

"Your mother's been sick for a long time. What's wrong with her?"

"I don't know. She won't go to the doctor."

"What do you mean 'sick?' Helen Demaio said that your mother has the consumption. Is she coughing?"

"No, she doesn't have the consumption and she's not coughing. Helen Demaio is a mean gossip," Berta said as they arrived at Sophia's and sat on the steps of the apartment building.

"Well, whatever it is it must not be contagious because you're not sick," Sophia pointed out. Berta said nothing for a moment and then tried to change the subject.

"I'm not sure I understand my math homework. I'd better get home and start working on it." But Berta didn't make a move to leave.

The two girls sat next to each other on Sophia's front stoop with their elbows planted on their laps and their hands under their chins. Finally Sophia turned to Berta and said, "It's not your fault that your mother's sick. I know that a lot of the kids and even some of the parents talk about her. You don't have to be embarrassed in front of me though," Sophia said gently.

"I'm not embarrassed," Berta said defensively. She turned her head to try to keep Sophia from seeing the tears that had welled up in her eyes.

"Berta, what's the matter?" Sophia asked. Berta turned and looked at Sophia.

"I think she's going crazy," Berta said, the tears finally spilling over and rolling down her cheeks.

Sophia put her arm around Berta. "It's alright, Berta. I'll help you, you'll see, everything will be fine." she said, trying to comfort her friend.

Sophia's mother came out of the front door and saw Berta crying.

"Berta, what's wrong?" Before Berta could answer Sophia spoke up.

"Berta's favorite uncle died last night and she's very upset about it. Her mother left for Queens this morning to help make arrangements. Berta is supposed to take the train to meet her. She said it was okay if Berta had a friend come with her. Can I go?"

"Berta, I'm so sorry to hear that," Mrs. Fabiano said. "I know how you feel. I was very close to my uncles too. It looks like you'll need the company of a good friend on a day like today. Where in Queens did your uncle live?"

Berta couldn't have answered if she wanted to. All the tears that she had held back over the months came pouring out as if a dam had burst and she was now sobbing. Sophia didn't miss a beat though. "Her uncle lived in Cambria Heights. We'll be staying with her Aunt Ethel, his wife, who'll need a lot of help. She has rheumatism you know. It's very sad. Berta's mother said we should be back home Sunday morning in plenty of time for mass."

Mrs. Fabiano leaned over and gave Berta a big hug and then said to Sophia. "Take good care of your friend. I'll get a bag together for you, Sophia."

"Thank you, Mama," Sophia smiled sweetly.

Mrs. Fabiano walked back up the steps and into the apartment. She came back out a few minutes later with a small cloth bag that held a change of clothes, a night gown, underwear, a comb and a toothbrush.

"Here Sophia," Mrs. Fabiano said as she handed Sophia the bag. "Be good and mind your manners."

"I will." Sophia said. Sophia turned to Berta and extended her hand. "Come on let's go. We don't want to miss the next train." Berta stood up and smiled; her face puffy and tear streaked.

"Thank you Mrs. Fabiano."

"Of course; my condolences to your family for their loss," Mrs. Fabiano said with heartfelt empathy.

Sophia and Berta walked slowly arm in arm toward Berta's. Sophia thought her mother might still be watching and wanted to make sure that they looked sad enough. It wouldn't do to go cheerfully skipping down the sidewalk. They walked solemnly down to the end of the block and turned the corner. As soon as they rounded the corner Sophia jumped up and down clapping her hands. "Berta, we're going to have so much fun! We have the whole weekend!"

Berta wasn't as enthusiastic. "I'm not sure this is a good idea Sophia. I don't know what my mother will say and if Vinny's home he might be mad that I invited a friend over without asking permission."

"Oh, stop being such a wet blanket. If your parents are that sore about it I'll just go home and tell my mother I have a sick stomach."

Sophia started skipping gleefully down the sidewalk but Berta was anxious. There was no telling what she and Sophia would be walking into when they got to the apartment. Berta didn't feel like skipping. Instead, she tried to ease her fears by focusing on not stepping on the cracks in the sidewalk.

"Come on Berta!" Sophia yelled. She was already half a block ahead of Berta. When the two girls arrived at the apartment Berta opened the door on a crack at first and peeked in. Sometimes her mother walked around the apartment in various stages of undress.

Berta didn't see her or Vinny and proceeded to open the door completely. The apartment was dimly lit by a small lamp on an end table in the living room. It was sunny out but the apartment was dreary, stuffy, and smelled vaguely of urine. All the shades were pulled down. Sophia's excitement evaporated.

"Mama...? Mama?" Berta called out softly as she walked from room to room.

Sophia watched Berta walk into her mother's bedroom and shut the door gently behind her. She could hear Berta talking.

"Mama, I have a friend over. Do you remember me telling you about my friend from school? Her name is Sophia. She's going to stay with us until Sunday. Is that alright Mama?" Sophia didn't hear any response from Berta's mother. Berta came back out of the bedroom and closed the door behind her.

"What did she say? Is it okay?" Sophia asked.

"It's okay," Berta replied.

The truth was that Rosa hadn't said anything. She just sat in the chair in the corner of the bedroom staring blankly at the floor. Sophia understood now why Berta was reluctant to have anyone over. The atmosphere in the apartment was almost unbearably depressing.

"Where's your father?" Sophia asked.

"He's not my father." Berta responded curtly.

"I know... You know what I mean. Anyway, where is he?"

"I don't know. He's usually here when I get home from school but he hasn't been home for a few days at least."

"Where did he go?"

"I don't know. I guess he's working."

"Where does he work?"

Berta hesitated for a moment. "He's a traveling salesman."

"Oh," is all Sophia said. Then she looked around the apartment and put her hands on her hips. "Well, the first thing we ought to do is put the shades up. Let's open some windows and let some fresh air in here too."

"Vinny doesn't like the shades up," Berta said, sounding nervous.

"Vinny isn't here," Sophia replied matter-of-factly as she went from window to window pulling up the shades and cracking the windows.

The crisp, cool fall air flooded in along with the sunshine. It had been a long time since Berta enjoyed looking out of the windows of the apartment. It elevated her mood immediately, although she was still worried that Vinny would come home and punish her for it. Sophia went over to the radio and turned it on.

"Yes! We have no bananas, we have no bananas today!" Sophia sang along to Billy Jones' hit song. Berta laughed at Sophia's theatrics. Sophia was doing a high stepping march around the couch in the living room and singing. It looked like so much fun Berta decided to join her. Around they went singing and laughing. "Yes! We have no bananas, we have no bananas today-ay-ay!"

Berta even jumped up on the sofa and walked from one end to the other doing her best Groucho Marx impersonation. Sophia was doubled over, hysterical with laughter. They danced and sang and laughed until they both collapsed on the floor. Berta was having so much fun she completely forgot about her mother.

"I'm starving. What do you have to eat?" Sophia asked as she headed into the kitchen.

Berta followed. "Do you want a sandwich? There's some tuna salad in the ice box."

Sophia ignored Berta's offer. She explored the kitchen; opening the cupboard doors and looking up into them assessing the contents.

"It looks like you have all the ingredients to bake something. Let's make a cake, Berta," Sophia said excitedly.

"I don't know," Berta said, obviously reluctant.

"Well, why not? You know how to make a cake don't you?" Sophia asked.

"I've never baked a cake. Vinny bakes. His family owns Capozza's bakery."

"Then Vinny must have taught you how to make a cake."

"Well, not really, but I've watched him."

"It's easy, you'll see." Sophia said cheerfully.

Sophia pulled a chair over to the kitchen counter. She stood up on it and reached into the shelves and pulled out what they needed. She handed the items down to Berta.

"Let's make some soup too while we're waiting for the cake to bake," Sophia said and passed down two cans of Campbell's tomato soup. "Oh, look, I almost didn't see these. They were pushed way back on the top shelf. I hope they're not stale." Sophia took down the large "Uneeda Biscuit" tin. It was nearly the size of a hat box. The lid had a picture of a little boy in a yellow southeaster rain cap and a yellow rain jacket. "Well, that ought to do it," Sophia said as she hopped off the chair. "I love these biscuits." Sophia exclaimed as she pulled off the lid.

Berta and Sophia both gasped. Their eyes grew wide as they looked down at the contents of the tin. Berta was speechless and the only thing Sophia could manage to say was, "Holy moly!"

CHAPTER THIRTY

Arthur Wallace was a name that most people in positions of power knew. It was a name that carried a lot of weight and had tremendous influence. Arthur made good use of it when he realized the magnitude of the problem. His wife was near hysterical and she wasn't a woman who cried easily. He'd never seen Katherine so upset in the entire course of their marriage. He knew that he had to take action and find Patrick and Chevonne O'Farrell. "Don't worry Katherine, we'll find them. You'll see," he reassured his wife as they drove down Fifth Ave toward their apartment.

As soon as they walked into the apartment, Arthur strode over to the phone and called his mid-town office. He spoke with his secretary. "Get Dick Enright on the phone right away. I need to speak with him immediately. Also, I need you to contact the Children's Aid Society and the New Foundling Hospital. I want a list of the families who signed up to take a child. We'll need the train schedules as well. Thank you Miss Davis," Arthur said to his secretary and hung up.

He went back to Katherine who was busy packing a suitcase. "What are you doing Katherine?" Arthur asked.

"I'm packing our bags. We're going to go get them."

"But Katherine, we have no idea where they are yet."

"I know that dear, but it shouldn't be long before we do and I want to be ready. I just can't sit and do nothing. I'll go crazy," Katherine said, as she walked back and forth from her bureau to the suitcase on the bed throwing clothes in it.

Bertram came into the room. "There's a Police Commissioner Richard Enwright on the phone for you sir," he announced.

Arthur went to the phone. "Dick, thank you for calling back. We have a situation that I think you may be able to help us with." Arthur went on to explain that they needed to locate two children who had boarded an orphan train. The commissioner assured the Wallaces that they would alert all the police departments and the sheriffs in all the towns along the train routes once that information was available. Also, detectives would be dispatched to Grand Central Terminal to speak with employees who may have seen Patrick and Chevonne. It was amazing how much people could remember when a badge was flashed.

Not more than three hours had gone by before the Wallaces learned that Patrick and Chevonne had boarded a train headed to Chicago. Now it was just a matter of finding out which stop they had gotten off at. It was less than an hour before that information became available as well. Katherine was overjoyed at learning that the police had called to tell Arthur where Patrick and Chevonne had disembarked. Arthur walked into the parlor after speaking with the Police Commissioner. He wore a pensive expression,

"Katherine, the children got off in a small town in rural Pennsylvania called Nazareth. It's about sixty miles from here," Arthur told his wife as he sat down next to her and took her hand in his.

"Oh thank God," Katherine said visibly relieved.

"Unfortunately, there's more."

"What do you mean?" Katherine asked anxiously.

"Katherine, I assure you the children will be found—"

Katherine interrupted. "The children have been found, you just told me that."

"Well, not exactly. They attempted to separate them from one another and they ran off."

"Ran off? For heaven's sake Arthur, how far could they have gotten? It sounds to me that they're in the middle of nowhere."

"Apparently they ran off into the woods with a Negro girl. I understand that the sheriff fired a few shots in the air to try to get them to stop."

"Fired shots? Oh Arthur, they must be terrified."

"It shouldn't be long before they're found. They've brought blood hounds from another county to track them. Chevonne's hair bow fell out while they were running so they have a scent to follow. A police car will be here in twenty minutes," Arthur assured his wife. "We can drive to Bremington but from there it's very rural. We'll take the train that passes through the town to the station that the children got off at. That'll be the quickest way. A gentleman by the name of Hodges will be putting us up for the night. He owns an Inn in Nazareth. My secretary has arranged for him to be waiting at the station for us. I'm guessing if we make good time and catch the train we'll be there in five or six hours. The sheriff and the deputy who were there when the children ran off will meet us at the train station too."

Katherine fought back her tears and focused on packing, making sure she thought of every eventuality. She even packed clothes for Patrick and Chevonne. There was no telling what kind of shape they'd be in after wandering around in the woods for hours. All Chevonne had on was a lightweight party dress. "Please God, don't let anything horrible happen to them," Katherine prayed. Arthur came into the bedroom.

"Katherine, why are you dressed like you're going on safari?"

"I'm not going to Nazareth so I can sit around sipping tea. I'm going to help find them and it doesn't hurt to be prepared." Katherine said, defensively. Arthur shook his head. "Alright then, let's go darling. Hopefully they'll find the children before nightfall."

Katherine and Arthur arrived in Nazareth just before ten o'clock at night. The sheriff and his deputy and a group of townspeople had been combing the woods for hours but to no avail. They were ready to call it a night when Katherine and Arthur arrived. Katherine looked around the train station and was even more frightened than she was before. It truly was the middle of nowhere. She noticed the crude staging on the other side of the tracks.

"Is that where you put the orphans on display for the townspeople?" Katherine said with venom in her voice. .

"Um… yes ma'am."

"Where did they run off to?" Katherine asked.

"Over there, ma'am," the sheriff pointed to the thickly wooded area a little ways in the distance.

The sheriff turned to Arthur and said, "I'm sorry sir. We've had the blood hounds out since six o'clock. We've just had no luck. It's like they disappeared into thin air. We can start up the search again at day break."

"They're liable to freeze. Why, it must be in the thirties now and those woods are teeming with predatory animals. How do you suppose they'll survive? Tell me that, would you?" Arthur demanded.

Arthur regretted his outburst almost immediately. He had let his emotions get the best of him and he was afraid all he'd done was upset Katherine.

"There's just nothing more we can do. We don't even have decent moonlight anymore because of the cloud cover," the sheriff said. Arthur looked at Katherine not knowing what else to do or say. Katherine said nothing, but she wore an expression of steely determination. She looked defiantly at Arthur and the sheriff and began walking toward the woods yelling. "Chevonne! Patrick! Can you hear me? Come out: it's alright, everything's going to be alright, we're here!"

Arthur looked at the sheriff. "Be back at the crack of dawn with a full search party and those blood hounds."

"Yes sir," the sheriff said solemnly.

Arthur followed Katherine. "Katherine, you can't go into the woods looking for them. You have no idea where you are and its pitch black." She took the French leather shooting bag she was carrying off of her shoulder, put in on the ground and knelt as she rummaged through it.

"Here, hold this," she said to Arthur and handed him a spool of string the size of a grapefruit. "And take this too." It was a flashlight. "Oh wait." Katherine reached into the deep pocket of her navy cashmere bush jacket. She pulled out a Dennison Birmingham pocket watch style compass. "Here, we'll need this."

"Katherine, I don't think this a good idea. There've been at least a dozen people looking for them since three o'clock this afternoon and they haven't been found."

"Those people weren't us. They don't know those people and they don't trust them. They're hiding from them," Katherine replied, sounding more indomitable than ever.

Chevonne, Patrick and Ginny had been huddled together for hours listening to the voices of the sheriff and his search party. They had been hoping for an opportunity to make their way out of the woods and eventually out of Nazareth but the search party never let up. They would have surely been captured if they came out from their hiding place. "Come on out! It's okay. Nobody's gonna hurt ya! Come on out!" they heard a strange man's voice yell.

Patrick didn't believe them for a moment and neither did the girls.

"You kids got some nice folks in New York lookin for ya. You wouldn't wanna worry them, now would ya?" the sheriff yelled.

Chevonne looked at Patrick. "Do you think the Wallace's are looking for us Patrick?" she said hopefully.

"I don't know why they would be, unless one of their rich friends is looking for Irish servants," Patrick said, not trying to hide the bitterness he felt. Chevonne looked at Patrick quizzically.

"Quiet" Ginny whispered.

The three of them sat perfectly still in silence waiting for the voices to fade. Eventually they did but now it was nighttime and they could barely see a hand in front of their face. They were all tired and it was getting very cold. Patrick took his jacket off and gave it to·Chevonne.

"What are we going to do?" Chevonne asked Patrick.

Patrick turned to Ginny, "How did you know this cave was here?"

"It's not a cave. It's a tunnel," Ginny answered.

CHAPTER THIRTY-ONE

ddy heard a high-pitched raspy wheeze and then coughing. He looked over the side of his bed to see the nurse he had strangled start to regain consciousness. Eddy leaned over the edge of the bed so that he could enjoy the look of horror on the nurse's face when she became lucid enough to realize that she was still just an arm's length away from the man who had nearly killed her only moments ago. He wasn't disappointed. The nurse opened her eyes, let out a piercing scream and scrambled to her feet and ran from the hospital ward. Eddy laughed at the sight, nearly forgetting the relentless throbbing in his left arm.

With her nursing cap askew and her starched white uniform twisted and rumpled, Nurse Jenkins ran and found Dr. Rovenstine. He was standing at the counter writing orders. "Dr. Rovenstine, I need to speak with you right away."

The doctor noted the nurse's disheveled appearance. She was near hysteria. "What is it, Nurse Jenkins; what's the matter?"

"It's that man. It's that man in bed three in the ward. He's crazy I tell you. He's a murderous lunatic." the nurse said breathlessly.

"What in the world are you talking about?"

"He tried to kill me. He nearly strangled me to death."

"Oh come now, Nurse Jenkins, why in the world would he want to kill you?"

"I'm telling you he's insane. You mustn't allow any of the nurses to go near him without an orderly with them."

Dr. Rovenstine tried to calm the frantic nurse. "There, there, Nurse Jenkins, you need to compose yourself. Remember that man has been through a traumatic event. He was in a horrible car accident. His friend is still in a coma. You've been a nurse long enough to know that patients do and say bizarre things when they're coming out of sedation. Why, it's quite common for patients to become confused and combative under those circumstances. I'm sure he's terribly embarrassed over his behavior."

"Oh no, no, no! He wasn't confused at all. He knew exactly what was he was doing. You should have seen the look in his eyes. I'm telling you he's very dangerous. In my opinion he should be on a psychiatric ward or better yet a prison infirmary," Nurse Jenkins said with intense certitude.

The doctor let out an impatient sigh. "Alright then, I'll have Dr. Wheeler from psychiatry take a look at him."

The nurse knew it was merely a consolatory gesture but it was something. "Thank you doctor, but I think the orderlies should take responsibly for his personal care until he can be cleared."

Dr. Rovenstine had gone back to writing orders and was obviously not interested in further discussion about the matter. It was the middle of the night and he was exhausted. "Fine," he said without looking up from his note pad.

Eddy woke up the next morning to a young man in his twenties placing a breakfast tray in front of him. "Good morning Mr. Johnson, I'm Kenneth. I'll be assisting you with your personal care today," said the tall blonde orderly. "Would you like me to cut up your meat?"

Eddy looked at the food. There was a slab of ham next to two poached eggs on toast and a cup of tea. "I guess you're gonna have to. I'm a little tied up at the moment," Eddy said with a smirk and pointed to the traction apparatus holding up his left arm.

"Yes, I see," Kenneth said and picked up the knife and fork and began slicing.

"I think I can handle it from here," Eddy said when Kenneth was finished cutting up the ham.

"Good. I'll be back in about twenty minutes to help you get washed up and change your sheets." Eddy nodded in the affirmative while chewing the bite of toast and egg he had put in his mouth. Once Kenneth was out of sight Eddy took the knife and slid it under his mattress.

Eddy had just finished eating when a man in a white lab coat approached his bed. "I'm sorry to interrupt your breakfast. I'm Dr. Wheeler. Do you mind if I ask you a few questions?"

"Actually, I do mind. I'm in a lot of pain right now and I'm not in the mood to chat."

"That's understandable. I think I can help you with that." Dr. Wheeler walked out of the ward. He was back within ten minutes. "I've got some diacetylmorphine here. I'm sure it'll take care of the pain, for a while at least."

The doctor pulled back the covers and pushed Eddy's hospital gown aside and grabbed a handful of his upper thigh and injected the medication.

"There, that ought to do it. You ought to be feeling a good deal more comfortable in a few minutes," the doctor said confidently. He was right. Eddy never felt so relaxed and content in his life.

"So Doc, what can I help you with?" Eddy asked dreamily.

"Unfortunately, one of the nurses claimed that you attacked her last night. She said you tried to strangle her. I'd like to know what you have to say in your defensive."

Eddy wore a stupid, lazy smile as was the effect of the medication. "Gee Doc, are ya sure she meant me? I'd never do a thing like that," Eddy lied.

"Yes, she meant you. I suppose it's possible that you were a bit amnesic following the anesthetic, and considering the trauma of the accident, an uncharacteristic outburst wouldn't be surprising. So you recall nothing?" Dr. Wheeler asked as he studied Eddy's face.

"Not a thing," Eddy shrugged.

"Well then, I suppose that's it. I'm sorry about your friend. I'll let the orderly know we're finished."

Eddy mulled over the doctor's words. *'I'm sorry about your friend.' What did he mean by that?* Eddy wondered. *Was Vinny dead?*

He was mildly curious, but whether Vinny was dead or not just didn't seem that important. Eddy felt warm all over and more comfortable than he could ever remember being. Kenneth carried a large porcelain bowl filled with hot soapy water and set it down on the over-bed table. He turned and pulled the privacy curtains closed. Clean sheets were stacked on the nightstand.

"I'm going to get you washed and change your sheets, Mr. Johnson." Kenneth said.

"Yeah, you mentioned that and it's about time. I've been lying in this mess for hours. I'm no bed wetter either. Christ, I haven't wet the bed since I was three years old," Eddy laughed softly, his eyes half-mast.

"Don't worry about it. It happens a lot with anesthesia. That's what we're here for," Kenneth said calmly.

Kenneth reached behind Eddy's neck and pulled the string of his hospital gown.

"We'll need to get this off of you to get you washed up." He pulled it off of Eddy's shoulder and down his arm, removing the hospital gown completely from the right side of Eddy's body. Kenneth un-tucked the soiled sheets and rolled them toward Eddy. "Turn on your side as much as you can," Kenneth directed. Eddy turned with his back to Kenneth as far as the traction apparatus holding up his left arm would permit. Kenneth untied Eddy's hospital gown at the back and gently tossed the gown over Eddy exposing the full length of his posterior body.

Eddy closed his eyes and relished the warmth of the soapy water on his back. Kenneth patted Eddy dry with a towel and massaged him with liniment oil. He started from Eddy's neck and shoulders and went to the small of his back.

Kenneth rolled the soiled lined in on itself and pushed it up close to Eddy. He then laid out the fresh sheets on the bare mattress and smoothed them out. Kenneth walked around to the other side of the bed.

"Lift yourself up a little, Mr. Johnson, so I can pull the dirty sheets out from under you and pull the clean sheets through." Eddy did as he was told. The fresh sheets felt smooth and cool against Eddy's skin. Kenneth unfastened the snaps along the left shoulder of Eddy's hospital gown and removed it.

"I'll get you a clean gown."

Eddy lay completely naked for a moment before Kenneth placed a thin white sheet over him.

"Christ Almighty," Eddy laughed. "Look at that; it looks like somebody set up a goddamn pup tent in the bed." He was right and it was impossible to ignore. His large penis stood erect like a stone statue. "Hand me the urinal will ya? Maybe if I try to take a leak it'll help settle things down."

Kenneth bore the expression of a hungry man who'd just had a hot meal placed in front of him.

"Maybe I can help," Kenneth said as he locked eyes with Eddy.

"Maybe ya can." Eddy smiled broadly. Kenneth took Eddy's penis in his hand, still slick with liniment oil. He stroked Eddy, moving his hand up and down slowly at first and then faster. Kenneth watched Eddy's face. His eyes were closed and his brow was furrowed. After only a few minutes, Eddy's body stiffened and he let out an almost inaudible grunt. Creamy, white viscous fluid shot nearly a foot in the air. Eddy's body jerked forward slightly and then fell back on the pillows.

They heard voices coming closer. Eddy covered himself with the sheet and Kenneth pulled back the privacy curtain. Dr. Rovenstine stood with his clipboard just a few feet away. Kenneth bent over to pick up the soiled laundry from the floor.

"Good morning, Dr. Rovenstine," Kenneth said politely and walked out of the ward.

"Good morning," Dr. Rovenstine replied.

The effects of the pain medication were wearing off but Eddy was pleasantly spent from his encounter with Kenneth.

"So, Mr. Johnson, how are things going?" Before Eddy could answer, the doctor continued. "I just spoke with Dr. Wheeler. He tells me that he believes you had an episode of combativeness coming out of the anesthesia. It happens from time to time. You seem to be completely lucid now. Your injuries are minor compared to your friend's. I'm sorry to tell you that he's fallen into a coma. Unfortunately, the longer a patient remains unconscious the less likely it is that he'll come out of it. I understand you hit a deer and lost control of the car. It could've happened to anyone you know. I hope you're not blaming yourself."

It never occurred to Eddy to feel badly.

"Yeah Doc, I'm real broke up about it. I feel just terrible." Eddy hung his head feigning sorrow.

"We need to contact Mr. Smith's family, Mr. Johnson. Do you know where we can reach them? He's wearing a wedding ring. He must have a wife," Dr. Rovenstine remarked.

"Well, I gotta tell ya, I never laid eyes on the guy before. I happened to strike up a conversation with him at the horse track and it turned out that he was a car buff like me, so I told him about my new car and he asked if I'd take him for a ride. Our horses lost, and we left. All he told me about himself was his name: Vinny Smith. Sorry Doc, that's all I know."

The pain medication had completely worn off and his own adrenalin was coursing through his veins. Eddy's mind started racing. The last thing he needed was for word to get out that Vinny Capozza and Eddy Belachi were in Bellevue Hospital. They were sitting ducks for anyone who wanted to bump them off. Eddy knew he needed to get out of the hospital. He didn't even know where his gun was and he couldn't have been more vulnerable. His left arm was tied up and he was stark naked under the bed sheets. Eddy was lost in thought but the doctor's words brought him back to the present.

"I'm sorry to hear that. He's been in a coma for days. I'm sure his family is very worried about him. I suppose they'll go to the police soon enough to report him missing and the police will check all the hospitals. That's how it goes. I know from experience. Unfortunately, I've accompanied more than a few police officers and grieving families to the morgue," the doctor said soberly.

Eddy's skin crawled at the thought of police officers coming to the hospital asking questions. "Hey Doc, when can I go home?"

"I'm not sure. The next few days will give us a better idea of how quickly you're going to heal and if there'll be complications we'll have to address."

Before Eddy could respond they we interrupted by screaming.

"Dr. Rovenstine! Dr. Rovenstine! Come quick! It's Mr. Smith, we need your help right away!"

CHAPTER THIRTY-TWO

Sophia and Berta stood at the kitchen counter with their mouths agape looking into the Uneeda Biscuit tin. "Whose is it?" Sophia asked still staring down into the tin.

"I don't know," Berta replied with her eyes fixed on the tightly coiled wads of money secured with rubber bands. The rolls of money were fit snugly in the tin. Sophia began to count each wad.

"There are twenty of them," Sophia said as she reached in and pulled out a roll of money.

"I don't think we should touch it..." Berta whispered.

Sophia looked vexed, "Why not? We're not going to take any. We're just going to count it and we'll put back just exactly as it was. Do you think your mother knows where the money came from?" Sophia whispered back.

"I don't think she'll know. She has a hard time remembering things," Berta said. She doubted that her mother knew anything about the money and was reluctant to tell her about it for fear she'd fly into some kind of paranoid, crazy rant.

Sophia took the rubber band off of one of the rolls of money she had pulled out of the tin.

"They're all ten dollar bills. Geez o'crow, I've never seen this much money before in my life." Sophia began counting, laying each bill out on the counter, one on top of the other to form a stack.

"Ten, twenty, thirty, forty, fifty..." Sophia laid the next increment of fifty dollars cross-ways so that each stack was easily separated from the other. She repeated the count five times.

"It looks like all the rolls are the same size. So there's probably two hundred and fifty dollars in each roll. Times twenty rolls equals... what?" Sophia asked, trying to calculate in her head.

"Well, four rolls equal a thousand dollars, so there's five thousand dollars in this biscuit tin," Berta said, quickly doing the mental math.

"Holy smokes! My aunt Marie and Uncle Mario bought a three bedroom house near Avenue M and 21st Street. My mother said they paid too much for it and it was seven thousand."

Sophia and Berta looked up and stared at one another for a moment.

"Do you think it could be Vinny's money?" Sophia asked.

"I don't know, but I think we should put it back and forget we ever found it," Berta opined.

"Maybe the people who used to live here left it behind," Sophia suggested, as she rolled the money back up and wound the rubber band around it and placed it back in the tin.

"Why in the world would someone leave five thousand dollars in a biscuit tin in their kitchen cupboard?" Berta said.

"Maybe they forgot it?" Sophia said, knowing how silly it sounded even before Berta pointed it out.

"That's ridiculous. Nobody in their right mind could forget that they had thousands of dollars stashed away in their kitchen."

"Well, for Pete's sake Berta, are you going to tell anybody?" Berta had a distant look on her face. "Hello, hey you, anybody home?" Sophia waved a hand in front of Berta's face.

Berta had become completely lost in thought. She thought about Vinny and how he went out nearly every night dressed to the nines. She thought about his gold cufflinks and expensive watch. She thought about the men who used to came to the house every once in a while, the ones he called his "associates." She thought about the gun she saw on his nightstand and how he didn't want the shades up… and she thought about his temper and how violent he could be. Berta knew that Vinny paid the bills, but she didn't know exactly how since his father fired him from the bakery. She suspected that Vinny made his living doing things that weren't exactly legal, but she tried not to think about it. Berta had no doubt that the money was Vinny's and she had no doubt that he never intended for her to find it. She wasn't sure what he'd do to her if he found out that she knew about it. Sophia's hand moving in front of her face finally snapped her out of her reverie.

Berta grabbed the lid and slammed it on the biscuit tin. She stepped up on the chair with it and pushed it way back, out of sight, on the top shelf where Sophia had found it. Berta stepped back down off the chair and grasped Sophia's arms with her hands and looked into Sophia's eyes.

"Sophia, you must never, ever tell anybody about the money. Promise me you won't."

Sophia looked confused and alarmed. "Berta, your hands are shaking. Why are you so scared? There's something you're not telling me. What is it? What's wrong?"

She took Sophia by the hand and walked slowly out of the kitchen with her friend in tow. Berta looked quickly around the apartment to make sure Vinny hadn't come home while they were in the kitchen. When she was sure that they were safe she pulled Sophia into her room and shut the door behind them. Berta sat on the bed. Sophia sat next to her. "Sophia, Vinny isn't a traveling salesman." Sophia said nothing and waited for Berta to find the words she was searching for. "You see, he used to work at the bakery with his father." Sophia was anxious to hear Berta's revelation.

"Yes, I know you told me that. So, what did you want to tell me?"

"His father fired him for marrying my mother and he hasn't really had a job since."

"So, are you saying it's not his money?"

Berta shook her head. "What I mean is he hasn't had a real job for a long time. I think he's a... well... I think he's a..."

"A what?" Sophia nearly yelled.

"A gangster," Berta blurted.

Sophia looked stunned momentarily, "You mean like Al Capone?" Sophia asked.

"Well, sort of," Berta said reluctantly.

Sophia looked excited, "My sister Mildred, said she heard my parents talking about your step-father. They said he was in the newspaper because he was in a shoot-out. Mildred said Vinny was in the mob. I didn't believe her though. I thought she was just making up stupid stories like she usually does. It's true?"

"I think so." Berta said quietly.

"Gosh, do you think he robbed a bank?"

Berta shrugged. "All I know is that if he or any of his friends ever find out that we know about the money he might think that he needs to do something to keep us quiet, if you know what I mean."

Sophia's eyes widened, "You mean..." Sophia's voice trailed off as she moved her index finger from one side of her neck to the other.

"Maybe..." Berta said, looking queasy.

Sophia sat silently for a few minutes weighing all of the options,

"There's no use calling the police. My father says that the mob owns the police around here, at least most of them. I think you're right Berta.

Let's just pretend it never happened." Berta looked worn out but Sophia was still determined to make the most of her weekend of freedom.

"I have an idea!" Sophia said enthusiastically.

"It seems like every time you have an idea we end up in trouble..." Berta muttered, sounding dubious.

"Oh, come on now, Berta, don't be such a sad sack. Remember, we're pretending nothing happened. We're putting it out of our minds, right?"

"Yeah, I guess so. So what's your idea?" Berta said grudgingly.

Sophia put her hand in her sweater pocket and pulled out a dollar. "Looky here," Sophia held the bill up holding it at each end between her index finger and thumb and pulled it taunt. "I got it from my grandparents for making my Confirmation and I've been saving for a special occasion. Let's go to the movies. Rudolph Valentino is playing in 'A Sainted Devil.'"

"You're going to spend your Confirmation money on a movie called "A Sainted Devil"? Are you sure that's not a sin?"

"Maybe it is. I'm not sure. I'll go to Confession and tell Father Giovanni next week. I'm sure it'll definitely be worth having to say a few Hail Mary's. Come on, get your jacket."

"Alright, but first I have to get something for my mother to eat. She doesn't like to eat much and she's losing weight. I'll feed her a sandwich and tell her we're going to the movies," Berta said and went into the kitchen.

Sophia sat on the couch and waited for Berta to make a sandwich. Berta walked past the couch with the plate and small glass of milk, and went in the bedroom. She could hear Berta speaking to her mother. "Here Mama, eat. I made you a sandwich. Sophia and I are going to see a movie. We'll come back right afterward."

Sophia felt sad for Berta. It was as if Berta was the parent and her mother was the child. Sophia said a silent prayer. *"Please God, let Berta's mother get better".* About ten minutes had past and Berta opened the bedroom door. She looked happy. "She ate the whole sandwich. She usually only eats about half and she drank all the milk," Berta said, sounding pleased at having accomplished the task of getting her mother to eat and drink. Sophia didn't know what to say. She just knew she wanted to get out of the apartment.

The girls walked down the sidewalk with an exuberant spring in their step. Sophia felt relieved to get away from the mysterious money and Berta's crazy mother. They chatted about nothing in particular while they waited to board the trolley.

"Do you know what my sister, Miserable Mildred, told me the other day?"

"No, what did she tell you?"

"That dumbbell tried to tell me that she met Rudolph Valentino at Luna Park and that he was so smitten with her that he wrote her a love letter." Sophia and Berta laughed out loud.

"Can you believe that? She's bonkers. No wonder my mother doesn't want her reading those movie magazines. She even showed me the letter. Of course, it was written in her own stupid handwriting. She tried to disguise it but I could tell right away. She's such a dumb Dora." Berta and Sophia were still laughing when one of the bulbous, drop-center, maroon and cream colored trolleys stopped in front of them. Sophia handed the driver the dollar. He looked annoyed. "Next time, bring change will ya? this ain't the Bank of New York, ya know."

The movie was wonderful. Sophia and Berta came out of B.F.Keith's Greenpoint Theatre feeling buoyant. "That was the best! I think he's the most handsome man on the face of the earth," Sophia exclaimed.

Berta laughed. "Sophia Valentino. Mr. and Mrs. Valentino. I think you and Rudolph would make a beautiful couple."

"I think so too," Sophia agreed, beaming. "I don't know about you, but I'm starving. We have sixty cents left. That's plenty, so let's get some ice cream." Berta and Sophia walked to Coney Island since it wasn't far from the theatre. It was late Friday afternoon and the boardwalk was bustling. They took a stroll around Luna Park and the penny arcade before going across the street to Feltman's. Feltman's stretched all the way from the Boardwalk to Surf Avenue. It was massive; an intertwining of two bars and nine restaurants with beautiful gardens with names like Wisteria Pergola and Deutscher Garten. Each had a live orchestra.

They found a booth and settled in across from one another. Oompah-pah music played cheerfully in the background. The smells of roasted peanuts and cotton candy wafted in from the boardwalk and made their mouths water. They ordered a banana split. It arrived in a large, long silver colored dish. Sophia and Berta picked up their spoons and dug into the huge pile of whipped cream, chocolate syrup, pineapple topping and crushed nuts.

"Ugh, I can hardly breathe, I'm so stuffed!" Sophia said as they savored the last bites of ice cream. Sophia looked at Berta and started to giggle.

"What? What's so funny?" Berta asked.

"You have a big ring of chocolate sauce around your mouth." Berta noticed Sophia's expression change suddenly from amusement to shock and surprise.

"Berta, get down!" Sophia hissed in a panicked whisper and quickly leaned way over. They were face to face under the table. Berta felt like her heart was going to pound out of her chest. In that instant, she had imagined that Vinny had found out that she had discovered his cache in the biscuit tin and had somehow tracked her to the restaurant. She envisioned her step-father in classic mobster regalia, complete with trench coat and machine gun, bursting into the restaurant and spraying the booth they sat in with bullets.

"What's the matter?" Berta whispered over the music, her voice trembling with fear.

"Mildred's here!"

"Mildred? Your sister?"

"Yes! She's here with Patty Petrino and Mary Sambona. If she sees us, I'm in big trouble, and I mean big," Sophia whispered urgently. She lifted her head slowly, just enough to see over the back of the booth and quickly ducked back down.

"What are we going to do?" Berta whispered.

"She has her back turned toward us right now. We're going to run toward the back door as fast as we can. Don't look back, it'll just give Mildred and her friends a chance to see your face," Sophia instructed, as she dug into her pocket and took out two dimes and reached up and put them on the table.

"Okay, are you ready?" Sophia asked. Berta nodded. "On the count of three: one, two, three!" Sophia counted, and they shot out of the booth.

They ran through the restaurant and out the door onto Surf Avenue and didn't stop until they reached the trolley stop. They were winded from their sprint.

"Phew! That was close," Berta said, panting.

"You said it," Sophia agreed, trying to catch her breath.

"Here comes the trolley," Berta pointed out. They got back to the apartment just before the sun went down. Berta went into her mother's bedroom with a glass of water and came back out a minute later.

"She's sleeping. I'm going to wash up and get in my pajamas, unless you want to go first," Berta said to Sophia.

"No, that's alright, you go ahead," her friend said as she fiddled with the dial of the radio.

It had been a long eventful day. In some ways it seemed like finding the money was some strange distant dream and that it had never really happened. Berta and Sophia settled down with cups of hot cocoa at the coffee table in the living room. "Do you want to play cards?" Berta asked Sophia.

"What do you want to play?" Sophia asked.

"I don't know; Old Maid?" Berta offered.

"Old Maid it is then," Sophia said. Berta had just stood up to get the deck of cards when a loud, abrupt rapping at the apartment door startled them.

A man's deep throaty voice yelled, "Hey, open up! I want my money! Come on Vinny! I know you're in there!"

CHAPTER THIRTY-THREE

$\mathcal{P}$atrick and Chevonne were stunned to hear that they were actually sitting in the mouth of a tunnel. It seemed like a very small, shallow cave. "What do you mean this is a tunnel?" Patrick asked Ginny.

"It was part of the Underground Railroad. It was dug out before the Civil War. I've never been in it. My daddy told me about it though."

"Where does it lead?" Patrick asked.

"Do you remember seeing a small white church off a ways from the train stop?"

"Yes, I remember."

"The tunnel was dug out by one of the pastors of the church and some other townspeople who wanted to help escaped slaves. It was a safe house. My daddy told me that there was a hatch that blended in with the floorboards behind the pastor's lectern. That's where the tunnel ends, or starts, I suppose, depending on where you comin from or where you goin."

Ginny, Chevonne and Patrick were huddled together shivering. It was so dark that it was hard to see anything at all. The thick tree canopy had obscured the moonlight almost completely. All the cajoling voices were gone, replaced by the howling of wolves and other mysterious nocturnal stirrings.

"That church looked to be about one hundred and fifty yards from the train stop. I suppose it might be a bit further from where we are right now," Patrick estimated.

"That's about right," Ginny replied.

"Do you think the tunnel is still unobstructed?" Patrick asked.

"I don't know. I don't think nobody would be using it nowadays. I suspect there ain't been anybody in that tunnel since the end of the Civil War, be my guess."

"I think you're probably right," Patrick agreed. "Hopefully, there hasn't been a collapse anywhere over the years. I don't think we have a choice though. We could freeze to death tonight if we don't find shelter."

The head clearance in the mouth of the tunnel was only seven or eight inches above Patrick as he sat cross legged in the dirt. Patrick wiggled backwards a few yards and felt along the wall. He felt what seemed to be fist sized round rocks. He put his hands over one and pulled it back and forth to loosen it. It came out easily along with a good bit of dirt. He pulled down another and another. It seemed that the opening of the tunnel had been hidden behind a pile of rocks with soil packed in between them.

"Patrick, what are you doing?" Chevonne asked.

"I'm moving these rocks out of the way so that we can get into the tunnel."

"It seems as if my eyes are shut tight but they're not. They're wide open and I just can't see anything but pure black. This must be what it's like to be completely blind," Chevonne said, sounding on the verge of panic. Ginny and Chevonne could hear Patrick breathing harder as he worked to tear down the small wall of rocks and push them off to the side.

"I think I've cleared out enough for us to get in," Patrick said.

"Patrick, I'm scared. I don't think I can do this," Chevonne said, her voice cracking.

"Maybe we should try to make our way back out of the woods and then head to the church."

Ginny spoke up. "That ravine we climbed down to get here is too steep. I don't think we'd be able to get back up it, especially in the dark. Besides, these woods are full of hungry animals that'd make a meal of us if they got the chance."

"Chevonne, you'll be alright. I won't let anything happen to you. I'll go first. Just stay close to me," Patrick said gently and started into the tunnel. Chevonne crawled in after him and Ginny crawled in after her. The pungent smell of moist earth enveloped them. The tunnel was incredibly narrow. Patrick's shoulders brushed against the walls. His head brushed the ceiling of the tunnel as he crawled on his hands and knees.

They crawled cautiously into the blackness, the sound of gravel falling from the low tunnel roof was unnerving. Nobody spoke for a long time.

"I think we must be about midway now," Ginny declared.

"Good," was all Patrick said in response. The truth was that Patrick was feeling claustrophobic and was consciously trying to push away the thought of being buried alive, gasping for breath as the heavy earth crushed the life out of him. He forced himself to imagine an open field on a sunny day or the vast expanse of the Atlantic Ocean, he often marveled at, as he sat on the docks down on South Street. They continued to crawl in silence for another minute or two before Patrick's head hit something solid and he could go forward no more.

"Stop," was all Patrick could manage to say. He felt as if he might pass out. The feeling of dread was almost completely overwhelming. He inhaled deeply and exhaled slowly. Patrick thought the amount of oxygen available in the tight space was likely insufficient, and contributed to his growing sense of trepidation.

"Patrick?" Chevonne's small questioning voice came from behind him. He fought to maintain a calm even tone.

"There's something solid in front of me. I'm not sure what it is yet," he said putting a hand up and feeling from top to bottom and side to side.

"It just feels like dirt."

"But we've got at least another two-hundred feet to go before we get to the church," Ginny pointed out nervously.

"I know," Patrick said as his mind raced to try to digest what was happening.

Going back wasn't an option. Patrick managed to twist his body around enough to lie on his back and put his feet up on the wall of earth that impeded their passage. He bent his knees back and brought them up to his chest, and with all his might slammed them into the dirt wall. He felt one of his feet break through. He repeated the assault on the crumbling dirt until he could sit up and reach through the hole. Patrick pulled down the excess dirt with his hands to make the opening just big enough to fit through. There was nothing but more darkness on the other side. Patrick felt around like a blind man, trying to understand the dimensions of the rest of the tunnel. It was narrower so he could no longer crawl. Instead, he had to lie on his stomach and use his elbows to propel himself along.

"Come on," he encouraged Chevonne and Ginny. Gradually the tunnel widened; much to everyone's relief. They continued to crawl quietly toward the church. Patrick reached another impasse, but this time when he reached out to feel what was blocking their way, it wasn't dirt.

What was in front of him was solid and hard, maybe wood. He patted the surface, running his hand along the length of what felt like the rung of a ladder.

"I think we're here," he called back over his shoulder. "I think I feel a ladder." Patrick was able to stand up. He began to climb. The creaking of the old wood seemed oddly loud in the confines of the tunnel. Patrick ascended the ladder, not knowing how many rungs there were or what he would find when he got to the top of it. In his head, he counted the rungs as he climbed... *One, two, three.* Then, with an ear splitting "crack", the fourth rung broke.

"Patrick, are you alright?" Chevonne called out.

"I'm fine," Patrick answered. "I'm just going to reach up as far as I can to see if I can feel the trap door. I can't feel anymore rungs. I might be at the top of the ladder, but I'm not sure." He reached as high as he was able. He felt nothing but the cold air above his head. There was no sign of light and it was still pitch black.

"Ginny, I have an idea. Do you think you can get around Chevonne?" Patrick asked.

"I don't know. It'll be awful tight," Ginny replied.

"I think you can squeeze past me," Chevonne said.

"Why?" Ginny asked.

"I think the trap door is above my head but I can't see it or feel it. It must be just out of my reach, or..." Patrick stopped speaking. He was about to say what he was really afraid of; that the hatch that opened into the church no longer existed.

"I think if you can manage to get on my shoulders you might be able to reach the trapdoor." Ginny focused on trying to get past Chevonne. The dirt fell as their bodies pressed and slid against the walls of the tunnel. Chevonne had had her eyes shut since they entered the tunnel. Open or closed, it didn't make a difference in what she saw but she squeezed them shut tightly to keep the dirt out.

Once Ginny managed to get past Chevonne she crawled until she felt Patrick's shoes.

"I'm going to squat down Ginny. Hook your legs over my shoulders."

She was a tall, muscular girl and weighed nearly as much as Patrick. Patrick grunted and strained as he slowly straightened his knees until he was in a standing position.

"Can you feel anything?" Patrick asked.

"Yes! Yes! I can feel the door!" Ginny exclaimed. She pushed, but it felt as if something heavy was on top of it. There was just enough give when she pushed hard for a fine sliver of faint gray light to peek fleetingly through the crack of the trap door.

"Push harder, Ginny," Patrick heartened.

"I don't think I can do it like this. I think I'm going to need to stand on your shoulders if I'm ever gonna push the hatch open."

"Go ahead," Patrick replied, his voice straining with Ginny's weight. The backs of Ginny's calves were resting on Patrick's chest. She braced her left hand up against the wall of the tunnel and brought her right foot up and attempted to place it on Patrick's shoulder but she started to lose balance. She grabbed a hand full of Patrick's thick red hair to steady herself.

"Sorry, I ain't got nothing else to hang on to." Ginny apologized.

Patrick's face contorted with pain but he remained silent. Ginny brought her left foot up and proceeded to stand. Her back hit the door. Ginny raised both hands over her head and placed her palms on the trapdoor and pushed. The door lifted again but this time the opening was a few inches wider. It seemed there was something heavy on top of the door. She pushed again. There was a loud crash and the door opened up easily. Ginny leaned over the opening, placing half her body on the old maple wood floor of the church and lifted a leg and swung it up on the altar and heaved herself out of the tunnel. She could see that the sturdy podium that had stood on top of the hatch had fallen over on its side, rolled down two steps and hit the first pew. A half dozen or so sheets of paper were strewn about, most likely Sunday's sermon.

They had been making their way through the tunnel for about an hour or so. It was dark in the church but the cloud cover had dissipated and a brilliant half-moon shone through the windows and illuminated the church in a translucent blue; it was a sanctuary of tranquility, a sharp contrast to the menacing, inky blackness of the tunnel. Ginny lay on her back staring up at the crucifix where Jesus hung, and gave thanks. "Thank you, Lord Jesus!" Ginny said emphatically, out loud. She took a moment to get her bearings and rolled over, wiggling on her stomach to the edge of the hatch opening. Patrick looked up at Ginny's triumphant face.

"Eureka!" Patrick yelled out wearing a jubilant smile. "I'll hold Chevonne up," Patrick yelled to Ginny.

Chevonne got on Patrick's shoulders. Above them, Ginny leaned in and grabbed Chevonne, pulling her up onto the altar. They both looked down at Patrick.

"Well, what you waitin for? You decide you like it down there or somthin? Come on up," Ginny teased.

Patrick was able to use the partially rotted ladder rungs to reach up high enough to grab the opening of the trap door and pull his body up.

Katherine and Arthur stood in the moonlight gathering the paraphernalia they needed to venture into the woods to find Patrick and Chevonne.

"What was that? Did you hear that?"

"Yes, I did. I think it came from over there," Katherine said, pointing toward the church. Arthur stared off into the distance and was silent for a moment. Then, as if he'd had an epiphany, he spoke.

"The church! Of course. They're not dressed for this cold weather. They'd need shelter and there's nowhere else to go. They're in the church. It's the safest place they could have gone under the circumstances. Come on let's go!"

They raced toward the church.

Patrick, Chevonne and Ginny lay on their backs, relieved beyond words to be out of the tunnel. The church was warm and smelled of oil soap.

"I don't know about you two, but I'm bushed," Patrick announced. "I could fall asleep right here on the altar. Now I lay me down to sleep I pray the Lord my—"

Ginny sat up abruptly. "Did you hear that?" she asked, sounding alarmed.

There were voices that sounded as if they were coming closer.

"Someone's coming. We have to hide," Patrick whispered. They scrambled to their feet. The church was small and afforded very few places where they could hide.

"Quick, get under here," Patrick whispered to Chevonne. Chevonne lay down under the third pew from the altar. Patrick lay down next to her and they held hands while Ginny crouched behind the fallen podium.

Katherine and Arthur got to the large arched doors of the church. Arthur hoped that the church would be unlocked, as was the tradition in England, but this was rural Pennsylvania. Arthur turned the door knob and was relieved that it opened to a long aisle with rows of pews on each side. The altar was modest with an area for candles to be lit. A large life-sized figure of Jesus on the cross hung high on the wall, centered with the long carpeted aisle.

"Patrick! Chevonne!" Katherine yelled.

Patrick brought his index finger up to his lips, cueing Chevonne to remain quiet. He watched, brokenhearted, as Chevonne's blue eyes began to fill with tears. They lay still, listening to the Wallaces call their names for a minute, until Chevonne could no longer bear it. Chevonne pulled her hand away from Patrick's and came out from under the pew.

"We're here! We're here!" she yelled.

The party dress that Katherine had bought her was torn and covered with dirt. Chevonne saw Arthur standing at the end of the aisle and ran toward him. Her face was dirty and tear-streaked, her blond hair filthy and in tangles. Chevonne wrapped her arms around Arthur's waist and clung to him and sobbed.

"There, there," Arthur said, feeling a bit stunned as he patted Chevonne's back. After a moment he pulled Chevonne away from him and held her at arm's length. "Are you alright Chevonne? Are you hurt?" Chevonne shook her head "no" but continued to cry. Arthur put his arms around her and continued to pat her back gently. "It's alright now. You're going to be just fine."

Katherine had arrived at the podium that was lying on its side on the floor and saw the colored girl crouched down behind it. Ginny looked up at Katherine but said nothing. Patrick stood up from the pew and Katherine turned to look at him when she heard his movement. "Patrick! Oh my God! Patrick!" Katherine ran toward him and embraced him. Patrick did not respond. She put her hands on Patrick's shoulders and looked into his eyes.

"Why did you run away? I was sick with worry, Patrick!"

Patrick looked down and said, "It was just time for us to go."

Then he looked up and directed his words to Arthur. "Chevonne and I don't need your charity. I don't know why you came after us. We're not going back to New York with you and your wife. We'll manage on our own."

CHAPTER THIRTY-FOUR

*E*ddy was eager to get out of the hospital but his conversation with the doctor, about when he would be able to leave, was interrupted by the nurses yelling for Dr. Rovenstine. "Excuse me," the doctor said abruptly, and dashed off. Eddy sat up and watched him run into the room down the hall. He could hear the doctor barking orders.

"Get me a tongue depressor!"

Vinny was having a grand mal seizure. His body was rigid and only the whites of his eyes were visible as they were rolled back and up to the left. His right side twitched rapidly and he was foaming at the mouth and gnashing his teeth. Vinny was choking. His tongue had fallen back in his mouth and it was obstructing his airway.

Dr. Rovenstine placed a firm hand on Vinny's forehead and chin and pried his jaw open. The young nurse arrived at the bedside with a thin, wide, flat, wooden stick. Dr. Rovenstine fought to keep Vinny's mouth open.

"Insert the depressor and move his tongue." The nurse stood frozen. "Do it!" the doctor screamed. The nurse jumped, but quickly looked down into Vinny's mouth and inserted the depressor to flatten out his tongue. Dr. Rovenstine let go of Vinny's jaw. His mouth snapped shut. The tongue depressor was left horizontally in Vinny's mouth, keeping his tongue in place. There was nothing more for the nurse or the doctor to do but stand by and ensure that Vinny didn't injure himself. Finally, after two or three minutes the seizure subsided.

"He'll need fifty milligrams of phenobarbital a day and turn him on his side in case he vomits," the doctor instructed and left the room.

Nurse Sally Lindburk stood at Vinny's bed side and examined his placid face.

"Do you need help with him?" a voice came from behind her.

"Oh, yes, I suppose I will," Sally said to Martha, a middle-aged woman who volunteered in the hospital on a regular basis.

"Isn't it sad?" she said to Martha, sounding melancholy as she looked down at Vinny. "He's been in a coma for days now. His family must be frantic."

Martha folded her arms and assessed Vinny with her eyes while she chewed her last piece of Wrigley's Doublemint gum. "The hospital administrator called all the police stations from here to Montauk. Nobody has reported a man by his description missing. You know what I think?" Martha asked rhetorically, "Maybe nobody misses him."

Sally and Martha got Vinny cleaned up and pushed a pillow under his back to keep him propped on his side. An orderly ducked his head into the room.

"Dr. Rovenstine wants Mr. Smith moved closer to the nurse's station for observation. He's going to go in the second bed in the ward. I'll go get the gurney."

"He'll be in the same room as the man who was driving the car. I'm not sure that's such a good idea. I think it'll be hard on Mr. Johnson. He must feel awful," Sally said.

"I don't think there are any other beds as close to the nurse's station, and if you ask me, something's fishy with that story. Think about it. Their names are Smith and Johnson. Sounds like alias' to me. And did you get a load of the duds they had on? I could probably pay half a year's rent for what one of those suits cost. Yup, something's fishy in Denmark, for sure. I think Mr. Johnson knows a lot more than he's letting on," Martha said sagely.

Eddy watched as Vinny was wheeled into the ward and placed in the bed next to him. "How's he doin'?" he asked the young nurse.

"I wish I could tell you that he was doing better, but that's not true. He's been unconscious since the accident and he's just had a seizure. Dr. Rovenstine thought Mr. Smith should be closer to the nurse's station, in case he has another fit. Unfortunately, there aren't any other beds available on the unit," Nurse Lindburk said apologetically.

Eddy stared at Vinny and said nothing. Nurse Lindburk busied herself with tucking in and smoothing Vinny's bed sheets and continued chatting. "I hope his family finds him soon. A detective from the local police department came in yesterday to see if he recognized Mr. Smith but he said it was no use trying to identify someone whose head looked like an oversized eggplant in a gauze turban. I suppose he's right. There's still a lot of bruising," Nurse Lindburk continued. She seemed to be talking aloud to herself. Eddy was relieved to hear that the police detective had come and gone without stopping in to see him.

Nurse Lindburk nattered on. "My boyfriend is a reporter. I told him about poor Mr. Smith. He said he was going to talk to his editor about doing a human interest story on him. Maybe when the swelling goes down they can put a picture of him in the newspaper. Can you imagine how happy and relieved his family will be?" Eddy's arm was beginning to throb. His head ached and he felt as if he'd explode if he had to listen to one more minute of Sally Lindburk's blathering.

"Hey, do me a favor, will ya? Knock off all the jaw-jackin and go get me some of that pain killer?"

Sally looked taken aback. "Oh, I'm sorry. I tend to talk too much sometimes."

"Ya don't say," Eddy said sarcastically.

"I'll go get you your medication," Nurse Lindburk assured Eddy and scurried off.

Eddy loved the effects of the pain med. "How often can I get these shots?" Eddy asked the nurse.   "Every few hours, but if you're still in pain I can let the doctor know so that he can increase your dosage."

"Yeah, yeah, that would be good. I'm hurtin real bad," Eddy said with a pained look on his face. Actually, Eddy wasn't feeling any pain, he was high. The pain had subsided completely after the first shot but Eddy thought if a little pain medication was good, more would be better. He was right. Eddy was euphoric. The sensation was like nothing he'd ever experienced. It was simply amazing.

Almost a week had passed. Eddy's days revolved around his pain medication and manipulating the nurses and doctors into giving him more and more. Vinny remained in the next bed with nurses coming in every two or three hours to turn and change him. The purple and blue bruises that covered his face had progressed to a yellow-green color and the swelling had subsided enough for him to be nearly recognizable. Eddy was lying on his right side with his left arm still up in the air in traction. He was facing Vinny, enjoying the warm, blissful ecstasy of his last injection when he noticed Vinny's eyelids flutter. At first he thought that he must be imagining it, then he looked closer. Vinny's eyelids fluttered and opened.

"Jesus Christ…Vinny, hey, Vinny," Eddy said drowsily and passed out, the effects of too much morphine.

Vinny started screaming, prompting the nurse tending to a patient on the other side of the ward to race to his bed side. "Mr. Smith! Calm down." He gazed at the nurse through his slightly swollen eyes and moaned. He brought his hands up to the thick bandages wrapped around his head and started to pull it off.

"No, no, don't do that," the nurse said reaching up to pull Vinny's hands down. Vinny attempted to reach up again. The nurse strained to hold his arms down.

"I need help in the ward!" she yelled.

Dr. Rovenstine and an orderly rushed into the room. "What's going on?" Dr. Rovenstine asked.

"He woke up screaming and he's trying to pull his bandages off."

Dr. Rovenstine looked to the orderly, "Get a straitjacket."

He nudged the nurse aside and took Vinny's arms and held them down. "Mr. Smith, please be still. You've had a head injury and it's important that you not remove your bandages."

Vinny looked at the doctor and stopped struggling. Dr. Rovenstine spoke soothingly. "Alright, alright... I'm going to let go of your arms Mr. Smith." Dr. Rovenstine slowly let go of Vinny's arms and watched Vinny's response. He made no attempt to move. "Good, very good, now tell me; are you having any pain?"

Vinny looked confused. His eyes were glazed over, his mouth hanging open. He appeared obtunded and shook his head slowly back and forth to indicate that he was not in pain. His lips were dry and chapped from lack of hydration. "Sit him up properly and start fluids. Go slowly, I don't want him aspirating," Dr. Rovenstine instructed the nurse. He began to check Vinny's pupils and reflexes. The orderly came back with the straitjacket. "That won't be necessary now. Leave it on his nightstand though; it may come in handy later. These kinds of patients are known to be emotionally labile."

Eddy had woken during the commotion. The immediate effects of the pain medication were fading and Eddy was a bit more alert. "Well, Mr. Johnson, it looks like your friend here is coming around. Of course, he's not out of the woods; not by a long a shot. It's likely that he'll have residual deficits in terms of his mental status. We won't know the extent until we do further tests," Dr. Rovenstine explained.

"What the hell does that mean? For Christ sake, speak English, will ya?" Eddy said, annoyed with the doctor's use of medical jargon.

"I'm sorry. What I mean is that he may not have the same mental capacity he did before the accident. He may have difficulty understanding things or remembering things."

Eddy thought about how that possibility affected him and how he might exploit the situation to his benefit.

A nurse arrived at Vinny's bed side with a glass of water. "Mr. Smith, you need to drink something," the nurse said as she patted his face firmly to get him to open his eyes and drink. "Here, suck on the straw." she cued him while putting the straw up against his lips. Vinny began drinking. Eddy watched closely.

"Excellent, Mr. Smith," the nurse said enthusiastically. "You'll be graduating to solid food before you know it."

"I need pain medication," Eddy called over to Vinny's nurse.

"Mr. Johnson, you're not due for pain medication. Dr. Rovenstine said you need to be weaned off of the diacetylmorphine injections. You can't have another shot for at least two more hours," the nurse informed Eddy.

"I can't wait that long. I'm dyin' here! Come on, have a heart," Eddy pleaded with the nurse.

"I'm sorry Mr. Johnson: doctor's orders," she replied firmly. Eddy thought about the knife under his mattress and considered his options.

The nurse left the ward. Vinny sat in his bed looking stuporous.

"Hey, Vinny, over here, it's Eddy." Vinny turned his head and looked at him.

"Well, aren't ya gonna say something? You can talk, can't ya?" Eddy asked.

Vinny nodded.

"Well, say something then."

"Where am I?" came Vinny's weak, hoarse voice.

"Bellevue, we been here for days now. Don't you remember the accident?"

"No."

"Well, you'd have been toast, except I dragged your fat ass outta the car and got you to the hospital. My arms busted up pretty good but other than that I'm alright. Listen Vinny, I told them our names were Smith and Johnson. The last thing we need is for word to get out that we're stuck in this hospital. I can think of more than a few mooks who might like to take advantage of the situation and bump us off. We're sitting ducks in here."

Vinny stared at Eddy, fighting to keep his eyes open. After a minute or two, Vinny succumbed to sleep and his head dropped back on the pillow. Eddy gave up on trying to apprise Vinny of their situation and turned his attention to procuring his next fix. Kenneth walked into the ward with an arm full of freshly laundered towels. "Kenneth, hey, buddy, I gotta ask ya a question." Kenneth said nothing and waited for Eddy to continue.

"Listen, I'm in a lot of pain, see. The doctor thinks I ought to be weaned off of my pain medication. See, they won't give me my medication and I really need it. Can you get some of that stuff for me? It's called diacetylmorphine. It's an injection. I got plenty of loot. I'll take care of ya."

Kenneth thought for a moment and then looked around to make sure nobody was in earshot of his reply. "There's probably some in the medication room behind the nurse's station but that old crank of a ward clerk and a few nurses are always sitting around there doing their charting. The really big stashes are in the dispensary downstairs. There's a druggist on duty though around the clock. They fill the orders and then there's a fella that brings the medication up to the floor but he has to account for every order. I don't see how I could get away with something like that," he explained. Eddy stared off into the distance seeing nothing but the machinations going on in his head as he tried to think of ways to get more of his beloved pain medication. Kenneth went on delivering towels, placing a fluffy white one at the foot of the next bed.

"Come on Mr. Smith, wake up now. You need to eat something." The nurse's high pitched voice snapped Eddy back to the present. Vinny wore his usual dull expression. Without looking at the nurse Vinny opened his mouth for her to shovel in another heaping spoonful of applesauce. "Very good Mr. Smith," she said cheerfully.

Vinny turned his head and looked at the nurse, obviously perplexed. "Why are you calling me that?" he asked drowsily.

"What do you mean?" asked the nurse.

"I'm not..."

Vinny was about to reveal his identity. Eddy couldn't allow that to happen so he began screaming to create a distraction.

"My stomach, my stomach! Nurse! Help me!"

The nurse immediately put the applesauce down and came to Eddy's bed side.

"What is it?" she asked anxiously.

"Get the doctor! Quick!" Eddy yelled.

"But Mr. Johnson...."

Eddy let out a guttural howl. The reaction was instant. The nurse ran out of the ward. The second she was out of sight, Eddy turned toward Vinny and hissed, "Vinny, what the hell is wrong with you? I told you, your last name's Smith. Got it? Smith! Now say it!"

Vinny looked confused. "Smith," he said slowly. Eddy wasn't sure that Vinny actually understood the concept or the purpose of their alias names but he hoped that the impromptu tutorial would buy him some time. Eddy's head felt like it was spinning. Vinny couldn't be trusted to keep his trap shut, and unfortunately, he was the one person who'd been an eye witness to nearly all of Eddy's gory deeds over the past few years. The cops would have a field day if they got their hands on Vinny. He knew he could end up spending the rest of his life in Sing Sing if Vinny spilled the beans. Vinny was a drooling moron, but he was a drooling moron who might still be able to tell them where the bodies were buried; literally. Even if Vinny did manage to remember his alias there was the possibility that the nurse's reporter boyfriend would be in to do his public interest piece and plaster a picture of Vinny's mug in the newspaper. Eddy knew he couldn't allow that.

Trying to keep from being knocked off or clipped by the Feds was enough of an incentive to get the hell out of Bellevue. But that wasn't Eddy's first concern. Getting his hands on the drugs that made him feel like he'd never felt before; blissful, as if nothing mattered was Eddy's first priority.

Eddy thought and thought. After a while an expansive Cheshire cat smile spread across his face.

"Yes, yes," Eddy said aloud, obviously pleased. He knew what he needed to do.

Eddy had a plan.

CHAPTER THIRTY-FIVE

erta and Sophia looked at one another, their eyes as big as saucers. The man at the door rapped harder. "Come on! I know you're in there. I can see the light underneath the door. Open up! I'm not leaving without my money!" the deep, angry voice bellowed.

The girls stood in the living room in their pajamas with their arms wrapped around each other, utterly terrified, staring at the door. Berta hadn't locked it behind them. They held their breath as they watched the doorknob turn.

A short, dumpy, bald man dressed modestly in workmen's clothes leaned into the apartment. He looked to be in his early sixties.

"What's the big idea?" he said with scowl. "Don't you know how to answer a door?"

They said nothing. He stepped into the living room and looked around.

"Where's Vinny?" he said gruffly.

"He's not home." Berta said timidly.

"Well, that's going to be a problem," the man said as he reached into his jacket pocket.

"Stop! We'll show you were the money is," Sophia said frantically. The man looked puzzled. "It's in there." Berta pointed to the kitchen. The man furrowed his brow and took the pen he'd just retrieved from inside his jacket pocket and tucked it behind his ear. He followed Berta and Sophia into the kitchen.

"This better not be some kind of a joke," he barked.

"It's up there," Berta said, pointing to the top shelf in the cupboard. Sophia pushed the chair over to the counter and stepped back.

The man looked at them suspiciously. "What's going on here?" he said with blatant annoyance.

"I swear, mister, we didn't take a penny of it," Sophia said, sounding frightened.

"It's in the tin," Berta added.

The man stood up on the chair and reached back on the shelf. "There's nothing up here," he said irritably.

"Its way, way back," Berta explained. The man stood on his tip toes and reached in as far as he could. He grunted, his face reddening with the exertion. Finally he pulled out the tin and stepped down from the chair and set it on the counter. He looked perplexed.

"It's in here?" the man asked. Berta and Sophia nodded simultaneously. The man pulled the lid off the tin and stared silently at the money, obviously stunned at the sight of all the cash.

"The rent's twenty dollars, plus a dollar a day for each day it's late. That makes twenty-six dollars," he announced.

At that moment, Berta and Sophia realized that the man wasn't a gangster. He was the landlord.

"I don't know what this is all about and frankly I don't want to know. I'm taking the rent money. Might as well take next month's rent too while I'm here. Forget about the late fee." The man peeled two twenty dollar bills off of a roll and shoved it in his pocket and left. Berta and Sophia looked at each other and started laughing uncontrollably. Partly because they were so relieved and partly because the landlord must have thought they were crazy.

"I thought we were goners for sure!" Sophia laughed, doubling over. Sophia and Berta went back out to the living room to finish their game of old maid.

"I never thought I'd say this but I hope Vinny comes home soon," Berta said, as they sat on the floor at the coffee table. "I'm not sure what I'm going to do. The egg man and the milk man left notes reminding Vinny that he hadn't paid them yet either. We're running low on groceries too," Berta said sounding worried.

"What's going to happen when Vinny finds out that some of the money is gone?" Sophia asked.

"I don't know. He's never been gone for this long before. I wonder if something happened to him... Maybe he got shot in one of those shoot outs, like the one they wrote about in the paper last year," Berta speculated.

"Probably not, it would have been in the papers again and I think big mouth Mildred would have mentioned it by now. She reads the paper every day," Sophia reassured Berta.

They continued playing Old Maid. "What if Vinny never comes back?' Sophia asked after another long silence.

"I hate Vinny. He's mean and I wouldn't miss him a bit," Berta responded.

"I know that, but your mother, well... She can't, you know... She's sick and you're only thirteen."

"I know. If something happens to my mother I don't really know where I'd go. I got a letter from my friend Chevonne. Remember, I told you about her. Chevonne and her brother Patrick took an orphan train. She said it was awful. She said they had to run away because some of the people who wanted children only wanted to use them to work on their farms for free or to...well, to make them do things that they didn't want to do." Berta stopped talking and put her head down and looked embarrassed.

Sophia and Berta sat quietly for a moment and then resumed playing cards. "Do you really think he's dead?" Sophia said, finally breaking the silence again.

"I don't know, but if anyone finds out my mother is crazy and my step-father is dead I could get sent away somewhere."

Sophia looked up and stared over Berta's shoulder. Berta turned to see what Sophia was looking at. It was Rosa. "Oh, Mama, this is my friend Sophia from school. You remember, I told you all about her," Berta said softly.

Sophia forced a nervous smile. "Hello Mrs. DeLuca," Sophia said, forgetting that Berta and her mother did not have the same last name.

Rosa looked at Sophia as if she were a curiosity. "Do you know Gaston?" Not knowing who Gaston was and why Berta's mother would ask, Sophia said nothing and looked at Berta questioningly.

"No, Mama, Sophia doesn't know Daddy. Daddy isn't... Mama, let me help you get ready for bed, alright?" Berta suggested. She didn't dare remind her mother that her late husband had died in a mining accident years ago. Berta worried that it would only serve to re-traumatize her and it could take hours to calm her down. She knew this from experience.

Rosa's ability to recall past events was nearly as bad as her capacity to retain new information. Berta had to do the shopping with Rosa now. Vinny usually picked things up from the store too because he often cooked. Rosa simply wasn't capable of the task any longer. Even when Vinny wrote down a list of things for Rosa to get from the store she'd get as far as the front stoop and sit, forgetting all about buying groceries.

"It's getting late Mama. Let me help you get ready for bed," Berta said. Sophia watched as Berta took her mother by the hand and went into the bathroom with her. Sophia could hear the water running. It muffled the words she was able to hear.

Berta opened the door about ten minutes later. Her mother's hair, thinning in spots, was combed and pulled back neatly. She wore a light blue nightgown and matching slippers. Sophia thought Berta's mother looked almost normal except for her blank expression and patchy hair.

"Alright, Mama, time for bed," Berta said cheerfully. She pulled down the covers and Rosa crawled into bed. She covered her mother up and kissed her on the forehead. "Goodnight, Mama. Sleep tight." Berta turned the light off and closed the door.

It seemed to Sophia that this had likely been a routine for a long time. Berta came back into the living room.

"Why did your mother ask me if I knew Gaston? Who's Gaston?"

"He's my father. Sometimes my mother forgets that he's dead. I think she still misses him a lot."

"That's so sad," Sophia said, her eyes starting to fill with tears.

"I know. It is sad, but there's nothing I can do about it. She's getting worse. Vinny doesn't notice it because he's hardly ever home and when he is, he doesn't even try to talk to her. She won't go to the doctor and he won't make her go," Berta explained, sounding frustrated.

"Maybe I should tell my mother or maybe you could tell one of the teachers at school," Sophia suggested.

"Maybe you're right," Berta conceded. "But let's wait until Vinny comes home. I don't know about you, but I'm bushed. I think it's time for bed."

"I'm tired too," Sophia agreed.

"There's not enough room in the bed for the two of us. You can have the bed Sophia. I'll take the cushions from the couch and sleep on the floor," Berta said.

"Why don't we both sleep on the floor in the living room? We can listen to the A&P Gypsies on the radio. We'll turn the volume down low so we don't bother your mother," Sophia said.

"That sounds like a great idea!" Berta said.

Sophia and Berta arranged the couch cushions, pillows and blankets to make a tent in the middle of the room. They stayed up late, giggling about boys in their class and finally fell asleep listening to the soothing music of Harry Horlick and his orchestra on the radio. Sophia and Berta were sound asleep when Rosa woke at the crack of dawn. She had been dreaming of Gaston, but it was impossible for her to know the difference between what was real and what wasn't now. All she knew was that she had to go to him. She knew he was waiting for her. She could see him in the distance, walking down that indiscriminate street. She would catch up to him this time.

Rosa got out of bed and sleepily slipped her skirt on over her nightgown. The nightgown was bunched around the waist of her skirt but she didn't notice. She walked over to the corner of the room and picked up the maroon sweater that was laying on the chair in the corner and put it on. She buttoned three of the eight buttons, failing to match them up with their corresponding buttonholes. Rosa put her slippers on and left the apartment, leaving the door open behind her.

The streets were quiet and empty at first. They became busier as the work day got underway. Rosa walked for blocks and blocks. She didn't notice the stares from the people passing by. She seemed not to notice the cars, trains, push carts and other spectacles of the avenues she walked. Rosa's wide-based gait was slow but she plodded on determinedly, motivated by the image of her late husband. Somehow, Rosa's subconscious mind prompted her toward the familiar and she ended up on Hester Street.

Rosa's feet were sore and so she sat on the steps of one of the brownstones. Gitta was running errands while the children were in Hebrew school. She was coming back from the market when she noticed a frail, disheveled woman sitting on the steps of a brownstone half a block from hers. "Rosa! Oy Vey! What are you doing here?" Gitta exclaimed, in shocked surprise with her heavy Yiddish accent.
Rosa stared off into space.
"Rosa, answer me, please!" Gitta pleaded.
Rosa simply looked at Gitta with eyes that seemed not to even see her. Rosa had changed so much since she'd seen her last, Gitta almost didn't recognize her.
"Rosa, how did you get here?"
Rosa didn't respond. Gitta took Rosa by the arm with one hand and carried the basket full of groceries with the other. To Gitta's relief, Rosa didn't resist. Once inside the brownstone, Rosa stopped on the stairs leading up to the apartment and sat down.
"Come on Rosa, we're almost there." Rosa slowly folded her arms and leaned forward and buried her head in her lap. "Rosa, please…"

Gitta heard the entryway door open. It was Yekl. He came home for lunch on most days. "What is this? What's going on?" Yekl asked. It took him a few minutes to realize that the emaciated woman sitting on the stairs leading to their second floor apartment was Rosa. Yekl turned to Gitta with a look of surprise on his face.

"I found her sitting on someone's steps half way down the block. She looks exhausted. I can't get her to walk any further." Gitta explained.

"You go ahead Gitta," Yekl said. Gitta picked up the basket of groceries and walked around Rosa and proceeded up to the small landing where the stairway took a sharp turn. She looked back to see Yekl lift Rosa's small frame. She went to the apartment door and opened it for Yekl so he could carry Rosa into the living room. Yekl laid her withered body on the couch. She was asleep in a matter of minutes.

"She is obviously very sick," Yekl said, as he stood looking down at her.

"She hasn't been herself for a very long time, Yekl. Look at her hair. It's falling out in patches around her head. She can't weigh more that ninety pounds. She seems completely demented now. What could be wrong with her? I cannot believe that her husband would allow her to deteriorate to this point. She looks like she should be in a hospital."

"She needs a doctor," Yekl said, decisively.

"Do you think your cousin Hyram will know what's wrong with her?" Gitta asked. "He was one of the best doctor's in all of Debrecen. I should think if anyone would know it would be him. I saw him this morning on Essex Street. He was going to see a patient."

Hyram Lachman and his wife lived upstairs from Gitta and Yekl and their children. They had immigrated to New York City from Hungary over a year ago. Although he had been a very prominent, well respected doctor for many years, the political climate after the Kishinev pogrom had finally forced Dr. Lachman and his wife to flee in 1922. He made his living making house calls in the Jewish community. He hadn't yet mastered the English language well enough to seek employment in one of the hospitals. It was a little after four o'clock in the afternoon when he got home. He was met in the hallway by his cousin Yekl, who seemed distressed.

"I'm sorry to bother you, Hyram, after your long day of seeing patients."

"What is it, Yekl?"

"A friend of ours is here. She's very sick. Could you look at her?"

"Of course, where is she?"

Yekl brought Hyram into the living room where Rosa had been sleeping for hours. Yekl pointed to the couch where Rosa's diminutive body was covered with a blanket. Gitta came into the living room.

"Oh Hyram, I'm so glad you are here," Gitta whispered, so as not to wake Rosa.

"Why don't we go into the kitchen where we can talk?" Hyram suggested. "Tell me about your friend." Hyram said once they were seated at the table.

"It's the saddest thing I've ever seen," Gitta began. She told Hyram all she knew about Rosa's gradual decline over the past few years. Hyram listened intently without interrupting. When Gitta had shared everything she knew, Hyram sat back in the chair and said, "It will take me about one minute of examination for me to tell you if your friend is suffering from what I suspect she is."

Hyram walked into the living room followed by Gitta and Yekl.

"Gitta, perhaps you should wake her? I know she is confused but it may startle her too much to be woken by a strange man." Hyram suggested.

"Yes, of course. Rosa, it's time to get up now," Gitta said softly as she patted Rosa's back gently.

Rosa woke, her eyes forlorn with an expression of bewilderment. She looked from one face to the other.

"Rosa, this is Yekl's cousin. His name is Hyram, he's a doctor. He is going to help you." Rosa looked over at Hyram and said nothing.

"Yekl, please close those blinds and bring one of the chairs over to the window," Hyram instructed. Yekl went over to the west facing window and adjusted the venetian blinds.

"I will need her to sit over here in the chair," Hyram indicated to Gitta. She took Rosa's arm and helped her off the couch and walked her to the chair next to the window. Hyram bent down so that he was face to face with Rosa.

"Rosa, look at me," Hyram said, as he lightly put his hand on Rosa's jaw and tilted her face up towards his. He put his index finger up in front of Rosa's nose and then pulled it back three or four inches.

"Rosa, look at my finger," Hyram instructed. At first, Rosa looked away, but Hyram was insistent. "Rosa, look at my finger," he commanded again in a more authoritarian tone. Rosa complied. Hyram focused on Rosa's eyes while he moved his finger to and from the middle of her face.

He finished the exam and stood up straight with a sigh. He wore an expression of concerned dismay. Again he took Rosa's face in his hand and turned it slightly toward the window.

"Yekl, open the blinds." Hyram looked closely at Rosa's eyes and then addressed Yekl and Gitta.

"I know exactly what is wrong with your friend."

CHAPTER THIRTY-SIX

 atrick's bitter words hung in the air and echoed from the rafters
of the small church. He held his gaze on Arthur after
announcing that he and Chevonne would not be returning to New York
City with the Wallaces. Patrick's jaw was set, his unblinking glare
steadfast.

Arthur knew that look. He'd seen it on the faces of men who were used
to being in charge, men who would not be persuaded or enticed to
comply. Patrick wasn't used to having adults interfere in his life. He'd been
on his own far too long. Arthur knew better than to argue. He could see
that Patrick O'Farrell would not stand for being coddled and his pride had
been wounded. Things hadn't gone as he'd anticipated.
"We didn't come here to kidnap you and your sister. You have the
perfect right to carry on as you'd planned, if that's what you choose,"
Arthur said firmly. Katherine started to speak, but Arthur put his hand up
to indicate that he had more to say. Arthur stood with one arm around
Chevonne. Her arms were still wrapped around his waist as if she feared
someone might try to pull her away from him. She was clearly shaken.
Her flimsy party dress was covered with dirt and torn. Patrick too was
filthy, covered with the damp soil of the tunnel.

"It's late. Tomorrow you can decide how you would like to proceed. I
think it would be wise of you to get a good night's rest and start fresh in
the morning. Of course, it's entirely up to you. We've arranged lodging in
a farm house about a mile from here. The owner is waiting for us at the
train stop. You're all welcome to come along. There should be enough
room in the carriage." Arthur said calmly. Patrick looked at Ginny and
then at Chevonne. He couldn't refuse and put them in the position of
having to forego a warm bed after what they'd been through. Patrick
nodded, indicating that he was in agreement. He then walked over to the

podium that lay on the floor and stood it upright. Katherine walked over to Chevonne and took her in her arms and held her tightly. Arthur stepped up onto the altar and looked down into the tunnel. He looked up at Patrick.

"What's this?" Arthur asked.

"That's a tunnel. It was once a part of the Underground Railroad. It starts out in the woods. Ginny's father told her about it. She was living with one of the farmers in town. She ran with us when Chevonne and I took off into the woods."

Arthur looked to Ginny. "Where's your family, Ginny?" Arthur asked.

"My mother, father and sister all died in the influenza. A farmer, Earl Clemmens, took me in. I was just ten and seeing I ain't got no family except a cousin or two somewhere in Georgia, I went and lived with him."

"Why did you run?" Arthur inquired.

"He beat me sometimes... and sometimes..." Ginny hesitated. "He's a bad man, Mr. Wallace, and I ain't goin back." Ginny put her head down and looked at the floor.

Arthur spoke reassuringly. "Well then, it's settled. You'll come with us. We'll get things sorted out in the morning."

They all left the church and walked toward the train station where Hodges, the elderly owner of the nearby farm house, waited in a horse drawn carriage. "I was beginning to think you'd been eaten by the black bears," Hodges said to Arthur as he sat with a thick red tartan wool blanket wrapped around him. Chevonne and Katherine sat up front. Patrick, Arthur and Ginny sat in back. They rode in silence. It was then that Patrick realized that he'd left his shoe shine kit on the train. It was a sinking feeling. He brought his shoe shine kit everywhere; it was almost like an appendage. Patrick felt as if he'd lost a loyal friend and thought if he were a few years younger he would have cried.

"Well, here we are," Hodges announced as they pulled up in front of the large farm house. A fire blazed in the enormous field stone fireplace. The house was gloriously warm. A heady aroma of home cooking emanated from a big cast iron pot full of beef stew that sat atop the stove. Bread was baking in the oven. Katherine was glad that she'd brought along an abundance of clothing and other necessities. She helped Ginny and Chevonne get cleaned up and gave Patrick some toiletries and clean clothes. Ginny, Chevonne and Patrick arrived at the table looking immaculate, dressed in newly bought outfits. Ginny fit perfectly into one of Katherine's one piece dresses and a pair of t-strapped shoes. It was hard to believe that just hours ago they were crawling through a tunnel not knowing if they would ever emerge above ground again.

The meal was delicious. They were all ravenous, not having eaten since breakfast. "It's almost mid-night. I can't keep my eyes open anymore," Katherine said covering a yawn. Ginny, Chevonne and Katherine went off to bed. Arthur and Patrick were left sitting at the table nursing hot cups of tea. Patrick got up and walked over to the small oval parlor table next to the fireplace and sat in one of the chairs. Arthur studied Patrick's face. He looked mesmerized by the fire and appeared exhausted. Arthur hoped that the hot bath and a full stomach had taken the edge off Patrick's anger. He walked over to the table and sat across from Patrick. Arthur waited a while before he spoke.

"Patrick, I think we need to talk," he started.

"Why? Did your silverware count come up short?" Patrick said. It was a sardonic jab that wasn't lost on Arthur.

Arthur hung his head briefly and thought back to the night he jokingly told his butler, Bertram to keep track of the silverware while the O'Farrell children were staying. Obviously Patrick overheard him. "I'm sorry. That wasn't fair. I apologize." Arthur said earnestly.

Arthur was a man of integrity and wasn't accustomed to feeling ashamed, but he was. Patrick didn't look away from the fire or respond. Arthur waited a moment and began anyway.

"Patrick, you're a bright, judicious young man, so I won't patronize you and tell you that I suddenly have a terrific urge to be a father and that I want you and your sister to come live with Katherine and me. Nothing could be farther from the truth. I rather enjoy my life just the way it is. I'm only here because my wife loves you and your sister like her own children, and I can't bear to see her heart broken. I'm willing to make that sacrifice for her. When you love someone you'll sacrifice for them. Do you love your sister Patrick?"

Patrick turned away from the fire and looked at Arthur.

"She's all I have. Chevonne is everything to me."

"That's what I thought."

Patrick turned his head and looked again into the fire. "I'm sorry sir. What's your point?" Patrick asked flatly.

"I have no doubt that you'll do very well in life Patrick. You're strong, industrious and brave. No, I have no doubt at all. You'll be just fine, but what about Chevonne? You know full well she won't stay with us if you don't. Can you offer her the finest education money can buy? Can you provide a safe place for her to live and put decent clothes on her back?

Can you guarantee that she won't be exploited by deviants, like that filthy farmer Ginny was subjected to, while you're busy making your way in the world? I don't think you can, but I think you would give your life for your sister and I don't think you could live with yourself, knowing that your pride got in the way of what was best for her."

Patrick continued to stare into the fire and said nothing. Arthur too, was silent. He wanted to give Patrick time to digest his words. They sat quietly for at least ten minutes until Arthur spoke again. "Let's make the best of it, shall we? I'll stay out of your way. Of course, you'll have to tolerate a fair degree of mothering from my wife, but I'm content to have a simple understanding between the two of us, for Chevonne and Katherine's sake. What do you say?"

There was a long silence. "Alright," Patrick said quietly, sounding defeated. He stood up and walked toward the bedroom without saying another word.

The trip back to the city was uneventful. Katherine and Arthur discussed Ginny's options with her during the train ride. Ginny wanted to be with family but the only family she had were distant cousins she knew very little about. Arthur told her that he would do his best to locate them.

"What are your cousins surnames Ginny?" Arthur asked.

"They're Creole. Their last name is Galafate, Honore and Esmene Galafate. Honore and my daddy grew up together. Daddy said they was like brothers. Esmene is his wife."

Arthur laughed, "Somehow I don't think there are a lot of people with those names. I think we'll be able to find them rather easily."

The chauffeur was sent to Grand Central Terminal to pick them up. They drove up to the curb where the doormen stood under the long burgundy awning, waiting to open the car doors and assist with the baggage. Even though Patrick had seen the Wallace's opulent home before, the lack of novelty didn't diminish its magnificence. Patrick watched Ginny's expression. Clearly, she'd never been witness to the kind of affluence the Wallace's enjoyed. "Not too shabby, is it?" Patrick said as he gently elbowed Ginny.

"I aint never seen nothin like it," Ginny said, looking around in amazement.

"Somehow I'm going to have to figure out how to get used to this," Patrick said drolly.

Ginny grinned, "You poor thing; how in the world are you goin to manage?" Ginny laughed.

"Collette, could you help Chevonne unpack? Oh, and Ginny will need clothes. She's my size, so have whatever she might need sent from Bergdorf's. We expect she'll be traveling south, so she'll need clothes appropriate for the warmer climate," Katherine instructed the maid.

Bertram busied himself with unpacking Arthur and Patrick's bags. Arthur went to his office to make some phone calls in the hopes of finding Ginny's cousins.

It took only a few calls to learn that Ginny's cousins ran a small five and dime store in Thunderbolt, Georgia, a shrimping town about five miles outside of Savannah. They had no idea that Ginny's parents and younger sister had died of influenza. The families had lost touch as people do. The last time they saw Ginny she was just a baby. They were understandably saddened and upset to learn that Ginny had been living with a virtual stranger for over three years and nobody had thought to contact them. They were happy to have Ginny, and Arthur was glad to report the good news.

"Well, your cousins are looking forward to meeting you." Arthur informed Ginny.

Ginny looked surprised. She was nearly speechless. "You mean... you mean... You found them?"

Arthur laughed. "Yes, as I suspected, it wasn't all that difficult. They're eager to see you, Ginny. If you'd like, I'll arrange for you to travel with Mr. Rowling and his wife. He's the grounds keeper at our Sand's Point home. He and his wife are going to Florida to visit relatives. It wouldn't be safe for you to travel alone. They've rented a Pullman car that sleeps four so there'll be plenty of room. The train leaves in the morning."

Tears streamed down Ginny's face.

"What's the matter?" Arthur asked, puzzled by Ginny's reaction to the news.

"Thank you Mr. Wallace. I thought I might end up spending my life in Nazareth with that dirty farmer. It's like a weight has been lifted from my heart, and it might burst with joy. To think that I have kin that want me, and I got my whole life to do with as I please instead seein' to that old man day and night, is more than I ever dared to hope for." The next morning Ginny left as planned. She hugged Chevonne and Patrick and thanked the Wallaces again. She was starting life anew and seemed almost giddy with excitement.

They were all starting anew.

Katherine and Arthur had taken on the responsibility of raising two children. Over dinner that evening schools were discussed. Patrick had very little experience in the way of formal education, so the idea of going to a school made Patrick nervous.

Chevonne, on the other hand, was excited about going to school and looked forward to it. "I think it makes sense for Chevonne to go to Brearly, don't you think so, Arthur?"

"Brearly? I don't think so," Arthur said earnestly.

"Why not?" Katherine asked, surprised by her husband's objection.

"I hear the uniforms are homely," Arthur said casually while cutting his roast beef.

Katherine laughed, "Arthur, be serious!"

Arthur grinned. He quite enjoyed teasing his wife.

"I think you're right. Brearly will be a good fit for Chevonne," Arthur conceded. "Darling, what grade are you in?" he asked Chevonne.

"I was in sixth grade at the orphanage," Chevonne said proudly.

"Patrick, how about you?"

Patrick's thoughts had drifted off. "Excuse me, sir. Did you say something?" Patrick looked up at Arthur as if he'd just come out of a deep trance.

Katherine didn't wait for Arthur to repeat the question. She spoke up before Patrick could respond, afraid he might be embarrassed. He'd never attended a real school. "I think placement testing would be a good idea. I'd imagine Patrick would be going into tenth grade."

Arthur seemed to have forgotten that Patrick had been living on the streets of New York City since he was eight years old and was mainly self-taught. Katherine had been informally tutoring him for years in the library and she knew how intelligent he was.

"I think it would be a good idea to have the children tutored until the start of the next semester. It'll give them a chance to get acclimated to their surroundings," Katherine imparted.

"That's a splendid idea. I'll call my old roommate from college tomorrow. You remember him don't you Katherine?"

"Do you mean Art Jones?" Katherine asked.

"That's right. I suppose he doesn't go by Jonesy anymore. He's Headmaster Jones at Browning now," Arthur said.

"That's wonderful. Browning is an excellent school. I've heard the curriculum is quite rigorous. The school is on East 62nd, only a few blocks away," Katherine responded.

"Of course there'll be extracurricular activities to think about as well," Arthur said thoughtfully. Patrick and Chevonne's heads went back and forth from Katherine to Arthur as if they were watching a tennis match as they continued the discussion.

Chevonne loved school and was looking forward to starting at Brearly.

Patrick was understandably apprehensive. He was out of his element. It was very different from the rough and tumble of the streets where he knew what to expect and felt in control. He'd need to learn to navigate in a whole new world; a world of privilege and power, and for Patrick, pitfalls.

CHAPTER THIRTY-SEVEN

*E*ddy was fed up with begging the nurses and doctors for his pain medication and babysitting Vinny so he wouldn't start flapping his gums and blow their cover. It was definitely time to check out of Bellevue.

"Hey Doc, when are ya gonna cut me loose?" Eddy asked Dr. Rovenstine during morning rounds.

"The bone you fractured needs time to knit together. You run the risk of a deformity if we discontinue the traction too early, Mr. Johnson."

Eddy shook his head in disgust. "For Christ sake, I feel like I've been in this stinking piss hole for a year already. I ain't got time for this crap..."

"Mr. Johnson, calm down. You're upsetting the other patients," Dr. Rovenstine chastened.

"Fuck them! Fuck you!" Eddy screamed. "You have me tied up here like a God damn animal and won't give me pain medication when I need it. It's inhumane, is what it is. What the hell kind of a doctor are you, you sadistic fuck!" Eddy continued yelling loud enough to be heard clearly at the nurse's station. It was change of shift.

"That one's a real peach," one of the nurses coming on for the morning shift remarked wryly as she removed her coat. Eddy's tantrums were nothing new.

"Let me guess, Mr. Johnson?" another nurse said as she stubbed out her cigarette.

"He's a terror, alright. He gets pretty ugly when he's due for his pain medication. I gave him a shot around three hours ago. I've been busy though, so he's overdue. I'm going to give you girls a break and medicate him before I leave," the night nurse said as she walked into the med room to draw up Eddy's diacetylmorphine.

"Be generous! I'd like to have an uneventful day," one of the nurses called in to the med room. They all laughed.

Eddy's demeanor improved drastically within minutes of getting his medication. The problem was that he needed more of it to get the amazing high that he had initially enjoyed. Now he needed his pain medication just to keep from feeling miserable and the feeling of euphoria was significantly diminished. The doctor had reduced his dosage and the nurses couldn't be counted on to bring him his medication when he asked for it. Eddy felt like he'd lose his mind when he needed his medication. He would start to sweat and become nauseous. A sense of impending doom would come over him.

It was like nothing he'd ever experienced. It was hell.

Eddy had never let anything or anyone control him, until now. In his saner moments he recalled stories about soldiers who had become dope fiends. Pathetic, desperate and debased after coming home from the Great War addicted to pain medication. He thought about the opium ghosts that wandered the streets of Chinatown, pale shadows of their former selves. He thought maybe, just maybe, the drugs had too much of a hold on him. But those thoughts were fleeting and quickly pushed aside when his body told him it was time for another injection.

"Hey Eddy!" Vinny called over.

"What do ya want, Vinny?" Eddy asked, impatiently.

"When we goin home Eddy?" Vinny asked in his slow, stupid sounding monotone voice.

"You just asked me that question fifteen minutes ago, ya dumb cluck. I told ya, soon. Now quit pesterin me, will ya?"

"My Pop is gonna be mad if I don't get home soon."

"Christ, Vinny, just relax and shut the hell up."

Vinny's memory didn't seem to include Rosa or Berta. It was as if Vinny had the intellect of a child. He worried about "getting in trouble" if he didn't get home in time for dinner. Vinny remembered Eddy as a childhood friend, but so far, showed no other signs of recalling anything more. All knowledge of their criminal activity remained safe, at least for now. The doctors said that his memory would likely come back slowly in bits and pieces. Of course, there was an upside to Vinny being an idiot. He did whatever Eddy told him to do without argument, questions or complaints and that was a convenience that Eddy enjoyed.

Eddy hated being in the hospital but he especially hated the nights. There was only a skeleton crew on. The lights were turned off at nine o'clock sharp and the nurses were scarce. Waiting for his shot seemed like an eternity. He didn't intend to have to spend another day pleading with nurses and doctors for his medication. It was nearly two o'clock in the morning and Eddy had managed to get a nurse to inject him around midnight. There was enough diacetylmorphine in his system to dull the pain and yet leave him clear headed enough to follow through with his plan. He closed his eyes and went over it in his head at least a dozen times. There was no room for error.

Eddy listened to sounds of the ward: snoring, sheets rustling, farting, coughing, moaning, vomiting, and urinating. Every night the obnoxious sounds and smells infuriated and disgusted him.

As usual, a flashlight shone at the end of the ward. It swept across the room, stopping briefly on each patient. It was blinding and made it impossible to see who was holding it. When it got to Eddy he put his right hand up to shield his eyes. "How the hell am I supposed to sleep in this joint when you ninnies come in here every Goddamn hour and shine that fucking light in my face?" Eddy barked.

The owner of the flashlight kept it squarely on Eddy and began walking toward his bed. The shadowy figure stopped a foot or so away from Eddy's bedside. "What's the big idea? Shut that thing off you son of a bitch or I'll take that flashlight and shove it right up your ass." Eddy threatened.

"Promises, promises," whispered a deep, breathy male voice. Kenneth turned off the flashlight and chuckled. He stood at Eddy's bedside looking pleased with himself.

"You said you wouldn't be here until five in the morning. What are you doing here now?" Eddy asked, trying not to sound alarmed. He wasn't ready yet and Kenneth's early arrival threatened to spoil everything.

"Just thought I'd come by and say hello. I'll be back, don't worry." Kenneth said reassuringly.

Eddy had regained his composure and reached up, putting his hand on the back of Kenneth's neck and gently pulled him toward his face and kissed him, exploring Kenneth's mouth slowly with his tongue. Finally, Eddy released him.

"See you later," Kenneth said with a sly smile.

Just a few more hours and I'll be home free, Eddy reminded himself as he watched the handsome orderly walk out of the ward.

CHAPTER THIRTY-EIGHT

Berta woke up late amidst the pillows, blankets and sheets she and Sophia had taken from her bedroom and brought into the living room the night before. Sophia lay on the floor next to her, sound asleep. It wasn't long after she awoke that her bladder insisted she get out from underneath the warm blankets. She rubbed her eyes lazily and stretched and yawned. Still half asleep, she ambled into the bathroom. Berta came out of the bathroom still dozy but something caught her eye. It was the door. It had been left slightly ajar.

She was almost positive that she had closed it tightly and locked it behind her when they got home last night. Berta walked toward the door and opened it fully, looking out into the hallway. It was empty. She closed the door softly so as not to wake Sophia or her mother.

Berta momentarily considered the possibility that her mother had left the apartment. No, no, she wouldn't have. No, Mama wouldn't leave the apartment. She was afraid to. *Mama hadn't taken the initiative to leave the apartment on her own for months,* Berta reminded herself in an attempt to quell her anxiety, but the sense of dread only increased with each step she took toward her mother's bedroom. The bedroom door was partially open.

Berta slowly peeked around the door and over to her mother's bed.

Her stomach contracted; there was nothing there but the rumpled sheets and blanket. Berta turned and ran into the kitchen, hoping to find her mother sitting at the breakfast nook. But Rosa wasn't there either. She was gone.

"Sophia! Wake up!" Berta shouted, as she threw her coat over her nightgown and shoved her bare feet into her patent leather Mary Jane shoes.

Sophia struggled to make sense of what was happening. "Berta, what's going on? Why are you yelling? What's the matter?" Sophia mumbled, as she propped herself up on her elbows, her eyes mere slits, not ready for full exposure to the morning light.

"Sophia, get up! We need to find my mother, she's gone!"

"Maybe she went out to get the newspaper or groceries or something." Sophia suggested sleepily.

"No, you don't understand. She doesn't go out by herself. She can't. She... she... Sophia, we have to find her, let's go!"

"All right already." Sophia said, as she pulled her sweater on over her nightgown.

Sophia and Berta raced out onto the sidewalk and looked down the block for Rosa. Berta's eye darted from one stoop to the next.

"I don't see her." Sophia said.

"Let's check the deli." Berta said. She and Sophia ran all the way there, to no avail. They asked the clerk behind the counter if he'd seen a small, thin woman, in her thirties, and described Rosa.

"Nope, can't say that I have." the clerk responded casually, as he wiped the counter with a rag. Berta swallowed hard and tried to fight back the tears. Berta didn't know what to do.

"What about the bakery?" Sophia suggested.

"What do you mean?" Berta asked.

"Do you think she might have gone to look for Vinny?"

"No...well...I don't think so. She knows that he doesn't work there anymore; but then again she might not remember that. I don't know." Berta's mind was racing.

"It can't hurt to check. Maybe Vinny's parents will know where he is and he can help us find your mother." Sophia offered.

"I suppose it's worth a try." Berta admitted.

There was a line at Capozza's Bakery. An older man with thick salt and pepper hair took orders and chatted with the customers. "Thank you Mr. Cappozza," said a woman as she took a box of pastries from the man. Berta and Sophia waited impatiently.

"Yes, young ladies. What can I do for you?" the man asked with a warm smile. Berta's mouth opened but no words would come out. She was terror stricken at the thought of talking to Vinny's father. Sophia spoke up, "We're looking for Vinny Capozza. Is he here?" Sophia asked sweetly. The man's smile evaporated immediately and his countenance changed suddenly. The tone of his voice became gruff and caustic.

"I don't know no Vinny. Now do you want to buy something or not?"

Sophia was undaunted. "We're looking for your son, Vinny. His wife is missing."

Like Sophia's father, Salvatore Capozza had a heavy Italian accent.

"I no see Vinny for a long time. I know nothing about his life except for what I read in the papers," he said with an air of disgust.

"This is Berta, Rosa's daughter," Sophia explained nodding toward Berta. Salvatore looked at Berta and realized that she was on the verge of tears. His expression softened.

"I am sorry, but I cannot help you. I do not know where Vinny is. I hope you will find your mother soon though. Now, if you'll excuse me, I have to get back to work." Salvatore hesitated for a moment and looked Sophia and Berta over. He turned and took two large, warm, buttery pastries off of the rack behind him.

"Wait, I think you girls left in a rush this morning, no?" It was only then that they felt self-conscious about their disheveled appearance.

"I think you no eat breakfast this morning. Here, take these, and good luck," Salvatore said softly, handing them the pastries before going back to waiting on his customers.

Berta and Sophia left the bakery and started back up 86th Street. "I'm starving," Sophia said as she chewed a large bite of the pastry.

"Berta, aren't you going to eat yours?"

"I'm not hungry," Berta said quietly.

Sophia saw the anguished look on Berta's face and tried to console her.

"Don't worry Berta, we'll find her. I know we will," Sophia said putting an arm around Berta. "Maybe we should check the apartment again. She might have come back by now," she suggested.

Berta felt completely overwhelmed and frightened. The two girls entered the apartment hoping to find Rosa but, she was nowhere to be found. "I think I should go to the police. I don't know what else to do," Berta said sounding hopeless.

"I suppose that's a good idea. Maybe while you're there you ought to ask them if they know where Vinny is too," Sophia said, only half joking. They took their coats off and changed out of their pajamas and got dressed. "I've never been in a police station, have you?" Sophia asked.

"No," Berta said, thinking about what she would say once she got there.

They walked in silence for twenty minutes or so. Sophia was worried that someone would see her and tell her parents and they'd find out that she wasn't at a funeral in Cambria Heights. But that concern seemed trivial compared to Berta's worries at the moment. Finally, they came to 1925 Bath Avenue, the 70th precinct. Sophia and Berta stood looking up. "Here we are." Sophia announced as they stood outside looking up at the imposing, three-story brick building.

Sophia and Berta walked into the police precinct. A police officer, obscured by the newspaper he was reading, sat behind a large highly polished wood desk. It was elevated about two feet off the floor and flanked with lit electric globes that read "Precinct 70." Berta and Sophia waited to be noticed. Sophia let out a faint cough to get his attention. The police officer brought the paper down. He wore a sergeant's badge.

"Good afternoon ladies; how can I help you today?" the officer said, pleasantly.

"I'd like to report a missing person, sir," Berta said, her voice shaking slightly.

"I see; and who might that be?" the officer asked.

"My mother," Berta replied.

The officer folded the paper, and put it aside and leaned forward to focus his full attention on Berta. "I'm Sergeant Travese. What's your name?"

"My name is Berta and this is my friend, Sophia."

"How long has your mother been missing?"

"She was gone when we woke up this morning."

"It's only three o'clock in the afternoon. She hasn't been gone long. Maybe she went shopping or out to run some errands," Sergeant Travese suggested.

"My mother's sick. She can't go out by herself," Berta explained.

Sergeant Travese looked puzzled. "I don't understand; what's the matter with her?"

Berta felt embarrassed. She didn't know how to explain it. "I don't really know. I just know that she's confused a lot."

The Sergeant sat back and thought for a moment. "I suppose I could take a report, but I think the best thing for you to do is to go home and wait. Most of the time the people that are reported missing show up; they come walking back in the door and they're surprised that anyone was looking for them. I have a feeling she'll be back before nightfall. Try not to worry too much." But Berta was worried. She was worried sick. She stood in front of the desk looking pale and dejected.

"I'm sorry, but that's the best I can do right now. Good luck," he said finally, and got up from the desk and walked over to a large file cabinet turning his back to Sophia and Berta.

"Thank you," Berta said, her voice came out in a hoarse whisper. He seemed not to hear her.

"I think he's right, Berta. Your mother hasn't been gone that long. Let's walk around the neighborhood some more. Is there anywhere else she might have gone?"

"I can't think of anywhere else... Well, maybe the movie theatre? She used to love to go to the movies."

"That's a good idea."

Sophia and Berta walked to the theatre. They asked the man in the ticket booth if he'd seen a woman fitting Rosa's description. The answer was "no." They walked through parks and alleys and along the docks. There was still no sign of Rosa. Finally, they went back to the apartment. It was dark out and the apartment was empty.

Berta and Sophia collapsed, exhausted on the couch. Berta's stomach rumbled: she hadn't eaten all day.

"Was that your stomach?" Sophia exclaimed.

"I guess so," Berta said glumly.

"You need to eat something. I'm going to see what I can find for us," Sophia said and went into the kitchen. There was a sauce pan full of cooked oatmeal in the ice box. She added milk and sugar and heated it up on the stove.

"Soup's on!" Sophia announced as she carried two large, steaming bowls of oatmeal into the living room and set them on the coffee table. Berta picked up the spoon and took a small bite.

"It's good," Berta said, taking another bite and another. The bowl was empty in no time.

"I'm so tired." she said, as she fought to keep her eyes open.

"Me too," Sophia murmured, lying her head on a throw pillow and drifting off to sleep.

It was nearly five thirty in the morning when Berta woke up next to Sophia on the couch. Berta rubbed her eyes. For a few moments, she thought that maybe she'd had a terrible nightmare. Maybe her mother wasn't missing at all, and everything she thought had happened since she woke up the previous morning, was just a bad dream. Berta got up and slowly walked into her mother's bedroom. Her heart sunk when she saw it. It was exactly how she remembered it – empty. Berta turned and walked out of the room.

She was thirsty and decided to go into the kitchen to get a glass of water. It was then that she noticed a piece of brown delicatessen paper on the floor in front of the door. She didn't know where it had come from. She or Sophia must have brought it in on their shoe. Berta picked it up and crumpled it in her hand. As she tossed it into the trash she noticed that there was writing on it. Quickly, she reached into the trash and plucked it back out and unfurled it.

Berta's knees became weak and her whole body began to shake as she read the words on the coarse brown paper.

CHAPTER THIRTY-NINE

Chevonne could hardly remember Roxbury, the place where she was born. She and her brother were taken away when they were very young and brought to New York City. The only home she really remembered was the orphanage, and there was nothing in her experience there that prepared her for life with Katherine and Arthur Wallace. Chevonne was keenly observant though and she admired Katherine and, of course, wanted to be just like her. Katherine never corrected Chevonne's grammar, or table manners and she never had to prompt her about her posture or telephone etiquette. She simply didn't need to.

Chevonne managed to emulate Katherine perfectly. She watched Katherine like a hawk. Arthur joked about it when they were in private.

"If imitation is the sincerest form of flattery, I'd say Chevonne has paid you quite a compliment. She sits like you and walks like you, she even uses the same inflections and intonations when she speaks as you do," Arthur laughed, as he sat in bed watching Katherine comb her long Auburn hair.

"Yes, I noticed. It's her way of coping with all this change. Change is difficult, even when it's a change for the better. I think it'll take a little while for her to feel comfortable. She's just getting to the age when young girls start to feel self-conscious. I'm sure she'll come into her own in no time." Katherine said, as she smiled at Arthur in the reflection of her dressing table mirror. Arthur smiled back, happy that Katherine was happy. She obviously enjoyed Chevonne's company, and he had to admit that he did too.

"Well, there's nothing like riding to boost a girl's confidence, is what I say."

Katherine smiled. "Really? Is that what you say? I never took you for a man who thought a lot about ways to build self-esteem in pre-adolescent girls."

Arthur looked sheepish for a moment, "I just think there's nothing like horsemanship to bolster ones confidence. There's a riding school on 39th and Fifth Avenue. Maybe we could take Chevonne over this weekend and see about a few lessons. What do you think?"

Katherine finished combing her hair and walked over to the foot of the bed, pulled her silk nightgown up to her mid-thighs and placed a knee on the mattress and crawled seductively up to Arthur and kissed him on the mouth. "I think you're going to try to turn her into a polo fanatic like you. That's what I think." Katherine purred, as she reached over to turn the light off. They made love and drifted off to sleep in each other's arms.

Katherine rolled over the following morning and reached for Arthur. She ran her delicate hands over the cool linen sheets where Arthur's body should have been. It was then that she remembered that her husband had scheduled an early business meeting. She slipped out of bed and got ready to head out to the library to volunteer her time as she had for so many years. It gave structure to her day and she loved the library. It was strange to think, that unlike so many of the days before, Patrick wouldn't be there. Instead, he was sitting in the solarium reading the newspaper and sipping a cup of coffee.

"Good morning Patrick," Katherine greeted as she walked into the solarium and sat down at the table.

"Good morning Ma'am," Patrick replied politely.

"Have you had breakfast yet?" Katherine inquired.

Patrick looked slightly uncomfortable. "No, I... well... I helped myself to some coffee. The pot was on the kitchen stove. I hope you don't mind."

Katherine leaned forward and took Patrick's hand in hers. "Of course I don't mind. Patrick, this is your home now too. You may help yourself to anything you like."

Patrick slid his hand out from under Katherine's and picked up his coffee cup. He turned his head to look out the window and he sipped his drink. "It looks as if it might rain. I see thunder clouds in the distance," Patrick said, casually changing the subject.

Katherine couldn't help but notice that Patrick had been distant and aloof and she still didn't understand why he and Chevonne had left so abruptly to board the orphan train.

"Patrick, what's the matter? You seem... I don't know, not yourself. You know you can tell me anything. Maybe I can help. What's on your mind?"

Patrick didn't see the point in explaining that he didn't feel "at home" and that he was staying with the Wallace's because of his sister, and that he'd just as soon fend for himself on the streets of New York City than depend on the charity of a bigot like Arthur Wallace.

"Everything's fine," Patrick said, forcing a smile.

"Alright, I suppose it's understandable. We'll all be going through a bit of an adjustment period," Katherine said, sounding worried. "I'm headed to the library. I'm only staying a few hours, so I'll be back by lunch. Your tutor will be here any minute."

Katherine picked up her purse from the table and walked out of the solarium. "Good luck!" she yelled from the door, and waved.

Patrick sat, deep in thought, wondering what life had in store for him, when Chevonne bounced into the room. Her corn silk blonde hair had been freshly coiffed and adorned with a large velvet ribbon. "Good morning Patrick! Come out to the dining room, there's a surprise for you," Chevonne announced cheerfully. He couldn't help but grin as he watched Chevonne skip down the hall in her pretty new dress and shoes. He followed her into the dining room where two place settings, complete with French-made china, rimmed with gold leaf and sterling silver flat ware, were waiting.Bertram stood by the table with two linen napkins draped over his left forearm. He pulled Chevonne's chair out with his right hand.

"Thank you Bertram." Chevonne said with a sunny smile as she hopped onto the chair. Bertram placed the linen napkin over Chevonne's lap. Patrick managed his own chair and sat down. Bertram took the other linen napkin and placed it over Patrick's lap.

"Thank you, sir." Patrick said feeling slightly awkward.

"Please, Master Patrick, call me Bertram."

"Thank you Bertram." Patrick said. Bertram left the room.

"So what's the surprise?" Patrick asked.

"Well, actually there are three. First, the cook made us a special breakfast. It's called Crepes Suzette and he said it's the most delicious thing you'll ever taste in your life. The second is a letter from Berta I haven't opened yet. If you're very sweet, I'll read it to you."

Patrick smiled, "How is the old girl? I know you miss her terribly."

"Yes, I do and I also know that you've always had a bit of a crush on her." Patrick looked embarrassed but didn't deny it. "Mrs. Wallace said that Berta could come and visit. It'll be like old times, won't it Patrick?" Chevonne said excitedly, clapping her hands together.

"I suppose it will be," Patrick said with a widening smile. "You said there were three surprises. What's the third?"

"It's under the table," Chevonne said with a giggle.

CHAPTER FOURTY

ddy reached under the mattress and felt for the steak knife he had slid under it days ago. He gingerly touched it, trying not to cut himself on the blade. When he was satisfied that he had identified the wooden handle, he grasped it firmly and pulled it out from under the mattress. Eddy brought his right arm across his chest and reached up to press the blade against the traction ropes holding up his left arm. Over and over he dragged the blade against the rope until it finally let go. Eddy's arm dropped suddenly. A searing, excruciating pain shot from his elbow to his shoulder. For a moment he thought he might vomit. Eddy turned his face and screamed into the pillow.

His left arm was slightly weak from muscle atrophy after being immobile for so long, but he could move it. He took the knife from his right hand with his left hand and slid it back under the mattress. A piece of rope about a foot and a half long, dangled from the traction pulley. Eddy pulled it down, rolled over on his stomach, and placed it under his pillow, not coiled up, but lengthwise from one end of the pillow to the other. His arm throbbed mercilessly. It had been too long since his last injection. Eddy returned to a supine position, shut his eyes and breathed in deeply, trying to gain control over the urge to yell for more pain medication.

Kenneth should be here any minute. It won't be long after that, Eddy reminded himself. He opened his eyes when he heard someone humming "Tea for Two" at his bedside.

It was Kenneth.

Eddy looked over at Vinny, who was snoring loudly in the next bed. "Pull the curtain around will ya," Eddy said, trying to sound more good-humored than he felt.

Kenneth quietly pulled the curtain around the bed and came back to the bedside.

"I see they cut you down," Kenneth said, looking at the traction apparatus.

"Yup. Now the two of us are gonna have even more fun," Eddy whispered. Kenneth put his hand under the blanket and felt for Eddy's penis: it was soft. Kenneth fondled Eddy's testicles and still, nothing.

"Get in bed with me," Eddy commanded.

Kenneth began to lift the covers to get underneath them.

"What are you doing?" Eddy asked.

"I'm getting in bed with you, like you asked me to," Kenneth replied, sounding surprised.

"Not with your clothes on, ya dope," Eddy laughed softly.

"I don't know about this Eddy. I don't want to get caught."

"Are you kidding me? I could be screaming bloody murder and those lazy nurses wouldn't get off their asses and come in here. Now take your clothes off, hot stuff," Eddy said with a salacious grin.

Kenneth hesitated for only a moment before pulling his crisp white tunic over his head. He folded it and placed in on Eddy's nightstand before pulling his pants down and stepping out of them. Eddy wore a broad grin as he watched Kenneth undress. Kenneth slipped under the covers, his naked body rubbing up against Eddy's. The two men embraced one another and kissed passionately. Kenneth reached down between Eddy's legs to find him rock hard.

"Get on your stomach," Eddy whispered in Kenneth's ear.

Kenneth obliged right away. Eddy positioned himself behind Kenneth and spit into his hand. He stroked his penis, using his saliva as a lubricant, and entered Kenneth slowly and fully. Eddy began moving his hips rhythmically, pumping and gyrating until he felt Kenneth's muscles tighten and saw Kenneth's fingers dig into the sheets. He reached over Kenneth's shoulders and under the pillow. Eddy placed one hand at each end of the rope and grasped it, sliding it under Kenneth's chin. He pulled the rope back hard around his neck, crossing it as he arched his back and drove himself deeper into Kenneth. Kenneth began to struggle but the sudden cessation of blood flow to his brain rendered him unconscious in less than a minute. Eddy ejaculated while continuing to pull the rope tight. Finally, he collapsed on Kenneth's back.

Eddy got out of bed, covered Kenneth's dead body with the blanket, and slipped on his orderly's uniform. It was baggy, but not so much that it would raise suspicion. He took the knife out from under the mattress again, secured it in his waist band, and picked up the comb from the nightstand. He ran it through his hair hastily, and went over to Vinny.

"Vinny, wake up, we gotta go," Eddy whispered as he shook Vinny's shoulder.

Vinny's blood shot eyes opened wide, he looked confused and startled.

"Don't talk, Vinny. I swear to God if you say one fucking word I'm gonna punch you in the mouth. You understand?" Eddy hissed. Vinny nodded. "Just do what I tell ya and we'll be out of this crap hole in no time."

Eddy walked quickly down to the end of the ward and retrieved a wheelchair, bringing it over to Vinny's bedside. Vinny could walk but the head injury had affected his balance. His stiff legged waddle was slow, and besides, Eddy felt he'd look more official wheeling a patient.

"Get in." Vinny pulled back his covers and stood up. He looked at the wheel chair and then at Eddy, quizzically. "Come on, Vinny, move it." Eddy whispered, insistently.

Eddy grabbed the straight jacket that had been left at Vinny's bedside after his seizure and threw it on Vinny's lap. "Here, hold that." Eddy instructed.

He took one of the blankets off Vinny's bed and wrapped him in it, pulling a portion of it over Vinny's head like a hood.

Eddy fought the urge to race down the corridor to the elevator. Instead, he pushed Vinny in the wheelchair, nonchalantly, with a blasé' expression on his face, emulating the countenance of so many of the jaded hospital staff. He waited in front of the elevator; the beads of sweat building on his brow, a knot in his stomach and his left arm in agonizing pain. He was beginning to go into full blown withdrawals.

The elevator arrived and an elderly man with thick glasses pulled the metal grated accordion door open. "Hop on." he said cordially. "What floor you want?" he asked, without looking at Eddy or Vinny.

"Ground floor," Eddy said flatly.

"You got it, pal." The man said, as he began to pull the levers. The elevator descended, stopping with a bounce. The elderly man yanked the lever down and reached over and heaved the door open with both hands. "Here you go," he said cheerfully. Eddy surveyed the hospital lobby. There wasn't a soul around. He pushed the wheelchair off the elevator, his eyes darting about. Kenneth had told him the dispensary was on the ground floor. Finally, he saw a plaque on the wall that read "Dispensary," with an arrow pointing down a long corridor. It wasn't quite six in the morning and the hallway was empty. The perspiration ran off of Eddy's brow and stung his eyes. He wiped his sleeve across his forehead and blinked. He felt slightly dizzy but he pushed on. He came to what looked like a bank teller's window with a door next to it.

Eddy peered through the window. He could see a slight man in a lab coat sitting on a stool hunched over a pile of pills. He watched the man count them out carefully and put them into a stone mortar. Eddy reached for the door knob and found it unlocked. He pushed it open and wheeled Vinny in. The druggist, a balding middle-aged man, wearing a red bow tie, spun around. "What's the meaning of this? Nobody's allowed back here! Now get out and go wait at the window."

Eddy walked over to the man and grabbed him by the collar. With trembling hands, he pulled the knife from his waist band and held it up against his neck. The druggist gasped.

"What's your name, sport?"

"F-Felix, Felix Bixby."

"Alright then Felix, you're gonna do me a little favor. You're gonna fill that black satchel over there with all the diacetylmorphine and syringes you got. Try anything funny and I'll carve your eyes out, got it?"

Felix nodded nervously and scurried over to the satchel and emptied the contents of it onto the floor.

"Come on, come on, we ain't got all day!" Eddy snapped.

Felix grabbed handfuls of vials from a cabinet and dropped them into the satchel. He went over to a drawer and reached in and pulled out syringes and threw them in too. Eddy looked at the other vials in the cabinet.

"What's that?" he asked pointing to the chloroform.

"It's used as an anesthetic."

"Throw them in," Eddy ordered. "What are those pills for?" he asked, indicating the pile of pills next to the mortar and pestle.

"It's called codeine. They're pain killers."

Eddy reached over and picked up two and swallowed them dry. He then proceeded to grab a handful and fill his front pocket.

Eddy snatched the satchel from Felix and slung it over his shoulder. "Take your clothes off," Eddy ordered, pointing the knife at the druggist.

"I will not." Felix said indignantly.

Eddy's arm felt like it was on fire. The pain was almost unbearable and his stomach felt as if it were in a vice grip. He hoped the pain killers would kick in soon. "Take your fucking clothes off or I'll slice you to pieces right here," Eddy growled. Felix could see that Eddy was desperate and realized that he would indeed follow through on his threat. Tentatively, Felix began to slowly loosen his bow tie.

"Hurry up!" Eddy barked, his nose running, spittle flying from his mouth. Felix removed the rest of his clothes quickly and stood terrified in his t-shirt and boxer shorts, his arms wrapped around himself.

"You and me are gonna get along just fine as long as you do what I tell ya to do. I'm gonna be back here and you're gonna make sure I got all the junk I need. Yeah, you and me are gonna be tight. Don't worry; I'll make it worth your while."

Vinny had been sitting in the wheelchair gape mouthed, listening to Eddy's tirade.

"Get up Vinny, and put that straight jacket on our friend here," Eddy instructed. Vinny picked the straight jacket up off his lap and held it up trying to figure out which way it was supposed to go.

"Gimme that thing you idiot," Eddy said as he ripped the straight jacket from Vinny's hands. "Get outta that stupid hospital gown and put those clothes on. Make it snappy, you imbecile," Eddy snarled. Vinny stood up from the wheelchair and walked over to the pile of clothes the druggist had just taken off. He began to put them on. Eddy put the knife between his teeth and held the straightjacket up in front of Felix.

"Put your arms in," Eddy said, panting. The pain took his breath away and he was sweating profusely and shaking.

"You'll never get away with this, you know," Felix said with an unmistakable tone of contempt. His fear of being murdered by a mad man had dissipated once he understood that Eddy's intention was to use him as a long term supplier. Eddy looked as if he could collapse at any moment. He dropped the straight jacket on the floor and took the knife out from between his teeth. Without warning he plunged it into the druggist's left eye, pulled the knife back out and wiped the blood off on Felix's t-shirt. Felix Bixby keeled over and landed on the floor with a thud.

Eddy placed the knife back into his waist band. "I don't have time for this shit," he grumbled. There'd be other druggists and they'd probably be more cooperative, Eddy told himself. Vinny stood, wearing Felix's clothes. They were clearly too small. "Get in the wheelchair. We're running out of time. We gotta get outta here before the next shift shows up." Vinny sat down. Eddy again placed the blanket over him like a shroud, obscuring his face. He grabbed the druggist's jacket off of the back of a chair, put it on and reached into the pockets to find a handkerchief and a dollar or so worth of loose change.

"Let's go," Eddy said as he pushed the wheelchair out of the dispensary and raced down the corridor. The lobby was still empty. Eddy turned the wheelchair around and pushed the hospital door open with his back, pulling the wheelchair over the threshold. Eddy inhaled the cold early morning air. It helped clear his head. He strode down the long brick walk way toward the curb, pushing Vinny in the wheelchair. There was nobody around, except for two teenage girls, walking quickly toward the entrance. The girl in the blue cloche hat looked familiar, but Eddy couldn't place her.

They locked eyes for only a moment.

Eddy proceeded on down the sidewalk. He had managed to time their escape perfectly: the first trains had just started running. Eddy pushed the wheelchair a few blocks down First Avenue until he saw the streetcar coming. "Get up Vinny," he ordered.

Vinny stood from the wheelchair; Eddy pushed it out of sight down into an alleyway.

Eddy and Vinny boarded the streetcar. It was still early; there were only a few passengers. Nobody seemed to notice them, but the image of the girl who'd looked squarely into Eddy's eyes on the walkway of the hospital nagged at him.

She looked at Eddy as if he looked as familiar to her as she looked to him.

CHAPTER FOURTY-ONE

Gitta stood watching her brother-in-law examine Rosa. When he announced that he knew exactly what was wrong with her, Gitta felt a sense of relief. Rosa had been ill for a long time and Yekl and Gitta had been frustrated and disappointed as they watched her steady deterioration.

"You know what's wrong with her? That's good. You can help her, right?" Gitta asked hopefully.

"I'm afraid I cannot. Your friend is very sick. I have seen many, many cases such as this."

Rosa turned her head and looked in the direction of Dr. Lachman but did not speak. He looked at Rosa with sad eyes and turned back to Gitta and Yekl,

"I think your friend here might like to finish her nap."

Rosa looked bewildered.

"Come with me, Rosa." Gitta said, as she took her hand and lead her back to the couch.

Gitta covered Rosa with a blanket. "You rest now," Gitta said as she gently smoothed the hair back from Rosa's forehead.

Hyram and Yekl sat at the kitchen table. Gitta pulled out a chair and sat down.

"Please, Hyram, will you tell us what is wrong with her?" Gitta entreated.

"It is called general paresis. Unfortunately there is no cure and no way to halt the disease. The asylums are full of people like your friend Rosa. It is not an uncommon disease."

"How can you be so sure that that is what it is?" Yekl asked.

"Ah, yes, well, you see it is easily differentiated from other types of psychosis. There is a characteristic abnormality in the eye, the pupillary reflexes, specifically. It has come to be called "Whore's Eye," which has a double meaning of sorts," Hyram explained calmly.

"I don't understand." Gitta said looking shocked. "Are you insinuating that Rosa is a woman of questionable morals? I can assure you that that is not the case."

Hyram sighed. "You see, the disease is transmitted during intimate relations with an infected person. Prostitutes are, of course, at much higher risk for contracting the disease. Also, the pupils of the patient with general paresis will constrict quickly when they focus on a near object. They accommodate, but they do not constrict when exposed to bright light. So, they accommodate, but do not react. This is how the test is remembered by medical students. I am sorry, it is such a crude analogy, but it is a very specific sign of neurosyphilis. General paresis is caused by a syphilis infection."

"This cannot be! After Rosa was widowed she worked in a textile mill until she re-married over three years ago. She would never have considered—"

Hyram interrupted, "Gitta, I am not suggesting that your friend is or has ever been a prostitute. Sadly, many women are infected by their husbands.

"This doesn't make sense, Hyram. Her husband seems to be in perfect health, so he could not have given her this awful disease you talk about." Yekl pointed out.

"You do not understand how syphilis behaves." Hyram responded and went on to explain in more detail.

"The majority of people infected show no signs of illness for many, many years. Usually, it is twenty years or more before symptoms begin to show. It is likely that her husband infected her but he himself has not presented with symptoms. Some people, like Rosa, start to show the effects within a year or so after becoming infected because the syphilis bacterium invades their brain tissues. Most everyone who contracts syphilis develops a painless chancre around the genital area that resolves after some weeks. Some people don't even notice it, then later on, an odd rash on the palms of the hands and feet. This rash also resolves."

Yekl and Gitta sat and listened in disbelief.

Hyram continued solemnly. "With neurosyphillis, there are personality changes and depression. The mental status declines further and we start to see everything from mania to paranoia to delusions of grandeur or persecution. Worsening dementia follows, and because the bacterium causing syphilis invades not just the brain, but the spinal cord as well, we

202

begin to see changes in a patient's gait and problems with balance. Also, there is often a characteristic thinning of the hair, to the extent that the scalp becomes visible in places."

"What will become of her?" Gitta asked with tears in her eyes.

The doctor sighed again and spoke quietly, "I'm afraid the picture is quite bleak. The patient becomes completely incapacitated. She will become bedridden and lose control over bowel and bladder. In time, she will not be able to communicate in any effective manner," he told them. "I suspect your friend will not survive more than a year or so. Because of the severity and complexity of her illness, I think she should be hospitalized at this point. Clearly, she needs constant supervision and care. Many patients admitted to the mental asylums are suffering from general paresis of the insane caused by syphilis. It is a horrid scourge."

Gitta covered her entire face in her handkerchief and began to sob softly. Yekl rubbed her back in an attempt to soothe his wife. He turned to his cousin.

"Rosa has a daughter, Berta, who is about fifteen years old now. Her father, Rosa's first husband, died when Berta was little. It will be difficult to tell this girl that her mother is dying and will spend her last days languishing in a hospital bed."

"There are very rare instances of remission, and of course, there is always divine intervention. You may not want to cause her to lose all hope. The important thing is that Rosa will get the care she needs. I will pray for your friend and her daughter."

"Thank you Hyram." Yekl said sincerely.

Gitta looked up. "How will we tell Vinny?"

"Vinny?" Hyram asked.

"Yes, he is Rosa's husband, the man that surely gave her this sickness." Gitta said; an angry timbre in her voice.

"I can arrange for Rosa to be admitted to Bellevue this afternoon. I have a colleague who is working there. I think it may be best to get her settled in and then the doctors can explain everything to her husband." Hyram suggested.

"Yes, I think that would be best." Yekl agreed.

Gitta was still crying. She nodded her head and blew her nose. "Yekl, you will need to go to their apartment to let Vinny and Berta know that Rosa is in the hospital. I need to pick the children up from Hebrew school in a few hours. Berta and Vinny must be frantic looking for Rosa. Please go right way," Gitta urged.

Yekl raced to the Cappozza's apartment, hoping Berta and Vinny would be there. No one was home. He waited for over two hours and finally, he knocked at a neighbor's door and asked for a piece of paper and pencil.

An old woman came to the door.

"I don't think I have any stationery" she said.

"I just need to leave a short note for someone. Please, any scrap of paper will do." Yekl beseeched.

The old woman tottered away and came back a few minutes later with a small piece of brown delicatessen paper and a pencil.

"Thank you." Yekl said and began to write.

The old woman watched as he wrote. He handed the pencil back to her and walked down the hallway to slip the note under the apartment door.

> *Dear Vinny and Berta,*
> *Rosa made her way to Hester Street. She looked ill and so she was taken to Bellevue Hospital. I am sorry to be the bearer of such news. Please let us know if there's anything we can do to help.*
> *Yours,*
> *Yekl*

Berta and Sophia had come back to the apartment exhausted after spending all day looking for Rosa. Berta didn't notice the small piece of brown deli paper on the floor, at least not until the wee hours of the next morning. She was both alarmed and relieved after reading it.

"Sophia! Sophia! Wake up!"

"Oh no, not again" Sophia said, lifting her head off the arm of the couch. "What time is it?" Sophia said, sleepily, rubbing her eyes.

"It's almost six in the morning," Berta told her offhandedly, more concerned about her mother's whereabouts. "There was a note on the floor. Mr. Lachman must have come over when we were out looking for my mother and slid it under the door. I just found it."

"What does it say?" Sophia asked.

"That my mother is at Bellevue Hospital. She must have gone to her friend Gitta's and they took her there. Come on, we have to go! We'll be able to catch the first streetcar if we hurry."

"Well, at least we're already dressed," Sophia muttered wryly. The weekend hadn't exactly turned out as she had hoped, but her heart broke for Berta, and she was happy that she was there for her friend, during such a difficult time.

It was cold out. Berta and Sophia stood shivering waiting for the streetcar. Berta pulled her blue cloche hat down further to try to cover her ears. They sat silently on the way to Bellevue. Sophia nodded off a few times during the ride. Berta was nervous. She had never been in a hospital and tried to imagine what it would be like. They got off at 27th Street, a few blocks away from the hospital and walked up First Avenue. They came to a huge brick building with a long walkway that led to the entrance, where a big stone arch, read "Bellevue Hospital." Berta wondered how she would find her mother.

Berta and Sophia stood at the end of the long walkway looking at the building. "Well, here we are." Sophia announced. There was nobody around except for a tall thin man who had just come through the hospital doors. He was walking quickly toward them, pushing someone in a wheelchair covered in a blanket. Berta could see that the man wore a white uniform under his tight tweed jacket. The sleeves were unusually short, falling at least two inches above his wrists.

Berta considered asking the man how she might go about locating a patient in the hospital, but the look on his face dissuaded her. He looked panicked. His face was flushed and even though it was cold out, his skin glistened with perspiration. He looked directly at Berta. They held each other's gaze far longer than was comfortable. The man looked at Berta as if she was a bug under a microscope. She wanted to look away but couldn't. He looked so familiar, she was sure she'd remember where she knew him from at any moment, but nothing came. Sophia's voice broke her train of thought, "Did the note say what floor she was on?" she asked. The enormity of the building was overwhelming. Finally, Berta and Sophia were directed to the woman's psychiatric ward. Berta and Sophia went to the nurse's station.

"Excuse me? I'm looking for my mother. Her name is Rosa Cappozza. Is she here?"

The young nurse looked up from her paperwork. "Um, yes, she came in last evening. What can I do to help you?"

"I'd like to see her."

"I'm afraid that isn't possible. She's been sedated. She was a bit agitated when she arrived. I'm sure she'll be feeling better when she wakes; why don't you come back later in the afternoon?"

"What's the matter with her?" Sophia asked the nurse.

The nurse ignored her and turned to Berta.

"You should come back with your father so that he can speak with the doctor."

Berta didn't bother telling the nurse that Vinny wasn't her father. "He's a traveling salesman. He's away on business." Bert explained.

"You must know what's wrong with her." Sophia said insistently.

"I'm afraid she has an infection." The nurse said reluctantly.

"What kind of infection?" Sophia queried.

"I've got patients to tend now. You'll need to come back another time", the nurse said tersely, and walked away.

Dejected, the two girls walked back down the long corridor. The gruesome sounds of the psychiatric ward echoed in the hallway. Women were screaming and screeching. There was maniacal laughing and nonsensical rambling. They could hear a nurse yelling at one of the patients, "Open your mouth this instant and take your pills or you'll have no breakfast this morning!" The smell of feces and stale urine, poorly masked by disinfectant, hung in the air. Berta felt like crying but managed to keep her composure. At least she knew where her mother was, she told herself, and maybe now, under the care of a doctor, she would get better.

Berta and Sophia got down to the lobby to find it swarming with police. "What's happened?" Sophia asked the nurses who were standing next to the elevator with their arms folded in front of them, looking anxious.

"There're two madmen on the loose. They murdered an orderly and a druggist. The men were patients here, recovering after a car accident. They think that they must have left the hospital early in the morning."

Berta's eyes grew wide and she gasped, "We saw..." Berta began.

Sophia grabbed Berta's arm and yanked her away.

"Thank you, we have to go catch the trolley now," Sophia said, with a forced smile, as she waved goodbye to the nurses.

"Berta, we can't go to the police," Sophia whispered, looking frightened.

CHAPTER FORTY-TWO

It had been almost a year since Chevonne and Patrick had come to live with the Wallace's.

Chevonne took to the life of a socialite, like a duck to water. She made friends easily at her new school. The disparity in social status seemed not to make a bit of difference to Chevonne's friends at Brearly and she fit in beautifully. Nobody would have guessed that she hadn't grown up with a silver spoon in her mouth. Katherine Wallace invited the daughters of the most powerful and wealthy families and their mothers, to tea parties and soirees, to meet Chevonne before she was enrolled in Brearly.

Katherine was completely forthright about Chevonne's background and how she and her brother had come to live with the Wallace's. Katherine beamed when she introduced Chevonne. She would say "this is my Chevonne," with an arm around her shoulder

Katherine Wallace knew all too well how things worked in the catty upper crust of the social circles she ran in, so she made it perfectly clear in her very subtle and understated way that Chevonne was to be afforded the same consideration and courtesies that would be extended to her if she were Katherine's own daughter. The parents of Chevonne's classmates were astute enough to make sure their daughters understood this. Katharine made it known that any slights would be met with retribution. Invites to important parties might not show up in the mail, or perhaps inclusion in Junior League committee meetings would cease. Being anything but gracious and respectful to Chevonne O'Farrell could mean being banished to societal Siberia.

Of course, Chevonne was oblivious to Katherine's guileful handling of the high society crowd. She enjoyed her new friends and all the wonderful experiences that came along with living among the privileged class. Patrick shunned the social gatherings that Chevonne relished and he seemed to have a genuine disdain for the pretenses and formalities of them. Neither Katherine nor Arthur could blame him. In fact, to a large degree, they recognized that much of the socializing was an exercise in futility and nothing more than an opportunity for one-upmanship and sophisticated backbiting, but they also understood that it was a necessary evil, particularly, when it came to charity work and business.

Unfortunately, Patrick didn't fare as well as Chevonne when it came to school. He excelled academically and perhaps there was a degree of jealousy because of it, fueling the ire of the other boys. The Browning School's alumni included students with last names like Rockafella, and the students were keenly aware of each other's station.

"Where are you from?" asked one the boys on Patrick's first day.

"I'm from Roxbury, Massachusetts originally", Patrick replied.

"Roxbury? I've never heard of it," the boy said with a smug, self-satisfied expression. He turned to another boy and said, "Have you ever heard of Roxbury?"

The other boy laughed, "No, and I doubt anyone in this school ever has. I heard you were a newspaper boy or a shoe shine boy from Wall Street... or some other street corner; a street urchin really, and a smelly Irish one at that."

The two boys laughed and strolled off.

Patrick was stoic about the treatment he received from the other boys. He didn't see the point in complaining about it. It wasn't until near the end of the school year the situation came to a head and became apparent to Arthur and Katherine. Patrick did his best to ignore the barbs and taunting. He had advanced from tenth into eleventh grade early on in the year but because he'd never really been to school officially, he was nervous about his abilities. It was clear that all the years he'd spent studying at the library with Mrs. Wallace had served him well but it wasn't academics that were the issue: it was dealing with the hostility directed at him from the other students, and even some of the teachers, that made his days at Browning hell.

Patrick had vowed to keep his head.

The physical assaults were subtle. Typically, another student would intentionally bump into him or trip him and say, "pardon me." This would be accompanied by laughter from an on-looking group of boys. Patrick knew they were baiting him. The thought that he'd be graduating at the end of next year helped to sustain him, but one day, Patrick snapped. A classmate poured his milk into his lap at the lunch table. The other boys at the table snickered. "Oh my, how clumsy of me," the boy said, wearing a cunning grin. Patrick stood up, grabbed the boy by the back of the collar and yanked him off the bench and on to the floor. He proceeded to dive on top of him and began pummeling the boy. Within seconds, however, the other boys sitting at the table jumped on top of Patrick.

The pig pile was broken up after a few minutes when one of the teachers came running from across the room.

"Here, here, what's this all about?" he shouted as he began pulling boys away.

"Patrick O'Farrell hit me!" the boy who had poured the milk in Patrick's lap, pointed at Patrick and shouted, as the blood dripped from his nose.

Patrick said nothing. He was angry at himself for losing his temper.

"Go to the infirmary and have them take a look at that nose. Hopefully it's not broken." the teacher said to the boy.

Then he turned to Patrick.

"You! You hoodlum, this kind of behavior might be acceptable where you're from, but it won't be tolerated here! Come with me. I'm sure Headmaster Jones will have plenty to say about this."

The teacher grasped Patrick's upper arm in an attempt to lead him toward the door. Patrick pulled away and walked ahead to the headmaster's office, leaving the teacher to trail behind him. Headmaster Jones sat behind the desk in his well-appointed office.

"Can I help you?" he asked the teacher, who had come to stand in the doorway with Patrick.

"I'm sorry to interrupt you, but there was an incident in the lunch room. It appears that Patrick O'Farrell attacked another student."

The headmaster looked Patrick up and down.

"This isn't the Bowery young man. This is a school for gentlemen of pedigree. Beating on people to settle your differences is barbaric. I'm going to contact your guardian, Arthur Wallace, and apprise him of the situation." The headmaster said haughtily. "Now wait outside in the hall."

Patrick sat outside of the headmaster's office on the floor in the hallway, stewing. Within twenty minutes Arthur Wallace came walking down the hall toward Patrick. He looked at Patrick, nodded and strode into the office.

"What seems to be the problem Jonesy?"

Patrick could hear the conversation clearly. The door was open.

"Arthur, this isn't going to work. Patrick just doesn't seem to be...well... he's not adjusting the way that we'd hoped he would."

"What in the world are you talking about?" Arthur asked sounding annoyed.

"I'm afraid this will be Patrick's last day at Browning. We just can't tolerate his behavior here. We have a reputation to think about, Arthur."

"What in bloody hell happened?"

"He attacked another student," the headmaster said solemnly. "He's not like us. He's not our kind of people, Arthur."

Patrick strained to hear Arthur's response.

For just a moment there was complete silence, then Arthur Wallace's rancorous words filled the room.

"Why you sniveling little wretch; if you only had an ounce of Patrick O'Farrell's grit and honor and integrity you might be half a man. Might I remind you that we go back far enough for me to know that your mother came from a family of sharecroppers and that you practically went to bed sucking your thumb the first few months of college. I know Patrick, and I know that if he did hit someone they bloody well deserved it."

"Now, Arthur, please calm down. I'm sure there's just been some misunderstanding" the headmaster said nervously.

Patrick heard Arthur chuckle. "Of course there's been a misunderstanding. You don't understand how miserable it will be to acquire the real estate the Browning School will need to expand the way you planned or to finance that expansion if things don't turn around for Patrick at this school. I'm not asking for special treatment for him. I'm demanding decency and fairness. Do you understand?"

"Yes, yes, naturally, of course; it's just the right thing to do." the headmaster acquiesced.

"Good, I'm glad you understand. Now get your boney ass up and go out into the hallway and apologize to him."

Patrick nearly fell over but managed to right himself and stand before the headmaster made his way out to the hall.

"I'm sorry about this unfortunate misunderstanding, Patrick. It won't happen again." The headmaster extended his hand.

Patrick shook it and nodded. He was speechless.

"Well, Jonesy, I suppose I should let you get back to work now." Arthur said amicably, as if they'd just finished chatting about the weather.

"I suppose I should." the headmaster said pleasantly. "Give my best to Katherine, will you?"

"I'll do that." Arthur said. He turned to Patrick, "Did you finish your lunch?"

"No sir."
"Well then, let's go home so you can get changed and have a bite to eat."

Katherine was at the library, Chevonne was at school and Bertram was out shopping.
"Well, it looks like we're on our own Patrick." Arthur said as he tossed Patrick an apple, poured two glasses of milk and took some sliced ham out of the icebox. They made sandwiches at the kitchen table. Patrick and Arthur ate in silence, comfortable enough with one another not to feel as if they needed to make idle chit chat.
Finally, Patrick spoke. "Thank you." he said simply.
"What are you thanking me for?" Arthur asked casually as he ate.
Patrick took another bite of his sandwich and thought for a moment.
"Well, for one thing, I never thanked you for tracking down my shoe shine kit. It meant a lot to me. It might seem silly to some people, but... well, it was like a trusted friend, I suppose." Patrick smiled.
Arthur laughed. "I thought Chevonne would jump out of her skin. She couldn't wait to see your reaction when you looked under the table."
"I know; nobody loves a surprise like Chevonne."
They both laughed.
"And, um, I'm sorry," Patrick said sheepishly.
Arthur laughed again. "My, you're awfully mawkish today, aren't you?"
Patrick chewed slowly, while examining the sandwich he held in his hand. Finally, he swallowed and said, "I think I may have misjudged you a bit."
"Don't mention it. I think we all have our preconceived notions. All we can hope for is the experience to see things from another point of view every now and again." Arthur said thoughtfully.
"I think that's true." Patrick said and continued eating his sandwich.

CHAPTER FORTY-THREE

*M*onths had passed since Eddy murdered Kenneth and the druggist and escaped from Bellevue with Vinny.

Except for a small, amber glass bottle labeled *chloroform*, the drugs stolen from the hospital infirmary were long gone. Eddy had injected, swallowed or sniffed all of it. His existence now revolved around ways to get more. He'd managed to go through thousands of dollars to support his habit; a few "business deals" gone badly took care of the rest. Eddy's reputation as a force to be reckoned with among New York City's most notorious mobsters had disintegrated. The high rollers steered clear of Eddy. They didn't take him seriously anymore.

After the vultures, two bit gangsters and small time bootleggers, had swooped in and enticed Eddy into investing in bogus, quick money making schemes, in which they got him to put up substantial amounts of front money, they had no more use for him.

Eddy Belachi was nothing more but a desperate dope fiend.

Vinny Capozza was his ever-present side kick who rarely spoke. He was Eddy's toady who spent his days tagging along with Eddy like a stray dog. But, their relationship had become more complicated than anyone would have suspected.

"I know plenty of guys like you, Vinny. The bath houses are full of them." Eddy said, one night when the two men were sitting on the sofa in Eddy's apartment listening to the radio and drinking whiskey.

Vinny still liked to drink. Most nights he passed out on the couch, stone cold drunk. He had only been back to his apartment in Bensonhurst once since they'd left Bellevue. Vinny remembered how Eddy had gone through the apartment hastily throwing some of Vinny's clothes and valuables like Vinny's watches and cuff links. Naturally, Eddy had long since pawned it all. Vinny still wore his wedding ring, but he couldn't remember getting married. Sometimes though, something he heard or saw would trigger a memory or even a flood of memories. He remembered his parents and the bakery clearly. Eddy told him that his father, Salvatore, threatened to call the police on him if he ever tried to contact him or dared to show up at the bakery. In his mind, images of Berta and Rosa were vague and disjointed, but they were slowly returning.

Every week Vinny remembered a little bit more about his life before the accident but finding the words to express his thoughts hadn't become any easier. He sounded dim-witted, and was aware enough to be self-conscious about it, so he avoided speaking as much as he could. Vinny sat on the couch next to Eddy and drank directly from the bottle of whiskey. He didn't respond to Eddy's statement about "guys like him and bath houses," he just looked at Eddy blankly and took another swig off the bottle of whiskey.

"You didn't get no thrill from sleepin with all those quiffs at Polly Adler's cathouse. You kept goin' back, hoping to get some satisfaction the next time. But for guys like you, fuckin a dame is just another bodily function, like takin' a crap. Of course, makin a show of chasing dames to try to convince yourself and everyone else that you ain't like me, is another little perk, huh, Vinny? But I know what you really like. I got your number buddy." Eddy said, as he placed a hand on Vinny's thigh; and that's how it started.

Since that time, Vinny had thought about what Eddy said.

Maybe Eddy was right. Maybe he was queer. He really wasn't sure but he knew it didn't matter. His days of wearing expensive, custom made suits and flashing wads of cash at clubs and whorehouses were over. He was grateful that Eddy kept him in booze and gave him money to walk around to the Chinese restaurant on Thirteenth Avenue and buy takeout. Vinny didn't cook anymore. He couldn't remember how; there were too many steps and remembering ingredients was too hard. The truth was that Vinny knew he wasn't capable of surviving on his own. He was completely dependent on Eddy. Eddy was his childhood friend; his only friend. Eddy was his everything.

Eddy sat on the couch taking hits off an opium pipe. It wasn't even nine in the morning yet. "We gotta score some cash somehow." Eddy said to Vinny, his eyelids heavy from the opium. Vinny said nothing as he sat next to Eddy drinking a beer. Eddy reached over and put a hand on Vinny's crotch; Vinny seemed not to notice. Eddy put the opium pipe down on the end table and stood up in front of Vinny and unbuttoned his fly, exposing himself.

"You know what to do." he said, offhandedly.

Vinny took Eddy in his mouth as he'd done so many times before.

When Eddy began to cum, Vinny started to pull his head away. Eddy grabbed a fist full of his hair and held his head in place while he emptied himself into Vinny's mouth. When Eddy was done, Vinny turned away and took a long guzzle of beer. Eddy buttoned his pants up, sat back down and picked up the opium pipe again. They sat quietly on the couch, Vinny drinking his beer and Eddy smoking his pipe.

"I think I remembered something. I think I hid some money in the apartment in Bensonhurst," Vinny said.

"How much money?" Eddy asked, looking at Vinny intently.

"I don't know. I think a lot," Vinny said.

"I think a lot," Eddy said mimicking Vinny's slow speaking, in disgust. "What the fuck is a lot?" Eddy asked, impatiently.

Vinny was silent for a moment. "Thousands," Vinny answered.

Eddy stared at Vinny with a look of astonishment on his face.

After a moment of silence he shook his head and waved a dismissive hand. "You're all wet. We gave that place the once over pretty good when we grabbed your stuff."

Eddy thought back to that day and how he had rifled through everything. The only thing left that was worth anything, at least potentially, was a life insurance policy Salvatore Capozza had taken out years earlier, in which Vinny and his mother were the benefactors. Eddy slyly slid the policy into his coat pocket and neglected to mention it to Vinny, thinking it might come in handy one day.

As far as Eddy was concerned, that day was fast approaching.

Eddy woke one Sunday morning with a familiar knot in his stomach. He rolled onto his side and reached over and picked up the small manila envelope on the nightstand. He looked inside at the soft gray powder. There was maybe a day or two worth of dope. He took a snort and fell back onto the pillow. He was tired of chasing dimes and nickels just to get enough heroin to keep from going through the agony of withdrawals. He reached under the bed and pulled out the hat box he'd kept hidden there and took out a beautifully engraved certificate from the Public Life Insurance Company. He'd buried it beneath some prized mementos of his nefarious deeds, like extortion letters and newspaper clippings.

Eddy had found the policy in Vinny's dresser drawer in the apartment in Bensonhurst. It had been almost a year since that day. According to the policy, Vinny would receive seven thousand dollars in one lump sum in the event his father died. If he died due to an accident, the amount paid out would double. Eddy smiled. *That could be arranged*, he thought to himself. Vinny would cash in, and of course, Eddy would be there to assist his ole' chum in the management of the windfall.

Salvatore Capozza and his wife would be dead by week's end, and as far as the supposed money in the apartment in Bensonhurst, well, it might just be worth a look see, Eddy decided.

CHAPTER FOURTY-FOUR

erta had become used to being alone in the apartment. She thought back to the first time she walked through the door after her mother had been admitted to Bellevue. Almost a year had gone by since that day. Vinny never came back. A few weeks after her mother had gone to the hospital, she came home from school to find that the door had been jimmied. Vinny's clothes, not all, but a lot of them had been taken, along with things like his expensive cuff links and watches.

She didn't know if Vinny had come back to get his things, or if the apartment had been robbed. It was hard to tell. Berta didn't own anything of value and neither did her mother, so none of their things were touched.

Berta thought that Vinny might have come back for his money, too. She went to the kitchen and pulled a chair up to the counter and stood on it. She reached up onto the top shelf. The biscuit tin was still there. Berta pulled it down and took off the lid. It hadn't been disturbed at all. She didn't know what to think. *Why would Vinny jimmy the door?* Berta thought to herself. *Maybe he lost his key,* she considered. *But why didn't he take his money?*

Maybe he felt guilty for abandoning his wife and step-daughter, and left the money behind for them to live on, Berta mused, but almost as soon as that thought crossed her mind, she discounted it.

Vinny had his generous moments, but he wasn't *that* generous, and why would he hide the money where it was unlikely to be found? Why not simply tell them that he was leaving? Nothing seemed to make sense.

The months rolled past and there was no word from Vinny, and her mother's health continued to fail. Berta went twice a week to visit her mother, who didn't speak at all anymore. Some days Berta sat for hours trying to get Rosa to eat.

"Here Mama, open up, it's Jell-O. You like Jell-O" Berta would cajole.

Rosa had wasted away to skin and bones. Sometimes Mrs. Lachman went with her to see Rosa, and afterward Berta would go back to the Lachman's and visit with them. Sylvia and Yetta, the Lachman's daughters, were always so excited to see her. Even their son, David, who was nearly five years old now, ran to hug Berta when she came to visit.

"I asked the doctor what was wrong with Mama. He told me the same thing the nurses did." Berta complained to Gitta and Yekl one day over dinner.

"Oh? What did he tell you?" Gitta asked, feigning ignorance.

Gitta and Yekl had assumed that the doctors had spoken to Vinny about Rosa's condition and that they'd decided it was best not to burden Berta with the disclosure. It was an incurable disease and a diagnosis of Syphilis carried a horrible stigma.

Berta continued, "He told me that she had an infection, but it was the kind of infection that I couldn't catch from her. I asked what the infection was called and he told me that it was a Latin word that meant the French disease, but that it wouldn't do me any good to commit it to memory. Then I asked if she'd be getting better, and he said all things are possible through Christ the Lord." Berta let out a frustrated sigh.

"The important thing is that she's getting proper care." Gitta said sympathetically, and changed the subject.

Berta loved going to the Lachman's for dinner. The food was delicious and there was always plenty of laughter and interesting conversation.

"So, Berta, how is Vinny?"

Berta could feel her cheeks getting warm. She hated lying to the Lachman's. They'd been so kind to her, but she was afraid of what might happen if she told them that Vinny was gone and that she was actually living alone. She was afraid that they might insist that she move in with them, and as much as she enjoyed being there she dreaded the idea of leaving her friends at PS 128. "He's been very busy, but he said to say "hello" for him." Berta said trying to sound blithe.

Sophia was the only one that knew about Vinny's disappearance. Sophia and Berta shared other secrets as well. The headlines in the New York Post the morning after they'd found out that Rosa was at Bellevue read, "Murderers Escape Bellevue."

The afternoon paper, The Brooklyn Eagle, had a front page headline that read, "Bellevue Butchers on the Loose."

Berta and Sophia were sure that they'd come face to face with the two men that cold morning on the walkway in front of the hospital.

They didn't go to the police though. They couldn't.

After all, they were supposed to be at Berta's favorite uncle's funeral in Cambria Heights that weekend. They were supposed to be with Berta's mother, comforting poor, old, arthritic Aunt Ethel. It wouldn't do to have the police come to the Fabiano's apartment wanting to talk about how she and Berta had ended up at Bellevue that day. Sophia knew she'd get the spanking of her life if her parent's ever found out, and they'd never let her go anywhere ever again.

Berta and Sophia read everything they could get their hands on about the "Bellevue Butchers." Berta still couldn't shake the thought that she knew the man pushing the wheelchair. According to the newspapers the men had gone by the names "Vincent Smith" and "Edward Johnson."

There were no leads.

Neither man had had any visitors while at the hospital. One of the men was in a coma for a while, but had woken up. The other man had a badly broken arm. Both men looked to be in their thirties. The article went on to give a physical description of both men. Berta only saw one of them, but the description matched the man she saw that morning, exactly.

Berta worried about using the money in the tin but she had no choice. She was frugal and most of the time used only what she absolutely had to. She spent a lot of time at Sophia's house and ate dinner there at least two or three nights a week. Their apartment was crowded and loud with spirited conversation, but it always smelled of good cooking and felt homey and comfortable.

One night after dinner Mrs. Fabiano brought a cake with candles burning on top, to the table. It was Berta's birthday. She'd completely forgotten about it, but Sophia didn't. They all sang "Happy Birthday" and clapped after Berta blew out the candles. It was her sixteenth birthday. It was hard to believe that over five years had gone by since she'd left Sacred Heart Orphan Asylum.

Berta walked back to the apartment that evening and got ready for bed. She examined her image in the mirror fastened to the back of her bedroom door. She noticed that her breasts had grown over the past year or so. She started wearing some of her mother's old braziers, the ones Rosa wore before she became ill and lost so much weight. She brushed her hair and studied her face, wondering if she was pretty or not.

"You'd look just like Clara Bow if you'd just do something with your hair and put on a little make-up, Berta," Sophia's sister, Mildred informed her one afternoon. But Berta didn't feel pretty; not like other girls seemed to. Sophia was boy crazy and flirting came naturally to her. Berta was shy and unsure of herself.

Chevonne and Berta continued to write to one another. The letters were less frequent though, than they had been in the beginning. They shared so much during their time in the orphanage, but now they lead very different lives.

Berta had been invited to the Wallace's to spend the weekend with Chevonne.

Saturday morning had finally arrived. Berta stood at her bedroom window looking down at the street. The car would be arriving at any moment. Berta looked forward to seeing Chevonne, she loved her like a sister, but there was a part of Berta that was reluctant to go. Berta thought back to the first time she went to the Wallace's. She couldn't believe her eyes. It was as if she'd stepped into a movie set. She half expected Gloria Swanson to come sweeping into the room.

The Wallace's home was so incredibly beautiful and lavish. Chevonne was as kind and sweet as Berta remembered. They hugged one another and cried. It had been so long since they'd seen each other. Chevonne was still strikingly attractive, except she wasn't a little girl anymore and she was different in other ways too. Chevonne spoke another language now, one that Berta didn't understand. Chevonne and her friends giggled about the stable boys, talked about dressage events and their riding lessons. They used words like cotillion, debutante, and canapé'.

Berta felt out of place. She would have been happier standing in line eating a hotdog, waiting for a ride on the Thunderbolt roller coaster at Coney Island with her rough and tumble friends from Bensonhurst.

Chevonne had invited her to visit for the weekend again, and although she enjoyed spending time with Chevonne, she had to admit that she was more interested in seeing Patrick. He, like Chevonne, had grown up. His hair was darker, a deep auburn and he was tall with broad shoulders. Patrick O'Farrell had grown up to be a very handsome young man. The first time she'd seen him after they had moved in with the Wallace's, he took her breath away. She hoped he didn't notice.

She stood in the lobby of the Wallace's home. Their chauffeur had been sent for her and she had been let in by the doorman. She watched, awestruck as Patrick ran toward her, his arms open wide with a warm smile. He grabbed her around the waist and swung her in circles as they laughed. "Berta! It's been so long. We've missed you." Patrick said. Berta's stomach felt as if it were full of butterflies.

"I missed you too… I mean, I missed you and Chevonne, terribly."

Patrick put an arm around Berta's shoulder. "Miss Fancy Pants is at a Junior League meeting. They're working on saving the world: a good cause I think." he laughed. "She should be home soon enough though. Come on, I'll show you our little Taj Mahal."

Patrick had always had a way of making people feel like they were the center of the universe. He'd always been charming and thoughtful, so Berta couldn't tell if Patrick was simply being polite, or if he was interested in her in the way that a young man might be interested in a young woman.

The blare of a car horn interrupted her thoughts and brought her back to the present.

She looked down at the street from her bedroom window to see Patrick getting out of the passenger's side of a black Rolls Royce. She watched as he bounded up the stairs of the front stoop. Berta's stomach did a flip. She ran over to the mirror and checked her hair. The door buzzer buzzed. Berta grabbed her bag and ran out of the apartment to meet Patrick at the front door.

She hurried down the stairs.

"There you are; are you ready?" Patrick asked, with a smile that made Berta's knees weak.

"Um, yes. I didn't expect you to come with the driver to pick me up though." Berta thought she saw Patrick blush just a little.

"Well, it's always fun to go for a ride and Chevonne still isn't back from Meadowbrook yet. Arthur took her and Katherine to watch a polo match. I hope you don't mind the company." Patrick said looking self-conscious.

"Oh, um, no, not at all… I, well, it's… I'm happy to see you." Berta stammered.

Patrick smiled broadly and opened the back door of the car for Berta to get in and hopped in after her. "I thought it might be fun to see the sights. What do you think?" Patrick asked.

"I think I'd like that," Berta replied.

Berta and Patrick sat in the back of the Rolls Royce as the chauffeur drove. They went over the Brooklyn Bridge, through Times Square and toward the Upper East Side. "Take us to Central Park please, Phillip" Patrick said to the chauffeur.

"I don't expect that Chevonne will be back for a few more hours. I thought it might be fun to go to the park. It's so nice out. We can walk back to the townhouse from there." Patrick suggested.

Berta felt like she would jump out of her skin, she was so excited at the idea of spending time alone with Patrick. "Alright," was the only thing Berta could manage to say; she was afraid her voice would shake.

"Phillip, drop us off at the Seventy Second Street entrance, please." Patrick directed the chauffer.

When they arrived, Patrick jumped out of the car and jaunted around to Berta's side to open the door for her.

The foliage was at its peak and it was a bit chilly, but warm for a late autumn afternoon. The colors of the oak trees and sugar maples were more vibrant than Berta had ever remembered them being. There was a light breeze. Leaves, scarlet, orange and gold, blew across the grass and were occasionally taken up in tiny whirlwinds. The air smelled faintly of burning wood from the crackling fireplaces that puffed white smoke from chimneys.

"I spent a lot of time in this park when I was a boy. Come on, I'll show you my favorite spot." Patrick said as he took Berta by the hand. Berta felt as if she might faint. She was so nervous and worried that her palms would become sweaty. Patrick held her hand as they walked in silence enjoying the scenery. Berta could feel her heart practically beating out of her chest. Finally, they came to a spectacular sight.

"Well, here she is." Patrick announced.

Berta stood awestruck looking up at it. It was enormous.

"It's beautiful. It must be the biggest fountain in the world." Berta was so enthralled at the sight that she'd nearly forgotten that she was holding Patrick's hand.

"I'm not sure about that, but it's the biggest in New York. It stands twenty-six feet high and ninety-six feet wide. The angel at the top, The Angel of Waters, is eight feet tall and made of bronze. The four smaller cherubim underneath the angel represent health, purity, temperance and peace," Patrick said, as he too, marveled at the Bethesda Fountain.

Berta and Patrick moved to sit on a nearby bench. Patrick pulled a handkerchief full of small pieces of stale bread out of his pocket and opened it and set it between them.

"I used to love to feed the birds." Patrick picked up a piece of bread and tossed it in the air. Within seconds a half dozen sparrows flocked around.

Berta followed suit, relieved to have something to do with her hands. "Chevonne told me that your mother was in the hospital. How is she?" Patrick asked, with a look of concern.

"She's not doing very well. She can't speak anymore and she's not eating."

"I'm sorry to hear that, Berta. How is your step-father?"

Berta stayed quiet for a minute, and thought how she might answer, without lying to Patrick. "I don't know. I haven't seen him in a long time." she said, as if it were a simple matter of fact.

Patrick stopped feeding the birds and looked at Berta. She kept her eyes on the sparrows, trying to decide if she should confide in Patrick or not.

"Where is he?" Patrick asked.

"I don't know," Berta said, as she tossed another piece of bread onto the grass.

CHAPTER FORTY-FIVE

$\mathcal{P}$atrick never thought of Berta as anything more than a good friend, but he'd developed a crush on her over the course of the last year. She had changed, gradually and somehow all at once. He had remembered her as a timid little girl in a frayed Sacred Heart school uniform, her chestnut hair pulled back in a ponytail. He remembered her speaking broken English, and how Chevonne had taken such a liking to her.

Patrick thought Berta was beautiful. She had large hazel eyes and delicate features. Her face lit up when she smiled, and the sound of her laughter made Patrick's heart soar. He looked forward to Berta's visits and thought back to how carefully he'd tried to arrange for them to finally have time alone together during that weekend visit.

"Did you say Berta was coming to visit this weekend?" Patrick had asked Chevonne.

Chevonne looked up from her school book and grinned.

"Yes, she is" she answered.

"I thought you were going to Meadowbrook to watch the Polo match." Patrick said.

"Why, that's right. I'd forgotten all about it. I suppose I should cancel." Chevonne said, toying with Patrick.

"No, no, you don't have to do that. I was thinking that I could keep her company until you got back." Patrick said, trying to sound casual.

"Oh Patrick, you're such a kind, thoughtful brother. Are you sure it wouldn't be too much of an imposition?" Chevonne asked, feigning sincerity.

"Not at all," Patrick said.

"Well, alright then. But please promise me you'll tell her how completely enamored you are with her, because I'm fairly certain that the feeling's mutual." Chevonne imparted wryly, and went back to her studies.

Patrick thought about what Chevonne had said and wondered if it was true. Berta was shy and she'd never given Patrick any indication that she was interested in him. Patrick made an effort to include himself in Chevonne and Berta's activities when she visited. They'd spent time with one another playing cards, backgammon or chess. They laughed and joked and ate meals together, but never alone. It was always the three of them. Patrick decided that that would need to change.

Finally, Saturday afternoon had arrived. Patrick combed his hair carefully. He looked in the mirror to inspect his teeth and exhaled into his hand to check his breath. Satisfied, he went down to the lobby of the townhouse and summoned the chauffeur.

"I'll be accompanying you on the ride to Berta DeLuca's in Bensonhurst, sir," Patrick said to the chauffeur.

"Please, call me Phillip," the chauffeur offered pleasantly.

"Yes, sir — I mean, Phillip." Patrick corrected himself. He sat nervously in the passenger's seat of the Rolls Royce and thought about where he would take Berta during their time alone together. He wanted to take her somewhere special. After a minute or two of staring out the window at the passing scenery thinking about it, Patrick had come to a decision. The Angel of Waters was breathtaking, and the views from the Bethesda Terrace were the most amazing in all of New York City.

Patrick was proud that he'd managed the nerve to take Berta's hand as they walked into the park at the Seventy Second Street entrance. They walked hand in hand all the way to the fountain. He could tell by the expression on Berta's face that he'd made the right decision. It was a sight to behold and one that Patrick knew Berta would never forget. But it was what Berta told him while they sat on the bench feeding the birds that would stay with him forever.

He knew that Berta's mother was ill and had been for a long time. He knew that her mother was in the Bellevue psychiatric ward, but when he asked how her step father was, Berta responded, "I don't know." Patrick could sense that Berta was holding something back but he didn't want to pry. For a long time they sat together feeding the birds in silence. Finally, Berta offered more information.

"Vinny disappeared a week or two before my mother was admitted to Bellevue. I think he just decided to leave. He took most of his clothes and a few other things, like his watches and jewelry."

Patrick was stunned.

"You've been living by yourself all this time?" Patrick asked.

Berta shrugged, "It's not so bad. Actually, I used to worry about my mother being alone in the apartment when I was at school, and Vinny, well, I steered clear of him when he was home and I don't miss him one bit."

Patrick thought about what Berta had just told him for a moment. "How have you been managing? I mean financially. I'd imagine there are bills to be paid, rent and utilities, food and what not," he wondered. Telling Patrick about Vinnys' disappearance had led to more questions. Berta revealed that she and her friend, Sophia, had found a biscuit tin full of money in the kitchen, and that she had been living off the money. She went on to explain that she thought the money must be Vinny's and she was afraid that one day he would come back for it.

"I haven't told anybody about Vinny leaving, or about the money. The only person who knows is Sophia, my friend from school. She's actually the one who found the money and she was with me when my mother went missing. She and I were even together when we ran into the Bellevue Butchers." Berta confessed.

Patrick laughed. "Wait a minute, did you say you ran into the Bellevue Butchers? Do you mean the two men who escaped Bellevue last year... the ones who murdered the orderly and the druggist?"

Berta nodded.

"They've never been caught, you know. They were using aliases. Nobody knew anything about them and they're still at large. I read all about it in the paper." Patrick said, somberly.

"I know. I saw one of the men very plainly. I know that I knew him from somewhere too but I just couldn't place him. It seemed as if he recognized me as well, from the way he looked at me," Berta told Patrick, sounding slightly nervous.

"Well I'm sure they're long gone now. Anyway, I think he was probably just admiring your lovely face." Patrick said, as he gently brought the tip of his index finger to rest beneath Berta's chin. He tilted her head up slightly and turned her face to his and kissed her softly, not on the lips, but just ever so gingerly, next to them. Her skin felt like roses petals.

Patrick and Berta had been inseparable over the weekend.

Chevonne managed, at least most of the time, to ignore their long adoring gazes and awkward flirtations.

"I'm sure you'll both be heartbroken over what I'm about to tell you." Chevonne announced over tea as Patrick and Berta sat mooning at each other. "But, I'm afraid I'm not going to be able to join you at the movies this afternoon. I know it's a terrible disappointment, so I promise to think of some way to make it up to you both." Chevonne finished, her words dripping with good natured sarcasm.

"I'm sorry, did you say something Chevonne?" Patrick teased.

Berta's face turned red. "I'm sorry Chevonne. We're being rude."

"Oh don't worry about it. I knew it was inevitable, and to be honest, you make a lovely couple." Chevonne smiled.

Sunday evening came much too soon. Berta and Patrick sat in the back of the Rolls Royce headed to Bensonhurst.

"I have something for you," Patrick said, as he reached into his coat pocket.

Berta watched him pull out a tiny corked vial filled with a clear liquid. Patrick held it up between his thumb and index finger, and seemed to make a proclamation, "'Now there is, at Jerusalem by the sheep market, a pool, which is called Bethesda. Whoever then first, after the troubling of the waters, stepped in, was made whole of whatsoever disease he had,'" Patrick finished.

Berta looked puzzled.

"That's a quote, a bible verse. I've been told that the water from the Bethesda Fountain has healing powers like the Bethesda pool in Jerusalem is said to have. I thought maybe you could take it with you when you go to see your mother." Patrick said, gently.

Berta turned her head to look out the window of the car and said nothing in response to Patrick's gesture.

"Berta?" Patrick didn't know what to think; he wondered if he had said something to upset her. "Berta, what is it?" Patrick asked, as he leaned forward in an attempt to see her face.

Finally, Berta turned to took look at him. Tears streamed down her cheeks.

"What's wrong?" Patrick asked sounding perplexed.

"Patrick, you're so sweet. Thank you. It would be wonderful if there were something that could make my mother well again. I miss her terribly." Berta said.

"Take us to Bellevue, please, Phillip," Patrick said to the chauffeur.

Berta started to laugh through her tears. Patrick looked thoroughly befuddled.

"I didn't mean that I wanted to go see my mother right away. I meant that my mother hasn't been herself for a very long time and I've missed her; you know, the way she used to be," Berta explained. She was touched by how eager Patrick was to comfort her.

Patrick smiled bashfully, "I suppose it would save you a train ride though. We're not far from the hospital."

Berta looked out the window. It had started to rain. "You don't mind?" she asked.

"Of course not. Would you like me to go with you?" Patrick offered.

"No, I don't think so." Berta said, looking down.

"I understand. I'll wait for you in the lobby." Patrick replied. Berta looked back over her shoulder at Patrick as she stood waiting for the elevator in the lobby of Bellevue hospital. After a few moments, it arrived. The operator pulled the metal accordion door open and Berta stepped on. "Third floor please." she said.

Berta placed the vial of water she'd been holding tightly in her hand, into her coat pocket and prayed for a miracle.

CHAPTER FORTY-SIX

ddy snorted the last of the heroine. He mixed it with cocaine knowing that he would need to be alert. Vinny was passed out on the couch. Eddy had cleaned himself up since it was important that he look presentable. The suit hung on his body. He'd lost at least twenty pounds since he'd last worn it. Eddy looked at his image in the mirror. He appeared gaunt but the drugs made him feel strong, euphoric and energetic. Carefully, he parted his hair down the middle and combed it back neatly, using a liberal amount of macassar oil.

There could be no evidence of a struggle or foul play. That would surely raise suspicions and put the life insurance pay out in jeopardy.

Eddy thought back to the days when he used to go to Vinny's house as a kid. Most people were creatures of habit, or at least Eddy hoped Salvatore Capozza and his wife were. Eddy knew the bakery closed at six o'clock every evening and that it took another forty minutes or so for Salvatore to clean up and prepare for the next day. His wife spent that time making dinner.

Eddy walked around to the back of the bakery, past the small vegetable garden, and down a short brick walk-way. He opened the rickety screen door and stepped into a tiny, dimly lit vestibule. To his left, was the back entrance to the bakery. A steep, narrow staircase immediately in front of him led to the second floor where the Capozza's lived. At the top of the stairs was a door that opened into the kitchen. Eddy walked quietly up the stairs and knocked lightly at the door. Within seconds it opened. Vinny's mother stood with her apron on drying her hands on a dish rag.

"Hello, Mrs. Capozza." Eddy said politely.

"What you doing here? You no welcome around here, Eddy Belachi! You a bad man." Anna Capozza said crossly in her heavy Italian accent.

Eddy bowed his head humbly. "I'm really sorry to bother you, Mrs. Capozza, but it's important. It's about Vinny." Eddy said softly, and with great reverence.

Anna Capozza looked Eddy over suspiciously.

"What about Vinny?" she asked sounding guarded.

"May I come in?" Eddy asked. Anna hesitated for a moment and then reluctantly opened the door all the way and stepped aside allowing Eddy into the apartment.

Eddy reached into his pocket and pulled out the chloroform soaked handkerchief. He grabbed Anna by the back of the neck and held the handkerchief firmly against her nose and mouth. Within seconds she was out. He guided her body down onto the floor and ran down the stairway and into the bakery.

"Mr. Cappoza! Help!" Eddy yelled.

Salvatore spun around and looked at Eddy. "What you doing in my bakery? Get out, you—"

Eddy interrupted, "Please, Mr. Capozza, your wife... there's something wrong. She collapsed." Salvatore's expression went from one of fury to bewilderment. He pushed past Eddy and hurried up the stairs to find his wife on the floor, unconscious. Salvatore quickly knelt down at her side.

He took his wife's face in his hands. "Anna! Anna! What's wrong? Wake up!" Again, Eddy took the chloroform soaked handkerchief from his pants pocket. He came up behind Salvatore and held it tightly over the elderly man's face. Salvatore keeled over next to his wife.

Eddy stuck his hand in Salvatore's pocket and pulled out a five dollar bill and some change and placed it in his suit coat pocket. He walked over to the cast iron gas stove and blew out the pilot and turned the gas all the way up. He then crumbled up a piece of newspaper and stuffed it into the toaster, plugged it in and pushed the lever down. Eddy took a quick look around, satisfied that he'd left no signs of any struggle. It would be considered nothing more than an unfortunate accident. Eddy noticed a pastry box with four small meat pies in it on the kitchen counter; he grabbed it, closed the door behind him and dashed down the stairs and out the back door. He walked nonchalantly around the building and crossed the street.

Eddy waited, knowing the gas was spewing from the stove and filling the room. Any minute the newspaper in the toaster would ignite, causing a violent explosion. Eddy wasn't disappointed. The windows in the second floor of Capozza's bakery shattered and flames burst from them.

Eddy left before a crowd could gather. He stopped at the local speakeasy, knocked back a shot of scotch, bought a bottle of whiskey, a few pills and some cocaine with the money he had taken from Salvatore.

His high from the cocaine he'd snorted before leaving for the Capozza's was wearing off, but he felt exuberant, nonetheless. Eddy was about to cash in. *Fourteen grand will be enough to live very comfortably for a long time,* Eddy thought.

He stuck his finger in the white powder and touched it to his tongue and then brought a finger full to his nostril and sniffed deeply.

CHAPTER FORTY-SEVEN

Vinny was asleep on the couch when Eddy got back to the apartment.

"Vinny. Ah, sleepin beauty, come on, wake up." Eddy nudged him.

Vinny sat up, groggy, his eyes still shut. Eddy sat the pastry box down on the coffee table and opened the whiskey. He poured two glasses and handed one to Vinny. "Here, drink up." Eddy encouraged.

Vinny took a sip and sleepily looked at him.

"Listen, Vinny, I got some tough news for ya; seems there's been an accident." Eddy said not bothering to sound sympathetic.

"What... what... kind of accident?" Vinny asked, in his usual slow speech.

"Well, I guess there was some kind of explosion or something, maybe a fire at the bakery. I dunno Vinny, but I heard through the grapevine that your parents... well, ya see, they're gone." Eddy explained.

"Gone?" Vinny said sounding confused.

"Yeah, Vinny, gone. They're dead." Eddy said flatly and took another gulp of whiskey.

Vinny said nothing more.

"That's the bad news. There's a silver lining though, thanks to your ole pal Eddy, here." Eddy said pointing to himself with his thumb.

Vinny sat on the couch trying to make sense of what Eddy had just told him; he didn't know what to say or do, so he finished his drink.

Eddy filled the glasses again. "I picked up some dinner for us. I think you ought to eat something, Vinny. I don't want ya getting too sloshed. We got some business to attend to." Eddy laughed uneasily. Vinny stared at Eddy, clearly flummoxed.

"It just so happens that your father had a little life insurance policy and named you as the benefactor." Eddy said gleefully.

Eddy waited for a response from Vinny but still he said nothing.

"You know what this means don't ya pal?" he asked.

Vinny shook his head "no."

Eddy laughed, "Don't worry, buddy. I'll take care of everything. You just do what I tell ya and we'll be rolling in the dough in no time." Eddy reached into the pastry box and pulled out a meat pie. He sunk his teeth into it and tore off a big bite and tossed it back into the box.

"Let me show ya something, Vinny." Eddy said, chewing vigorously.

Eddy left the room and came back carrying the hatbox he kept under the bed. He set it on the coffee table and rummaged through the contents until he found the life insurance policy and certificate.

"Look, Vinny, here it is, see? It's a life insurance policy. You gotta sign it so we can bring it to the insurance company with the death notice. Then they'll give you a check and we'll bring it to the bank." Eddy explained excitedly.

Vinny looked at Eddy blankly trying to understanding what was happening.

Eddy continued, "I think this is your lucky day, Vinny, and it's not over yet. It's not even seven o'clock. Why don't you get cleaned up a little and we'll head over to your apartment in Bensonhurst. Maybe we can find that loot you got stashed. It could be a while before we get our hands on the insurance money and it sure would be nice to have some scratch in the meantime." Eddy stood up.

"I gotta take a dump," he announced and headed to the bathroom.

Vinny looked down at the beautifully engraved life insurance certificate with its intricate border and thought about his father. He remembered back, to when he was a little boy in the bakery. Every Sunday he and his father made meat pie pastries together.

"Vincenzo, you going to be a very good baker when you grow up, you know that? Papa will teach you everything," Salvatore would tell him.

Capozza's meat pies were unique: his father never used green peppers the way they were traditionally made because Vinny didn't like green peppers. Instead, Salvatore added spinach to the pies. Vinny picked up the meat pie Eddy had taken a bite of. He examined its contents closely.

No green peppers.

It was made with spinach... and it was Sunday.

Vinny sat for a few moments thinking about the pastries. Then he looked into the hatbox that Eddy had left on the coffee table. It was full of newspaper clipping and letters. Vinny began looking through them. There was a newspaper articles about the shoot-out at a liquor exchange. There was a newspaper clipping about the assassination attempt on Joe Messeria. Memories started flooding back. Vinny remembered how Eddy had drawn him into the Five Points Gang like a spider draws prey into its sticky web.

Then Vinny came across a letter.

It was the letter that the butcher had given him; left by a man who'd said it was a "special recipe." But there was no special recipe. It was a letter demanding two thousand dollars or "something bad" would happen to Salvatore: retribution for Salvatore's refusal to join the "Bensonhurst Business Association." Vinny thought back to that day and how he showed the letter to Eddy, hoping that his friend would know what to do. Eddy took the handwritten letter, with its peculiar left slant and numerous misspellings, and assured Vinny that he would take care of it. A few days later Eddy explained that, through his connections, he'd managed to get the demanded amount cut in half. Vinny gladly gave Eddy the thousand dollar pay off to give to the blackmailers, relieved to put the incident behind him.

Vinny saw other letters in the box too, at least a dozen, handwritten with the same peculiar slant demanding money; extortion letters.

All of them were signed "anonomis."

The sound of Eddy's voice drew Vinny's attention away from the revelations of the hatbox.

"I hope this little treasure hunt pans out," Eddy said, as he rubbed his hands together and sniffed.

Vinny could see the remnants of the cocaine around one of Eddy's nostrils. Eddy strode over to the window and pulled back the curtain. "Shit, it's starting to rain. Come on, Capozza, let's get going."

Vinny stood up and lumbered across the living room and put his jacket on, still thinking about the pastries and the letters and the newspaper clippings. His sluggish movements belying the speed in which the images and recollections were coming back to him.

CHAPTER FORTY-EIGHT

The psychiatric unit was noisy, as usual, but Berta had become accustomed to the cacophony. The shrieks and screams that used to terrify her had become mere background noise; she hardly noticed it anymore. Rosa hadn't been out of bed in weeks. Berta often sat at her mother's bedside and combed Rosa's sparse hair, talking about her day as if her mother understood every word. Rosa usually slept during the visits, or stared off into the distance.

Berta anticipated that this visit would be no different, except she'd tell her mother all about her wonderful weekend with Patrick and, of course, there was the Bethesda fountain water in her pocket. Berta entered her mother's ward. There were four narrow iron framed beds on each side of the room. The headboards were pushed up against the walls. The beds were spaced approximately five feet apart from one another; each had a simple night stand next to it. Berta's mother had occupied the last bed on the right since she'd been admitted, but it was empty. Berta stood looking at the bed. It had been stripped down. Only the thin, blue ticking mattress with its various amber stains was left.

"Excuse me." a soft voice came from behind.

Berta didn't turn to look at the person who had spoken. She knew that this would be the voice that would tell her that her mother had died, and as long as she didn't hear the words she could have hope.

Berta felt a hand on her shoulder.

"You must be Rosa's daughter, I'm Sister Lucilla."

Finally, Berta looked at the nun.

"What's your name?" the nun asked.

"My name is Berta."

The nun looked at Berta with deep compassion in her eyes. "Berta, I'm sorry, the Lord has called your mother home. One of the nurses told Father Keenan that her time was coming near, so he administered the

Sacrament of the Sick and Extreme Unction this afternoon. She passed shortly afterward. She's been taken to the morgue."

Berta and the young nun stood shoulder to shoulder, looking at the empty bed for a few moments.

"Would you like to say a prayer with me?" the nun asked, breaking the silence. Berta nodded, indicating that she would.

They bowed their heads and Sister Lucilla began to recite the Pater Noster.

"Thank you; I'll make arrangements for my mother tomorrow. I have a friend waiting for me in the lobby." Berta informed Sister Lucilla when they were done praying.

Berta felt numb.

Her mother was gone.

She stepped off the elevator into the hospital lobby where Patrick was waiting. He walked toward Berta with a worried look on his face.

"Berta, you're as white as a sheet. You look as if you might faint right where you're standing." Patrick said as he took her arm. "What's wrong?" he asked.

Berta forced the words out of her mouth. "She's gone. My mother died this afternoon."

Patrick said nothing. He searched her face with his eyes, kissed her gently on the forehead and took her hand and walked her out to the car.

Berta looked out of the car window. A heavy mist fell from the dark, cloudy, moonless sky. She wanted to cry, but couldn't. She thought about her mother and everything Rosa had endured. It didn't seem fair that someone should have had to suffer as much as her mother had.

"I don't think you should be alone tonight Berta. Come back to the Wallace's with me," Patrick offered.

"Thank you, Patrick, but I just want to lie down in my own bed. I feel exhausted. I need some time to think, to sort things out in my mind a bit. I'll be fine." Berta assured him.

The Rolls Royce pulled up in front of the apartment building in Bensonhurst. Patrick opened the car door, helped Berta out and walked her to the front door. They embraced one another.

"Goodnight Berta." Patrick whispered against her ear.

Berta pulled back slightly to look into Patrick's eyes. She smiled faintly, "Good night." she said.

Berta turned and walked into the building and up to the second floor. She came to the apartment door and realized that she'd become so flustered when she saw that Patrick had come to pick her up, that she had forgotten to lock the door when she left.

Berta opened the door, making sure she locked it behind her, and went directly to her bedroom. She undressed and slipped on her nightgown. It wasn't until Berta went to brush her teeth that it occurred to her that she'd left her tote bag in the back of the Rolls Royce on the floor. Berta chided herself for being so forgetful and decided to have a glass of milk before getting into bed. She went to the kitchen, opened the ice box door and leaned in to reach for the milk. Berta closed the door and stood erect with the bottle of milk in her hand. She gasped and dropped it, a look of shocked surprise on her face. The milk bottle shattered on the floor.

"Vinny?" Berta said, her mouth hanging open. Vinny didn't say anything. He stood motionless with an odd, dull expression on his face. It looked as if he hadn't shaved in a week and he was dressed in clothes that were ill fitting. He looked slovenly.

"For Christ sake, what the hell is all the racket about in here?" Eddy demanded as he walked into the kitchen behind Vinny. Berta's eyes grew wide.

She recognized Eddy immediately. He was the Bellevue Butcher.

He looked familiar because she had met him once a few years earlier. He was Vinny's good friend Eddy, Eddy Belachi.

Eddy stopped dead in his tracks. His eyes narrowed as he examined Berta's face.

"Well, well, well, what do we have here?" Eddy said coolly. "So that's why you looked so familiar to me when I saw you going into Bellevue that morning. You're Rosa's kid. I haven't seen ya in years. I gotta say, ya grew up to be a looker."

"What do you want?" Berta asked nervously.

"What do I want? I want the dough that Vinny stashed somewhere in this apartment."

"It's up there." Berta pointed to the cupboard.

Eddy looked up and then looked at Berta again. "Oh, and I wanna make sure that you can't rat me out to the cops. Ya see, I got a lot of loot to enjoy and getting thrown in the slammer just wouldn't do. You understand don't ya?" Eddy asked, sounding affable.

Berta stood paralyzed with fear. Vinny had yet to utter a word.

Berta was cornered in the kitchen. She decided that there was nothing else for her to do but try to make a run for it. Eddy put his arm out to catch her but she kicked him swiftly in the shin. The sudden pain forced Eddy to let go.

"God damn it!" Eddy wailed.

Berta ran to the door in a terrified panic. She fumbled with the lock, but Eddy had recovered and dashed into the living room after her. He gripped the back of Berta's night gown and flung her hard across the room. Berta landed next to the fireplace. Eddy let out a malicious laugh.

"You're a feisty one, aren't ya." he said as he took one slow, deliberate step after another toward her. Berta was splayed out on the floor. She looked up in horror.

Eddy stood over her with the paring knife he'd picked up off of the kitchen counter. Berta sat up and struggled to get to her feet. Eddy lunged at her.

Berta let out a blood curdling scream. "Help! Somebody help!"

CHAPTER FOURTY-NINE

Patrick thought about Berta and how she had nobody now; at least no family. Patrick had Chevonne and the Wallace's had been wonderful to them but Berta had been on her own for so long. Patrick sat in the back of the Rolls Royce. They were about to go over the Brooklyn Bridge when he looked down on the floor of the car and noticed that Berta had left her over-night bag behind. Patrick knew that Berta wanted time alone but he was happy that he had an excuse to see her again.

"Phillip, please go back to Bensonhurst. Berta left her over-night bag in the car." Patrick informed the chauffeur.

Patrick felt silly. It hadn't even been fifteen minutes since he'd seen Berta and he missed her already. He couldn't wait to see her face and hear her voice. Patrick jumped out of the car. The heavy mist that had been falling had turned into a torrential downpour. He grabbed the bag and sprinted for the door. One of the tenants was leaving the building. Patrick slipped through the doorway as they were coming out, and bounded up the stairs, two at a time, to the second floor.

Patrick could hear a woman screaming for help but wasn't sure where it was coming from, at first. Berta lived in apartment 2E. Patrick hurried down the hall looking at the numbers on the doors. 2A... 2B... The screaming became louder. Finally, Patrick came to Berta's apartment. The screaming was coming from inside the apartment. Patrick tossed the overnight bag aside and turned the door knob. "Berta!" he yelled. The door was locked. He took a few steps back and drove his right shoulder into the door as hard as he could. It didn't budge. He raised his leg and began kicking the door in. Patrick managed to kick a hole in the door next to the door knob. He reached in and turned the lock. He opened the door to find a tall thin man holding Berta around the neck with a knife in his hand.

"Alright lover boy, take a seat over there."

Eddy motioned to the couch.

Patrick hesitated.

"Do it, or I'll slice her throat." Eddy snarled.

"Patrick, he's the Bellevue Butcher. He knows I can identify him, so there's no chance he'll let us out of this apartment alive."

Tears welled up in Berta's eyes. "Run Patrick; please go," she pleaded.

"I'm not leaving you here," Patrick said resolutely.

"Why, listen to you two, just like Romeo and Juliet... and we know how that ended too, don't we?" Eddy snickered.

Berta turned her head and tucked her chin down just a little. Eddy didn't seem to notice. He pressed his boney forearm firmly against her throat and held the paring knife tightly in his hand. Berta opened her mouth as wide as she could and sunk her teeth into Eddy's wrist. Eddy let out a guttural howl and released Berta from his grip. Berta ran to Patrick. They headed for the door but Eddy grabbed the poker from the fireplace and swung it with all his might, hitting Patrick in the temple. Berta watched in horror as Patrick's knees buckled, his eyes rolled back into his head and he slid to the floor.

Eddy quickly pounced. He straddled Patrick and brought the paring knife up over his head poised to plunge it directly into Patrick's heart.

The girl is right, Eddy thought to himself.

He couldn't let either one of them out of the apartment alive. Now Romeo was out cold in front of the door and Juliet was screaming bloody murder. She'd taken hold of Eddy's wrist in an attempt to prevent him from plunging the knife into her boyfriend.

"Vinny! Get your ass out here you moron!" Eddy bellowed.

Vinny walked out of the kitchen. He held a rolling pin in his left hand.

"Get this bitch off of me!" Eddy screamed.

Vinny plodded over to Berta and grabbed a fist full of her hair and threw her off to the side.

Berta scrambled to get to her feet. She watched in horror as Vinny brought the rolling pin up over his head.

She screamed, "Vinny, no!"

Berta tried to get to Vinny before the rolling pin could come down on Patrick. Patrick was still unconscious from Eddy's assault with the fireplace poker. Berta noticed that the odd, dull expression Vinny had worn was gone. His face was contorted with rage, his lips taut across his teeth. Vinny grasped the rolling pin with both hands and brought it down with powerful, brute force. The sound of cracking bone it made on contact was stomach churning.

CHAPTER FIFTY

Berta looked on astonished. Eddy's skull split open like a ripe melon. His body slumped over, the pool of blood surrounding it growing rapidly. Vinny brought the rolling pin up over his head again and again, smashing it down over and over, bludgeoning Eddy to death.

"You...you...Eddy...you did it...you did it all, Eddy!" Vinny cried. Tears ran down his face as he sobbed uncontrollably, wielded the rolling pin.

Berta was terrified, but mustered the courage to push Eddy's flaccid body off of Patrick. She managed to open the door wide enough to pull Patrick's unconscious body across the parquet floor and out into the hallway.

Vinny seemed oblivious to her or anything else around him. He was focused on Eddy. He seemed completely possessed, consumed by a visceral fury as he beat Eddy's head with the rolling pin.

"Patrick, Patrick... please Patrick, wake up." Berta begged.

Patrick's eyes opened slowly. "What happened?" he asked groggily.

"Eddy hit you in the head with the fireplace poker. You were unconscious. We have to go Patrick. Vinny's in the apartment; he's killing Eddy, but I don't know what he'll do afterward. We have to get to the police station." Berta said frantically as she tried to pull Patrick up from the floor.

After a minute or so Patrick regained his equilibrium and they ran down to the car where Phillip was waiting in the Rolls Royce.

Berta wore only her thin cotton night gown. She hadn't had time to feel self-conscious until they got down to the car. Patrick took off his coat,

"Here, put this on." he said as he draped it over her shoulders. He opened the car door for Berta and jumped in after her in the back seat.

"Phillip, we need to go to the police station." Berta informed the chauffeur.

"Yes, miss. Could you tell me where the nearest one is?" Phillip asked. Berta directed the chauffeur to the 71st precinct. She and Patrick hurried into the police station. Sergeant Trevese sat behind the desk engrossed in his paper work.

"Excuse me officer." Patrick interrupted.

"What can I help you with?" the sergeant asked.

"We'd like to report a crime in progress." Patrick said.

"Is that so? What kind of crime?" the sergeant asked.

"A murder," Patrick said flatly.

Sergeant Travese furrowed his brow. "A murder? What are you talking about?"

It took a while to convince the officer that two renowned mobsters were in an apartment just a few blocks away.

"You see, one of the gangsters, Eddy Belachi, tried to kill us. But for some reason the other gangster, Vinny Capozza, killed him instead. Vinny Capozza, is my step-father. Oh, and they're the Bellevue Butchers too," Berta explained.

Sergeant Travese shook his head in disbelief. "Is this some kind of joke? You two are gonna be in a lotta hot water if this story aint on the level," the sergeant warned sternly.

"I swear officer, everything we're telling you is the God's honest truth," Berta replied.

Eventually, the sergeant decided that Berta and Patrick seemed credible. He picked up the phone receiver and spoke, "Operator, connect me to the Federal Bureau of Investigation."

Berta and Patrick stood listening closely as Sergeant Travese explained the situation.

"Yes, they're still here. Yes, sir, I'll let them know. Thank you," Sergeant Travese said, and hung the receiver back on the phone.

"There are some nice gentlemen, special agents, who are coming here from the field office uptown to see you. They'd like to ask you two a few questions. We'll send a couple of our officers over to your apartment, too. You can have a seat over there." Sergeant Travese pointed to a long wooden bench near the front of the precinct. Berta and Patrick sat and waited.

The F.B.I. agents that came to speak with them were indeed nice. Berta told them everything. She even told them about the money in the biscuit tin and how she suspected that it was Vinny's. They told her that she couldn't go back to the apartment until they had examined all the evidence that might be there.Berta didn't want to go back to the apartment; not then, not ever. She wasn't sure where she would go but she knew that the images she's seen in the apartment in Bensonhurst would haunt her for a lifetime.

That night Berta decided to go back to the Wallace's with Patrick. It was late when they arrived. Katherine Wallace was waiting up in the study.

"Patrick, I was worried. What happened?" Katherine asked anxiously. She then turned to Berta, "Are you alright Berta?"

Berta looked overcome with fatigue. Patrick answered before Berta could speak knowing that she had spent the last two hours recounting everything she could recall about Vinny and Eddy.

"Yes, we're alright. We went to a police station to report a crime," Patrick said sounding exhausted.

Arthur appeared in the doorway of the study.

"Patrick, Berta, is everything alright?" Arthur asked, as he walked into the room tying his robe.

"It's a long story. I'm guessing it'll be in all the papers soon enough. The important thing is that we're both fine. It's late; can we discuss it in the morning?" Patrick asked.

Katherine and Arthur looked at one another and then back at Patrick and Berta.

"Well, the suspense is killing me, but I suppose we'll have to wait until then. Berta, I'll have the guest bed turned down for you and a bath drawn. You look like you could use a nice relaxing soak," Katherine said.

"Yes, that would be wonderful. Thank you, Mrs. Wallace," Berta responded.

Berta woke the next morning under a warm satin covered goose down blanket. The sun shone through the enormous floor to ceiling windows of the guest bedroom. The smell of freshly baked croissants wafted in the air. What had happened the day before seemed surreal to Berta. But, the newspaper confirmed it all.

"Bellevue Butchers Identified," read the front page headline with a lengthy article about the two ruthless gangsters and their exploits.

During breakfast, Patrick and Berta told the Wallace's and Chevonne everything, including Rosa's death.

Chevonne began to cry. "Berta, I'm so sorry! I'm sorry you've had to go through so much by yourself," she wept.

Berta was quiet for a moment and then she smiled.

"But I wasn't by myself. You were there, Chevonne. You weren't just there when I was a frightened little girl at the orphanage. Your letters meant so much to me. I knew that you were thinking about me. You were there. You helped make the sad times bearable. You and so many other people were there when I needed someone. I think that there are angels everywhere, angels on Earth. Everybody is an angel to someone at some time," Berta said with a full, grateful heart.

EPILOGUE

Vinny was still bashing Eddy's head in when the police arrived. He was covered in Eddy's blood. Eddy had been beaten to an unrecognizable pulp; the blood around his body extended out over six feet in a gelatinous, dark burgundy pool. Brain matter and pieces of skull stuck to the walls. Bright red arcs of blood were splattered on the ceiling. The police handcuffed Vinny and took him down to the station for questioning, but Vinny wouldn't talk. Vinny never spoke another word ever again.

"It appears he's in a catatonic stupor," his defense attorney complained to the judge, at the hearing.

The criminal proceedings were brief. The judge refused to believe that Vinny's attack on his friend, Eddy Belachi, was the result of temporary insanity or that his silence was due to acute psychosis.

"It appears that Mr. Belachi and Mr. Capozza's chickens have finally come home to roost. The state of New York remands Vincenzo Capozza to twenty five years, direct, to be served in the penitentiary on Blackwell's Island." the judge ordered, and slammed his gavel down on the sounding block.

Vinny's lawyer looked over to his client. There was no reaction. Vinny was led away by two bailiffs. His time in prison was short though, less than three weeks. Inmates reported that it was hard to believe that the docile mute that sat perfectly still in the prison yard while a rival gang member stabbed him to death, was the infamous Vinny Capozza.

Rosa was buried in the New Utrecht Cemetery in Bensonhurst. Her headstone was beautiful. Berta had it custom made with a small replica of the Angels of Waters atop it. The mass before the wake was heartwarming and uplifting. Fragrant flower bouquets covered the polished mahogany casket with its ornate brass handles. Yekl Lachman, Patrick, Arthur Wallace and Mr. Fabinao served as pall bearers.

Berta still hadn't cried. She watched as the casket was slowly lowered into the ground. She made the sign of the cross and said a prayer. Berta knew that her father, Gaston waited on the other side for his beloved wife and that they would spend eternity in the kingdom God. That was certainly better than wasting away in a hospital bed.

Her parents risked everything for the hope of a brighter future for themselves and their only child. Berta promised herself that she would live a life that was worthy of her parents sacrifice. She would be an angel on Earth, or at least, she'd be someone's angel whenever she could.

The money left in the biscuit tin found its way to the safe at the 70th police precinct, thanks to Sergeant Travese and an honest F.B.I. agent. It was labeled as evidence. It was determined, that because Vincenzo Capozza was gainfully employed as a legitimate business owner, in partnership with his father, for years prior to his involvement with the Five Points Gang, that it could not be proven that the money was the product of illegal activities. The courts decided that it should, therefore, be released to Vincenzo Capozza's only heir, Berta DeLuca.

Salvatore Capozza's life insurance policy stipulated that in the event the sole beneficiary expired, the payout would go to his or her heirs. As Mrs. Capozza was deceased, Vincenzo Capozza's only heir was his step-daughter, Berta DeLuca. Arthur Wallace arranged for the monies to be put into a trust that would allow for all appropriate living expenses and education. Shrewd investments would ensure that Berta had enough money to live comfortably for many years to come.

It would be another year and a half before Berta would graduate from high school. She rented a studio apartment in the same building the Fabiano's lived. She felt like a member of their family, eating dinner with them most nights and attending mass with them on Sundays. Gitta and Yekl were named as Berta's legal guardians. Rosa, in her lucid years, had asked the Lachmans to look out for Berta in the event that something happened to her. They were happy to oblige and were always there to offer wise advice and support.

Patrick had been accepted at Arthur Wallace's alma mater, Harvard University. He refused to go though, unless Berta promised to marry him when he graduated.

It was a promise she intended to keep.

Dear Reader,

I'd like to thank you for spending your hard earned money on this book. As you've probably noticed this is Book One of the Angles on Earth Series. This book is self-published, which means that the author, me, paid to have my manuscript put into book form and sold in various venues. Writing these books was a labor of love as I do not make my living writing novels –yet!

Writing novels has turned out to be a costly "hobby" so to speak. There's no advance from a publishing house or other compensation save revenue from book sales. I hope that you enjoyed this book (actually I hope that you loved it and couldn't put it down) and will recommend it enthusiastically to all your friends and family. Social networks are an amazing tool to spread the word. The more books sold the faster I'll be able to pay publishing costs and get Book Two of the Angels on Earth Series out to you!

Yours Truly,

Terry Suchanek

CPSIA information can be obtained at www.ICGtesting.com
Printed in the USA
LVOW052109270912

300665LV00001B/12/P